Praise for *The Tiger's Daughter*

"Rich, expansive, and grounded in human truth. It is a story of star-crossed loves, of fate and power and passion, and it is simply exquisite."　　　　—V. E. Schwab, *New York Times* bestselling author of the Shades of Magic series

"The epistolary tale at the heart of *The Tiger's Daughter* unfolds with deceptive elegance, leading the reader to a conclusion at once unexpected, touching, and apt."
　　　　—Jacqueline Carey, author of the bestselling Kushiel's Legacy series

"An incredible debut that takes all my favorite fantasy elements and adds the queer romance I've been waiting for in my magical fiction for years. If you love women who love women standing side by side to face off against a seemingly impervious foe, you will love *The Tiger's Daughter*."
　　　　—Sam Maggs, author of *The Fangirl's Guide to the Galaxy* and *Wonder Women*

"A layered and mesmerizing tale of love and legends, this fierce story will settle in your bones like a chill and leave your heart aching."　　　　—Roshani Chokshi, *New York Times* bestselling author of *The Star-Touched Queen*

"Delicate, intricate, inevitable . . . a stunning debut. It took my breath away."　　　　—Seanan McGuire

THE
TIGER'S
DAUGHTER

K ARSENAULT RIVERA

TOR

A TOM DOHERTY ASSOCIATES BOOK

NEW YORK

THE TIGER'S DAUGHTER

Copyright © 2017 by K Arsenault Rivera

Edited by Miriam Weinberg

A Tor Book
Published by Tom Doherty Associates
175 Fifth Avenue, New York, NY 10010

www.tor-forge.com

Tor® is a registered trademark of
Macmillan Publishing Group, LLC.

The Library of Congress Cataloging-in-Publication
Data is available upon request.

ISBN 978-0-7653-9253-4 (trade paperback)
ISBN 978-0-7653-9254-1 (ebook)

Our books may be purchased in bulk for
promotional, educational, or business use. Please
contact your local bookseller or the Macmillan
Corporate and Premium Sales Department at
1-800-221-7945, extension 5442, or by email at
MacmillanSpecialMarkets@macmillan.com.

First Edition: October 2017

Printed in the United States of America

0 9 8 7 6 5 4 3 2 1

To those who need to know they're not alone

ACKNOWLEDGMENTS

I used to dream about what I'd put on a page like this. Turns out when you sit down to actually write one, the words are more slippery than you'd expect. It's hard to adequately thank all the people who've shepherded this book along, who've helped turn this dream I was too shy to admit in public into a reality—but I'll try.

Sara Megibow, my agent, is an absolute ball of sunshine who is as unstoppable as she is approachable. Had she not fallen in love with this book, it would probably be sitting on my hard drive to this day. Well. Not the same hard drive. I have a tendency to spill mac and cheese on my laptops, and that was two laptops ago.

If you aren't familiar with Miriam Weinberg, then you've got some reading to do. Not only is she *my* editor, she's worked with other authors I'm honored to share shelf space with. I'm grateful for her insightful comments as much as I am that she joins me in flailing about Utena.

To Michelle Evans, who stayed up all night with me more than once talking about headcanons, who sprayed me with proverbial water whenever I thought about cutting too many scenes, thank you.

To #CovenSquad—Renee Beauvoir, Marissa Fucci, and Rena Finkel—thank you. When I decided to go hang out with strangers at the Alice in Wonderland Statue, I could never have known I'd get lifelong friends out of it. You've been with me through thick, thin, and vaguely pagan nondenominational rituals. So despite our differing opinions on leopard print, Jackson Pollock, and *Supernatural,* I can say I'm proud to know every one of you, and I love you from the bottom of my heart.

To Didi Feuer and Gavi Feuer, thank you for indulging my love of card games. I'm telling you, no one does a better impression of Thom Yorke than Didi, and no one can better debate the intricacies of *Game of Thrones* than Gavi.

To my gaming group—Sergej Babushka, Tyler Everett, Louis Galasso, Matt LaForet, Jace Parker, and Kaleb Shulla—thank you for giving me a place to create ridiculous characters with overly long backstories. More importantly, thank you for giving them a place to grow. We've told a whole world's worth of stories together, stories I'll always hold near and dear. Like the time Lennart bisected that druid.

To Leah Williams, thank you for your early confidence and support. I can't wait to see what you've got cooking up in the future, so you're going to have to send me a copy of your next project, all right?

To Morgane Audoin, Lauren Craig, and Madeline Vara, whom I met through my love of fictional noncanon lesbians in video games—here are some canon lesbians you've been waiting for.

You know, I used to be afraid of planes, but I think flying to Toronto to meet with you helped change that. Thank you for all the fond maple-syrup memories, and I'm sorry, Lauren, that I almost killed your cat.

To my parents, who fostered my love of reading and writing when it was not financially easy to do so.

To Stephanie Brown, lover of art and beautiful things, I hope this book qualifies as both.

And, lastly, to the person who told me they were happy I was writing again, to the person who tells me they hate my puns even as they laugh, to the person who cooks with me despite the fire hazard, and the person who loves me despite my unfortunate allergy to dogs—I love you, Charlie, and thank you for being my home.

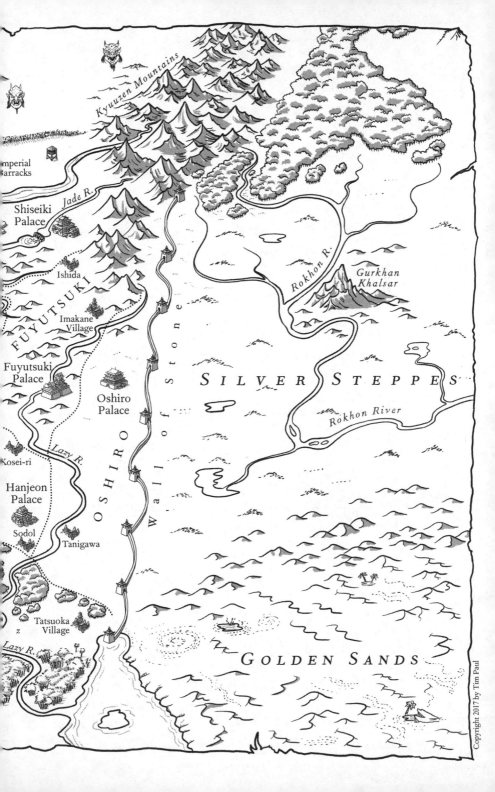

Kyuuzen Mountains

Imperial
Barracks

Jade R.

Shiseiki
Palace

Ishida

FUYUTSUKI

Imakane
Village

Rokhon R.

Gurkhan
Khalsar

Fuyutsuki
Palace

Oshiro
Palace

S I L V E R   S T E P P E S

Rokhon River

Lazy R.

Kosei-ri

OSHIRO

Wall of Stone

Hanjeon
Palace

Sodol

Tanigawa

Tatsuoka
Village

z

Lazy R.

G O L D E N   S A N D S

THE TIGER'S DAUGHTER

THE EMPRESS

ONE

Empress Yui wrestles with her broken zither. She'd rather deal with the tiger again. Or the demons. Or her uncle. Anything short of going north, anything short of war. But a snapped string? One cannot reason with a snapped string, nor can one chop it in half and be rid of the problem.

When she stops to think on it—chopping things in half is part of why she's alone with the stupid instrument to begin with. Did she not say she'd stop dueling? What was she thinking, accepting Rayama-tun's challenge? He is only a boy.

And now he will be the boy who dueled One-Stroke Shizuka, the boy whose sword she cut in half before he managed to draw it. That story will haunt him for the rest of his life.

The Phoenix Empress, Daughter of Heaven, the Light of Hokkaro, Celestial Flame—no, she is alone, let her wear her own name—O-Shizuka pinches her scarred nose. When was the last day she behaved the way an Empress should?

Shizuka—can she truly be Shizuka, for an hour?—twists the silk between her first two fingers and threads it through the offending peg. Honestly. The nerve! Sitting in her rooms, taking up her valuable space. Taunting her. She can hear her father's voice now: *Shizuka, it will only be an hour, won't you play me something?*

But O-Itsuki, Imperial Poet, brother to the Emperor, heard music wherever he heard words. Scholars say that the Hokkaran language itself was not really born until O-Itsuki began to write in it. What use did he have for his daughter's haphazard playing?

Shizuka, your mother is so tired and upset; surely your music will lift her spirits and calm her!

But it was never the music that cheered her mother. It was merely seeing Shizuka play. The sight of her daughter doing something other than swinging a sword. O-Shizuru did little else with her time, given her position as Imperial Executioner. Wherever she went, the Crows followed in her footsteps. Already thirty-six by the time she gave birth to her only child, O-Shizuru wore her world-weariness like a crown.

And who could blame her, with the things she had done?

Ah—but Shizuka hadn't understood, back then, why her mother was always so exhausted. Why she bickered with the Emperor whenever she saw him. Why it was so important to her that her daughter was more than a duelist, more than a fighter, more like her father, and less like . . .

The Empress frowns. She runs the string along the length of the zither, toward the other peg. Thanks to her modest height, it takes a bit of doing. She manages. She always does.

Perhaps she will be a musician yet. She will play the music Handa wrote for *View from Rolling Hills*, she thinks.

The melody is simple enough that she's memorized it already, soothing enough that she can lose herself in its gentle rise and fall.

Funny how you can hate a poem until the day you relate to it. Then it becomes your favorite.

She strikes the first notes—and that is when the footfalls meet her ears.

Footfalls meet her ears, and her frown only grows deeper.

No visitors, she said. No treating with courtiers, no inane trade meetings, no audiences with the public, nothing. Just her and the zither for an hour. One hour! Was that so difficult to understand?

She shakes her head. Beneath her breath she mutters an apology to her father.

One of the newer pages scurries to the threshold. He's wearing black and silver robes emblazoned with Dao Doan Province's seal. Is this Jiro-tul's latest son? He has so many, she can't keep track anymore. Eventually she's going to have to make an effort to remember the servants' names.

The new boy prostrates himself. He offers her a package wrapped in dark cloth and tied together with twine. It's so bulky the boy's hands quiver just holding it.

Some idiot suitor's latest gift. Only one thing makes a person foolhardy enough to contradict the Empress's will, and that is infatuation. Not love. Love has the decency to send up a note, not whatever this was.

"You may speak," she says.

"Your Imperial Majesty," he says, "this package was, we think, addressed to you—"

"You think?" She crooks a brow. "Rise."

The boy rises to his knees. She beckons him closer, and he scrambles forward, dropping the package in the process. It's a book. It must be. That sort of heavy thwack can come only from a book.

"Doan-tun," she says, "you are not in trouble, but tell me: Why are you bringing me something you can't be certain is mine?"

He's close enough now that she can see the wisps of black hair clinging to his upper lip. Good. From a distance, it looked like he'd taken a punch to the face.

"Your Imperial Majesty, Most Serene Empress Phoenix—"

" 'Your Imperial Majesty' suffices in private conversation."

He swallows. "Your Imperial Majesty," he says, "the handwriting is, if you will forgive my bluntness, atrocious. When I received it, I had a great deal of difficulty deciphering it."

O-Shizuka turns toward the zither as the boy speaks. For not the first time in recent years, she considers trimming her nails. But she likes the look of them, likes the glittering dust left behind by the crushed gems she dipped them in each morning. "Continue."

As he speaks she runs her fingertips along the strings of her zither. If she closes her eyes she can still hear *View from Rolling Hills*.

"I sought out the aid of the elder servants," he says. "One of them pointed out that this is in the horse script."

O-Shizuka stops mid-motion.

No one writes to her in Qorin. No Hokkaran courtiers bother learning it. Horselords are beneath them, and thus there is no reason to learn their tongue. It's the same reason only Xianese lords learn to read and write that language, the same reason Jeon is a cipher more than a tongue, the same reason one only ever reads of Doanese Kings in faded, musty scrolls.

The saying goes that to survive is Qorin—but the same can be said of the Hokkaran Empire, scavenging parts from the nations it swallows up, swearing that these borrowed clothes have been Imperial Finery all along. How did that drivel go? Hokkaro is a mother to unruly young nations, ever watchful, ever present. Shizuka always hated it.

So the letter cannot be from a Hokkaran, for what Hokkaran would deign to debase themselves in such a way? Burqila's calligraphy is serviceable, if not perfect; the servants would have no trouble with anything she sent. Which leaves only one Qorin who might write to her in the rough horse-tongue.

It's been eight years, she thinks, eight years since . . .

"I asked one of your older handmaidens, Keiko-lao, and she said your old friend Oshiro-sun couldn't write Hokkaran at all, so I thought—"

Sun. There are thirty-two different honorifics in Hokkaran— eight sets of four. Each set is used only in specific circumstances. Using the wrong one is akin to walking up to someone and spitting into their mouth.

So why was it that, to this day, Shefali remained Oshiro-sun? The boy should know better. Sun is for outsiders, and Shefali was . . .

"Give it to me," O-Shizuka snaps.

He offers it to her again, and when she takes it, her hands brush against his. That fleeting contact with the Empress is more than any other boy his age could dream of.

Naturally, he will tell all the others about it the moment he has a chance. His stories will be a bit more salacious, as he is a young man, and she is the Virgin Empress, and they are alone together save the guards standing outside.

O-Shizuka's hands tremble as she reaches for the paper attached to the package. Yes, she who is known as the Lady of Ink, the finest calligrapher in the Empire: her hands tremble like an old woman's.

The Hokkaran calligraphy is closer to a pig's muddy footprints than to anything legible, but the bold Qorin characters are unmistakable.

For O-Shizuka of Hokkaro, from Barsalyya Shefali Alshar.

That name!

Nothing could make her smile like this, not even hearing the Sister's secret song itself.

"Doan-tun," she says, her voice little more than a whisper. "Cancel all my appointments for the next two days."

"What?" he says. "Your Imperial Majesty, the Merchant Prince of Sur-Shar arrives tomorrow!"

"And he can make himself quite comfortable in whichever brothel he chooses until I am prepared to speak to him," O-Shizuka says. "Unless my uncle has finally done me the favor of dying, I am not to be bothered. You are dismissed."

"But, Your Imperial Majesty—"

"Dismissed," repeats Shizuka, this time sharp as the nails of her right hand. The boy leaves.

And she is alone.

Alone as she has been for eight years. Alone with her crown, her zither, her paper, her ink, her Imperial bed.

Alone.

But as she unwraps the package and uncovers the book under-neath, she can hear Shefali's voice in her mind. She can smell her: horses and sweat, milk and leather. And there, pressed between the first two pages—

Two pine needles.

When her eyes first land on the Qorin characters in the book, O-Shizuka's heart begins to sing.

THE COLORS OF THE FLOWERS

Shizuka, my Shizuka. If Grandmother Sky is good, then this finds
you sitting on your throne, eating far too many sweets, and com-
plaining about all the meetings you must attend.

My apologies for the awful calligraphy. I know you are shaking your head even as you read this, saying something about my
brushstrokes not being decisive enough.

I have so many questions for you, and I'm certain you have
just as many for me. Here in the East, I hear rumors of what
you've been up to. Is it true you returned to Shiseiki Province
and slew a Demon General? You must tell me the story. And
do not brush off the details, Shizuka. I can almost hear your
voice.

"It really was nothing. . . ."

The day will come when we share stories over kumaq and rice
wine. I know it will. But until then, paper and ink are all we have.

They are old friends of yours, and have kindly agreed to keep you company in my absence.

Do you remember the first time we met, Shizuka, or has that long faded from your memory? It is my favorite story in all the world to tell. Oh, you know it well. But let me tell it all the same. Let me have my comfort. Without you, I am in the dark. It has been so long, Shizuka, that I might mistake a candle for the sun.

Our births—that is where I should start, though I doubt there exists a soul who has not heard about yours. Hokkarans rely on numbers and superstition more than they rely on sense, so when you popped out of your mother's womb on the Eighth of Ji-Dao, the whole Empire boomed with joy. Your existence alone was cause for celebration. Your uncle, the Emperor, had let fourteen years go by without producing an heir.

And there was the matter of your parents, as well. The most well-loved poet of his time and the national hero who slew a Demon General with nothing but her fabled sword and my mother's assistance, those were your father and mother. When you were born, both were nearing forty.

I cannot imagine the elation the Empire felt after holding its breath for so long. Fourteen years without an heir, fourteen years spent tiptoeing on eggshells. All it would take was one errant arrow to bring your entire dynasty to its knees.

So you saved them. From the first moment of your life, Shizuka, you have been saving people. But you have never been subtle, never been modest, and so you chose the eighth of Ji-Dao to be born.

The eighth day of the eighth month, in the year dedicated to the Daughter—the eighth member of the Heavenly Family. Legend has it, you were born eight minutes into Last Bell, as well, though no one can really know for certain. I cannot say it would surprise me. You do not do anything halfway.

But there was another thing about your birth—something we shared.

The moment my mother put you in your mother's hands, two pine needles fell on your forehead, right between your eyes.

One month later, on the first of Qurukai, I was born beneath the Eternal Sky. Like all Qorin, I was born with a patch of blue on my bottom; unlike the others, mine was so pale, it was nearly white. I was not screaming, and I did not cry until my mother slapped me. The sanvaartains present told her that this was a bad sign—that a baby who did not cry at birth would make up for it when she died in agony.

I can imagine you shaking your head. It's true—Qorin portents are never pleasant.

But my mother scoffed, just as your mother scoffed, and presented me to the sanvaartain for blessings anyway. Just as the sanvaartain held the bowl of milk above my head, just as the first drops splashed onto my brow, she saw them.

Two pine needles stuck together between my eyes.

There are no pine trees in that part of the steppes.

When my mother told yours about what had happened, our fates were decided. The pine needles were an omen—we would always be friends, you and I, always together. To celebrate our good fortune, your father wrote a poem on the subject. Don't you find it amusing, Shizuka? Everyone thinks that poem was about your parents, but it was about us the whole time.

When we were three, our mothers introduced us. Shizuru and Alshara wrote to each other for months about it. For all your mother's incredible abilities, for all her skills and talents, conceiving was almost impossible for her. Your mother, the youngest of five bamboo mat salespeople, worried you'd grow up lonely. Burqila Alshara wasn't having that. She offered to take you in for a summer on the steppes, so that we might share our earliest memories together.

But the moment you laid eyes on me, something within you snapped. I cannot know what it was—I have no way of seeing into your thoughts—but I can only imagine the intensity of it.

All I know is that the first thing I can remember seeing, the first sight to embed itself like an arrow in the trunk of my mind, is your face contorted with rage.

And when I say rage, you must understand the sort of anger I am discussing. Normal children get upset when they lose a toy or when their parents leave the room. They weep, they beat their little fists against the ground, they scream.

But it was not so with you. Your lips were drawn back like a cat's, your teeth flashing in the light. Your whole face was taut with fury. Your scream was wordless and dark, sharp as a knife.

You moved so fast, they could not stop you. A rush of red, yes—the color of your robes. Flickering golden ornaments in your hair. Dragons, or phoenixes, it matters not. Snarling, you wrapped your hands around my throat. Spittle dripped onto my forehead. When you shook me, my head knocked against the floor.

I struggled, but I could not throw you off. You'd latched on. Whatever hate drove you made you ten times as vicious as any child has a right to be. In desperation I tried rolling away from you.

On the third roll, we knocked into a brazier. Burning oil spilled out and seared your shoulder. Only that immense pain was enough to distract you. By the time your mother pulled you off me, I had bruises along my throat, and you had a scar on your shoulder.

O-Shizuru apologized, or maybe O-Itsuki. I think it must have been both of them. Your mother chided you for what you'd done, while your father swore to Alshara that you'd never done anything like this before.

Before that day, before you tried to kill me, no one ever said no to you.

You did not come to stay with us that summer.

Soon, Shizuru scheduled your first appointment with your music tutor. The problem, in her mind, was that you were too much like her. If only you fell in love with poetry, like your father; or music or calligraphy; cooking or engineering or the medical arts; even acting! Anything.

Anything but warfare.

And as for my mother's reaction? As far as my mother was concerned, O-Shizuru's only sin in life was not learning how to speak Qorin after all their years as friends. That attitude extended to you, as well, though you had not earned it. O-Shizuru and Burqila Alshara spent eight days being tortured together, and years after that rescuing one another. When the Emperor insisted that O-Shizuru tour the Empire with an honor guard at her back, your mother scoffed in his face.

"Dearest Brother-in-Law," she said, "I'll run around the border like a show horse, if that's what you want me to do, but I'm not taking the whole stable with me. Burqila and I lived, so Burqila and I will travel, and let the Mother carry to sleep any idiot who says otherwise. Your honored self included."

Legend has it that O-Shizuru did not wait for an answer, or even bow on the way out of the palace. She left for the stables, saddled her horse, and rode out to Oshiro as soon as she could. Thus began our mothers' long journey through the Empire, with your father doing his best to try to keep up.

So—no, there was nothing your mother could do wrong. And when you stand in so great a shadow as O-Shizuru's, well—my mother was bound to overlook your failings.

But my mother did insist on one thing—taking a clipping of your hair, and braiding it into mine. She gave your mother a clipping of my hair and instruction, for the same reason. Old Qorin tradition, you see—part of your soul stays in your hair when the wind blows through it. By braiding ours together, she hoped to end our bickering.

I can't say that she was right or wrong—only that as a child, I liked touching your hair. It's so much thicker than mine, Shizuka, and so much glossier. I wish I still had that lock of hair—I treasure all my remnants of you, but to have your hair in a place so far from home . . .

Let me tell you another story, the ending of which you know, but let us take our time arriving there. May you hear this in my voice, and not the careful accent of a gossiping courtier. May you hear the story itself, and not the rumors the rest may have whispered to you.

WHEN I WAS FIVE, my mother took my brother and me back to the steppes. We spent too long in the palace at Oshiro, she said; our minds sprouted roots. She did not actually say that out loud, of course—my brother spoke for her. In those days, he was the one who read her signing. My mother uses a form of signing employed by deaf Qorin, passed down from one to another through the years. Kenshiro did not spend much time traveling with the clan, due to my father's objections, but my brother has always been too studious for his own good. If he could only see our mother once every eight years, then he wanted to be able to impress her.

Thus, he taught himself to sign.

Was my mother impressed? This is a difficult question. As commendable as it was that my brother went to such lengths, he was Not Qorin. He could never be, when he wore a face so like my father's, when he wore his Hokkaran name with such pride.

But he was my brother, and I loved him dearly, and when he told me this was going to be the best year of our lives, I believed him.

On our first night on the whistling Silver Steppes, I almost froze to death. The temperature there drops faster than—well, you've been there, Shizuka, you know. It's customary for mothers to rub their children down with urine just to keep them warm. No one sleeps alone; ten to fifteen of us all huddle together beneath our white felt gers. Even then the nights are frozen. Until I was eight and returned to Hokkaro, I slept in my brother's bedroll, and huddled against him to keep the cold away.

On one such night, he spoke to me of our names.

"Shefali," he said, "when you are out here, you are not Oshiro-sun. You know that, right?"

I stared at him. I was five. That is what five-year-olds do. He mussed my hair as he spoke again.

"Well, you know now," he said. "Our mother's the Kharsa, sort of. That means she's like the Emperor, but for Qorin people."

"No throne," I said.

"She doesn't need one," said Kenshiro. "She has her mare and the respect of her people."

Ah. Your uncle was a ruler, and so was my mother. They must be the same.

I did not know much about your family back then. Oh, everyone knew your uncle was the Son of Heaven, and his will in all things was absolute. And everyone knew your mother and my mother, together, killed one of the four Demon Generals and lived to tell the tale.

But I didn't much care about any of that. It didn't affect me as much as *you* did, as much as the memory of you did. For you were never far from my mother's mind, and she was always quick to say that the two of us must be like two pine needles.

Yes, she said "pine needles"—the woman who lived for plains and open sky. I always thought it strange, and when I learned it was a line of your father's poetry, I thought it stranger.

But still, I grew to think of you as . . .

Not the way I thought of Kenshiro. He was my brother. He taught me things, and spoke to me, and helped me hunt. But you?

I did not know how to express it, but when I touched the clipping of your hair braided into mine, I knew we were going to be together again. That we were always going to be together. As Moon chases Sun, so would I chase you.

But during my first journey around the steppes, I learned how different our two nations were.

Kenshiro was teaching me how to shoot. The day before this, Grandmother Sky blessed us with rain, and I hadn't thought to pack my bow away in its case. The second I tried to draw it back, it came apart in my hands; the string sliced me across the cheek and ear.

As I was a child, I broke out crying. Kenshiro did his best to calm me.

Two men who were watching us cackled.

"Look at that filthy mongrel!" called the taller one. He was thin and bowlegged, and he wore a warm wool hat with drooping earflaps. When he spoke, I caught sight of his teeth. What few he had left were brown. His deel was green and decorated with circles. Two braids hung in front of his right earflap, with bright beads at the end. "I tell you, it is because she was born indoors. Burqila is a fool for keeping her."

My brother was eleven then. For a Qorin boy, he was short. For a Hokkaran, he was tall and gangly, all elbows and knees. He stood in front of me, and I thought he was big as a tree.

"She was born outside," he said. "Everyone knows that, Boorchu. And if she wasn't, it wouldn't make her any less Qorin."

"And why should I listen to a boy with roots for feet?" said Boorchu. "If she had a real teacher—"

"Her bow was wet," he said. "Of course it broke. It could've happened to you, too."

"No, boy," said the tall man. "I know better. Because I was born on the steppes, and I grew beneath the sky, without a roof to suffocate me. You and your sister are pale-faced rice-eaters, and that is the plain truth."

The shorter one—who was squat and had only one braid—only snorted. I don't know why. "Rice-eater" is not a piercing insult. "Ricetongue" is far worse. And on top of that, they called both Kenshiro and me pale-faced, when only Kenshiro is pale. I'm dark as a bay. Anyone can see that.

"Boorchu," said the shorter one then, grabbing his friend's arm. "Boorchu, you should—"

"I'm not going to stop," said the tall one. "Burqila never should've married that inkdrinker. A good Qorin man, that is what she needs. One who'll give her strong sons and stubborn daughters, who don't snap their strings like fat little—"

All at once Boorchu grew quiet. Shock dawned on him, and soon he was the pale-faced one.

Someone touched my head. When I turned, my mother had emerged from the ger. A silent snarl curled her lips. She snapped to get Kenshiro's attention, and then her fingers spoke for her, flying into shapes I could not read.

"My mother says you are to repeat what you just said," Kenshiro translated. His voice shook. He squeezed me a bit tighter, and when he next spoke, he did so in Hokkaran. "Mother, if you're going to hurt him—"

She cut him off with more gestures. Her horsewhip hung from her belt, opposite her sword; to a child, both were frightening.

Kenshiro made a soft, sad sound.

Boorchu stammered. "I said that, I said, er, that your daughter . . ."

"A good Qorin man?" Kenshiro said, reading my mother's signs. "I don't see any here. Come forward, Boorchu." Then he broke into Hokkaran again. "Mother, please. She's only five."

What were they talking about? Why was Boorchu sweating so much, why had his friend run away, why was my brother trembling?

Boorchu dragged his feet. "Burqila," he said, "I just want them to be strong. If you never let them hear what people think of them, they'll weep at everything. You don't want them to be spoiled, do you?"

My mother clapped her hands. One of the guards—a woman with short hair and a scar across her face, with more braids than loose hair—snapped to attention.

"Bring the felt," Kenshiro translated.

And the guard ran to get it. In a minute, no more, she returned. She bound Boorchu's hands together with rope and wrapped him in the felt blanket. He kept screaming. The sound, Shizuka! Though it was soon muffled, it reverberated in my ears, my chest. It was getting harder to breathe.

"Ken," I said, "Ken, what's happening?"

"You should turn away," he replied. "You don't have to watch this."

But I couldn't. The sight and sound fixed me in place. My eyes watered, not from sadness, but from fear; my brain rattled in my skull.

"Shefali," he said, "look away."

My mother drew her sword. She didn't bother signing anymore. No, she walked up to the man in the felt binding and ran him through. Just like that. I remember how red spread out from the hilt of her sword like a flower blossoming. I remember the wet crunch of bones giving way, the slurp as she pulled her sword back.

Kenshiro ran his hands through my hair. "Shefali," he said, "I'm sorry. You shouldn't have . . . I'm sorry."

I wasn't paying attention.

I couldn't look away from the bundle of white-turning-red. I saw something coming out of it, glimmering in the air, swirling like smoke. As I watched, it scattered to the winds.

This was unspoken horror. This was water falling from the ground into the sky. This was a river of stone, this was a bird with fur, this was wet fire. I felt deep in my body that I was seeing something I was never meant to see.

I pointed out the flickering lights to Kenshiro with a trembling hand. "What's that?"

He glanced over, then turned his attention back to me. He stroked my cheeks. "The sky, Shefali," he said. "The Endless Sky, who sees all."

But that wasn't what I saw. I knew the sky. I was born with a patch of it on my lower back, and though the birthmark faded, the memory remained. Grandmother Sky never made me feel like this.

I felt like an arrow, trembling against a bowstring. Like the last drop of dew clinging to a leaf. Like a warhorn being sounded for the first time.

"Ken-ken," I said, "do you see the sparkles?"

And, ah—the moment I spoke, I knew something within me had changed. I felt the strangest urge to look North, toward the Wall of Flowers. At the time, I'd heard only the barest stories about it. I knew that it was beautiful, and I knew that it was full of the Daughter's magic.

How could I have known that the Wall was where blackbloods went to die?

How was I to know?

Kenshiro furrowed his brow. "You're just stressed, Shefali," he whispered. "You saw something you shouldn't have. But you'll be all right, I promise."

I bit my lip, hard. Kenshiro couldn't see it.

Maybe he was right. Kenshiro was right about a lot of things. He always knew where the sun was going to rise in the morning, and he knew the names for all the constellations.

But that didn't change the awful feeling in my stomach, or the rumbling I now heard in the distance, or the whisper telling me "go north." I looked around the camp for an oncoming horde, but I saw none. Yet there was the sound rolling between my ears; there was the clatter of a thousand horses.

It wasn't there, I told myself, it wasn't there, and I was safe with my mother and Kenshiro.

But for the rest of that day, I couldn't shake the feeling that something awful had happened.

Kenshiro told me Tumenbayar stories to pass the time. Tumenbayar is something like your ancestor Minami Shiori—there are hundreds of stories about her. All of them are true, of course, especially the ones that contradict each other.

It was one week later that I received your first letter. When the messenger first brought it out of his bag, I knew it was yours by sight alone. You sent it sealed in a bright red envelope, emblazoned with golden ink. I snatched it out of his hands in a way that made Kenshiro apologize for my rudeness, and I pressed it to my nose so I could smell you.

You might find it strange that I was so excited for a letter from a girl who tried to kill me. The truth is, I never bore you any ill will for what you did. When you first saw me, you were struck with unspeakable rage.

But when I saw you, I . . .

Imagine you are a rider, Shizuka, a Qorin rider. You have been out in the forests to the north for some time, trying to find something to feed your clanmates. Two days you've been hunting. Hunger twists your stomach into knots. You can hardly will yourself to move. Behind you, you hear something in the trees. You turn, you fire, and you slow down enough to see your catch: two fat marmots, speared together by your arrow.

Seeing you was like seeing those marmots. I knew everything would be all right, so long as I had you near me.

So your letter understandably excited me, and getting to smell it thrilled me even more so. A person's soul is in their scent. For the first time since Boorchu died, when I took a breath of your perfumed paper, I felt safe.

Until I tried to read the letter. Then I only felt frustrated. I stared at the characters and pretended I could read them. I traced them with one finger, and imagined what you might say to me.

Kenshiro caught me at it. "Is that—?"

He tried to take the letter from me. Only Grandmother Sky could've pried it away from my grubby little hands. After some coaxing, he convinced me to hold it out so he could read it.

His bushy brows rose halfway up his forehead. "Shefali," he said, "is this from the Peacock Princess?"

I nodded.

He let out a whistle. "You've made an important friend! Can you read this?" When I shook my head, he sat down next to me. "Then it's time for some tutoring. Follow along with my finger."

To be honest, I couldn't follow any of the writing at all. Your calligraphy was beautiful even then, but I could never make sense of it.

You can read Qorin letters, Shizuka. Imagine if every time you blinked, everything changed. Where the letters were. What they looked like. Imagine if they went from right side up to upside down and backwards. That is what happens to me when I read Hokkaran.

I made Kenshiro read it to me so many times that I remember it still.

> *Oshiro Shefali,*
>> *My parents are making me write this because they think I need to apologize to you. I think that's silly. You know that I*

am sorry, so why do I have to tell you again? But my mother
wants us to be friends, so I have to write to you.

Big lumpy Qorin horses don't interest me, and neither does
archery. I don't know what we can talk about. Do you like
flowers? I don't know if they have flowers on the Silver
Steppes. Peonies and chrysanthemums are my favorites.
Most of the time I can guess what everyone else's favorite is,
but whenever I try to think of yours, I can't do it. If you don't
like chrysanthemums at least, then you're wrong, and I'll
have to show you all of mine when I see you next.

I'm going to see you again. You're not getting out of that.
My uncle is the Son of Heaven, you know. I don't really like
him but that means people have to do what I tell them.

Respectfully,
O-Shizuka

After horse riding, reading your letter was my favorite way to
spend my time. Kenshiro had other things to take care of, though.
My mother insisted he learn how to wrestle and shoot and ride in
the traditional way.

The trouble was, I didn't have any friends while my brother was
away.

While Hokkarans hate me because I am dark and flaxen haired
and remind them of a horse, the Qorin dislike me because they
think I am too pampered. When I was a child, it was worse.

My nose didn't help.

I have my mother's round cheeks, which you always seemed to
have an unending fascination for. I have her wavy hair, her skin, her
height, her bowleggedness, her large hands, her grass green eyes.

But of all the features on my wide, flat face, my nose stands out. It is narrow, pinched, and begging for a fist to reshape it. My father's stamp on me.

Qorin children are not known for being well behaved. One day I was out riding on a borrowed colt, and when I returned, I found a half circle of my cousins waiting for me. At their head stood a pudgy ten-year-old whose face was round as a soup bowl and flecked with freckles.

"You're Burqila's daughter!" she said. "The one with the stupid nose!"

I frowned and covered my face. I tried to nudge my horse forward, but my cousins did not move.

"Needlenose," called my cousin. "Come off your horse, Needlenose! We've got to wrestle!"

Wrestling is my least favorite of the three manly arts. Riding? I can, and have, ridden a horse all day. Archery is more a passion than a chore. But wrestling? I'm still a lean little thing, Shizuka; my cousins have always been able to throw me clean across the ring.

"What?" sneered my cousin. She slapped her broad chest, smacked her belly. "Are you afraid?"

I touched my horse's shoulder. Horseflesh is always solid and firm and warm.

"No."

"Then you'd better get down off that horse!" she said. "Don't make us get you!"

I raised a brow. I was on a horse. The entire purpose of riding was to be able to get away from things fast.

But maybe I was a bit too cocky about that, seeing as I was surrounded by people who spend their whole lives around horses. Who own horses. And, as fate would have it, the colt I was riding belonged to one of my bully cousins. My mother thought I should learn how to handle a stranger's mount as well as I could my own. I thought that was silly—as if I was ever going to ride anything but my grey. Still, she plopped me down on this colt and set me off for the day. My cousin couldn't have been happier. He whistled and pulled out a treat from his deel pocket, and the horse trotted right up to him.

Which meant I was now close enough for my half dozen cousins to pull me off my horse and slam me to the ground.

What followed was a beating that I shall not waste any words on. You know how savage children can be. Qorin traditions forbid us from shedding one another's blood, but that has never stopped us from beating the tar out of each other. Kicking, punching, hair pulling—none of these draw blood. So it was.

I limped back to the ger in tears. The moment my mother laid eyes on me, she sprang to her feet and wrapped me in an embrace. Through sign language and interpreters, she told me she'd take care of things.

It wasn't hard for her to find out who put me in such a state, given how few Qorin are left. Within two hours, my mother corraled a half dozen of my cousins near her ger. Mother paced in front of them. Her fingers spoke in sharp, punctuated gestures.

"I understand the lot of you beat my daughter," Kenshiro translated.

My cousins shifted on the balls of their feet. A boy toward the end of the line cried. I stood behind my mother and sniffled.

"You are children," Kenshiro continued. "My sisters' children,

at that. If you were anyone else's brats, I'd have the beating returned two times over. But my sisters have always supported me,
even if they have spawned lawless brutes."

She came to a stop and pointed to the tallest cousin, the chubby
girl who wanted to wrestle me. As she stepped forward, I wrapped
my arms around my mother's leg.

"Otgar," said Kenshiro, "Zurgaanqar Bayaar is the meekest of
my sisters. When she was young, she was quiet as Shefali, and half
her size. Tell me, would you have pulled her from her horse and
beaten her senseless?"

Otgar crossed her arms. "Mom doesn't have a stupid nose," she
said.

What was it with her and noses? Hers was dumb-looking, too!
Her whole face was dumb!

"Otgar Bayasaaq," said Kenshiro, "you speak Hokkaran, don't
you?"

Otgar nodded. "Who doesn't?"

"A lot of children your age don't," Kenshiro said. Ironic. My
mother chuckled at her joke, making my brother speak those
words. "And you can read it?"

"Yes," Otgar said. "My father is a merchant, Aunt Burqila, you
know this!"

My mother nodded.

"Very well," she said through Kenshiro. "Since you have such
a fascination with my daughter, you are now assigned to be her
companion. For your first task, you will help her learn to read and
write the Ricetongue. She's received a letter from Naisuran's
daughter. Start with that."

"What?" Otgar and I shouted at once.

"She's scrawny and dumb-looking!" Otgar protested.

"She hates me!" I said.

But my mother shook her head.

"My word is final," Kenshiro spoke. "Get into the ger now, or I will throw you in it."

We trudged into the ger, all right, but it was some time before either of us spoke to each other. Two hours in, I decided that even if she was uncouth, if she could read Hokkaran, she could help me.

So I handed her your letter.

She yanked it from me and read it with a frown. "Grandmother's tits," she said with all the grace of a ten-year-old. "It really is Naisuran's daughter. Guess I shouldn't expect any less from a spoiled tree-baby like you."

"Don't like trees," I said. "Too tall."

"Yeah, well, they don't move around either," said Otgar. "And neither do you." She sighed. "Fine. Let's take a look, I guess. Can you write?"

I shook my head.

"Can you read this?"

Again, I shook my head.

She tilted her head back and groaned. "I didn't think Burqila hated me this much," she said. "But I guess we've got work to do."

I can't remember how long it took us to write back. I knew what I wanted to say to you, of course. Otgar wrote it down for me and walked me through each character ten, twenty times. She'd write them in the soot and ash of the campfire.

The trouble came when I tried to write them myself. Invariably I'd write a different character from the one I was instructed, and it would be flipped or upside down. Missing strokes, superfluous strokes; it was a mess, Shizuka. And after weeks of trying, I hadn't learned a single one.

Otgar was at her wits' end over it. "You speak Ricetongue like a native."

Pointing out my Hokkaran blood upset people, and she was beginning to think of me as more Qorin than Hokkaran. I kept quiet.

"It's the writing," she said. She cracked her knuckles. "Needlenose, you don't plan on going back there, do you?"

I shook my head. From the way my mother kept talking about things, I'd be spending more time with her on the steppes in the future. According to her marriage contract, she was not allowed to style herself Grand Kharsa of the Qorin, but her children were not bound by such rules. My father wanted Kenshiro to succeed him as Lord of Oshiro. That left me to take up her lost title.

I didn't know what any of that meant, except for two things: One day I'd be as terrifying as my mother, and the steppes were home now.

Otgar nodded. She reached for one of the precious few pieces of vellum we had. It was a rough thing, jagged at the edges, that reeked of old skin. She grabbed an old ink block and sat down in front of me.

"Repeat what you wanted to write," she said. "I'll do it for you. If you do go back to Hokkaro, you'll have servants to write things down for you anyway."

Then, as if she realized what she was saying, she grunted.

"But I'm not a servant," she said. "Don't you ever forget that, Needlenose. I'm your cousin. I'm helping you because we're family, and because Burqila asked—"

"—told—"

She pursed her lips. "Asked me to," she finished. "Now, let's hear it one more time."

So I spoke, and so Otgar wrote.

> *O-Shizuka,*
>
> *Thank you for saying sorry, even though you didn't have to. I've never seen a peony, or a chrysanthemum. There aren't many flowers here. Mostly it's grass and wolves, and sometimes marmots. Every now and again, we will see one or two flowers. Of the ones I've seen, I like mountain lilies the most. They grow only on the great mountain Gurkhan Khalsar. Gurkhan Khalsar is the closest place there is to the Endless Sky, so those flowers are very sacred.*
>
> *If you teach me more about flowers, I can teach you how to wrestle, but I'm not very good.*
>
> *My cousin is helping me write to you. Hokkaran is hard.*
>
> *Shefali Alsharyya*

I sent that off and waited every day for your reply. Our messengers all hated me. Whenever I saw one, I'd tug their deel and ask if there was anything for me.

We take some pride in our messengers. Before we began acting as couriers, it was almost impossible to get a message from the Empire to Sur-Shar. My mother saw how foolish that was. After she'd traveled the steppes to unite us, she established one messenger's post every one week's ride. With the help of the Surians she recruited into the clan, each post was given a unique lockbox that only the messengers could open. Anyone could drop any letters they needed mailed inside the lockboxes. For a higher fee, you could have one of the messengers come personally pick up whatever it was.

Everyone used our couriers—Surians, Ikhthians, Xianese, and even your people. Oh, the nobles would never admit to it, and we had to employ Ricetongues in the Empire itself—but they used us all the same.

Which meant they paid us.

People seem to think my mother is wealthy because of the plunder from breaking open the Wall. In fact, she is wealthy because of the couriers. That and the trading. You'd be surprised how canny a trader Burqila Alshara can be.

But the fact remains that I pestered our messengers so much that they came to hate visiting us. Every single day, I'd ask for news.

For months, there wasn't any.

But one day there was. Another bright red envelope dipped in priceless perfume. Once I read it, it joined its sibling in my bedroll, so that I could smell it as I went to sleep.

> *Alsharyya Shefali,*
>
> *Your calligraphy is terrible. Father says I shouldn't be mad at you, because it is very strange that I can write as well as I do. I'm mad at you anyway. You are going to kill blackbloods with me someday. You should have better handwriting! Don't worry, I'll teach you. If I write you a new letter every day, and you reply to all of them, then you'll be better in no time.*
>
> *Where are you now? Mother says you're traveling. Qorin do that a lot. I don't understand it. Why take a tent with you, when you have a warm bed at home? Do you have a bed? Do you have a room, or do you have to stay in your mother's tent? Do you have your own big lumpy horse already? My father says I can't have a proper one until I can take care of it, which is silly, because I'm the Imperial Niece*

and there will always be someone to take care of my horse
for me.

Maybe you can do it. Mostly I just want to go into the
Imperial Forest. Father says there are tigers.

My tutors tell me that I should be afraid of you and your
mother. They say that Burqila Alshara blew a hole in the
Wall of Stone and burned down Oshiro, and it took years
before it was back to normal. They tell me that if your mother
hadn't married your father, then we'd all be dead.

I don't want us all to be dead, but if your mother could talk
to my uncle—he keeps arguing with my father and making
everyone upset. Do you think your mother could scare him?

Are you afraid of your mother? I'm not afraid of mine, and
people keep whispering about how dangerous she is. No one
tells me not to talk to my mother, but everyone tells me not to
talk to you. I think it's because you're Qorin.

My tutors won't tell me why they don't like Qorin, but I've
heard the way they talk about your people. I'm five years old.
I'm not stupid. They don't like Xianese people, either, but
they'll wear Xianese clothes and play Xianese music all the
time.

It doesn't matter. I like you in spite of your awful hand-
writing, so they have to like you too.

I hope you're doing well.

O-Shizuka

So began our correspondence. You'd write to me; Otgar would
read the letter out loud, and I'd say what I wanted them to write
in return. I'll have you know Otgar was indignant when you insulted her calligraphy. She was a ten-year-old, and she was trying

hard! Not everyone is born with brush and sword in hand, Shi-zuka. There are scholars who write little better than Otgar did at the time.

(She's improved. You'll be happy to know that, I think. The last time I had her write to you was when we were thirteen, and you commented on the marked improvement. She pretended not to take it to heart, but she made a copy of that letter before giving me the original.)

Through the letters our friendship grew. You wrote to me of your endless lessons, of your mother's insistence that you take up the zither despite your hatred of it. You'd tell me about the court-iers you met over the course of your day. Soon the letters grew several pages long.

When I was seven, my mother announced we'd be returning to Oshiro for the summer. I told you all about it.

"We will be sure to meet you at the gates," you wrote. "I will have a surprise for you. Do not be late."

I cannot tell you how much that simple statement vexed me. A surprise. A surprise for me, from the Emperor's niece. Kenshiro said it must be a pretty set of robes—something you'd like, that I would hate. Otgar said it would be something foolish like a moun-tain of rice.

I remember when I came riding back to Oshiro. I didn't see you at the gates, as you promised. Rage filled my young heart; doubt wrung it dry. What if we were late? I'd pestered my mother into moving faster than she'd planned, and I was riding ahead of the caravan by a few hours. What if that wasn't enough?

I took my first steps up the stairs into my father's palace. Ser-vants greeted me with bows and hushed whispers of "Oshiro-sur, welcome home." My bare feet touched the floors.

And that was when I saw it. The first pink peony, laid out with utmost care at the threshold. I picked it up. It smelled just like your letters. I smiled so hard, it hurt my face, and looked around. Yes, there was another, and another!

I ran along the trail of flowers as fast as I could. Soon I was standing before our gardens, where I came to an abrupt stop.

For there you were, standing in the doorway in your shining golden robes, your hair dark as night, your ornaments like stars. There you were, smiling like dawn itself. Behind you were hundreds of flowers, more than I'd ever seen in my entire life, in colors I could not name. There was the angry red of our first meeting, next to the deep scarlet of our last; there was day's first yellow, swaying in the wind next to a gloaming violet.

But it is you I remember most, Shizuka. Your face. Your happiness upon seeing me. And all the flowers somehow staring right at you, as if you were teaching them how to be so bright and cheerful.

"There you are," you said. "How do you like your flowers?"

To this day, I do not know how you got them all to Oshiro. Whoever heard of transporting an entire Imperial Garden? Who would believe me, if I told them? The future Empress of Hokkaro and all her Children, doing such a thing to impress a Qorin girl? Oh, the servants believe it, and I'm sure they're talking about it to this day.

It is just like you, I think, to casually do the impossible.

THE EMPRESS

TWO

Flowers. Yes, Empress Yui—no, no, that was not the name she chose for herself, and it was not the name Shefali called her. Yui, a single character meant to shame her.

Solitude.

Her greatest friend, as her uncle saw things.

But he was wrong. Besides Shefali and Baozhai, Shizuka's greatest friends have always been the flowers.

All her life, they have been at her side. One glance outside will show her the Imperial Gardens, where she spent so much of her youth. If she leans back, she can see them, swaying in the breeze outside like the dancers her father so treasured.

It was her father who took her to the gardens. He'd always had a fondness for them. When she imagines his face, she sees a dogwood tree in the background and a sprig of the blooms tucked behind his ear. He is smiling in the midday sun, humming a tune he is too shy to share with anyone else.

"My little tigress," he'd say, helping her up onto the branches of a cherry blossom tree. He'd touch her on the nose, then pick the brightest flowers for her. Soon they wore matching adornments. "The Daughter is the finest poet in the land," he said, "and see how her flowers always turn to greet you! She must have excellent taste, for you have always been my favorite poem."

How many times has she clung to that phrase?

Is it still true?

She shakes her head. O-Itsuki is long gone, she tells herself. Only his poetry remains, dropping from the lips of amorous scholars, lending bravery to the timid.

Only his poetry, and his brother.

Thinking of her uncle makes the Empress wince. Yoshimoto is nothing like his late brother. He does not even have the common decency to share a resemblance. Where Itsuki was tall and thin, Yoshimoto had always been short and stout. Where Itsuki's cheeks were smooth, Yoshimoto wore a thick beard to hide his youth. Itsuki was a wild maple tree, Yoshimoto was . . .

Shizuka has never been fond of potted plants. She receives them more than any other gift—but no, she has never liked them.

She leans toward the window, lost in thought, lost in memory. Her eyes dance over poppies and jasmine, irises and hibiscus, champa and magnolia. And, yes—if she looks—she can see the golden daffodil.

Her mother hated that daffodil. So did her uncle.

It stands alone, at least two horselengths from the nearest bush, from the nearest tree. The grass around it is, for the most part, untouched. No one dares venture near it. Shizuka didn't even know of the daffodil's existence until one of her walks in the garden.

She was five at the time, she thinks, or perhaps six—before she uprooted the gardens for Shefali's sake, but after they'd first met. Her cousin Daishi Akiko came to visit from Fuyutsuki Province for the summer. Daishi was so far removed from the bloodline that her children would no longer count as Imperial, but she was the closest thing to a friend Shizuka had.

Well, besides Shefali, but then she has always been an exception.

Daishi was only two years older than she, but full of an eight-year-old's audacity. And while their parents were off at court, Daishi convinced her to raid the gardens.

"Raid." That was the word she used. They were going to the corpse blossom, she said, and they were going to steal one of its massive petals. Then they'd sneak into the throne room at night to hide it beneath the Dragon Throne. Imagine Yoshimoto's face! Imagine O-Hanae's!

But the moment they stepped in the garden, with the sun hanging overhead—Shizuka knew something was different.

As the two girls strolled past a rosebush, Daishi suddenly stopped and covered her mouth. "Did you see that?" she asked.

Shizuka, six, pouted and crossed her arms. "Those are roses," she said, "not corpse flowers."

"Walk by them again," said Daishi.

Grumbling, Shizuka did so, and that was when the shock on Daishi's face turned to awe. She pointed with her rough little hands. "They're turning toward you!"

Shizuka rolled her eyes. "Of course they are," she said. "I'm the heir."

Daishi would've slapped her if she could have—but they both

knew she couldn't. That only made Shizuka more bold. "If I tell them to change colors, then they have to do that, too," she boasted, and as she spoke, she reached for a pink one.

But then—ah, it was as if the rose fell into a bowl of golden ink, for the color spread through its petals before their eyes.

Daishi fell backwards, gasping, her hair flying out of its neat bun. Shizuka stood staring at the gilt leaves. She reached out to touch them again, only to find that they were as soft as any other rose's—yet when the light hit them, they shone like her aunt's hair ornaments.

"What did you do?" Daishi said. "How did you—? That isn't something people can just do!"

And though Shizuka's heart was a hummingbird, though her mouth was dry and her fingers trembled, she could not let herself be afraid.

"Don't doubt me, Aki-lun," she said.

Daishi wiped her nose and frowned. After getting to her feet, she, too, touched the flower.

Shizuka yanked it out of her hand. "It's mine," she said, and tucked it behind her ear as her father did. Daishi could hardly argue the point.

But she did smile. "You've got to make me one, too," she said.

And so Shizuka did.

By the start of Seventh Bell, when court finished, Shizuka had changed half the Eastern Garden. O-Shizuru found them laughing, rolling along a patch of golden grass.

But O-Shizuru did not laugh, not at all.

When Shizuka pictures her mother, she sees that look: jaw clenched, thick brows nearly meeting, a look of fear and fury in her eyes.

The moment they saw her, the girls froze, their smiles scattered like dandelion seeds to the wind.

"Daishi-lun," said O-Shizuru, "go to your father."

Daishi swallowed. She bowed to Shizuka, apologized under her breath, and ran as fast as her legs could take her.

And so they were alone, mother and daughter. Shizuka's face felt hot. She hadn't done anything wrong. Why was her mother so upset?

O-Shizuru thumbed her nose. She looked away for a moment, thinking of something her daughter couldn't fathom. Then she shook her head. "Who told you about the daffodil, Shizuka?" she said.

Shizuka paused. "No one," she says. "These are roses, Mother, they're different—"

"I'm well past the age of knowing what a rose looks like," Shizuru cut in.

Shizuka winced. Her mother's warm voice was a sword when she was upset.

O-Shizuru must've realized she was too severe, for she sighed and took her daughter's hand. "Come with me," she said. "I suppose it's time you heard the story."

At the time, that walk had seemed eternal. Frightening, too. Her father never took her to that part of the garden. The farther in they went, the more Shizuka saw random objects sticking up out of the ground—a statue of the Daughter, jade coins. Was that a bamboo mat? What were these things doing in the garden?

But then she saw it, standing alone.

A single golden daffodil.

Shizuru sniffed. "When your father and I were wishing for you," she said, "an old scholar told me I had to bury something I loved." She gestured vaguely at all the detritus around the garden. "I tried, and tried, with all sorts of things. But when I buried my short sword—that's when the flower showed up, gold as the sword's pommel. And then you did, not long after that. It's been here ever since."

And Shizuka remembers the breeze through the garden, remembers the daffodil's quiet dance to unseen music.

She reached out for the flower, but her mother touched her hand.

"Don't touch it," she said sharply. "The scholar said—Shizuka." She took a deep breath. "The day you touch that flower is your last day in the Empire. That's what he said. Do you know what that means?"

"That I'd be going to live with Shefali and the Qorin," Shizuka said, as if it were the most obvious thing in the world.

Shizuru palmed her face. "Shizuka," she said. "You and that girl. Like two pine needles."

At the time, Shizuka had no idea what it meant. After all, she hadn't seen Shefali in years, and when she spoke of running off to join the Qorin, it was just something that popped into her head.

But she knew it sounded right.

"I don't like this," said Shizuru, more to herself than to her daughter. "Changing the colors of things. Priests telling me they can't read your fortune, flowers following you around. You should have a good life. A nice, quiet life, with none of my foolishness and too much of your father's."

A pause. And then.

"Whatever happens," said O-Shizuru, "keep Shefali with you. Whatever is going on with you will also be going on with her.

Now, come on. Your uncle's not going to like this, and the Mother knows we'll hear about it tomorrow."

Years later, Shizuka can say that her mother was right. The next morning, in full view of the court, the Emperor railed against the perils of hubris, against the ungodly affront to His Divine Power in his garden. His thundering reprimands rained down on O-Shizuru—but she remained kneeling, and if she wanted to gut her brother-in-law like a catfish, she had the good sense not to show it.

Shizuka did not attend court that day. Instead, her parents swamped her with tutors. Calligraphy, poetry, zither, dance. One of them had to catch her interest. One of them would teach her calm, and caution, and to consider her actions.

One did, of course. Calligraphy. But Shizuka had never needed a tutor for that, beyond her brush and inkwell.

But once all that was through—once she made her way home— that was when she heard the words for the first time.

Her mother's voice near to breaking, her father's smooth and comforting. They had not yet noticed her.

"What if that Qorin woman was right, Itsuki, what if our girl is—?"

"Then who better to mother her, Zuru? Who better to keep her humble and noble? Better we raise her than Iori. And she will have Shefali, and the two of them will be like two pine needles. She will never be alone."

Iori. Had that been the Emperor's name, before the throne? It matched Itsuki, as was traditional for Imperial children. This was the first time she'd ever heard it, but the sad venom in her father's voice left little room for doubt.

Shizuka's breath caught. What were they talking about? Was this about her birthday? For she was born on the eighth day of Ji-Dao, the eighth month, at eight minutes into Last Bell in the Daughter's year. All the palace soothsayers told her it was a good omen.

Though they didn't use those words.

They just said she was destined for greatness. They said the Daughter had been born on the same day, at the same time.

Is that what her mother meant, in the garden?

A crow's creaking startled her parents. They saw her then, and their faces softened.

"Shizuka," said Itsuki, first to rise. He did not wear his normal smile that day. "Shizuka, how were your lessons today?"

Did you mean what you said? Shizuka wanted to ask him. "Boring."

"Better boring than difficult!" said Itsuki. "What I would give to have a boring day, my dear."

He hugged her, fixed her hair ornaments, doted on her as he always did.

But something felt different. As if she were wearing another girl's clothes, as if they were afraid of touching her.

She did not sleep that night. Instead, she stood by the window, staring out at the golden daffodil surrounded by her mother's old things.

In the morning, her uncle's men came for her. Twice-eight tall men in Dragon armor, twice-eight faceless warriors with wicked spears, politely asking her to come to the gardens with them. Her mother insulting them. Her father, squeezing Shizuru's shoulder, telling her that it would pass.

When they arrived, her uncle was already there. His litter was there, at least, held up by eight men, curtained off from the early-morning sun. Shizuka's mother forced her head down when they approached him.

"Brother," said Itsuki. "What a beautiful day the Daughter has made! You should come for a walk with us. The scenery will do you good."

The scenery.

They stood in front of the gold rosebush, and the men in armor had torches.

"Is that what you call this, Itsuki?" said the Emperor. "A beautiful day, and not an affront to our divine authority?"

Shizuka's chest went tight. "Mother, what is he doing?"

"Whatever you're planning," said O-Shizuru, her voice harsh, "you know she meant no offense. We've been over this. She is six years old, Iori, six years old, and if you hurt her—"

From inside the litter, the Emperor clapped. Two soldiers stood on each side of Shizuru. Itsuki grabbed his daughter by the shoulders.

"Willful child," said the Emperor. "Was this your doing?"

She spoke before she could think about it. Things never went well when she honed her thoughts. Then speaking became like dragging knives across her tongue. *Talk,* she thought. *Just talk. The words will come, and they'll fix everything. They always do.*

"Yes," she said. "It was. All I did was change their color. If you are the Son of Heaven, you can change them back. Gods can do whatever they wish."

Her father squeezed her tighter. That wasn't the reaction she wanted! He was supposed to be proud of her, he was supposed to relax!

"The Son of Heaven," she continued, "shouldn't have to tell his guards to hold my mother back, either. Are you afraid of her?"

"Discipline her," said the Emperor.

An eternal moment hung in the air, punctuated by black caws. Shizuka's heart punched against her ribs.

O-Shizuru stepped in front of her husband and daughter. She didn't draw the white sword at her side—but her hand was on its pommel. "Go on," she barked at the guards. "Lay a hand on my daughter, and I'll lay your hand on the ground."

"Shizuru—," said Itsuki.

"I mean it!" roared Shizuru. "Try me, if you are so brave!"

The guards all wore masks; Shizuka could not see their faces. Still, she knew they were pale.

"Wearing war masks to fight humans," said Shizuru. "To discipline a six-year-old girl. How dare you?"

"Hold the girl down," snapped the Emperor, "or face Imperial justice."

Shizuka remembers to this day the rattling of the guard's armor. Remembers how they stood trembling in front of her mother, remembers the fear in their eyes.

And she remembers her father whispering in her ear. "Shizuka, I'm sorry, but your mother is going to hurt those men unless you kneel. Please play along, and this will be over soon."

She remembers thinking, distinctly, that she didn't care if those men were hurt, because they served her uncle.

But if her mother hurt them, then . . . what would her uncle do? If she gave him a reason, a real reason? What if he sent O-Shizuru North, what if he told the guards to kill her?

Shizuka's jaw hurt. She didn't like being this afraid. She knelt.

Shizuru started shouting at her, at her father, at her uncle, at the world. Every harsh syllable made Shizuka's head pound. Fear choked her. Something awful was about to happen, wasn't it?

Yes.

One of the guards lit a torch, then another, then another, then another.

One by one, they marched toward the bushes.

And the others?

The others set fire to the roses. To the jasmine, to the dogwood, to the lilies; to cherry and plum; to all the flowers she'd come to know like old friends.

To all her father's favorites. Her father held her as they watched, as Shizuka screamed and screamed and screamed.

That day, thinks Shizuka—that was the day she learned to truly hate her uncle.

She sniffs.

To a lesser extent, that was when the public learned to hate him as well. The Hokkarans, that is. The Qorin knew Yoshimoto for a snake before he assumed the throne, but only the destruction of beauty appealed to courtly, art-obsessed Hokkarans.

By the time Shefali next visited, the gardens were coming back to life—but only just. Not that Shefali seems to have noticed. For the better, then.

The daffodil still stands, untouched, unharmed by the fire so many years ago.

Shizuka—no, Empress Yui—shakes herself away from the past. She has spent long enough staring, long enough dwelling in painful memories.

The book in her hands smells of pine and horses. She holds it to her nose and takes a deep breath.

Part of a person's soul is in their scent, as Shefali would say.

Shizuka has long missed this one.

LET THE WINDS
OF HEAVEN BLOW

When we were eight and I stayed with you for the winter, your father gave you a choice.

"Either you learn the naginata or the sword," he said. "You may choose only one."

You did not have to think about it. "The sword," you said. "It is about time Mother recognized my talent."

Your father smiled in his soft way. He reached out to muss your hair. Perhaps he decided not to; he drew back after half a second. But the smile stayed.

"Are you certain, my little tigress?" he said. "The sword may be your mother's weapon, but it is far more dangerous. You must be closer to your opponent. If we lived in the best times, you would never have to draw your sword; if we lived in better times, you would only fight humans. But . . ."

"I do not care whom I have to fight," you said.

O-Itsuki looked away. The smile on his face didn't change—or at least the shape of his mouth did not.

Once, when he was a young man, O-Itsuki took the field against the Qorin. He did not do much fighting. For the most part, he sat in his brother's tent, listening to their generals panic.

Many times, when he was a bit older, O-Itsuki accompanied his wife into battle. He did not do much fighting then, either. But he watched good men and women writhe in agony. He watched Shizuru put them down rather than let them become monsters. He watched Shizuru slay creatures twice her size. Perhaps these things were on his mind. But they were not on yours.

"I was born to hold a sword. If the gods saw fit to give my mother one, they've seen fit to give me one, too."

"The gods did not give your mother her sword," Itsuki said. "Her ancestors did."

"My mother is an ancestor. I'll have her sword one day," you countered. You crossed your arms.

If your father had any more arguments, he did not voice them. Your teacher was selected, and swordplay was added to the schedule of your daily lessons. You left the room triumphant. For the rest of the day, it was all you could talk about. During our walk around your gardens, you spoke of it.

"A sword, Shefali!" you said. "At last! Now that I'm being properly taught, my mother will have to recognize my talent."

Only the plum trees were blossoming. We stopped beneath one of them. Was it my imagination, or did the flowers turn toward you as we approached?

I plucked one of the sprigs of flowers, already tall enough to do so. I can't say what possessed me to do it—the penalty for defacing the Imperial Garden is twenty lashes, at minimum. Perhaps

I knew you'd never go through with such a punishment. What I did know, as soon as the flower was in my hand, was that it deserved to be in your hair. I stopped us with a small motion, swept your hair back between your ear, and slipped the flower there. The bright pink petals echoed the ones on your favorite winter dress.

What a pretty sight you were. I got the feeling it would be strange to tell you that you were pretty—that you might take it differently than you did when other people said it. So I changed the subject.

"Why not a naginata?"

You scoffed. "The weapon of cowards," you replied. "The weapon of those who think our only enemies come from the North."

And so we stood beneath the plum tree and spoke of other things. You spoke, and as always, I listened.

Two days later, your mother returned from her assignment in Shiratori Province. In those days she left often. On that particular morning, your mother returned with a man on a stretcher. We were not told what had happened, and in fact, we did not learn your mother was back until she called the two of us to meet her.

We stood in the healer's rooms. She was a stooped old relic, with more bald skin than hair and more hair than teeth. And yet, despite her appearance, she was no older than twenty-two. Such was the life of a healer.

When we entered the room, she tried to shoo us away from the man in the stretcher. "This is not a sight for young eyes," she said.

But I'd seen men die before this. I did not move. And you were made of iron and fire; you did not move, either.

"Leave them be, Chihiro-lao," your mother said. "They are here on my command."

"I am going to put this man down, O-Shizuru-mon. You cannot wish for them to see that," she said.

But your mother paid this no heed, and came to kneel at our side. "Shizuka," she said, "I understand you've chosen the sword."

"I have," you said. "And nothing you can show me will change my mind."

"I thought you might say that," said Shizuru. "Shefali-lun. Have you seen what happens to those who challenge your mother?"

I thought of Boorchu and nodded.

"Was it fast?"

Again, I nodded.

"That is because your mother is an honorable woman," Shizuru said. "At least as long as the situation calls for it. What I am about to show you is different. If you both insist on leading a warrior's life, you must know what happens when you are not careful."

I'd done no such insisting. On the steppes, you are either a warrior or a merchant or a sanvaartain, until you are old enough to simply be an old person. But I did not want to correct a woman who slew demons for a living.

"Step aside, Chihiro-lao."

The healer lumbered out of the way.

The man in front of us was a man in the loosest sense of the term. How long had it been since he was infected? Black coursed through his veins, black pulsed at his temples, black blossomed at his throat. His skin was pale and clammy. An unbandaged stump remained where his arm should've been. His eyes were closed, but his face contorted in pain. As we watched, shadows played beneath his skin, forming faces with two mouths and too many teeth.

Sometimes we'd hear a popping sound, and one of his limbs would snap out of place—with the man himself not moving at all.

"This man slew a demon today," your mother said. "But he made the mistake of letting its blood mingle with his. When he dealt the beast its killing blow, a gout of it landed on the stump of his arm."

The man thrashed. Your mother drew her sword.

My eyes flickered over to you. There you were, still as the noon-time sun. You clenched your jaw and creased your robes with white-knuckled hands. Ah, Shizuka, you tried so hard to tear yourself away from what you were seeing!

"He is having a violent reaction," your mother continued, stepping toward him. "Normally he would lie in bed and rot of a fever before he began thrashing."

The healer smothered him with a pillow while your mother wrapped her hands in cloth.

You reached for me.

Your mother made a clean slice.

There was a soft sound, then an awful smell. It was done. Shimmers clung to the underside of the pillow as the blood seeped up into it.

Chihiro-lao winced. She looked right at the two of us and mouthed, "I'm sorry." You weren't looking at her, but I was, and I appreciated that moment of warmth. Children remember who showed them kindness when the world tried to make them cruel.

This was necessary cruelty, but it was cruelty all the same.

I gave her a little bow from the chest. It was the least I could do to thank her. Satisfied that my soul wasn't lost, she made the sign of the eight over the man's body. Then she bowed to your mother and left.

She must have gone to fetch people to move the body. You needed at least four to do it safely, and though she was young her body was not. It would have to be five.

O-Shizuru tore the cloth off her hands and wiped her blade clean. When she glanced at us, we still had linked hands.

"When you use a sword, Shizuka," she said, "you must get close to your opponent. And when your opponent's blood is a poison to the gods themselves, you must be careful."

Shizuru must've expected you to buckle. Instead, you ground your bare heel into the floor.

"Careful?" you roared. "I am O-Shizuka, born on the eighth day of the eighth month, eight minutes past Last Bell. I don't need to be careful of the Traitor, Mother. He needs to be careful of us!"

And so you turned and stormed off before your mother could say anything.

You did not run. Instead, you walked as fast as you could while maintaining a degree of grace. Soon the plum tree rose above us, and soon we stood beneath it again. You stared up at it as if it offended you, and you finally snatched a fruit from it the way a queen backhands an unruly servant.

"Shefali," you said, "promise me something."

I nodded.

"If I am ever foolish enough to have that happen to me, you will put me out of my misery within the day."

And at this, too, I nodded.

I nodded because I was eight, and you were asking me to promise something that I never thought would happen. Because we were eight, and battle was still a distant dream in our minds, no matter how often we'd seen its effects. Because we were eight and standing beneath a plum tree, and nothing could hurt us.

* * *

THE NEXT DAY you began your formal swordplay lessons. And, yes, it's true—from the moment the wooden sword touched your hands, you were a natural. As a horse is made to run, so you were made to wield a blade. Your strokes painted bruises on your instructor like ink on paper.

But I was not so talented.

Hokkarans favor straight swords. They're well suited to your obsession with showy duels. On horseback it is different: a straight blade gets caught in your enemy's neck, and you can hardly stop to retrieve it. A curved blade is more practical.

Your instructor was an old man from Shiratori Province. The long years of his life bent his back and hobbled his knees, but with a sword in hand, he was spry as a youth. Complicated forms were to him as simple as rising up in the morning. Perhaps easier, given his age. He'd fought in the Qorin wars against my mother. Everyone his age had. But the color of my skin was the least of his concerns.

"Oshiro-sur!" he'd shout, the veins in his neck pulsing. "Have you no grace? I ask you to be flowing water; you are a cliff face!"

I frowned. I could be flowing water. When arrows left my bow, they were rain falling from the sky. When I was on my horse, we were the rampaging rapids of the Rokhon.

But put me on my feet, put a straight sword in my hand, and ask me to move like a dancer?

You noticed my discomfort.

As the days wore on into months and the Daughter brought spring back to the lands, you insisted we go riding after sword lessons. The forests around Fujino were dense, and from your castle we could see the morning fog like a cloud come down from the heavens. It stayed until midday, when Grandmother Sky called it back. White on emerald green, vibrant and pale; the sight itself refreshing and enticing.

It was your great-grandfather who commissioned that forest. In his day, it was only a thick circle of green around the palace. He was an avid hunter and wanted a place to keep his more dangerous game. Here, where he kept wolves and tigers and bears, you wished to hunt.

"Come," you said. "My men always go hunting in that forest; they never take me along. Too dangerous for an Imperial Flower, they say."

Forests intimidated me as much as castles did. No roof is a good roof, whether it be carved stone or a branch. I kept calm by remembering I'd see patches of blue, at least. Maybe I could stitch them together and make a patchwork sky.

I was too distracted by my little mental sewing experiment to keep track of where we went. Only when the scent of horses came to me did I realize you'd led us all the way to the stables. How you did it without anyone questioning us is beyond me—but then again, who would ever question you?

Once I realized our horses were nearby, a grin spread wide across my face. I could feel my gray nearby, I could feel her in my bones. How far would we ride? The forest was large. My gray didn't have much experience navigating thorns and brambles. Would she be all right? Perhaps I should pack extra sweets . . . she likes them far more than any horse of her caliber should. They're ruining her teeth. But how am I to deny her? How can anyone look into those soulful pools of brown and deny them a sweet?

"Your Imperial Highness, are you well?"

Ah. Right. In Hokkaro, you had hostlers instead of tending horses yourselves. This man was their leader if the plume on his cap was any indication. I'd forgotten his existence, and his voice startled me.

Before you opened your mouth to berate him, I touched your hand. You stopped and looked at me; I pointed to our horses.

"Ah, that's right," you said. Then you called to him. "Boy, ready our horses."

"O-Shizuka-shon," said the head hostler. "That Qorin girl touched you—"

You waved. He scrambled to his feet and prostrated himself before you. "That Qorin girl is Oshiro Shefali, my good friend, and you will treat her with the same respect you treat me."

By then I had already begun preparing your red gelding. Hokkaran saddles are different; where we have stirrups, a horn, and a high seat, you have little more than a flap of leather. Hokkarans believe that a rider and horse should communicate without words. That is the Qorin way of thinking, too; except that we recognize the usefulness of gestures.

You banished the head hostler to his chambers. I helped you up onto your horse and swung into my own saddle. My horse nickered. I ran my fingers through her mane. Again, she nickered—but this time she stamped her hoof, too. A dark mood, then.

So I leaned forward and whispered to her. In hushed Qorin, I spoke to her of the sweets that awaited her at the end of the day, of the verdant places we were going, of home, of grass and wind.

As the words left me, my throat thrummed with more than air. No, this was a great wind. This was the voice of something larger than myself, compressed into a whisper.

It was then I realized I was no longer speaking Qorin. Imagine a language like swaying grass. Imagine vowels sounded like a seer's horn, consonants the rattle of bones in her cup. My tongue was thick with the taste of loam.

My horse calmed.

I felt like an empty river. I opened my mouth and stared at my hands and tried to understand what had just happened. And, as I did whenever I was confused, I turned to you.

And there you were, sitting atop your horse like a throne. When you saw the expression on my face, your brows knit together. "Shefali?"

I closed my eyes and squeezed my hands together. Opening them took some effort. Were they still mine, or were they, too, the tools of something else?

You urged your horse toward me. There, just outside the royal stables, you squeezed my shoulder. Golden butterflies pinned to your hair fluttered the closer you moved.

"Shefali," you said.

I licked my dry lips. A deep, rattling breath shook me. "I am all right," I said.

"You aren't," you said. "Do not lie to me. I know you as I know my reflection. What happened?"

I met your eyes. I could not meet them long. The second we locked gazes, my chest throbbed and ached and rang with a note I did not recognize.

You, too, flinched. Your ring-covered hand flew to your heart. "Did you . . . ?" you asked.

I nodded. When you turned to look around us, the ornaments in your hair sounded like temple bells.

A messenger rode up toward the stable cloaked in yellow and

white—the colors of Shiseiki Province. Upon seeing you, he bowed at the waist, still mounted. "O-Shizuka-shon! Flower of the Empire! You honor me with your presence!"

Even at eight, you did not bat an eye at such praise. If anything, I think it exhausted you. When it came to you, the public knew only three ways to speak. The hostler earlier demonstrated mindless concern well; to those people, you were not a girl but a precious, frail object. The second thing a person might do was praise your parents. This did not trouble you much on its own, but by the third or fourth time you heard someone remark on your semblance to your mother, you made your excuses to leave. And here was the last: mindless praise from a passing messenger.

Seeing you alone was considered a great honor; you did not have to further honor him with words. No doubt this messenger would tell his family all he could about you: the colors you were wearing, the way you carried yourself, the small nod you gave him as he left.

Perhaps he'd mention how long your sleeves were, or the elaborate dragons embroidered in gold thread upon them. If he was an astute man, he'd mention the chrysanthemums secreted away by your wrists.

But he would not have mentioned how your hand gripped my wrist, how you squeezed mine when he called to you.

Long sleeves hide many secrets.

"We're going," you said. "We cannot talk here."

I nodded.

Together we made our way out of your lands. In spite of our age, no one questioned us. Why would they? You, the Imperial Niece, were old enough to go out on a ride if you so wished. You had company. Qorin company, yes, but that was perhaps for the best. Everyone knows my people are born on horseback and sired by stallions.

On any other day, you consider silence an enemy you must cut down. As our horses took us from the palace of Fujino to the deep green forests surrounding it, you spoke not a word.

But then, neither did I.

I was marveling at the trees, for one. Wondering how anything the gods created could be so tall. Wondering what it was like to climb up onto the highest branches of the tallest tree we passed. What did your palace look like from there? Which was taller— a tree that grew from a sapling over dozens of years, or a palace men raised with their own hands?

After five hours of riding in silence, I called for a stop. Our horses needed water and rest.

We stopped in a relatively light portion of the forest. A small pool lay beneath the trees. From it our horses drank, from the grass surrounding it, they ate.

And as for us?

I laid out a thick felt blanket made by my grandmother. At one time, it had been white, but the grit and grime and sweat and smoke of our lives tinged it gray. My mother let me take it from her ger before leaving me with you. Such a thing was normally not permitted—but then, I would normally not be leaving the ger for so long.

On this blanket you sat. On this blanket, with wool taken from my grandmother's flock. Your dress was blood on smoke.

"Shefali," you said, "have you ever seen a man die? Besides the tainted one my mother killed?"

I started. What sort of question was that?

And yet . . .

Boorchu calling me a coward. Claiming my Hokkaran blood made me weak. The sight of him crumpling to the ground.

I nodded.

Clouds shaded your brow; the bright ornaments of your hair could not illuminate the darkness of your mood. When you spoke next, you stared at the ground.

"Shefali," you said. As an inkbrush tints the water it touches, so did fear darken your voice. "What do you see when men die?"

My lips were dry. Dew on every leaf near us—but my lips were dry.

Because I knew the answer.

"Their souls," I said. "I see their souls."

On the blanket your hand twitched. You huddled in on yourself.

"Shizuka?"

"Right before I was born," you said, "my mother was with yours, out on the steppes."

I tilted my head. This I had not known. What was Shizuru doing on the steppes in such a state? For my mother, it is to be expected. But for a Hokkaran woman with a moon belly to be riding? To be riding in the *winter*?

And people say that you are foolhardy.

"Alshara insisted on taking my mother to an oracle before the week was out," you continued. "And in this, as in all things, my mother listened to yours."

"The oracle could not read my future," you said. "When her bones fell to the ground, they shattered into dozens of tiny pieces. She said she'd heard of that happening in stories, in the presence of gods. So they went to another oracle, and another. Every time they tried to read my fortune, the same thing happened. Hokkaran fortune-tellers only said my birthday was important; they couldn't say anything about my future."

Around us, a hundred creatures lived their small lives. Trees and roots and mushrooms alike bathed in the fading light of the sun. Trickling down through the branches, the sun painted us, too, with streaks of white and yellow, with bright patches like oases on our shaded faces.

As the priests told things, each of those animals, each of those plants, and even the rocks around us were gods. Some gods are grains of sand; some are Grandmother Sky. A god can be anything it wishes—as small or large as it pleases. A god may live in a sing-ing girl's zither, imbuing each note with the sweetness of a ripe plum. A god may choose a scabbard as its home, and lend any blade it touches sharpness unmatched. Or a god might also live in a crock and burn everything it comes into contact with.

Gods can be anything.

But could we be gods?

Two pine needles, my mother always said, like two pine needles . . .

You pointed to a particular tree some distance away. Perched on one of its branches was a bright green songbird, the sort people travel into the forest specifically to catch. At the right market, it would fetch a fine price.

"If I asked you to shoot that bird," you asked, "you would be able to, would you not?"

I frowned. I didn't really want to shoot that bird—someone hungrier than we were might need it in the future. Nevertheless, I swallowed my protests and nodded.

"Sitting here with me on this blanket," you said, "you could draw your bow, fire an arrow, and rob this forest of a singer."

It would not be an easy thing to do. Qorin bows are made to be fired from compact spaces; sitting was not the issue. Drawing it without startling the creature would be the problem.

And yet I knew I could do it. As that same bird was born knowing a hundred songs, I was born knowing a hundred ways to fire a bow.

"Does it not occur to you how strange that is?"

Strange was a walking fish. Strange was water spreading out across the horizon no matter where you looked. Being able to hunt was not strange. It was a skill I needed if I was going to feed myself out on the steppes.

"You are eight."

I gave you a level look.

"You are eight and you can strike a target as small as my fist from this far away," you said. "Shefali, there are grown men who cannot do that."

"Then they would starve," I said.

You sighed and shook your head. "Earlier," you said, "when you spoke to your horse—did you not feel strange? Did you not feel like someone else's inkbrush?"

I stared at the backs of my hands. Warm, brown skin, pockmarked here and there with unhealing white. If I made a fist, I could see my pulse throbbing. I counted the beats, waited for you to continue. If someone was using me as their brush, what were they writing?

You swallowed. Near to us was a shrub full of blossoms I could not name. They were all bright violet—so bright, I did not like to look at them. You reached out toward one of them. It struck me that your hand shook, that there was this fear in your eyes you cut down like an enemy on the field.

When your fingertips met the petals, they turned from violet to gold.

A soft sound escaped me, and I covered my mouth in surprise.

"Shefali," you said, and you took my hand in yours. I could not help but stare at you—your pleading mouth, your wide eyes. "As candles are not stars, we are not like the others. You must promise me, no matter what, that we will always find our way back to each other."

Your words hammered against the bell of my soul.

"I promise," I said. "Together."

"Swear it," you said. The fire of youthful conviction filled you. "Swear it to me."

Without hesitation, I stood up and walked to the great white tree on which the songbird sat.

When you walked to me, it was without fear, without a trace of nervousness.

I drew an arrow from the quiver hanging at my hip. I held out my hand, the flat of the arrowhead resting on my palm. Then, together, we cut our palms against it.

Sharp pain jolted through us.

And yet neither of us flinched.

When I drew my hand back, the arrowhead was dark with blood. It stuck to my palm, and it was only with some effort that I removed it. Then I nocked the arrow. Sweat and grime from my grip pressed into the weeping wound we'd just made.

When I drew back the bowstring, when the pressure against my palm set my whole arm alight, when the pain screamed inside me—when all these things happened, I pointed my bow at the sun.

"I swear by sky and blood," I said. "I swear by my mother's ger, and my grandmother's spirit. I swear by the blood of Grandmother

Sky, who birthed the Qorin and taught us to saddle lightning. To-gether. I swear this."

Only then did I loose.

Like the songbird, the arrow soared overhead, straight on toward the sun. I turned before it reached the peak of its arch. Once Grandmother Sky tastes your blood, you may not hide from your oath. Where can you go to hide from her bright gold eye, or the dull silver one? All things return to the sky in time.

As we walked back to the blanket we called our camp, I won-dered if we would return to the sky.

Only the stars and the clouds deserved to be in your company. Only the sky could be home to you. Only the sky was a splendid enough throne for you.

WE STAYED IN that clearing that night. I urged you to let us ride back, or at least to ride toward somewhere a little better populated. But you insisted in your bullheaded way that we could stay wher-ever we pleased. After all, hadn't you just told me that we were not normal?

I did not like that. It was the sort of thing said by a girl who has never had to keep watch for wolves in the dark of the night.

And so, as you crept into my tent to sleep, I set about bundling together our belongings and hanging them from a tree. Once this was done, I sat before the fire and resigned myself to a sleepless night.

It rained not long after you went to bed. My fire, reduced to smoldering cinders, did not give me much light. I slipped my arms inside my lined coat and huddled closer to the embers.

Yes, I remember the orange of the cinders, the low rumbles of the night creatures. I remember rain on leaves and their fresh green smell. I remember closing my eyes and listening to the hundred thousand sounds of life. I tilted my head back and let the rain fall into my mouth.

When it rained in the steppes, we'd put out every bowl we could to catch it. A hundred li away, my mother and cousins were running out into the darkness. They'd turn and dance and sing praises to the sky. In Xian-Lai—so far away, I could not imagine its distance—my father and brother slept in their warm beds. Kenshiro might be awake. Knowing him, he'd be sitting up in bed, looking out the window. In his hand I pictured a brush; on his mind, poetry. He kept writing to me of Lord Lai's youngest daughter. Kenshiro said she was more beautiful than the wind through a silver horse's mane, which might be the wrongest thing I've ever heard. How could he look on you and say such a thing about any other woman?

But love makes fools, as they say—and in my brother's case, it drove him to write terrible courtship poetry.

Thick drops of rain fall like beats. One, two, three, four, five . . .

And then there was you, asleep in my tent, not even a length away from me, yet given over to the world of dreams. I wondered what you dreamed of. I wondered if you were safe.

BY THE TIME dawn came upon me, my eyes were heavy with sand. I rose and moved toward the tent.

It was then that I saw the tiger.

You must understand I did not hear it, did not see it before this moment. A creature three, four times my size moved with the silence of death itself.

Your ancestor Minami Shiori hunted tigers for sport. Looking at the beast now, I did not know how she did it. Every sinew in its body, every muscle, tensed for attack. Great green eyes froze me in place. So astounded was I that I did not notice the beast was hurt.

Yes, yes, as it turned toward me, I saw dried blood on its paws like rust. On its side, a yawning mouth of a wound; on its side, claw marks. Red was its muzzle, red its teeth.

I did not know if tigers traveled in packs. I'd only heard of them in stories. There was only ever one tiger in the stories. Perhaps they were not like lone wolves, or lone Qorin.

But this one?

This one was. I knew that look in its eyes.

I licked my lips. The tiger crouched down. I'd seen cats do the same sort of thing, when they were about to pounce on mice.

I did what any Qorin would do: I mounted my horse and drew my bow, in a smooth ripple of movement. My palm still ached from the wound, but I did not have time to dwell on it.

"Shizuka!" I shouted. Hopefully, the sound of me raising my voice was enough to rouse you. If not, perhaps hooves pounding against the undergrowth would.

The tiger leaped forward, landing not far from me and my horse. In the moment before I kicked into a gallop, I found myself in awe.

On the steppes we have only these animals: stoats, sheep, dogs, wolves, birds, and horses. For most of my life, I was surrounded by these creatures. I knew the best place to aim for when hunting a stoat. I knew how to skin a wolf. I could talk to horses, if I wanted.

But never in my life had I seen anything so graceful as that tiger. The Sun herself sang its praises, spinning gold from the orange of its fur, turning the black to brushstrokes. As it stalked us, I saw its thick muscles sliding beneath its skin, like eels beneath a river.

We were wolves once, we Qorin—but there was nothing wolfish about that creature. When I looked into its great eyes, I did not see anything human. I didn't see anything I recognized. How could something so large move with such fluidity? With those bright stripes, how could it hide in the forest? What did it eat?

It did not belong here, I decided. That was why it was so lean, that was why it was covered in battle wounds. Whoever the game master of this forest was had captured it and placed it here—but this was never its choice.

I frowned.

I knew, a bit, what it was like to be dropped into a forest you hate.

And so something about its terrible beauty was familiar to me, like a favorite song forgotten.

But it was trying to kill me. I could not admire it for long.

I loosed an arrow at it as my horse pulled ahead. With a satisfying thunk, the arrow pierced the beast's pelt. A solid blow to its chest. A gout of blood watered the roots. The tiger roared, clawed at the ground.

And then it began running.

Riding through the forest is a difficult thing to do given the best conditions. Qorin horses are trained for speed and endurance, not sure-footedness. A good Hokkaran gelding would be ideal here. But I did not have a good Hokkaran gelding; I had a Qorin mare with a blackened steel coat and fire in her heart. As we barreled through the trees, I ducked low-hanging branches, whispered to her, told her we were going to make it out of this. I had to trust her. How else could I fire at the tiger? I could not guide us through the forest and aim. It was one or the other.

I thought of you scrambling awake in the tent. I thought of you watching the tiger follow me into the vast green growth.

Inside me was the thrumming power of a hundred horsemen; the light of a hundred dawns; the fire of a hundred clans meeting together. In the moment I realized this, a strange calm came over me. My horse could handle the woods, as long as I handled the tiger.

Another arrow, another, another. Each found its mark. First one of its paws, then its haunches, then its flank. Whatever agony the beast was in, it did not stop chasing me. My horse may be the fastest of the Burqila line, but it cannot outrun something that has lived and breathed this forest as I have lived and breathed sand and grass and snow.

The tiger jumped up onto a tree.

I nocked an arrow.

Could I hit a target small as my palm while it was moving?

Could I hit it while I was moving?

Could I hit it while seated?

I loosed.

The arrow whistled through the air. There! It hit the tiger in the eye. The beast recoiled.

But it did not stop.

My heart hammered in my chest. It was going to jump. It was going to jump from the tree and it was going to land on my horse and me and there was nothing I could do to stop it.

I held her mane in my hand and flattened myself against her

warm back. I took a deep breath and braced myself for what was coming. Would my mother be proud of me?

Wood creaking. The tiger, in the air. Claws tearing through my deel, tearing through my skin, baring my bone to the world. Red. Red. Red. Rank breath thick with the smell of corpses. Hot blood washing over my arm. A roar . . .

"Shefali!"

I forced my eyes open.

You stood before us.

But how? Unless . . . Yes, this was the camp. My horse, wily as ever, had led us in a circle.

There you were with your blunted training sword, there you were standing tall and proud in the face of this horrible creature. I opened my mouth to shout at you, to tell you to run.

You charged ahead.

The beast, woozy from lack of blood, clawed at you. As fire crackling, you moved away.

I could not let you do this alone, no matter how much pain I was in. Drawing my bow was so agonizing, I thought I might pass out, but I could not allow myself to, not when you were in danger. My hands shook.

This would not hit. This was not going to hit. There was no way. I loosed.

Another arrow landed in the beast's neck, near its shoulder.

You let out a roar to rival the tiger's. Then you plunged your sword into its stomach.

I was dizzy, swaying, straining to open my eyes as my body fought to shut them. Coldness cut through me like winter's harsh knife. Pain grabbed me by the shoulder and pulled, pulled, until my boot slid out of the stirrups and—

The last thing I saw before I fell off my horse: you under the morning sun, covered in the tiger's blood, your dull blade alight with dawn's fire.

When I awoke, you sat next to my bed. Worry lines dug their way onto your heart-shaped young face. Either your attendants had not seen you, or you did not let them touch you; the many knots and ornaments in your hair hung in disarray. Still you wore the red and gold dress.

"Shefali!" you said as you touched my shoulder. If I wore the ragged remnants of sleep, that touch and its resulting pain tore them off me. I screamed. You drew back and bit your lip. "I did not mean to hurt you," you said. "It's the tiger's fault for wounding you there."

I frowned.

You glanced away, hiding your hands within your wet sleeves.

These were your rooms in Fujino. In each corner, a different treasure, given to you by a courtier to try to curry favor. A golden statue of the Mother. An intricate porcelain doll, dressed in identical clothing to yours. A calligraphy set. Fine parchments. Gold-leaf ink. A bamboo screen, painted with O-Shizuru's story.

"My mother will be here soon," you said. "Be ready. She's not pleased with either of us, though I imagine she will take it easier on you."

I tilted my head, gestured around the room with my good hand. You understood me without my having to speak.

"After the incident," you said, "I rode out to find the nearest guards. When I explained what happened, they followed me to camp. I carried you back and graciously allowed them to carry the tiger. My parents have no idea what to do with it. I have informed them that it is your decision to make, by any rules that matter."

Your mother was not going to listen to that, and you knew it. But your father would. No doubt he found the whole situation poetic. A boon for us, then, if your father put ink to parchment in our behalf.

I pointed to my shoulder.

"Torn," you said. "We brought in a healer. Not a very good one."

You shifted in your seat. Picked at your nails. At court, the latest fashion was to dust one's fingertips in crushed gems mixed with oils and lotions. Between when I passed out and that moment, you'd dipped yours in crushed garnets.

"She said that healing you was beyond her power," you said. "It's my opinion that if you call yourself a thing, and you cannot do that thing, then you are nothing at all. But that is my opinion. And as always, my parents do not want to listen to me. So the healer was compensated for her utter lack of work."

With some effort—and some help from you—I sat up. Breath came in rattles.

When I was six, one of the Burqila clan riders came back from a hunt with his left arm in his right hand. His entire left arm. His left shoulder was a bloody stump; he and his horse were cloaked in rusty brown. Everyone ran to him. The women carried him off his horse and took him to the oracle's tent. Two sheep were brought in, too, and I remember hearing the shrill cries they made. When my mother sent me to get the oracle's blessings on her choice of camp a few days later, I saw the man. Sweat beaded on his brow like dew; fever painted his brown face red.

But his arm was attached again.

I reached for my own arm. It was still there. Why, then, was I beyond healing?

I thought of our promise again.

I grunted.

"I agree," you said. "On the bright side, we do not have to attend court until you are healed."

Small victories. Standing on my feet beneath a jade ceiling listening to Hokkarans prattle—was there any worse fate? At least they would not stare at me.

"Shizuka, you say that as if it's a fitting reward for your foolish decisions."

Ah. O-Shizuru opened the door. You sat a bit straighter, though I'm not certain you meant to.

"You will accompany me to court tomorrow. Your uncle has been asking about you, at any rate. Before the night is through, you shall write one of your father's poems for him on fine white paper."

You tugged at your sleeves rather than roll your eyes. If you rolled your eyes, you were lost.

Your mother was a force to be reckoned with when she was in the most pleasant of moods. Now worry and anger clouded her features. My mother may have conquered half of Hokkaro with nothing but horsemen and Dragon's Fire, but bandits had whole rituals dedicated to keeping your mother at bay. Right then, I would've liked a ritual or two.

Your mother fixed me with a harsh, unyielding glare. Her brown eyes became slabs of earth, her mouth a canyon. "Shara," said O-Shizuru, the only person who could call my mother that and live, "is never going to believe me."

I drew back. The clouds broke; she cracked a smile.

"Two eight-year-olds attacked by a tiger, and neither of them dead," she said. "If I told her that story, she'd give me a look, her look. And yet. Here we are."

What was I to say to that? Not a word of it was wrong. Just— when she put it that way, we did sound foolish.

Your mother cleared her throat. "How is your shoulder?"

I held up my hand and closed it tight into a fist.

She nodded. "Yes," she said, "it's going to hurt for some time. The healer couldn't do much; the doctors say it'll be at least a few months before you can shoot a bow with that arm again."

Wrong. I'd be shooting a bow again within a few weeks at most. My young brain could not imagine a life where I went any longer than that without firing it.

"I'd ask you what happened," said your mother, "but you've never been one for words. So I will tell you this."

Now the solemnity crept back in; now her words were heavy as the first rain of the season.

"What you did was foolish. Beyond foolish. If a man strapped raw meat to his person and ran to the Emperor's dogs—that would be less foolish. You are children; there are grown warriors who'd never dream of fighting a tiger. You lived this time. Next time, you will not. It is by the Mother's intervention alone that you live."

I wanted to say something. At the base of my throat, I felt it building. I wanted to tell her that, no, it was not the Mother's grace, it was my own skill at riding, it was my horse, it was your blade striking the final blow. It was us.

But no, no, it was not the time.

So I sat. I sat and I listened as your mother outlined all the things we'd done wrong. As she told us again and again how foolish we'd been.

"There are bandits in those woods," she said. "What would you have done if they came for you?"

"Shot them," you said. However long she'd lectured you before

I awoke, you could take no more. "She would've shot them, Mother. As she shot the tiger. Repeatedly."

"Men are not tigers," O-Shizuru snapped. "I'd rather fight a beast. At least they have dignity. Those men would've cut your horse's legs out from—"

I yelped and drew the covers around my knees. My brown face went lighter, my mouth hung open, my breath left me in harsh gasps.

Your mother reached out a hand. No doubt it was meant to be reassuring, but the thought of my horse being hurt was still on my mind—the image of her crumpling as some godless bandit cut into her. Her cries of pain rang in my ears. I pressed my head against the pillows to drown it out.

You whispered something to your mother.

The Queen of Crows eyed me and sighed. "Shefali-lun," she said, "no one is going to hurt your horse."

I peeked out from my self-imposed exile and wrinkled my face.

Your mother pinched the bridge of her nose. "Don't give me that look," she said. "You are on our lands. If anyone hurt your horse while you were lying here, I would execute them myself."

Slowly, slowly, I began to relax. But the look in her eyes still brooked no arguments.

"This changes nothing," she said. "However incredible it is you slew the tiger, it was a foolish thing to do. You should've run, Shefali. You should've taken Shizuka up on your horse and the two of you should've gotten away, somewhere safe."

I hung my head.

"People will tell you what you did was brave," Shizuru said. "My husband among them. But you must remember how easily it could've gone wrong. This wound you bear will scar. When you feel stiff skin tugging in your shoulder—you will remember."

And I drew the sheets closer to myself. I clutched them close. My throat tightened. So many things I wished to say. As she spoke, I watched you squirm in your seat. Each time you parted your lips, your eyes fell on my bandages, and you fell silent.

When your mother left, so did you. Urgent business, she said, that the both of you had to attend to. I watched you go. You looked back at me as you walked out of the room.

And then I sat up. I watched the moon rise. I thought of the tiger somewhere in the castle, rotting. What was I going to do with it? I'd never heard of anyone eating a tiger. An old Qorin poem came to mind. The Kharsa's daughter has tiger-striped arms. . . . I could not remember the rest. I racked my brains for it, but I might've been milking a stallion for all the good it did me. Eventually my frustration surrendered to exhaustion. I fell asleep and dreamed of the steppes.

At least until you crept into bed next to me.

Still half asleep, I thought I must've dreamed you—your hair unbound, your skin flush with anger or embarrassment or . . .

"Shefali," you said, lying next to me. How small you were for an eight-year-old, how tall I was. "I'm sorry."

I must've been dreaming.

"I should've moved faster."

I must have been dreaming. Those words would never leave you in the waking world.

"I won't let it happen again."

Sleep, then.

* * *

I WENT TO court more than once. I did not like it. There, in the halls of jade, I was stared at by scholars and advisers and sycophants.

"Ah, O-Shizuka-shon!" they might say, when they saw you. They'd bow so low that their beards swiped against the ground. "The Tiger-Slayer! Heaven's blood runs pure in you."

"I did not kill the tiger," you'd say. You said this each time we went to court, at least five times. "I struck the last blow, but I did not kill it."

"Do not be so modest," they might say. Or "Your humility is an inspiration."

With a sharp gesture, you'd wave them away. Under your breath, you would mutter curses at them. A bit louder, you would apologize to me on their behalf.

But me?

"Oshiro-sun," they might say, if they were being charitable. "Yun" was far more common from them than "sun," as if I possessed the Traitor's cunning simply for being born darker than they were. "Your father is a fine man, and your brother fares well."

But these courtiers never seemed to have any words for me. Nothing for Shefali. No praise. Did they know my name? Was I simply Oshiro to them? I must be. Not once during those summer months did I hear my personal name, save from your family.

And that honorific—"sun." I do not pretend to understand Hokkaran honorifics. Some things are beyond explanation. My people have twenty different words for the color brown, most of which relate to the color of a horse's coat. Your people have eight sets of four honorifics, one for each god. Using the wrong one in the wrong context was as bad as spitting in the eye of a person's mother right in front of them. To make matters worse, half of them sounded the same.

I knew only a few. "Sun" was the lowest form of the Grand-mother's honorific. Depending on the person speaking it, it might be affectionate. Most of the time, however, it indicated that the speaker thought themselves far above the subject.

The other ones I knew were "mor," which was the highest for the Mother; "lor," the second highest for the Sister and your father's favorite; "tono," used for the Emperor alone; and "shon."

Shon was the Daughter's highest. Who better to wear it than the girl born on the eighth day of the eighth month of the eighth year, at Last Bell?

You are doomed to be Shizuka-shon all your life, as I am destined to be Barsalai-sul for all of mine.

Honorifics were the least of our concerns, however. If we were annoyed by them, that meant we were at court, and if we were at court, there were other matters to distract us. Court itself, for instance. I had no clothes to wear. Your father was kind enough to buy me a new dress, for I was too tall to use any of yours. It was not so bad, for a Hokkaran dress—green, with painted horses along the sleeves and hem.

There was the matter of etiquette, of which I knew little. I solved that problem by letting you do all the talking, and bowing only when you glanced toward me expectantly.

And though it involved me little, there was also the matter of what people were saying.

AS THE SPACE between a hammer and a pot, that was the court in those days. Emperor Yoshimoto could do little to stop the worries faced by his people.

"We will increase patrols along the Wall of Flowers," he said.

Two weeks later, those patrols were found mangled and broken just outside the Wall.

"We will consult the oracles," he said.

When the Hokkaran oracle was brought in to read the future in her vapors, she frothed at the mouth, screamed, and died on the gilded floor.

And then came Yoshimoto's famous motto:

"We will endure."

It became something of a saying among the peasants.

A farmer struck his hoe against the ground—a new hoe he had made himself with fresh wood not a week ago. Sure enough, it would splinter. He'd pick up the metal end and heft it high overhead. After getting his wife's attention, he would grin a sad, gap-toothed grin.

"We will endure," he'd say.

A fisherman strikes out to sea. He takes with him a good net and a good rod. He sails far out and casts his net. Soon it is filled with pink salmon, flopping about, taking their last breaths. Just as he closes his eyes to thank the kami for his bounty, he smells something off. He opens his eyes.

The fish are rotten.

"We will endure" is his bitter laugh.

Already the words began to haunt us.

NOT LONG AFTER I started healing, your mother left for another one of her missions. The magistrates out in Shiratori were having issues with a rebellion—they'd already caught the leader, but wanted your mother to make an example of him for the crowd. She did not look happy when she left—although your father managed to make her smile, whispering some secret promise in her ear.

Your father sat at the head of the dinner table and spoke blessings over our food. He teased you constantly. In his easy way, he would smile and call you the most read woman in Fujino.

"After all," he said. "Your notices hang on every door. Your poetry is clear and simple, as refreshing as spring water—"

"Father," you'd say, scrunching up your face as if you'd tasted something sour. "They are your brother's words."

For, yes, your uncle forced you to write all his notices. WE WILL ENDURE, eight hundred times each morning.

"Ah, yes," Itsuki said. He held his teacup beneath his nose. Its sweet aromas filled his lungs and lent his smile a warmer air. "But your brushstrokes are the poetry."

You palmed your face and I laughed. O-Itsuki watched you with a bemused look. This was how he always was: calm and relaxed, somehow above stress or worry. I cannot remember a wrinkle crossing his face, save for the lines winging his eyes when he laughed. And he laughed often. Whenever he and Shizuru attended court, he could not contain himself—always a twinkle in his eye, always some unheard joke rolling around his mind.

Many nights we passed like that, speaking with your father. The jokes were a welcome change from his brother's proclamations. That was the year your uncle announced the eightfold path to plenty. All farmers had to bury specific stones attuned to their patron god in their fields—one every li, in each direction. For farms less than a li square, eight idols had to be buried, each one-eighth of the distance apart.

A superstitious gesture at best, meant to play on current fears. Your uncle claimed that it was Hokkaro's lack of faith that prompted the Heavenly Family's abandonment. Only proper veneration would bring them back. Anyone who failed to perform their pious duties would face Imperial justice.

Of course, burying things in a field like that, planting things the way he said to plant them, following all those rules . . .

I am no farmer, Shizuka. When I die and you leave me out for the vultures—that is the closest I shall come to farming, for flowers will grow where I last lay. But even I saw starving commoners curse your uncle.

Oh, when we were eight, it was not so bad. When we were eight, one could eke out a living, just barely.

But do you remember, Shizuka, when we traveled after—?

I am getting ahead of myself. That part, too, will come.

I had my own set of rooms in Fujino, but that did not stop me from visiting yours. I slept in my own bed perhaps twice in the entire three seasons I was with you.

In the dark of night, when the moon was high, I worked on my project. I'd had the tiger's pelt brought up to me. With my clumsy hands, I sewed and cut and sewed and cut. The end result was not going to be impressive—but it would be mine.

My mother arrived on the twenty-second of Tsu-Shao. With her came about a third of the Burqila clan, including two of my aunts. And Otgar, of course. I suspect she would've come even if she was in the sands at the time. I met them at the gates on my horse.

Otgar came riding up next to my mother. In the absence of my

brother, she was a capable interpreter. All that time spent in our
ger clued her in to my mother's language of gestures.

"Needlenose!" she shouted in Qorin. "You live! I heard a tiger
ate you!"

You blinked. You sat on your horse next to me. I do not think
you'd seen other Qorin before, or at least not so many. Otgar's
loud, long greeting—several times longer in Qorin than it
would've been in Hokkaran—might've startled you.

I waved at her as she pulled in. She clapped me hard on the
shoulder and mussed my hair. A little over a year it'd been since I
saw her, yet in that time she'd grown into her body far more than
I had. Seeing her wide face, her red cheeks, her beautifully embroidered deel, made me feel more at home already. Then she took
me close and pressed her nose against my cheeks.

She recoiled. "You smell like flowers!"

I laughed and pointed to you. You drew back.

"What is the matter?" you said. "Why was that girl smelling
you?"

"To make sure she is the same Shefali," Otgar said. Time light-
ened her Hokkaran accent; she almost sounded native. "Smell
never changes, no matter how long she is with pale foreigners."

Something changed in your posture. "You speak Hokkaran,"
you said.

"I do!" she said. "I am Dorbentei Otgar Bayasaaq, and it is my
honor to serve as Burqila's interpreter."

Next to us, our mothers exchanged their customary greetings.
Despite the crowd, my mother embraced yours, held her tight,
with her fingers in O-Shizuru's hair.

But I was more concerned with what Otgar had said.

"Dorbentei," I repeated. "You are an adult?"

Otgar beamed from ear to notched ear, proudly displaying her missing tooth. "I am!" she said. "When I learned to speak Surian. No braids yet, but soon!"

"I am O-Shizuka," you said, though no one had asked. "Daughter of O-Itsuki and O-Shizuru, Imperial Niece, Blood of Heaven—"

"Yes, yes," said Otgar, waving you off. "You are Barsatoq. We know of you already, we have heard the stories."

I tilted my head. Barsatoq. An adult name, like Dorbentei. But where Dorbentei meant "Possessing Three," Barsatoq meant . . .

Well, it meant "Tiger Thief."

I'm sorry you had to find out this way.

"So you've discussed me!" you said. Color filled your cheeks, and something of your old demeanor returned. "Yes, yes, I am Barsatoq Shizuka."

I covered my mouth rather than laugh. Tiger Thief. My clan bestowed upon you the great honor of an adult name—something only a handful of foreigners received—and they named you Tiger Thief. You were so quick to embrace it! Someone must've told you what a mark of acceptance it is to be named by the Qorin.

And yet.

Tiger Thief.

I was saved from hiding my amusement when my mother rode over. As animals sense storms, so I sensed her coming, and all the mirth fell from my face. My mother's eyes were vipers, her quick gestures as fangs in my flesh. Otgar, too, lost her mirth.

"Shefali," she said, "Burqila is displeased that you would act in such a foolhardy fashion."

"She is your daughter, Alshara," said O-Shizuru. "You are

lucky she did not stuff the tiger with fireworks and set it soaring through the sky."

Alshara shook her head. Another series of gestures, though less sharp.

"Burqila will host a banquet tonight, in her ger, to celebrate her daughter's well-being," Otgar said. "You are all welcome."

Good lamb stew! A warm fire, with my clan sitting around it! My grandmother's nagging; my aunts beating more felt into the ger; my uncles trying to convince them to do other things instead. The acrid smell of the fire pit, strips of meat hanging just above it to cure. Wind whistling outside, rattling the small red door. I'd get to see our hunting dogs again, too—how big were they now? The russet bitch must've had her pups.

And the kumaq. By Grandmother Sky, the kumaq!

I bounced in my saddle the whole way to camp, no matter how upset my mother was.

Home.

I was going home again.

WHEN IN DREAMS I GO TO YOU

Home, for me, means two things. The first is you. Above all, you are my white felt ger, you are my bright red door, and you are my warm fire. But if I cannot have you, then I will have silver—the silver of the steppes' swaying grass, the silver of winter, the silver clouds coloring Grandmother Sky.

In Fujino, you see, everything is green. One look outside your window will tell you why. Your Imperial Forest is so deep a green that it reminds me of the Father's ocean—and it is only one of many. Your province is covered in too many to name. Your father once called Fujino the land of sun and pine.

He also called it the land of rolling hills.

I hate hills, Shizuka. Did you know? You cannot build a ger on a hill; everything will slide right off your furniture. You cannot camp at the bottom of a hill; the rain can get in and extinguish your fire. You cannot wrestle on a hill without your cousin tumbling down and cracking her head on a rock, as I learned when Otgar tossed me off one when we were ten.

But I admit there is more to it than my own opinion. The sanvaartains tell us that you can find true peace only when Sky and Earth are mirrors of each other. That is when you encounter eternity. Standing at the base of the Rokhon, with Gurkhan Khalsar behind you—is there anything more infinite than that? That is, I think, my favorite spot in the whole world.

And to think, I never got to show it to you.

Well. As far as hills go, and green, Oshiro is a far sight better than Fujino. Oshiro exists on the gentlest slope in the Empire. What few trees mark the landscape are bright white, or warm brown. The people are the same. In Fujino, it's my appearance that makes people stare: my hay-colored hair, my bowed legs, my skin so dark and cheeks so wide. In Oshiro, I see those features staring back at me on Hokkaran faces—a guard with flecks of green in his eyes, babies born with blue marks on their bottoms and cheeks meant for nibbling. Oshiro is not home, no, for it will always remind me of my father—but I love it when it reminds me of my mother.

And there is the Wall. You cannot discuss Oshiro without discussing the wreckage. The Wall of Stone was built three hundred years ago, at the height of Qorin culture, when Brave Arslandaar led us as Kharsaq. One of your ancestors decided the only way to keep us from raiding Oshiro and the border villages was to build a wall.

But, you see, he did not build the Wall simply to keep us out. He thought that such a feat of engineering would amaze us. He thought we would gaze upon it and weep; he thought we would cast aside our weapons and our horses, and join the superior Hokkaran Empire.

But what he did not know was this: Qorin engineers exist. Qorin stonemasons, Qorin builders. Wherever we go, we welcome additions to the clan, should they prove stout enough to survive the winter. Those newcomers might not be Qorin—but their children are. And so the trade is passed down the family line.

This comes in handy when we encounter other travelers—we can offer services instead of just goods. More than once, we've stopped near a Surian town and helped construct a house or two; more than once, we've offered medical assistance to the desert nomads; more than once, we've been contacted by Xianese scholars for our thoughts on astronomic conundrums.

That is why the remains of the Wall make me smile. The wreckage reminds me of what a woman can do when she becomes an arrow in flight—reminds me that we are so much more than what the Hokkarans think us to be. And if you stand in the right spot— the white palace at your back and the hole in the Wall right in front of you—then you are *almost* eternal.

Almost.

Do you remember, Shizuka, the feast that awaited us beyond that wall? Your parents huddled beneath a white felt roof, surrounded by carpets and tapestries. Shizuru pinched her nose with one hand. With the other, she held a skin full of kumaq. My uncles challenged her to drink all of it in one go. She did, of course. Your mother was never one to refuse a drink, or a dare.

If she stepped out of the ger to vomit, hours later, no one pointed it out. No one would dare.

Your father drank more than she did, of course. Two and a half skins of kumaq for him, and he did not have to hold his nose. But he did not draw attention to it. Only the red on his cheeks gave him away; the Imperial Poet could never allow himself to slur his words. Not that he did much speaking. Your father knew more Qorin than his wife did, but I can't remember hearing him speak it. Our language reminded him of the war, I think; of the early days of his brother's reign. But he would never say such a thing out loud. It had been many, many years since O-Itsuki spoke of the Qorin war.

All the highest-ranking members of the Burqila clan attended. That night I saw generals dance around the fire. I saw men and women the Hokkarans paint as bloodthirsty barbarians tell bawdy jokes. I ate, and ate, and ate, and I did it with my fingers instead of fumbling with chopsticks, and there was no rice to fall between my fingers, no fishbones to stab me in the tongue. There was soup, and pickled sheep's head, and my cousins sat around the fire throwing anklebones.

You watched me.

In between hugs from my clanmates, I caught sight of you. Flickering flames painted your amber eyes orange.

And as Otgar whispered in my ear, as my mother kept a keen eye on her drunk siblings, I watched you.

Among the dark-skinned, light-haired Qorin, you sat—pale and inky-haired. I remember you—or do I remember only the disguise all that kumaq draped around you? For I thought to myself that you were so pale and so still, you must be a masked actress. At any moment, your face would fall clean off to reveal your true nature, if only I kept watching. But you stared into the flames and squeezed your hands until your knuckles went white, and if the director called for you to shed your mask, you did not hear him.

A man on the Wall of Stone spots riders coming. Wasting no time, he hefts his hammer and strikes his great iron bell. He did not think to cover his ears, and so for hours afterwards, they ring. At night when he lies down to sleep, he hears it, feels it in his bones. He cannot escape the sound.

So it was that when I looked at you, my chest rang with your discomfort.

I reached out and touched your shoulder.

You sniffed. "It is strange," you said, "to feel the way you do in Fujino."

At least here no one looked at you as if you were going to murder them on a moment's notice. The first time someone gave me that look in Fujino, I was ten.

But I knew what it was like, and I did my best to comfort you.

"Otgar is my best friend," I said. You stiffened. "Besides you," I added. This was why I did not like talking. I meant to imply that you two should talk. If I liked both of you, then you were bound to like each other.

At the mention of her name, Otgar slid over to us. "Besides Barsatoq?" she said. "You wound me, Needlenose. Too much time in one place. Your mind is getting stagnant."

I chuckled, but you did not think it was funny. "Shefali's been staying with my family," you said. "We've the finest tutors in all Hokkaro."

I was afraid Otgar would roll her eyes at this. Instead, she laughed in a good-natured way. "Yes, Barsatoq, of that I am sure!" she said. "But we are Qorin: traveling is in our blood. You learn nothing staying in one place. Only by struggling against the earth do you learn anything of worth."

"Is that how you learned your languages?" you said.

"It is," Otgar said. "Burqila traveled the spice road to Sur-Shar. On the way, we met a Surian merchant, with no stores save those he meant to sell. Burqila allowed him to come with us on the condition she received a portion of the money from whatever he sold. Except he spoke no Qorin."

"So you learned Surian," you said. "To translate for him."

"No, my mother slept with him," said Otgar. "And he left some of his books behind when he left, so I cracked them open. I had to learn, you see, so I could translate for Burqila." Otgar corrected, waving her finger. "The Kharsa is always the highest priority."

Except that my mother never formally accepted the title of Kharsa, as part of the terms of her marriage. No one paid that any heed here. She was a Kharsa in all but name.

You said nothing to this. For all your talent with Hokkaran, you spoke not a word of Qorin. Oh, you could write it. My mother wanted our alphabet to be simple enough for a child to learn. You knew it and you knew which symbols corresponded to which sounds. But the words themselves, the grammar?

No. That you could not do.

So you sat and you shifted. I imagine you were about to say something cutting when my mother raised her hand in the air, and the ger fell silent. Otgar rushed to her side.

I sidled up closer to you. My mother was giving me that viper look again. Her serpents coiled about my heart and squeezed. She would not throw a celebration like this if she meant to tear into me in front of the clan, would she?

My mother's fingers made shapes too fast for me to keep up with them. Before my stay with you, I knew a great many of her gestures, but now I found I could no longer keep up. It's a strange feeling, being unable to understand your own mother.

"Burqila Alshara Nadyyasar welcomes you all," Otgar said. "Both those of her clan and of Naisuran Shizuru's."

I'd heard your mother's Qorin name before, but it'd been some time. The sound of it startled me. Nai, for "eight"; Suran for "trials." Eight Trial Shizuru, for the eight days of hardship she and Alshara endured past the Wall of Flowers. Looking at her rosy, drunk face now, it was hard to imagine her cutting down one of the Traitor's Generals. But, then again—legend has it she learned the name of the General by charming one of his underlings. And your mother has always been a very charming drunk.

I tried to picture it—my mother and yours huddled together in a damp prison cell, an unspeakable monstrosity dangling rotten food just out of their grasp. Your mother calling him closer, and closer, beckoning with her husky voice—

My mother grabbing the thing's arm and slamming it against the bars.

One day we shall hear that story in full, Shizuka. I have heard tell that my brother wrote of it from a few of the nobles here—would that I could find a copy, and have it read to me. Sky knows my mother refused to elaborate on what had happened. So much of it is left to our imaginations, Shizuka, and imaginations are the worst kinds of liars.

But even so—it was hard to imagine you and I killed a tiger.

"She hopes you will enjoy the kumaq to its fullest extent, and advises that anyone caught vomiting in her ger will be punished," Otgar continued, "as she hates the smell."

All eyes fell on your mother. The laughter that left her, unbridled and boisterous, was more Qorin than Hokkaran.

"Don't give me that look, Alshara!" she said. "I outdrank Kikomura-zul, I can keep this down!"

I am not certain if your mother knew the gravity of referring to my mother by her birth name. As a Hokkaran man might only call his wife, daughter, and mother by their personal names, so a Qorin would never think of addressing anyone but his immediate family by their child name. An adult name was earned. An adult name told you everything you needed to know about a person. My mother, for instance, is the Destroyer—for what she did to the Wall of Stone.

And yet Shizuru called her the same thing my grandmother called her. The same thing I might call her, if I wanted to catch a backhand. You will not tell my mother I've been using her personal name this whole time, will you?

The Burqila chiefs stared at your mother. Some cleared their throats. None said a word against her. Such was our mothers' friendship—anyone who spoke up against Shizuru spoke up against Alshara.

My mother shook her head. She made four more gestures, then pointed to the red door, a wry smile on her harsh face.

"Burqila says that you are welcome to vomit outside, Naisuran, as she knows you will," Otgar said in Hokkaran.

Your mother guffawed, slapped her knee. Itsuki covered his mouth. I had to remind myself that this was the Queen of Crows and the Imperial Poet laughing like children. I had to remind myself that your parents were far older than mine. And you were their only daughter.

Was it lonely, Shizuka, growing up without a sibling? Kenshiro was not always with me—and by then, he had already left for Xian-Lai—but I had more cousins than I knew what to do with. I've heard you mention yours only once or twice. If only we did not live so far apart! I know my family is loud, and I know they stay up too late, and I know how fond you are of time alone—but

I wish I could have kept you company. I wish we had spent more hours together than apart.

Was that why you were so sour? Because I was leaving?

My mother continued her gesturing. Now her movements were slow and deliberate. As she "spoke," she made eye contact with everyone in the room.

Including me.

At that moment I wished I were a horse, so I might run away faster.

"But before the festivities can continue, there is one thing Burqila would like to say," said Otgar. "You have by now all heard the story of Shefali and the tiger. It is her opinion that such a deed entitles Shefali to a proper, adult name."

My breath caught. Next to me, you sat dumbfounded; it occurred to me Otgar was speaking in Qorin and you could not understand her.

Mother beckoned me closer. I stood, reaching for the bundle of cloth behind me, and walked to her.

"From this day forth," said Otgar.

My mother reached for a strand of my hair. With callused fingers she braided it, then hid it behind my ear.

"You are Barsalai."

Barsalai—"Tiger-Striped." Silently I moved my mouth to form the word. My name. Barsalai. Truth be told, I was afraid I'd be Needlenose as an adult. This new name settled on my shoulders like a well-worn cloak.

Ah, that was right. My project.

I presented my mother with the bundle of cloth. Slowly, deliberately, she unfolded it. Within was a deel lined with tiger fur. I will not lie and say it was of exquisite make; embroidery has never been my strong suit. But it was warm, and made of sturdy cloth, and the colors were pleasing to the eye. If it was plain, the tiger fur made up for it.

My mother's lips widened into a smile. I saw a rare sight that night: wrinkles around her mouth and eyes. She covered my head with her hand and kissed my cheek.

The ger erupted into cheers. Uncle Ganzorig spilled his kumaq onto the fire; it exploded upward. Suddenly I was afloat in a sea of people clapping me on the shoulder or pinching my cheeks or sniffing me. More than one of my cousins dragged me closer to the fire. In the frantic steps of Qorin dances we lost ourselves. Your parents did their best imitation of us. I'm embarrassed to say that O-Itsuki managed a perfect impression despite going through the whole thing without a word. At one point, your mother almost fell into the campfire, only for your father to swoop her away at the last moment. O-Shizuru laughed and kissed him.

But their joy did not extend to you.

I can count on one hand the number of times I've been upset with you, Shizuka. That night, acid filled my throat; that night, a foul anger clouded an otherwise wonderful celebration. Every time I saw you, the taste in my mouth grew more bitter. And I was not the only one to notice.

"Your friend," Otgar whispered to me, "is she always like this?" I shook my head.

"I don't know why we ever let you stay with the Hokkarans," Otgar said. "No sense for a good party!"

She was a far better dancer than I was. Four more years of experience did that. I struggled to keep up with her steps, and hoped all the kumaq in my belly wouldn't topple me over into the fire.

Whenever I took a false step, Otgar caught me. If I fell, it was mostly her responsibility, but I like to think she didn't want me to hurt myself.

During one such false step, I fell backwards and landed on my bottom. A chorus of laughs followed. My relatives teased me for having more kumaq than I could handle. Otgar helped me up, just as a gust of wind flickered the fire. Hardened warriors spat on the ground. Superstition. Winds were not meant to enter the ger, for they brought with them the foul spirits that haunted the steppes at night.

I spat on the ground, too.

But I also saw the tail of your dress as you left through the red door. My chest burned, my stomach churned; the speech I wanted to give you formed in my mind. I got to my feet, told Otgar I'd return soon, and followed you out.

Outside, spring winds cut through my Hokkaran clothing. I wished I'd brought my deel. I'd be warm in my deel, and I could've smuggled some kumaq out. But no, I wore the clothing you bought me. Earlier this morning, it made me feel braver.

Now I just felt cold.

Wordlessly I followed you. At some time, you'd stop. At some time, the cold would get to you, or the faint smell of horse manure, or one of the animals would startle you.

But no. You kept walking. And by the time you stopped, I'd been following you for what felt like an hour.

"You have a party to attend, do you not?" you sneered.

A puff of vapor left my nostrils. The tips of my ears fast turned red. I scowled at you and dug in my heels.

You hid your hands within your sleeves. The Moon cast her silver light onto you, and lent an unearthly air to your complexion.

In that moment, I saw some traces of the woman you'd become: I saw your sharp lips painted red as your sword; I saw your cheeks pink as petals; I saw the brown-gold of your cutting eyes.

And I saw the eight-year-old girl shaking in the freezing cold.

Despite the fire of anger in me, I could not just stand there and watch you freeze. I walked up to you and wrapped an arm around you.

"You're leaving in the morning, aren't you?"

I nodded. Another puff of vapor left my lips and spiraled into the air between us. You looked out at the pure white gers alight from within, looked out at the horses and the dogs and the guards.

"I will see you again," you said. "I know I will. But until that time, you will keep yourself safe. I know there are no tigers on the steppes; do not go chasing anything large and fanged and terrible. You aren't allowed to get hurt until I see you again. You just aren't."

You leaned your head on my shoulder as you spoke.

I tried very hard to hold on to my anger, but it was like holding water. Only my fingers were still wet.

"Celebrate," I said.

You scoffed. "Celebrate your leaving?" You shook your head. "No. I will not celebrate that."

Ahh, there it was again, a bit more water in my palms. "My name. Barsalai."

You paused. You took my hand and hid it in your flower-scented sleeves. I was struck by how small your wrists were.

"Then I will not celebrate your going, Barsalai, but we will celebrate in the halls of Fujino when you return. And I will call you Shefali, and you will call me Shizuka, even when we are adults."

And I said nothing, lest my voice ruin the beauty of the moment. Because we were together beneath the great silver moon, together on the steppes, and I did not know when I would next be near you.

"WRITE TO ME," you said.

I did.

Over the next three years, I wrote to you whenever I had the chance. I did not have the chance often. Paper was too delicate to last long traveling with us; Qorin favored oral messages when possible. But every now and again, we would meet with a merchant on his way to Sur-Shar, and I would buy as much paper as I could, and have Otgar write you.

When our travels took us to the great mountain Gurkhan Khalsar, I secretly cut a few mountain flowers and sent them to you. That night I prayed to Grandfather Earth to forgive me for what I'd done, but I cannot say I truly regretted it.

You, who had an entire Imperial Garden delivered from Fujino to Oshiro simply so I could see—certainly you deserved something sacred in return.

I did not tell you in that letter what Gurkhan Khalsar means to us.

You see, it is the highest point on the steppes. In front of it runs the river Rokhon, which flows from the harsh tundra of the North all the way down to the Golden Sands. As such, at the peak of Gurkhan Khalsar you are closest to Grandmother Sky, and at its base you are very near the waters given to us by Grandfather Earth. On Gurkhan Khalsar alone do you find this perfect union. So it is that Kharsas and Kharsaqs climb the mountain once a year to meditate. Only there, at the peak, will they hear the whispers of the future.

So the story goes.

And while my mother was busy meditating, I chose to pluck a livid flower from the earth and tuck it away within my deel. I did this knowing some of my ancestors are buried on this mountain. I did this knowing my mother would've slain anyone who dared to alter Gurkhan Khalsar in any way.

I did it because I thought you deserved it.

I hope the flower arrived intact. In your return letter, you wrote that it was still fragrant when it arrived. What did you think when you held it in your hands—this sacred object? If I had stolen a prayer tag from a temple and sent it to you, it would've been less sacrilegious. When you pressed it to your nose, what did you smell? For my people believe the soul of a person is in their scent, in their hair. On the mountain, there are dozens of banners made from the mane of Kharsaqs, Kharsas, and their horses. The wind whips through them and carries their souls forever across the great plains. One day I will take you to the mountain and you shall see them, all lined up, all swaying like dancers, and you will think of the flower I gave you when we were children.

WINTER LONELINESS
IN A MOUNTAIN VILLAGE

I wrote to you of the things I saw, the places I'd traveled. There weren't many. At least, not many different ones. The steppes enthrall me, Shizuka, and they always have—but there are only so many times I can write about endless silver grass before it gets boring.

I wrote about it anyway. Anything I could think of—how Otgar's new bows were coming along, a long rant about where a saddle should sit on a horse's back, my Uncle Ganzorig's latest stew recipe—went into those letters. Otgar hated transcribing them. She must have gotten used to it, though, since we did it every day for two years straight.

Seven hundred and twenty letters. When I was writing them, they all felt like one long conversation. Your replies always found us within a reasonable span—my mother enlisted four messengers dedicated only to our correspondence—until we reached the northern forests.

The Qorin there almost looked like Hokkarans, their skin was so pale—but their hair was lighter than mine was, and they still greeted us with kumaq and old war songs.

The chief of the northern tribes was, at the time, a man named Surenqalan. Old and graying, with as many scars as a dappled mare has spots, he greeted us from horseback. Only three pale braids circled his head, tied from the hair at the base of his crown. Across the flat of his bald head was a nasty streak of scarred flesh.

We shared his fire that first night, and stayed in his ger for the customary meal. On the first night of my mother's visits, she does not discuss business. Instead, Surenqalan spoke to us of his daughters and his sons, of marriages and funerals. I listened though I knew none of the people being discussed. Otgar translated for my mother, and gave me summaries of the people. I had distant cousins here, too, thanks to my absurd number of aunts.

But the reason I remember this night so well—the reason I can still picture old Surenqalan poking at the fire, the reason I can feel the tip of my nose go numb when I think about that night, is what happened after we left to our own ger.

I saw something out of the corner of my eye, dashing between the gers. Tall, slender, cloaked in black and red; it moved as quickly as a shadow flickering between trees.

Wolves sometimes attack us, but they would not do so this far north. And they would not get so close to the camps, when they know we'd shoot them on sight. Nor could I say the figure looked Qorin—it did not wear a deel, or any winter clothing at all.

I froze in place. My mother turned toward me, one hand on the hilt of her scimitar. She wrinkled her nose and bared her teeth. I pointed where I'd seen the figure, and my mother made a few more gestures.

"Search the area," Otgar said.

The riders scrambled off. I watched them go, opening and closing my fists. I had the sinking feeling they were not going to find anything. What if this, like the glimmer near the dying, was something only I could see?

I strung my bow and pulled an arrow from my quiver.

"Shefali," Otgar said, "what are you doing?"

I started walking between the gers. That thing was somewhere around here, lurking near my people, and I would not allow it to continue stalking us.

"Has it occured to you," Otgar said, "that you are ten years old?"

I continued. No use arguing; I did not have the time. Black and red, black and red . . . there! I saw it—her—clearly now, a living darkness against the pure white ger.

I drew back my bow and aimed.

"What are you firing at?" Otgar asked.

I was right; she couldn't see the dark thing! More reason to let fly!

Except . . . well, there were people in that ger, and if my arrow pierced through its walls, they might be hurt.

A moment's hesitation doomed me.

Because the figure noticed that I'd noticed her.

It is difficult to say that a shadow smiled. If you imagine a silhouette in darkest ink against finest paper, that was the figure I saw. No features, no light, nothing to indicate she had any expression at all. Yet I knew she was looking at me, and my bones rattled with her amusement.

"Hello, Steel-Eye."

Ice ran through my veins.

Who was Steel-Eye? For I'd earned my name already. Tiger-Striped, I was, with my mother's viper-green eyes.

And yet in my chest I felt a *rightness*. That, more than the voice itself, terrified me.

I wanted to run. I wanted, more than anything, to run.

But I was Barsalai Shefali now, an adult of the Burqila clan. And the Burqila clan did not become dominant by running from their enemies.

So I thought at this thing clearly and loudly: *Whatever you are, you are not welcome in my lands.*

"They are not your lands yet, Steel-Eye," she said. "And you are still a child. You cannot stop me."

I can, I thought.

Again, I raised my bow. Otgar squeezed my forearm, her face wrought with concern. "Shefali," she said, "there is nothing there. You're staring at a blank patch of the ger."

Laughter, if you could call it that. The sound of a lump of coal shattering.

"See how they doubt you? So they will for years and years. It would be much easier if you joined us now," it said.

Its words triggered a roiling anger within me. I no longer cared if anyone was hurt; I fired. The shadow peeled away from the ger. Arrow met felt. That sound of breaking coal rang through the air. The figure slipped inside, I took a step forward—

Otgar blocked my path.

"Shefali," she said in a level voice, "listen to me. Whatever you saw, don't let it affect you like this. You are going to be Kharsa one day. You cannot let the shadows rule you."

By then my mother returned with her empty-handed riders. She saw the arrow sticking out from the ger—saw it was mine—and frowned. When she sharply gestured that I should apologize to the inhabitants, I was not surprised.

I looked from her to Otgar. My cousin was fourteen then. In a few more years, she'd be ready to marry. She was not a pretty girl, but she was smart as a whip. Someone would be coming to stay with her soon—some boy working off his bride-price.

And she was looking at me like I was a child who ran off from camp and nearly got eaten by wolves.

I lowered my bow and shrank about three sizes.

I knew what I saw.

And I knew it had a name, the same way I knew your name from the moment I could speak.

Shao. Her name was Shao.

My mother forced me to apologize, and I did that as curtly as I could. A small family lived inside that ger. A man, his wife, his grandmother. Very small. No doubt the man's brothers died off before my mother came to power, during the wars. So many of us died to the blackblood that we were trying to make up for it. Each family was encouraged to have as many children as they could, and then sanvaartains got involved. Did you know, Shizuka, that many of the Qorin children you see these days are fatherless? Given the proper rituals, sanvaartains can induce pregnancy—but still, I saw no children here.

Otgar did her best to calm me. She told me the story of Tumenbayar again—the Kharsa who used the moon as her bow, with hair of shining silver and skin like rich clay.

THAT NIGHT I listened to another of Otgar's stories and pretended to take an interest in it. Tumenbayar saddled her golden mare and rode to the north. Friendly winds told her of a clan in danger there. When she arrived, she found demons rampaging through the camp, scooping up horses and snapping into them like jerky. Dozens of them, the largest horde anyone had ever seen up to that point—and this Ages ago, when demons did not roam the countryside as they do now. An entire clan could not hope to defeat this many.

But Tumenbayar and her golden mare were worth twenty clans together. So she strung her crescent-moon bow and fired her windcutter arrows. As she fired at the beasts, she rode in a circle around them, faster and faster each time. The demons caught on to this and threw people at her, threw horses at her, threw anything they could to try to slow her down.

Tumenbayar reached into her thousand-pocket saddlebags. She pulled out her skin of mare's milk, and with the tip of her arrow, she slit it open. Milk dripped along her path. Tumenbayar, raised by a cadre of sanvaartain, spoke holy words as she rode.

Demons charged at her, but could not pass the barrier of the milk. Tumenbayar rode just outside their grasp. In an hour's time, no more, she felled all the demons. When they were dead, she herself set fire to their bodies, so that their foul blood could not corrupt Grandfather Earth. She did this wearing the deel given to her by Grandmother Sky herself, which protected her from all manner of harm.

It was a good story. Not the best Tumenbayar story, but good. Enough to get my mind off things, if it were any other night, or any other thing I'd seen. Otgar did her best to lend the tale more weight. One day, you shall hear her Tumenbayar voice, and you will laugh loud and long.

Tumenbayar is something like your ancestor Shiori to us.

I've heard a thousand stories about her, and despite my better judgment, I believe every one. For who is to say whether or not Tumenbayar really did fire arrows of wind, or if the ridge of mountains north of the Rokhon really are her horse's footprints? These things are legends. In their own way, all legends are true.

You must be laughing now. I'm certain you've heard a few legends about us. Those are true, as well, but true in a different way. I've begun to think of the Barsalai my clan whispers about as a different person. Did you know, Shizuka; I've heard children telling Tumenbayar stories, but with me instead of her?

SOMETIME AFTER MIDNIGHT, Otgar gave in to sleep. I stayed up awhile later. If Shao returned, I wanted to be ready. This time, I told myself, I would not hesitate.

So I told myself. In reality, we'd been riding most of the day, and most of the day before that. Exhaustion gripped me, and try as I might, I could not fight it. I, too, fell asleep.

I awoke to women screaming.

"Burqila! Burqila, save us!"

As I scrambled to my feet, my mother was dashing out our door with sword in hand. Ringing pain split my ears; I reached for my bow and followed her out. My chest ached. Without looking, I knew which ger we'd be going to.

The one I saw Shao outside of.

A dozen Qorin clustered outside its red door. Color drained from dark faces. An old grandmother sank to her knees in the snow weeping, raking her cheeks and pulling her hair. She was the one screaming for my mother.

Alshara pushed her way to the door, then pushed her way past that. I saw her go in and I tried to follow—only to find crossed swords barring my path.

"Barsalai," said the taller woman. "A demon visited us last night. That ger is no place for a child."

I pointed to my braid. My one braid. The woman I was speaking to had three.

"Braid or no, name or no," she said, "you are ten. I cannot let you pass."

I knew this woman, though not by name. She rode in my mother's personal guard. Short for a Qorin, she had short hair the color of hay and a scar on her chin. On her left hand, she was missing one finger. Years she'd been with us. I remember seeing her when I still had to be strapped into my horse. A good, loyal guard is hard to find.

At that moment, I wished she were a bit less loyal. I could not strike her down. I was not you—I could not command her. I was not even Otgar.

Where was Otgar?

Bounding up toward the ger, hastily fastening her deel with one hand and holding her hat to her head with the other. The guard looked to her and crossed her arms.

"Dorbentei, until I receive orders otherwise, I cannot allow you to enter—"

"Who is going to give you the orders?" Otgar said. "Burqila? She is not going to break her oath of silence to speak to you."

The guard pressed her lips into a line. "Dorbentei, the body might be corrupt."

"Burqila does not fear corruption and neither do I," said Otgar. "I do not intend to touch the corpse. We will be fine."

But I did not want to wait for her to negotiate. While Otgar spoke to the guard, I slipped in.

My mother stood at the western side of the ger. At her feet, a corpse. Calling it a "corpse" is, perhaps, exaggerating.

You are out in your Imperial Garden enjoying a plum. Suddenly business calls you away—you leave the plum on a bench and tend to your affairs. Hours later when you return home, the plum is forgotten. Days pass into weeks. When you next sit on the bench, the plum is still there, but it is a dry, withered thing, and you mistake it for a stone.

So it was with the corpse. Once it might've been a man. Now it was simply skin and bones. No meat. No substance. On its face an eternal scream. Dark pits where its eyes should've been, dark pits for nostrils. Any hair the man had was gone, too, as well as any clothing.

Worst of all, I saw no glimmering near him.

My stomach churned. I tasted bile at the back of my throat. A Kharsa cannot retch at the sight of a body; I tried my best to conceal it. Still I let out a small noise.

My mother sheathed her sword. She stomped on the ground once, to catch my attention. When she saw I looked at her, she pointed to the corpse, then the door. I nodded and left and tried not to think of the shadow I'd seen the night before.

When I left the ger, Otgar and the guard were still talking. Both turned toward me.

"Barsalai!" said the guard. "I told you not to go in there!"

The old woman continued her wailing, her screaming. *Burqila, save us.* Over and over again. As if my mother could bring her dead son back to life. I screwed my eyes shut against the sound, and waved for Otgar to come closer.

"Burn the body," I whispered to her. "Remove it. Burn it."

Otgar nodded. Orders were passed along. I did not stay to watch it all happen. No need to. Instead, I followed my mother and Otgar as they made their way to Surenqalan's ger. The old man was already awake. My mother did not bother taking off her boots, and so neither did we.

As he bowed to us, the old chief shook.

My mother made three sharp gestures.

"Surenqalan," said Otgar. "How long has this been happening?"

The man's ger was empty. Completely empty. I cannot remember another time I've seen something like it—stark white felt walls, with no furniture to speak of save the door and the frame keeping everything up. After seeing the corpse of that man from earlier, I shivered.

Something was very wrong with this clan.

"Great Kharsa," said Surenqalan, tapping his forehead against my mother's boots. "Wall-breaker, slayer of men, Burqila Alshara, I am unworthy to be in your presence."

Otgar rolled her eyes. My mother tapped her lips, then held her fingers out.

"Get to the point," Otgar said.

The old man took fistfuls of the rug at his feet. Shaking, he looked up at my mother. Did he see a woman, I wonder, or a legend? Did he see the Uncrowned Kharsa, the woman who breathed Dragon's Fire? Or did he see something darker—perhaps the woman who killed her own brothers rather than submit to their authority? For my mother was all those things and more, and sometimes I had trouble figuring out which woman I spoke to.

But from his eyes wide as pebbles and his cheeks paler than the walls of the ger, I had an idea what he saw.

The Destroyer.

"Burqila," he said with a trembling voice, "I fear the Generals have come for my clan."

"Don't be silly," Otgar said. My mother's hands were still; this was Otgar's opinion alone. "Of the six remaining clans, yours is the smallest. One of the Generals would never bother coming all the way up north unless they wanted a fine fur coat. We cannot be dealing with a General."

I nodded. The Generals—four demon lords in the service of the Traitor—made appearances only in the most dire of times. When armies of blackbloods marched, a General led them. When the Traitor's forces tore through old Shiseiki as an arrow through paper, the Generals strung their bows.

But for a few hundred Qorin up near the mountains, barely scraping by on whatever food they could scavenge?

It made no sense. What would a General want with this clan?

Not to mention the remaining three were trapped beyond the Wall of Flowers. Everyone knew that. The Daughter's creation kept them from rampaging through the rest of Shiseiki Province, kept them sealed within the borders of northern Hokkaro. The last time actual demons set foot on the steppes was when Tumenbayar was Grand Kharsa.

Blackbloods would not be surprising.

But blackbloods did not leave this sort of mess. They left carnage, blood and broken bones—not empty husks.

If demons were out on the steppes again . . .

My mother's fingers moved in soft, small gestures—meant for Otgar and not Surenqalan. I did not catch all of them, but I understood enough. *We will make a diplomat out of you yet.*

"What else could do this to a man? To many men?" Surenqalan protested. As he continued, his voice cracked like a child's. I felt a pang of pity for him. For my people. There were not many of us left; less than the population of even a small Hokkaran city. Every life lost was notable now.

"A demon," Otgar said. "But it's not a General. There are only four of those, old man, and Burqila killed one with Naisuran. We would have seen it by now if it were a blackblood, too—they're not good at hiding. So it must be a demon. It cannot be a blackblood."

"A demon?" said Surenqalan. He attempted to get to his feet. My mother tapped her foot, and he stayed where he was. "How could they get past the Wall of Flowers? Demons are a Ricetongue problem, not one of ours."

Moving shadows against the ger's walls. A featureless face smiling at me.

"Not for long," I said.

Otgar and Alshara both shot me a look. I shifted my weight from one foot to the other.

Curiosity written on my mother's features—who taught me anything about demons?

I licked my lips.

My mother is silent because of an oath, but I simply don't like talking.

More to the point—I had no idea where that bit of information had come from. Do flowers know, I wonder, when it is going to rain? If so, I imagine they felt the same way I did whenever I thought of the demon.

THERE I WAS, my mother and Otgar staring at me, waiting for me to elaborate.

I cleared my throat. Say what you mean the first time, and say it plainly.

"I saw the demon last night," I said. "Our deaths amuse it."

Alshara beckoned me closer. I stood next to her. She sniffed both my cheeks and squeezed my shoulders. Gone was the accusing look. In its place, concern. In its place, hiding beneath the surface of her dark skin: worry and fear.

Otgar, too, hugged herself a bit tighter. She spat on the ground. By some miracle, she did not hit Surenqalan, who still prostrated himself at my mother's feet.

"Barsalai," he said, "you have seen the thing that stalks us?"

I nodded.

"Can we kill it?" he asked.

I looked to my mother. Alshara and Shizuru slew one of the Generals in their youth. Of the Sixteen Swords that set out from Fujino, only they returned. If anyone could kill Shao, it was my mother.

She nodded. She raised her hands to about chest level and gestured again, her fingers flying through forms and motions as a tongue shapes syllables.

"Burqila will slay this demon," Otgar said. "She will set out tonight and she will return with its head. In exchange, you shall provide her with one of your sons, or your grandsons—

whichever is the right age to perform his bridal duties. He will stay with—"

Otgar paused though my mother continued signing. And then she did something I did not expect.

She began signing back.

The two of them went back and forth for some time. Otgar's motions were choppy waves; my mother's rising tides. Otgar's whole arm moved when her hand did, throwing more volume behind her silent words. Eventually she stomped her right foot, crossed her arms, and glowered for a few moments.

"He will stay in our ger and perform his duties there," Otgar mumbled. "And in two years' time, if he is not horrible, he might find himself married to me."

Surenqalan did not know what to say. He chose the wise man's course and said as little as possible.

"As you wish, Burqila."

My mother continued signing, but Otgar refused to translate. She turned on her heel and left the ger, her footfalls like a colt's. When my mother saw this, she stopped mid-motion and put a palm to her forehead. She grunted. For her, it might as well have been a speech.

For my part, I did not want to focus on personal matters when there was a demon on the loose. Especially not a demon that knew me.

So I shrugged in the direction Otgar had gone and reached for my bow.

My mother nodded. To get Surenqalan's attention, she tapped her foot by his head. He looked up; she inclined her head. That was all the good-bye we offered.

Outside, the preparations began. My mother gathered up her

riders. Without an interpreter, things were a bit more difficult, but many of our guards have been with us for years. If they couldn't read Alshara's signs, they could read her body language. Simple enough to convey "get your weapons" or "follow me."

I watched from horseback. I watched them string their bows and sharpen their swords, watched them don their three-mirror armor, their bronze war masks. Two dozen humans became two dozen animals. I gazed upon the faces of wolves and tigers, of lions and eagles.

Not a trace of their skin showed through.

I did not have a war mask. I did not have three-mirror armor, or gauntlets thick enough to shield me from any demon blood. If I followed them on this trip, I'd be exposing myself to great risk— the sort of risk my mother wouldn't abide. The smallest drop of demon blood spreads through a body like paint in water. For this reason, we cover ourselves. For this reason, Hokkarans use naginatas in place of swords.

Qorin do not much believe in polearms—instead, we prefer to pick enemies off from afar. And for the most part, this works.

But you must sever a demon's head for it to truly die.

And that requires getting very close indeed.

Whoever slew the creature must be both the bravest and the most foolish. My mother, more likely than anything. She is the only person I know whose war mask is modeled on her own face. She would be the one to hold Shao's hair and swing her sword and sever her head. She would be the one whose clothing would be burned when this was through.

The more I thought about it, the more I wanted to see it. The more I wanted to be there. And this want grew into a need, into a burning thing in my chest.

I slunk over to the supply tent. I did not have a war mask, but I could find one here. Indeed, a few were lined up on a table just inside. Wolf, fox, falcon. Family, guile, speed. I picked up the fox mask. Not that I consider myself a trickster—several others wore them. It was best if I fit in. And, no, there was no three-mirror armor—but there was lamellar. I wriggled into it and looked in the mirror.

I stood fifteen hands tall. My armor was intended for someone sixteen and a half hands at the shortest. It hung loose around my torso; I had to hold my gauntlets up to keep them on. When I moved my head, my war mask rattled. I could see, yes. Barely. Enough to know I looked ridiculous. Imagine it, Shizuka: a kitten wearing a lion's mane.

But in the dark, on horseback, in the heat of battle—who is paying attention to what their comrade looks like?

This would have to do.

I stuffed the armor into my saddlebags. My mother wouldn't depart until later on, when the moon was high in the sky. Demons do not travel by day. I had until then to convince Otgar to translate again.

Otgar was in our ger when I found her, huddled against the northern wall. She poked at the fire with a stick. Glowered at it. In that moment, she reminded me of you. A darker, paler-haired version of you. When I entered, she glanced up, then continued staring at the fire.

"Needlenose," she said. "Your mother wants to marry me off."

I took a seat next to her. The fire made my cheeks tingle as they came back to life; I held out my hands to warm them.

"Can you imagine some ten-year-old running around our ger, trying to get his chores done?" she continued. I was ten, which I did not point out. "Messing everything up. He's going to mess everything up. Why's she doing this?"

"You're old enough," I said.

Otgar threw her stick into the fire. It crackled and roared, devouring the wood in an instant. She slumped forward and hugged her knees.

If only I were you—if only I could instill confidence in someone with the slightest effort. You'd know what to say.

Granted you did not like Otgar.

But in general, you would've known what to say.

"Otgar."

"Yes, Needlenose?"

"You don't have to," I said. "You can say no."

She puffed her cheeks out. Here in the ger, it was warm enough that no vapor left her. I half expected to see it anyway. "You want me to say no to the Kharsa."

"Your aunt."

"The Kharsa."

I shrugged.

Otgar shook her head. For some time she stayed slumped forward like that. I watched the fire in her place, wondering how long it would take her to feel better. There would be time to discuss this after the demon was dead. Plenty of time. Two years, in fact, when we could send the boy away if he ever displeased us. Such was the way bride-price worked: a boy came to work for his mother-in-law for a certain amount of time, as a sort of audition. If at any point his mother-in-law decided he was not worthy, he'd be sent back to his mother's ger. Otgar was only slightly less picky than you were. She'd find some reason to send him away.

I wanted her to feel better, I did. But I wanted the demon to die first. That was more important than Otgar, more important than me. If a letter arrived with your seal, I'd stop to read that—but otherwise, the death of my people took precedence.

After what felt like hours, Otgar sighed again. "You need me to translate, don't you?"

I nodded.

"You have some nerve, Shefali," Otgar said. "I'm worried, you know, about the boy, and here you are, asking me to translate."

There are bigger things, I wanted to say, *than you or I.*

Instead, I gave her a flat look.

Otgar pinched her temples. Finally she stood and kicked a bucket of sand onto the fire. "I will do it," she said. "But it's because we don't have many more people left to lose. And you have to promise to support me when I speak to your mother."

Again, I nodded. I could not think of anything less appealing to me than standing up to my mother, but I nodded. It was not about me.

So I gathered Otgar's and my things, and we mounted our horses, and we met my mother outside the camp before sundown. The two dozen riders joined us. My mother was in front of them, gesturing in as clear a way as she could what she wanted them to do.

But the moment my mother laid eyes on Otgar, she brightened and beckoned her close. She held one hand high in the air, her fingers crossed, then tapped her eyes.

"She is happy to see us," Otgar said.

I elbowed her.

With a sigh, she returned the gesture.

When we were close enough, my mother mussed Otgar's hair. This time she made her signs far closer to her chest, and faster—

only Otgar could get a good look at them. I watched in silence as they communicated. It is a strange thing to be unable to speak with your own mother. It felt unfair. I hardly spoke. Shouldn't I be able to understand them, too? Shouldn't I know what they were saying?

My father wrote to Kenshiro in Hokkaran, and he always used characters I could not read. Kenshiro tried his best to explain them, but . . . they never seem to take hold in my mind, never seem to stay. He'd read his letters out loud and point to each character as he went, so that I would not feel excluded.

Yet the letters were addressed to Kenshiro and spoke only to Kenshiro. They never mentioned me.

And here I was, watching my cousin and my mother talk in a sign language I barely understood, addressing only each other.

I held my reins a little tighter. Let them talk, then. I'd use the opportunity to slip away and get my armor on.

In the time it took me to get on my armor and ride back, the battle plans were settled. I'd heard precisely none of it. Instead, I heard the echoes of your voice. We were more than others. Gods, you said. The notes rang within me that night. As dusk fell and the sea of stars rolled into view beneath a fat full moon, I imagined myself among them. You and I were going to do great deeds, were going to be the brightest stars in the sky.

What need did I have for plans, when I knew in my bones I was going to rule one day?

So I said nothing and did my best to look inconspicuous on horseback. My mother sorted everyone into three groups of five. She led one with Otgar, and two of our senior riders led the others. One of the younger boys went around passing out torches, and one of my older cousins lit them. I took one. When no one was looking, I snuffed it. Darkness did not trouble me the way it troubled my clanmates, and I wanted both hands free.

I was not in my mother's group. No matter. I did not need my mother's guidance. I had my bow and my own strength; those would be enough.

Surenqalan's clan stayed inside their gers, as they had been instructed. Besides our horses and the clinking of our armor, the whistling wind was the only sound. My war mask hid my face but did not warm it; the tips of my ears stuck to the metal. My cheeks burned. At least my hands were warm, tucked away in oversized gloves. A cold face I can ignore. Cold fingers ruin good shots.

The five of us advanced through the camp. We circled each ger. The rider leading us—the stern woman from earlier—sprinkled milk around the walls. Under her breath she muttered holy words, too, and when she was done, she kissed her fingers and held them up to the sky. So it was with every ger we saw.

Hours of this. I did not know how I ended up with the blessing team, but I did not like it. While our leader blessed the gers, we waited nearby. If anything happened, we were to act, I suppose. The thought rankled me. I did not sneak into this mission to watch someone else bless tents. I grunted, checked my bow.

"Temurin," said one of the riders to my right. He jerked a finger toward me. I did my best to sit up straight. All thoughts of boredom left my mind; I'd forgotten I was not meant to be here. "Do you recognize that one? Armor doesn't fit right."

Our leader—so that was her name—rode right up to me. She was so close that I had to squint against the light of her torch as she studied me. I puffed myself up, stuck out my chest, pulled back my shoulders. With one hand I gripped my bow, and with the other the pommel of my stolen sword. I nodded to her with all the mock bravado I could muster.

Temurin clucked her tongue.

"Rider," she said. "Unmask yourself."

Beneath bronze, I bit my lip. If I hadn't grunted so loudly, this wouldn't be happening. And it was not as if I could avoid taking my mask off. Temurin wouldn't hesitate to shoot me. An unknown rider could mean anything. I could very well be the demon, for all she knew. From the way her dark green eyes pierced into me, she needed only an excuse to turn me into a pincushion.

I raised both hands to show I meant no harm. Then I lifted off the mask.

The rider nearest me guffawed. "It's Burqila's girl!"

The other three riders soon joined him in laughter, all while I sat there trying my best to look official. Temurin groaned and threw her head back. When she spoke, I could picture her brows knitting together.

"Barsalai," she said. "Burqila may have given you an adult name, but she did not change your age. You are ten. We are hunting a demon, and you weren't even sensible enough to take a torch. Mongke will lead you back to camp, where you will stay in your ger until your mother returns."

I shook my head.

Temurin stared me down. "Listen to me, girl," she said. "Follow Mongke back to camp. In another five years, perhaps you can accompany us—but now you must stay safe. Burqila cannot be named Kharsa. You can. Do not forget that."

What did it matter if my mother could not bear the title? She was Kharsa in every other way. How could I know what it meant for my mother to sacrifice that? Since the dawn of time, since we learned to ride, our leaders have been Kharsas and Kharsaqs. All children learn their names and deeds. Broad Khalja, who won a wrestling match against the Son himself; Clever Dzoldzaya, who made Grandmother Sky weep with his stories when the clans needed rain; Toluqai the Talker, the man who negotiated our trade pact with the Surians.

All of them paled in comparison to my mother.

The seven clans turned to her for leadership. She called them together once a year, she provided for them, she hunted with them, she commanded them.

In her rise to power, my mother had overcome obstacle after obstacle: the blackblood plague spreading among her people; her brothers fighting each other like starving wolves over a scrap of meat; her oath of silence; the Wall of Stone itself. When she finally laid down her bow and sword, it was not because she wanted to. If Alshara had her way, there would be no Hokkaro anymore. No, when she laid down her weapons, it was because she'd lost too many of her people, and could not bear to see more of us die.

So she married my father. So she agreed never to name herself Kharsa of the Silver Steppes. So she birthed two children with a man she never cared for, and allowed them to be given Hokkaran names.

When the time came for my mother's name to be sung with Dzoldzaya's, and Khalja's, and Toluqai's—why should she receive any less respect than they did? Why should anyone question her? At the time, "Kharsa" was only a word to me. Two short sounds, straining to encompass within them all the things my mother had done for her people.

But I would not say that to Temurin, who lived through the

plagues; I would not say that to Temurin, who was there on the day my mother swore her oath of silence.

"Stop dallying!" she said.

I opened my mouth to protest, though I knew nothing I said would convince her. Adults never listened. She reached out and turned my head toward Mongke, who held up his torch as if that would make him easier to see.

"Go," said Temurin.

Maybe you would've fought, but I knew a lost cause when I saw one. I rode over to Mongke with one last sad look over my shoulder. This was only the blessing party anyway, I told myself; they were never going to come to real harm. They didn't need my help. No demon would come near blessed milk.

Mongke knew better than to pat me on the shoulder, but as soon as we were out of earshot he leaned toward me. "You should talk to your mother about a suit of armor. Can't have our future Kharsa clanging around like this."

And—well, it was silly. Only the dark made my disguise passable, and it *was* dark.

Wait. Shouldn't the moon be shining bright, as it was when we began this expedition? My eyes were playing tricks on me. I must have seen the wrong moon overhead. It must be a new moon, and not a full one, for it to be this black. Mongke's torch was a pinprick at best.

Something was wrong. I stopped, looked back toward the rest of the group. My tongue stuck to the roof of my mouth. Five minutes away, no more, and yet the distance between us felt as profound as the distance between my ger and your rooms at the palace.

But the darkness didn't bother Mongke. He reached into his

saddlebags for a skin. "Though, if you keep this stuff up, people are going to start calling you—"

But screaming drowned out his words. I reached for my bow and nocked an arrow before I began to process what was happening.

It was as if he'd fallen into a pit of ink. The darkness itself swallowed him up so quick and so sudden that he was gone in a blink. From the bubbling scar of black before me emerged a smooth sphere, about the size of a man's head. Another blink. The surface bubbled again, and now the thing was growing, and growing, and the horse . . .

I screamed. I screamed as loud as I could. You might think I wanted to alert the others, but in truth there is little that frightens me like the death of a horse. No—this was not simply death; this was consumption. One moment the horse was there and then it was not. Not even hoofprints remained.

Riders scrambled. Someone pulled a horn from their pack and sounded an alarm. Hooves against snow. My heart hammered in my chest.

I fired a shot at the sphere. It swallowed my arrow, too. The hairs on the back of my neck stood on end. Weren't demons supposed to be person shaped? How were we meant to kill that?

And what was it going to do next?

The sphere hurtled straight toward me.

When you take a hard enough blow to the head, darkness comes upon you. You do not expect it, you do not foresee it—one moment you see color, and the next you do not. So it was when the sphere enveloped my head. Cold, wet, slimy. I could not breathe. I tried and tried, but I might've been breathing in rocks for all the good it did me. My lungs burned. I heard nothing but a churning sound, a gurgling sound that made me sick to my stomach.

And there was Shao's voice in my mind again.

Steel-Eye. You're going to have to do better than this.

That name again. Why did it hurt whenever I heard it?

My hands were still free, and so were my legs. Beneath me was my horse, solid and warm and breathing. As long as I had my horse, I could live through this.

You hardly fought at all.

Arrows plinked against the sphere's smooth surface. I tried to pry it off my head, but the damned thing clamped on tighter, and as brave as I was trying to be, I could not hold my breath forever. Was it the sphere making me dizzy, or the lack of breath? Hard to tell, but it did not stop my struggling. I pulled and pulled, the muscles in my arms screaming in agony, but I could not break free. Someone tried to cut me loose. I could not hear their shouting, but I did feel the flat of their blade stuck to the sphere.

Do you have anything to say for yourself before you die here, an untested child?

Panic's cold fingers around my throat. What if I couldn't do it? What if I was—we were—wrong all along? What if we weren't gods, Shizuka, what if I was going to die there on my horse with a demon eating my face and my mother found my corpse and it was burned, burned, not fed to the steppe animals as it should be, what if what if what if—?

No.

No, I would not allow it.

You would not allow it.

In that moment, I swear I heard your voice in my head. Perhaps it was the lack of air. Whatever the cause, I heard you: *No, no, you must fight.*

In a blind frenzy, I reached for the knife on my belt and plunged it into the sphere, without a care in the world if I hit myself. The pressure on my head tightened. Again, I stabbed, again, again, again. My hands were going numb, but I bent them to my will.

After perhaps the fifth strike, the sphere uncoiled just enough for me to catch a breath. As a man lost in the sands guzzles water, so did I greedily slurp down this air. It gave me life enough to keep striking back.

The next time I plunged the knife into it, the sphere flew off my face. Gasping and dizzy, I tried to take in what was going on. There it was, there she was: the woman-shaped shadow standing in the center of the riders. Shao.

She held the sword she'd stolen in one hand. I did not recognize her stance, but I did know that graceful ease she held herself with.

She was staring at me. I cannot tell you how I know this, Shizuka. Have you ever felt someone staring at you? Felt eyes on you, though no one was watching? If a thousand such eyes watched me, they would not equal Shao's intensity. She did not stare only at me. She stared through me, through all the versions of myself at once.

Shao held out her sword in challenge. "Steel-Eye!" she called.

This time everyone heard her. The warriors around me recoiled, the sound of her voice like falling glass.

"Is that a knife, Steel-Eye, or a tooth? Tiger's Daughter, using your milk teeth on big game—"

Here it came, my inglorious end—

My mother charged toward us.

I had to keep Shao distracted. If she moved, my mother wouldn't be able to behead her.

So I did what any foolish, angry, ten-year-old Qorin would do.

I jumped off my horse and I tackled her. I didn't bother trying to steer myself at all; I was not interested in kicks or strikes or anything fancy. Only the brute force of my falling weight. I slammed into her. Like slamming into a hill, it was, like crashing against unturned earth. My teeth rattled in my skull.

I could not stagger a thing with no breath, but it seemed I could surprise it. Shao dropped her sword. Shadows wrapped around my throat. I held my breath and braced myself. Either I was going to hurt very much, or I was going to feel nothing and my story was going to end.

I did not see my mother behead the demon, as I was facing down at the time. I could tell you in great detail how my boots looked against the snow. I could tell you about the horses embroidered in dull yellow thread. I could tell you how the toes curled up.

But I can tell you how my whole body shook with the strength of the blow. I can tell you how coldness splattered onto me thick as blood, heavy as iron. I can tell you of how I fell face-first into the snow when the demon ceased to exist.

When I rolled over, my mother held Shao's head in her hand. It was a shriveled thing, not much bigger than her fist—a lump of coal with hair attached. Far more frightening was the look on my mother's face. Far more terrifying, the striking green of her eyes against her dusky brown skin; far more terrifying, the anger, the fear.

Shao's featureless face unnerved me. But I knew my mother's face so well that the smallest glimpses of it beneath her war mask spoke volumes to me. In the crinkles near her eyes hid a thousand words.

For the first time I hated my vision. If I were normal, if the night did not favor me, I never would have seen that look in her eyes.

I cowered. I do not like to admit it, but I cowered at the sight of my mother astride her liver mare.

With her sword hand, she beckoned me to stand.

I feared I could not do it—my legs were still shaky—and no one was going to help me up when I was covered in demon blood. In the back of my mind, I knew this was bad. My armor soaked up most of it.

Except for my head. My uncovered head.

That man two years ago, lying on a bed just before your mother killed him. Glassy eyes. A fever. Black veins pulsing. His whole body struggling to rid itself of the Traitor's influence.

Shaking, I ran my hands through my hair. When my gauntlets came off, I tried not to scream. I huddled in on myself, cold and clammy, and rocked back and forth. Blood. So much blood, on me, just looking for a way to get in and . . .

My mother dismounted. The demon's head fell into the snow. She swaddled me in a blanket pulled from her saddlebags, scooped me up, and started walking.

If I told you she did not speak to me, you'd laugh and say of course. Such a thing is obvious. But when I write these words now, take heed: My mother did not speak to me for days. Not through Otgar. Not in hastily scrawled letters on her sheet of slate. Not in gestures.

No one else was permitted inside the ger. Only me, only my mother. More than once, I opened my mouth to speak to her. She'd fix me with a look, and I'd swallow my tongue. I felt so small, Shizuka. I felt so small and so scared. At night with the winds whistling outside, I'd hug myself tight and pray to Grandmother Sky that I would stay myself.

I tried to write to you. My mother kept a writing set in the ger, for she is fond of letters. On that first lonely evening, I sat in front of it and thought of all I might say to you. *Yes, we might be gods, but I might be dying. If I do, you can keep my horse.*

That is what I wanted to say.

But you know well, Shizuka, the struggle it is for me to write in Hokkaran. Frustration only set fire to my fear, to my anger and shame. I fell asleep with smears of ink on my hands, and unreadable scratch on my mother's fine paper.

On the morning of the fourth day, Otgar came into the ger, and it was then I breathed a heavy sigh of relief. For when I awoke, my mother was gone, too, and this meant I could finally talk to someone.

But Otgar wasn't pleased with me either.

"Barsalai Shefali," she said. "Do you have any idea just how much of an idiot you are?"

I stared into my bowl. It was one of the plain ones, not the painted ceramic from Sur-Shar.

"Mongke died," she said. "Temurin didn't notice a ten-year-old among her group, and so she can't return to the camp until she skins ten wolves. The riders won't stop talking about it, not for a moment. They all saw that thing grab hold of you. Five minutes, they said. You held your breath for five whole minutes, and they could not get it off you. Anyone else would've died. Yet here you are, staring into your soup."

The more Otgar spoke, the more I longed for silence again. All I wanted to do was help. All I wanted to do was prove that I was . . . that I was something more.

Otgar shook her head and kicked the carpet. Then she tapped the bowl I stared into, to get me to meet her eyes.

"That being said, I am glad you lived."

I tilted my head. After the danger I'd put myself in? After the way I acted—she was glad I was alive?

"When you grow up, Needlenose, you will be a fine warrior. You'll have more sense then," Otgar said. "People cannot decide whether they are upset with you for endangering yourself, or if they admire you for fighting against so wretched a beast. Me? I think you are ten, and my cousin. If I had the same Sky-given luck you did, I'd try to kill a demon, too."

Sheepish, I looked away.

Otgar ruffled my hair. "When you are feeling up to it, you will tell me what happened," she said. "Someone has to know the true story. All the riders are saying you spoke the name of the Mother."

There she was, my cousin, whom I'd ignored in favor of my foolish crusade.

I slumped forward.

She hugged me. Then she patted me on the shoulder. "Come on, Shefali," she said. "Don't think you're out of the woods yet. Your mother is going to punish you."

Otgar helped me up. She led me to the seat of my mother's war council—her and four or five riders clustered around a fire.

My mother held my bow. When she saw me, she lifted it above her head with one hand and held it there, so that everyone could see that it was mine. There were the beads I made from clay I found near the sands. There was a paper charm you made me, kept safely inside a jade cat no larger than my thumbnail. Vulture feathers. Pieces of silk from Sur-Shar in colors I'd never seen before.

My mother's fingers spoke. Otgar cleared her throat.

"Barsalai Shefali," Otgar said. "A man is dead because of your reckless actions and insubordination. Had you stayed behind as instructed, Mongke would not have had to leave the group to escort you back. Temurin failed to spot you among her number, yes, and she made the decision to send Mongke back with a ten-year-old. She's already faced my justice for that. If you want to bear an adult name, you must bear adult consequences. You must think beyond your own lust for glory. You faced a tiger in combat and did not think it enough. This behavior—this recklessness—ill suits you, and ill suits a future Kharsa. You must relearn patience and humility, since you seem to have forgotten them. Perhaps making a new bow will teach you."

And with that, she threw my bow—the bow Kenshiro and I made together—onto the fire. I watched it burn and covered my mouth to keep from screaming. In front of the war chiefs, I could not allow myself to cry, but my eyes watered anyway. I tried to be stoic, Shizuka, I did, but I hadn't seen Kenshiro since I was six, and that bow was the last thing we made together.

Watching it go up in flames pierced through me.

Years.

It would take me two months to make a bow, and almost as long for Temurin to return from her hunt. When she returned, she gave me a skin filled with what I thought was kumaq. It was, mostly. But there was enough raw milk mixed in to banish me to the latrines for a day and a half.

When I survived, Temurin decided we were even.

She did not help me with the bow, and I did not ask for her

assistance. You've seen me make them enough times—the whole process is a personal one for me, and one that always brings me peace. So, while the clan did their best to avoid me, I sneaked out at night and worked.

You might find it strange that I chose to work in the dark, alone, when being alone is so abhorrent to my people. When I'd just had such an awful experience.

I say this: The Moon kept me company for two long years. We have always been good friends, she and I. And—well. There was something else.

You wrote to me, of course. You always wrote. I took your letters with me whenever I ran off at night. If I grew lonely or frightened, I'd hold the paper beneath my nose so I could smell your perfume. Often I'd take a break from bow making just to drink in your calligraphy. It didn't matter that I couldn't read the characters themselves when I'd had Otgar read them to me so many times.

That was how I'd learned that you challenged your mother to a duel after five years of sword-training lessons. O-Shizuru broke your arm in a single stroke, and still you were not discouraged.

"One day," you wrote to me, "I will defeat her. One day I will tap her throat with my wooden sword and she will be forced to acknowledge what I have always known: I was born to hold a sword. I was born to duel. I live for that day, Shefali. It is coming. Soon."

I smiled when Otgar read that, for I knew you were right—but at the same time, I felt a heavy dread I could not explain.

Long after I shot my first triumphant arrow, a messenger came from Fujino.

He wore all white, and he carried with him no letter. Among our brightly colored people, he was a ghost.

He entered my mother's tent. I was out riding with Otgar at the time.

She stiffened. "Shefali," she said, "when was the last time you got a letter from that friend of yours?"

"Hai-tsu," I said. Three months ago. A month late. You did not deviate from your schedules, and you wrote back as soon as you received my letters.

Ice in my heart.

I kicked my horse into a gallop. When I dismounted, it was more leap than step, and when I opened the tent, I heard him say the words.

"O-Shizuru and O-Itsuki are dead."

THE EMPRESS

THREE

She must stop. Those characters are arrows in her heart, nails through her fingers. O-Shizuka drops the book and presses her palms against her eyes. Still she sees the words. Still she hears them in Shefali's soft voice.

It has been ten years since they left. (O-Shizuka will use that word, for now; the other one will cut open her tongue if she thinks of it.) Ten years without her father's hand on her shoulder, ten years without her mother shouting at her about her sword forms, ten years since she . . .

A throbbing pain starts up at her temple when she tries to remember. A sharper ache rises to meet it when she tries to forget. The ninth of Nishen is a firebrand within her mind, painful to behold and painful to ignore.

Before the ninth—before the day her mother left—there was

the fifth. Even if her parents had lived to this day, the fifth of Nishen would be a sword against their flesh for all their days.

That was the day O-Shizuru had enough of her brother-in-law.

It had happened at court. Itsuki coaxed Shizuka into going by allowing her a day off from zither lessons. Court was the lesser of the two evils at the time.

Things began in the normal manner. Everyone milled about, exchanging pleasantries while they waited for her uncle. But there was already one difference—suitors. Shiratori Ryuji, lord of Shiratori Province, asked her father, with a smile, when Shizuka could meet his son.

"A quiet little tomcat," he said, "to balance out your tigress."

Shizuka opened her mouth, but her father squeezed her shoulder.

"You're right, Ryuji-tun!" he said. "Shizuka is at her best with someone quiet to balance her. Is your son quieter than Oshiro-tur's daughter?"

And Shizuka covered her mouth to keep from laughing, covered her cheeks to hide when they turned red.

Shiratori Ryuji's smile grew strained all of a sudden, but Ituski's did not falter. He clapped Ryuji on the shoulder. As they walked away from him, Itsuki and Shizuka shared guilty smiles at Ryuji's expense.

But neither of them laughed when, later that evening, Yoshimoto introduced Uemura Kaito as his new Champion. Shizuka's brows climbed halfway up her forehead. She and Uemura studied with the same sword tutor. He was a baby-faced seventeen, if she did not miss her guess; the hair on his upper lip looked more like dirt than a beard.

"Uemura-zun?" Shizuka called. "You?"

He offered her a friendly smile and wave. Yes, he was just a boy.

"How old are you, then? Eleven? Twelve? Maybe a full thirteen?" O-Shizuru said, for she had never been one to keep her thoughts bottled up inside her, and Uemura did not quite look his age. Until that moment, Shizuru stood at the Emperor's side in silence. The white robes of her station stood in stark contrast to her charcoal hair and ink-dark mood.

When she heard a boy proclaimed the new Champion, O-Shizuru clapped once, twice, thrice, as loud as she could. One by one, the others gawked at such a brazen breach of etiquette.

"Ara, ara," she said. "Let's hear it for Yoshimoto's newest guardian—a child! Have you ever been cut in a duel before, boy? Not a scar on you. Look at that."

The young Shizuka-zul covered her mouth to stifle a laugh. She didn't quite succeed. Uemura seemed to grow more nervous than he already was, standing in front of the throne in armor that flapped against his bony frame.

"With all due respect, O-Shizuka-mor," he stammered, "I won my position in a duel like every other Champion—"

"I could beat you," Shizuka cut in from the crowd. "You lack decisiveness, Uemura-zun, you know that. Batting away your sword is as easy as—"

Itsuki squeezed her shoulders. "Is this wise, Brother?" he asked. "Surely there is someone more experienced to guard your honored head?"

"He doesn't want someone more experienced, Itsuki," said Shizuru. "He wants someone too scared to question him."

Shizuka had said a great many insulting things in her life—but then, she had the benefit of divine blood.

O-Shizuru, who was born Minami Shizuru, who later married the poet prince Itsuki, did not.

Yoshimoto clapped. Silence overtook shock. He drummed his fingertips on the arm of the Dragon Throne, his fat pink lips like a gash on an overripe fruit. "You question us enough for any twenty people, our honored sister-in-law," he said.

The way he had pronounced the word "honored" made Shizuka's skin crawl.

"This attitude is unbecoming of a northerner. With such a boorish role model, it is no wonder your daughter acts more like a horsewife than a proper lady. You've left her in the company of Oshiro's wife—"

For many years, it was illegal to speak of what happened next—of Shizuru drawing the Daybreak blade and leveling it at the Emperor himself, of the words that left her lips.

"Her name is Burqila Alshara, and the most notable thing Oshiro Yuichi ever did in his life was marry her," said her mother. "The bravest woman I've ever met, and the finest warrior. Do you know what she did, when she realized her people were dying off in droves? She united them. If my daughter is even *half* that kind of woman, she'll be eight times the ruler you are. May the Mother herself take me if I lie."

O-Shizuka thought she knew silence. In a way, she did. The day Shefali almost died in the Imperial Forest, the day her best friend lay bleeding and motionless in her arms—silence accompanied her then.

But this was the silence of anticipation. This was the silence of a healer's bed, this was the silence of rotting fields, this was the silence of a sword drawn from a leather sheath.

"Iori," said Itsuki. "Iori, don't be rash."

The Emperor scoffed. His eyes—Imperial Amber—were so flat and dark that they reminded Shizuka of cinders.

"Unlike your wife," he said, "we are capable of caution. Forgiveness, even, if she shows proper atonement. We have known you so many years, Minami Shizuru. What a lasting shame it would be if this were our final meeting."

Shizuka's ears burned. She sniffed. Burning roses scratched at the back of her throat. Hokkaran is a language of signs, a language where one word may have twenty meanings.

One did not need Itsuki's talents to understand Yoshimoto's implications.

O-Shizuru understood. She sheathed her sword and shook her head. "What a lasting shame indeed," she said. "It is a good thing I've yet to meet my equal."

Itsuki took his wife's hand in full view of the court. He leaned over and whispered something to her. Shizuka was left standing alone with a single thought.

I am her equal already.

But this was not the time to crow about it. Not when half the court was waiting to see what would happen next and the other half was turning purple with fury at Itsuki and Shizuru's display of affection.

They did not have to wait long.

"That is true," said Yoshimoto. "So it will not burden you, then, to travel five hundred li north of Fujino. One of the villages bordering Shiseiki has begged our assistance. We've heard tell that a pack of blackbloods are trying to make it over the Wall of Flowers. If you have yet to meet your equal, then it will be a small matter for you."

O-Shizuru, one year off from fifty, listened to her brother-in-law's words with her typical stoicism. It was Itsuki who started to tremble. It was Itsuki's smile that fell to the ground; it was Itsuki who leaned over as if he has been struck.

"She will have a company?" said Itsuki. "A small one, at least—"

"Did you not hear your wife?" said Yoshimoto. "She says she has no equal. Let her prove it, then, and inspire more of your pretty lines."

"Iori," growled Itsuki, but Shizuru raised her hand to cut him off.

"Your brother wants me to go kill some blackbloods," she said. "What else is new? I'll do it, Your Imperial Majesty. It shall be done. But we will meet again, upon my return."

"When you return," echoed Yoshimoto.

When they arrived home that day, Shizuka's parents did not speak. Not while she was present, at least. They sent her up to her own private rooms. Her curiosity got the better of her—she has never been one to sit on her hands—and so she sneaked downstairs.

And she saw her mother lying in her father's arms, a bottle of rice wine in one hand. She saw her father pressing teary kisses into her mother's hair. And she heard Shizuru saying over and over and over—

"We'll be fine, we are always fine."

Shizuka, until now, had always known what to do. She always knew what to say, always knew how to jump into action, how to make people stand at attention.

But that night, she slumped herself against the wall and watched.

In the morning, before she left, O-Shizuru held her daughter close. "Remember what I said about you and Shefali-lun," she said. "Together. Don't let anyone tear you apart. I don't care what racist nonsense your uncle tries to fill your head with. That girl is more family to you than your cousins are, do you understand?"

Why was she saying this? It angered Shizuka. It was as if Shizuru herself did not believe she was coming back.

"I'm not a child, Mother," Shizuka said. "And I'm not going to stop talking to Shefali. No one else is worth talking to, anyway."

"Good," said Shizuru. She kissed her daughter's forehead. "Don't let your uncle marry you off while I'm away."

"He's welcome to try," said Shizuka. "I'll duel whoever he sends."

Shizuru laughed, once. "That's my girl," she said. "When I get back, I'll see if I can whip your swordsmanship into shape."

This was it—the moment Shizuka had been waiting for. Personal lessons from the finest sword in Hokkaro. At last, her mother thought she was worth teaching.

But Shizuru also thought she was going to die.

What a bitter taste that left in Shizuka's mouth.

"What am I going to learn from an old woman like you?" Shizuka snapped, but her heart was not really in it, and her mother knew.

"How to live this long when all you do is run face-first at danger, Shizuka," her mother said with a wry smile. "Be safe, and pay attention to your tutors. We love you."

We love you.

Did they still love her? she now wondered. Would they, knowing all the things she'd done, all the things she'd seen?

It did not matter if they loved her, did it? The Empire loved her well enough, and so did Shefali—wherever she'd found herself. And there was the other love—the one she dared not remember, even alone in her chambers, for she still had Shefali's book sitting in her lap. What did filial affection matter to an Eternal Empress?

Why did it leave such an ache in her heart?

EMPRESS YUI OF HOKKARO lies back on her pillows. She presses her fingertips to her face, lays her hand along the thick scar over her nose.

She takes a deep, rattling breath. Shefali's letter brings to mind things she's long since forgotten. The struggle of taking the entire Imperial Garden to Oshiro, for one; a stunt she had to pay for with public zither performances. At the time, there was no higher price. Performing, in public, for people she hated, doing something she loathed? To this day courtiers reminisced about seeing her.

How many times has she heard this man or that woman say she remembers the day perfectly? Don't they understand how it makes her feel? She was eight at the time. Eight, drowning under the weight of a proper woman's robes, wearing a crown that hurt her neck, looking out on a crowd that did not see a girl before them.

They saw a symbol.

She remembers that day well. Her uncle had the stage covered in roses, to taunt her. He introduced her as Princess Solitude for the first time then, and everyone applauded, as if that were the finest name they'd ever heard.

Solitude, he said, would be her only true companion in life.

Yet, looking back, O-Shizuka wonders just how much it cost to hire five hundred servants to carry her flowers. She tries to figure it out in her mind. How much was it that her father used to pay their household? And what was the average?

How much was a single cash seal worth, again?

But it was worth it. No matter how much it cost (and O-Shizuka has never had a head for money), it was worth it to see Shefali's warm brown face light up.

That was a good memory, she thinks. That one was worth holding on to. Yet there are other memories she'd drown if she could.

She calls for a bottle of rice wine. Spirits to drown spirits, as they say. So what if Baozhai disapproved?

But while she waits for it to arrive—she will read.

IF I SHOULD HEAR THE SOUND
OF PINE TREES

I must have heard him wrong.

O-Shizuru, Queen of Crows, who sent more to the Mother's cold embrace than any other—dead? And her husband— O-Itsuki, the man who made stones weep and trees grow with only his words—who would kill him? No. This was wrong. They couldn't be dead. Your parents could not be dead.

My mother drew away. With complete disgust, she made sharp, cutting gestures. Her face contorted into a war mask.

"Get out of my sight," Otgar translated. She was doing her best to keep my mother's tone, but her voice wavered. "You come into my ger and spread lies? How dare you! I should have you executed on the spot!"

But the messenger did not leave. He stood there with his arms crossed behind his back, his shoulders bowed as if bearing the weight of his news. He had the audacity to meet my mother's eyes.

"O-Itsuki and O-Shizuru are dead," he repeated. "By now, their funeral will have passed. His Serene Majesty the Son of Heaven has taken O-Shizuka in for now—but it was O-Shizuru's wish that you raise her, should the unthinkable happen."

Numb. I could not feel my fingers. Otgar steadied me with her free arm. In the privacy of our ger, my mother shook.

She was pale, Shizuka. The earthy brown of her skin changed to tea. Sweat trickled down her brow.

One gesture. Alshara's hand trembled like a branch in a storm.

Otgar's voice cracked. "You lie."

Tears watered the messenger's eyes, but he did not falter. His voice was clear as a funeral bell.

"On the sixth of Nishen, O-Shizuru and her husband departed on a mission from the Son of Heaven," the messenger said. "They did not return. I wish I could tell you otherwise, Great Kharsa, but I cannot. I speak to you the truth. They are dead—"

My mother rose to her feet. Wordlessly she left the ger. Lightning in her footfalls, thunder in the slam of the door. Otgar, the messenger, and I remained.

My mouth went dry.

"Shizuka," I whispered.

"Barsatoq will be all right," Otgar whispered. "She is a stubborn girl. This will not slow her down."

But Otgar did not know how much you idolized your parents. She did not know—

Again, the sharp aching in my chest painted my vision red. My lips went cold. All I could do was imagine you in your rooms at Fujino, weeping and raking your cheeks, too proud to admit you need company. Too proud to let anyone near you.

"I'm going to Fujino," I said.

And I, too, left the ger. Otgar followed behind.

I saddled my horse. We were a month's ride, perhaps two, if the entire clan was coming. But with only myself and Otgar, we could make the trip in a week or two if we rode hard enough. I availed myself of two geldings; I was going to need a change of horse if I planned to make it to you quickly.

"Barsalai," said Otgar, "do you not think we should take a few riders with us? We might meet bandits on the way, or wolves."

I shook my head.

Otgar ran her hand through her hair. She had two braids now, though she did not earn them in battle. My mother allowed her to wear one for each new language she picked up. One for learning to read and write Ikhthian, one for learning the tongue of the Pale People from a book written in Ikhthian. We hadn't met any Pale People yet. She wanted to be prepared.

"I'm not going to convince you, am I?"

Again, I shook my head. With my whip, I eased my horse into a trot.

"Then let me go with you," Otgar said. "I won't stay unless you want me to. But someone has to make sure you get there all right."

"Temurin," I said.

Otgar drew back, hurt written on her face. "You don't want me with you?"

"Mother needs you."

Otgar looked at her reins. From the pout of her lips, I could tell she did not like this; from the furrow of her brow, I could tell she knew I was right.

"Burqila will leave for Fujino, too," she said. "And then we will be going the same way."

"Not right now," I said. "She will mourn."

Otgar's mouth made a thin line. Could I never get my words right? Why couldn't people be more like horses? They got on just fine without talking.

"Stay with her," I said. "She needs someone to talk to."

"You need someone to talk to," Otgar said, her voice dark.

I stopped my horse. I rode over to her, and I squeezed her hand. "I will be fine," I said. "Mother will not."

As an old man senses when rain is coming, so I sensed that my mother would not return to camp for some time. Alshara swore an oath of silence. It changed her into something of a symbol: a looming, silent statue of a woman. Hokkarans liked to say her sword did all the talking for her.

No one heard my mother speak. No one saw her do anything but glower at people. Where others' emotions fluctuated, she was as consistent as the dawn. She did not cry. She smiled only in the presence of Shizuru.

And she never wept.

That was not going to change. No one would see her weep, no one would see her beat her chest, no one would see the tears streaming down her face or her bloodshot eyes. No one would hear her scream herself raw.

That was why she needed Otgar. Someone was going to have to meet her when she returned, haggard and drained. Someone was going to have to speak for her when she did not have the energy to sign. Someone had to comfort her as I could not.

Otgar was the only one I trusted with such a task.

And so I left her to it on the cold, windy steppes, and I did my best not to look back on the white felt gers as I left.

Temurin said little on the way, save to chide me for being so single-minded.

"You should've waited for Burqila," she said, "and arrived with the clan at your back, as befits a future Kharsa."

But when I arrived in Fujino, it was not as a future Kharsa. It was barely as Oshiro Shefali—were it not for the Imperial Seal you gave me, they never would've let me into the palace.

A string's tied us together all our lives, Shizuka. No matter how far we are, I can feel you tugging at it.

Perhaps it was that tugging I followed, for on that day, the very first door in the Jade Palace I threw open somehow was yours.

There you were, dressed in white from head to toe. No ornaments in your hair. No jewelry on your neck or your fingers. Since I last saw you, you had not grown much in height—but your figure was beginning to fill out, and your face was changing into a woman's.

Our eyes met, yours rimmed with red.

"Shefali," you said.

I stepped forward and opened my arms.

You embraced me. "I was worried you would not come," you said.

"I always will," I whispered.

If you ask any Qorin what home is, the answer would vary. Their mother's ger. This spot by the Rokhon where the sun caught the silver grass just so. On the back of their mare, their cheeks worn red, a good bow in hand.

But my answer has been the same since that moment when we were thirteen.

Home is holding you. Home is the smell of your hair. I would give up the howling gales of the steppe to listen to you breathe. All the stars in the sky, all the fallen Qorin guiding us through the night, could not compare to the brightness of your eyes when you looked at me. Your eyes were wide, so wide, like campfires burning.

There are certain moments that tie themselves into your soul. Like a mother beating felt into the walls of the ger, they hammer themselves into you. So it was, then, with you in my arms and no one around to watch us.

So it was, then, when you flushed the color of cherry blossoms.

So it was, then, when my heart hammered from being so near to you.

The two of us may well have been statues, for neither of us could move. My neck felt hot. My hackles rose, and suddenly my lips were so dry, I just had to lick them, and yours were red, red, red.

Fireworks shot off between my ears. Touching you made me wonder when you were going to leave me in a pile of cinders. I felt in my bones that I had to be nearer to you. That I had to consume you, and let you consume me.

When we parted, I went cold as a Qorin night. We spoke to hide the crackling of our emotions.

We did not speak of what had happened to your parents. I will not repeat the details here. In all the years since their passing, you've never mentioned them. You keep a shrine, of course, in your rooms. A piece of your mother's war mask sits next to a scroll of your father's poetry. Every morning you kneel, you light incense, you speak prayers in hushed tones. The shrine was there when I arrived that day, and I have no doubt you've taken it with you to your current holdings.

Wherever they may be.

No, we did not speak of your parents. You asked me what I'd done out on the steppes, and you chided me for my awful handwriting.

"Four years away from me, and this is what happens?" you said, holding one of my letters. "All my hard work undone."

Though I laughed to boost your mood, I shifted in my seat. I knew what the letters said; I could recite them from memory. But reading them . . .

I opened my hand and closed it. Maybe I was just dumb.

You furrowed your brow. "Shefali?" you said. "Is something the matter?"

As if I had anything to worry about. As if your parents had not just died.

I shook my head, but you weren't having it.

"Shefali," you said, "I do not have to tell you to be honest with me. I cannot lie to you, and you must be the same. We are the same."

You reached for a brush, inkblock, bowl, and paper. They were always within arm's reach of you, as if you might wake in the night with a powerful urge to practice calligraphy.

"I want you to write my name," you said. "And do not stress too much over it. I want to see something."

Do not stress over it, you said. The finest calligrapher in Hokkaro wanted to inspect my handwriting, but it was nothing to stress over.

Breathe in. Raise brush. Make the stroke, then breathe out. Except that line didn't look right. What did that symbol look like? I racked my mind for it. How many times had I seen your name?

I bit my lip. You were staring at me, at the paper.

By then I was trembling. I added another line. That wasn't right either. With my free hand, I took hold of my braid.

What did your name look like?

You squeezed my shoulder.

"All right," you said. You reached for a sheet of clean paper and set that out in front of me. "Now, in Qorin, I want you to write everything I say starting . . . now."

I inked the brush and waited for you to begin. You stood, got on your tiptoes, and picked up my bow.

"My name is Barsalai Shefali Alsharyya. My favorite hobbies are hunting, shooting things full of arrows, and sitting quietly at dinner parties. My best friend is the illustrious O-Shizuka of Fujino, Imperial Niece, and the finest swordsman to walk the earth since Minami Shiori. Together we are going to slay a god. But first we are conducting a simple test. I like horses. Especially gray ones."

By the time you finished, you grinned from ear to ear. I was fighting off a smile myself. The whole thing was so silly. There you were in a mourning dress, doing a terrible impression of me, and there I was, taking down everything you said.

Yet when I looked down at the parchment, there was every word. No false starts, no terrible handwriting.

You leaned over and studied it. You knew enough Qorin to make your conclusion. "I think," you said, "that you cannot write in Hokkaran."

You did not say this as an accusation. Somehow hearing someone else say it relieved me. I nodded.

"When I write to you, your friend Dorbentei reads it for you," you said. "And you tell her what you wish to say."

I made no motion to argue.

You studied me for a moment. I worried you'd say something dismissive.

"Do you think," you said, "we could write Hokkaran words in the Qorin alphabet? Would that be easier?"

I tilted my head. But the Qorin alphabet was much simpler; it did not have as many letters. That was the whole reason I liked it.

Yet . . . the more I thought about it, it was possible, if we added one or two more letters.

"Yes," I said.

"Very well, then," you said. "I tire of Hokkaran characters, anyway. A change of pace will be welcome."

I found myself grinning. I spent so long worried what you'd think when you pieced it together.

You smiled a soft, infant smile and sat down next to me.

Long hours gave way to night. It occurred to me I did not have anywhere to stay in the Imperial Palace. Before I brought it up, you called for your servants and commanded them to bring up an additional bed. Not to prepare another room, oh no. You wanted a bed brought into this one.

I pointed out the hallway. Was there not another room we could use—one with two beds?

For your answer, you waved me off. "We stay here," you said firmly.

Though I thought it unjust—what you were doing to your service staff—I said nothing. There was a certain look about you. Had you left this room since the incident? You must have. This was you. This was O-Shizuka, Flower of the Empire. You wouldn't lock yourself away to wilt.

Except . . .

That pile of papers on your desk tall as a helmet. The more I looked at your dress, the more wrinkles I saw. You slept in it. Your hair free of ornaments, your fingers stained with ink . . .

You hadn't left your room, in all this time?

"Shizuka?"

Moments before this, you had sat on the painted bench near your bed. Now you bent in on yourself like a branch bearing too much weight.

"For tonight," you said. "We stay here."

A strange thing happens when one speaks aloud: words take on their own meaning. They move in through the listener's ears and make themselves home, decorating their meaning with whatever memories they find lying around. And you did not want Shizuru and Itsuki to leave you just yet.

So as you broke down—as your shoulders shook with the force of your tears, as your breath came to you in shallow gulps and gasps—I held you.

"These are the finest rooms in the palace," you choked out. I put a finger to your lips to try to stop you from forcing yourself to talk. You batted my hand away. You fought to sit upright, but you were too dizzy to keep up for long. "My uncle picked them out himself."

Your tears soaked my deel. I ran my hands through your hair. I took a deep breath of your perfume, hoping I might siphon some of your sorrows away. But it did not help. Nothing helped.

Though you opened your trembling mouth, you could speak no more. So I rocked you back and forth for what seemed an hour. When the servants came with my bed, I pointed to an unoccupied corner of the room and dismissed them, rather than let them see you.

So I lay with you that night until you fell asleep. I did not bother changing out of my deel. When Grandmother Sky's golden eye peeked in on us, you were turned toward me, your head nuzzled against my chest.

I woke before you. Hunters wake before dawn as a force of habit.

As a lotus petal floating on placid water, so you floated on the bed-sheets. Your dress spread out around you, your hair a black fan against white. No traces of worry, no traces of sorrow. Only peace remained on your features.

Looking at you in the morning light, Shizuka, watching you sleep—it is like cresting a hill and finding a valley sprawling be-fore you, full of flowers, teeming with life and colors you cannot name. I was awestruck.

And in the back of my mind, I wondered when your hairline got so bright, when your lips became bows, when the Daughter herself painted spring onto your cheeks.

I touched your cheek, and I immediately disturbed your sacred slumber. Your eyes fluttered open. Dawn cast them gold.

"Shefali?" you muttered.

I sat up quick as I could, hoping you were too sleepy to notice I was gawking. Why was I gawking? I knit my brows together; why? Why was I so fascinated by your face?

You lurched up and rubbed at your eyes. "What time is it?"

I held up two fists, one finger raised on the first and two on the second.

"The first hour of Second Bell?" you said. You pulled the cov-ers over your head. "What are you doing awake?"

I shrugged. You could not see me, but I shrugged.

"You are a fool," you said. "A fool who needs her rest. Go back to bed, Shefali. We will have to go to court today."

The idea of spending *even more* time mired in etiquette and pro-priety was less appealing than riding for ten days straight with no saddle and no time for breaks—but you needed me. So I swal-lowed up my discomfort, my trepidation, and I thought of how miserable you'd be if you had to go alone.

A bit past Second Bell, servants woke us. They gathered around you like moths to a flame. A dozen hands undressed you, and redressed you. One girl carried the white dress away; another brought in a vibrant blue gown. Peacock feathers adorned the collar and sleeves. The back and train bore iridescent paint in gold and green and black. One of the girls held a tray of crushed gems properly treated; you dipped your fingers in sapphires.

I was fascinated by it. Every one of them had a different job, and they all set about doing them at the same time. Like worms making silk, like women weaving. Your face they painted pale white; on the back of your neck, two sharp blue points; on your forehead, gold leaf shaped into a peacock feather.

By the time they finished with you, the Shizuka I grew up with was gone. In her place was a young empress. In her place stood the Daughter made flesh. In her place, the image of spring; in her place, the Sky in all her splendor.

The servants surrounded you and bowed. You held one hand up and dismissed them.

"Now that my armor is ready," you said, "I suppose we will have to face my uncle." You fixed me with your amber eyes. "You will keep me company?"

I was in the same deel I wore yesterday—the one my grandmother made me, embroidered with colorful shapes. I hadn't bathed in a week, at least. My hair was greasy, my braid a knotted mess. I smelled like horses and rotten milk.

But you wanted me to go with you to see the Emperor.

I flapped my deel's collar.

You came closer. With your shining fingers, you reached for my braid. "You rode all the way from the steppes," you said. "If anyone chides you, they will deal with me." You smoothed my deel. "Besides," you said, "this is a very fine coat."

My cheeks flushed. I cleared my throat and nodded. It was then that I noticed you weren't wearing your sword. I touched the wide belt around your waist, then touched my scabbard.

You covered my hand with your own. "If I wear my mother's blade," you said, "people will think it's an invitation. And I don't mean to get blood on this dress."

Temurin accompanied us on the way to the throne room. So did half a dozen Imperial Guard, who did not speak to you. As mist in the morning, they appeared behind us. You paid them no mind, but I found myself glancing at them. Sharp, crescent blades crowned their pikes. When did those come into style? And why did they need to carry them inside the palace, when a sword would do? No blackbloods wandered the Imperial Halls; no demons.

"Barsalai," said Temurin, eyes darting behind her. "These men have been standing outside Barsatoq's door all night."

I crooked a brow. "And you, too?"

Temurin frowned. "That's not the point. They were waiting for her to leave. Six men to guard a single girl? Six men in full armor, with pikes indoors? I do not like it. This is not an honor guard."

ONE OF THE guards spoke, rattling his pike as he did. "All conversations in the Imperial Palace must be conducted in Hokkaran, as the gods intended."

He must not have known very much about us, if he thought that was intimidating.

"The gods are not stopping us," you said briskly. "I see no reason for a tall boy in armor to stop us, either. You will cease interrupting my companions."

You did not look at them as you spoke. Instead, you kept right on walking, your shoulders back and your head held high.

"O-Shizuka-shon, we are under strict orders—"

"Your orders do not concern me," you said. "Your manners do."

If the guard had anything more to say, he bit his tongue.

The path to the throne room was long and winding. I followed you, walking just behind you, and fought the urge to keep your dress from dragging along the ground. Surely something that cost so much should not be exposed to dirt. But you did not seem concerned about it, and neither did any of the guards.

The courtiers we saw on the way were another story. There were so many! For every twenty steps you took, another begged your attention. Young magistrates, old lords and ladies, generals, and diplomats. Anyone who laid eyes on you wanted to speak to you.

"O-Shizuka-shon!" they'd call. "You grace us with your presence! May we come to court with you?"

"You may not," you would say, and you would keep going rather than entertain their arguments. What of the fine silks they could send to you? What of the dress they'd sent for, just for you? What of the jewels? What of the poetry?

They were nothing to you.

And so you kept walking, leaving only the scent of your perfume in your wake.

When we entered the throne room, a gong rang.

Before its brassy ring finished sounding, one of the servants announced you. "O-Shizuka-shon, daughter of O-Itsuki-lor and O-Shizuru-mor, enters! May flowers sprout in her steps!"

You flinched at the mention of your parents' names. Then, in an instant, the look of despair was gone, and only your Imperial mask remained.

As well it should. A warrior might put on a mask of bronze to face demons and blackbloods, but to face these jackals in men's clothing, one needed a different sort of protection.

No, come to think of it, I prefer jackals. At least they are honest about their hunger. The people milling about the throne room that day had the same desperation in their eyes for you, the same bright avarice. Yet they had the nerve to smile to you, to bow when your name was mentioned.

But for the moment, you ignored them and turned your attention to the young man by the gong. "Crier," you said. "You did not announce my companion."

I shifted. Did I really need to be announced? I did not think of myself as a noble. At least, not the learned Hokkaran noble. I passed no exams, I received only minimal tutoring. My father did nothing to teach me how to run my lands; indeed, being in Oshiro too long chafed. My name meant nothing to these people.

"The Qorin?" said the crier. He studied me and Temurin both, as if trying to decide which one of us was more likely to be a barbarian.

"Oshiro Shefali, daughter of Oshiro Yuichi and Burqila Alshara," you said. Strange to hear my mother's child name coming from anyone but your mother or my grandmother. Most of the time, she was "that woman," or "that demon."

The crier stiffened. He clenched his jaw. Seeing him, I felt my stomach twist. Either my mother killed part of his family, or he was racist—or perhaps both. I did not wish to deal with either.

You narrowed your eyes. Just behind you, some courtiers were coming; you did not have much time before you had to brush them off. "Is something the matter?" you said.

The crier could not lie to you. Lying to the Blood of Heaven was lying to the Gods themselves. But he could not insult me either, since I technically had higher status than he did. And so, however bitter his qualms, he swallowed them.

"Oshiro Shefali-sun," he said, "daughter of Oshiro Yuichi-tur. May her life be long and peaceful."

It was then that the courtiers approached you: a middle-aged man with a topknot and his young wife, in black and yellow. Fuyutsuki Province, then. Were they the lord and lady? I did not know. Both of them wore a honeybee crest on their clothing. I racked my mind; had I seen it before? A dull ache dissuaded me from thinking too hard.

"O-Shizuka-shon," said the man. "We are pleased to see you. It's been so long since you attended court."

Was it the crest that was bothering me? I felt a darkness in the room, a wrongness. Whenever I took a breath, the back of my tongue tasted terrible. I ended up holding my breath rather than deal with the nausea.

"We are sorry for the loss of your parents. They shall be missed," said the woman. "O-Itsuki-lor's work immortalizes him."

Perhaps it was the environment? All the courtiers together, speaking their honeyed falsehoods? Why did I feel as if I'd caught scent of a tiger?

Again, you flinched. "Thank you, Fuyutsuki-tun," you said. Wasn't that the lowest form of address for a lord? "Have you met

Barsalai-sur?" And a third-degree honorific for me. Shizuka, sometimes I wonder how you did not invite duels from everyone you met.

Fuyutsuki appraised me and my worn-out deel. His wife didn't bother.

"Are you Yuichi-tul's daughter?" he said. "I've heard stories about you."

I said nothing, simply nodded. I did not like being in the spotlight.

"O-Shizuka-shon," said Lady Fuyutsuki. "You know you are always welcome in our lands. My son, Keichi, is about your age. I'm certain you'd enjoy dueling him."

"I would enjoy defeating him, if that is what you mean," you said.

Lord Fuyutsuki laughed. It was a loud, pompous sort of laugh— one single "ha." "Is there anyone you cannot defeat?"

Next to me, Temurin grumbled. "These Hokkarans and their simpering," she said. "Barsalai, must we stay for this?"

"Barsatoq asked," I said quietly.

Temurin crossed her arms. I did not blame her. In her position, I'd do everything I could to leave early. Expansive though the throne room may be, it still had a ceiling.

I do not need to describe the throne room to you, Shizuka. You know its secrets better than I do. Its hundred jade columns are as familiar to you as the rivers and brooks of the steppes are to me. Gold tiles line the ceiling, lending everything a brighter look; braziers shine like alarm fires. Around the perimeter of the room is an undulating jade dragon statue. I'm sure you tried to ride it as a child. In the center, near its yawning head, is the Dragon Throne.

On it sat your uncle in Imperial Green. Next to him, one of your three aunts. His first wife, nearing forty-two now, gray hairs tucked behind her ears like flowers. The current lord of Shiseiki was her nephew if I remembered correctly. My father liked to ramble about her when he'd had too much to drink.

"Now, there is a woman," he'd say. "The beauty of a phoenix, cunning as a fox. O-Yoshimoto-tono is in safe hands with her."

What was her name? Sand slipping between my fingers. Only the image of my father's drunken face remained, of his pale gold cheeks flushing red, of the glassy look in his eyes. He and the Empress knew each other as children, thanks to my father's friendship with your father. Maybe they played together as we did. He did not speak of her much except when the liquor got into him.

I lost track of the conversation while staring at the Empress, at the woman my father so prized. What few wrinkles she had only emphasized her handsome features. Not that it was easy to focus on her face. Where you were cloaked in peacock feathers, the Empress wore genuine phoenix feathers, passed down through the Imperial line for Ages. The slightest movement sent them swaying. Bright red, deep crimson; dawn's gold and dusk's orange trailed in their wake.

I could not look away from those feathers. Each plume bore a single green spot, almost like an eye, near the top. I found myself leaning toward them. As the smell of fresh brewed tea incites thirst, these feathers incited . . .

I could not be sure. My fingertips tingled; my forehead felt hot. What was it like to touch them? Would they sear my flesh?

And yet I knew I had to have them, and when I glanced down at my hands, I saw it there in my palms, and all around me were thousands of candles in different shapes and sizes, and my hand was not my hand, it was gray and twisted and topped with sharp claws—

"Barsalai," said Temurin. "You gawk."

Clearing my throat, I tore myself away. Lord and Lady Fuyutsuki left our company while I was busy making a fool of myself.

Only you remained, your hands tucked into your sleeves. You looked down your nose at me. "Shefali," you said, "you are as bad as my suitors."

Suitors? I grimaced. We were thirteen, and you had suitors? Your parents had just died—and you had suitors?

"Do not be so surprised," you said. Venom crept into your voice as you glanced around the room. I saw them now—the men standing by the jade columns, looking over to you just often enough. Demure smiles. Dangerous eyes. "Three wives in, and Uncle has not conceived a child. There are fools who think they can use me to get on the throne."

You kept going back to one of the men. He wore white and bright green, the colors of Shiratori. He was not tall, but he bore himself as if he were, all broad shoulders and puffed-out chest. Night-dark hair pulled into a horsetail complemented the shadow of a beard on his chin. At his hip hung a straight sword with an elaborate jade hilt.

Something about him soured my stomach. Have you ever seen a sick dog, Shizuka? Have you seen it shamble about, frothing at the mouth? Have you seen ticks coating a dog's flank, so many and so fat that they look like mushrooms growing on a tree?

So I felt when I looked at him. He made my teeth hurt and my ears ring.

Four, five times you looked at him. Each time, you shivered as if something wet crawled down your neck. "Do not," you whispered, "let him look at me."

I stood in front of you to block his view.

Qorin height had its advantages. In the entirety of the throne room, only Temurin and a handful of guards were taller than I. I made it my duty to know where that man stood at all times, and as you went about your business entertaining conversations with people you did not care about, I stood between the two of you.

For the barest of moments, you slipped your hands free of your sleeves, and your fingertips brushed against mine.

And then I felt two pinpricks of heat on my back. I reached for the bow I left in your chambers out of habit as I turned. I was careful to keep you behind me.

He was there. So close. Shorter than I was, as a thirteen-year-old. I was struck by how clammy his skin looked, like raw fish. Beads of sweat collected on his forehead. When he smiled, his teeth were painted black. Fashionable two decades ago. Strange. He was no older than thirty, by the look of him.

He bowed and his coalfire eyes met mine. I did not allow myself to shiver, but the hackles on my neck rose all the same.

"Oshiro-sun, I take it?" he said. "I do not believe we've met."

I fought the urge to bare my teeth. Temurin took a step closer to me, one hand on her scimitar.

The man glanced at her and scoffed. "Shizuka-shan," he said, "you should call off your dogs."

Instantly you pushed in front of me. Though you were cloaked in peacock feathers and sapphires, you burned with anger. "Call me that one more time, Kagemori-yon," you snarled, "and I will show the entire court just where you belong." Yon. I'd never heard that one before, but only the Brother's titles started with that sound.

But Kagemori did not flinch. He laughed, once, as a man laughs at a child's flailing. "And where is that, Shizuka-shan?" he said. "What ferocity. Did you slay the tiger, Shizuka-shan, or did you switch souls with it?"

In the years to come, many people would write about this moment. They'd swear they saw you draw a shimmering sword from the light itself and point it at his throat. I've seen paintings of it, you know. None include me. Some include Temurin. Temurin is more important to the story.

For it was Temurin's scimitar you drew, Temurin's curved blade catching the golden light of the throne room. To say you drew it in the blink of an eye would be to do you a disservice. One moment, you were empty-handed. The very next, you were not.

The sound of steel rang throughout the gilt room. Guards moved in, their pikes lowered, forming a tight circle around us. You kept the sword leveled at Kagemori's throat.

"O-Shizuka-shon! Are you all right?" called the guard captain.

"I have been insulted," you said. "And disrespected by this foul excuse for a human being."

At once they turned their pikes toward Kagemori.

He sneered. "What a willful child you are," he said, "drawing steel in the Emperor's presence."

"Uncle!" you shouted.

No one addressed the Emperor. The proper thing to do was to wait for him to speak in any given situation.

But you have never been one for waiting.

Your uncle bristled. He did not rise from his throne. Instead, he waved a hand, and the guards stepped back. The other court-iers went quiet in anticipation of his holy words.

"Shizuka," he said, "you have demanded our attention. Out of respect for your father's memory, we shall allow it, but you are to keep a closer guard on your tongue in the future." Each syllable was heavy, each word formed according to the most formal rules of Hokkaran.

"This man refers to me as a child," you said. "He speaks to me with familiarity he has not and will never earn. He has not heeded me when I have told him to leave me alone. I demand the right granted me by our divine blood. I demand a duel."

As a stone dropped in a puddle sends out ripples, so you sent out waves of hushed whispers through the crowd. Kagemori—still held at sword-point—knit his brows.

Your uncle did not stand. To stand would show too much emo-tion. Nor did his wife have any visible reaction, save to reach for one of the phoenix feathers and stroke it.

"You cannot be serious," your uncle said. "You are thirteen. He is a grown man."

"Three months ago, I faced older men, and soldiers," you said, your voice crackling with pride. "My age was not an issue then. It should not be an issue now. I am worth twenty of him with one hand tied behind my back and blindfolded. I demand a duel."

This was the first I'd heard of it. But then, it had been three months since you last wrote to me. You must've been composing the letter when . . .

"That was a tournament," Yoshimoto intoned. "One your mother did not wish for you to attend—"

"Uncle, do not speak to me of my mother's wishes," you snapped. Sky save you, you were snapping at the Emperor. Did it at all matter to you that he ruled Hokkaro? "If my mother were here, I would not be asking your permission for a duel, I would be watching his body be dragged from the throne room. I demand a duel."

The silence in the room was like glass shattering.

I longed to touch you, to give you some sort of reassurance. But you stood in front of me, and all eyes were on us. I could not touch you without further sullying your reputation.

Instead, I whispered your name so low, only you could hear it. And I swear, I saw the taut muscles of your hand relax.

"Uncle," you repeated, your voice calmer, "if I am old enough to receive marriage proposals, I am old enough to duel."

Yoshimoto said nothing. The Emperor is supposed to be serenity made flesh, but in your uncle's doughy brow, I read nothing but anger. The Empress leaned over and whispered in his ear. He said something sharp and cutting to her I could not hear. She spoke again, more timidly this time.

Finally he sighed. "Very well," he said. "If you so insist, Shizuka, then we shall grant your request. You may duel to first blood in the courtyard."

So the courtiers filed one by one out of the throne room. Still you stood before Kagemori; still you held the blade to his throat.

He bared his blackened teeth. "There was no need to bring the Emperor into our little lovers' quarrel," he said.

Lovers' quarrel. He spoke in such a way to a thirteen-year-old girl! I growled at him.

His eyes flickered over to me and he scoffed. "I did not know your dog spoke Hokkaran," he said to you.

"Get to the courtyard," you roared, "before I behead you where you stand."

Another soft laugh. As he stepped away, he hummed to himself. "If you insist," he said. "It will not change fate's path. You will be mine one day, Shizuka-shan."

Only you, I, Temurin, and your guards remained in the throne room. Even the Emperor had departed on his palanquin.

You bit your lip. "I will kill him," you said. "Not today. But one day, when I am older, I will kill him."

I squeezed your shoulder.

Next to us, Temurin shifted from foot to foot. "Barsalai, I may not speak Ricetongue, but I know a challenge when I see it. Does Barsatoq need our assistance? Say the word, and I will gladly use him to test my arrows."

You gave Temurin the respect of looking at her when she spoke, though you did not share a language. I was going to ask if you wanted us to help you in the duel (though I had no idea how that would work) when you spoke to her.

"Guard," you said, "I do not know your name. Barsalai will tell me soon, I am sure. I thank you for the use of your sword."

"Temurin," I said, pointing to her. Then I tapped on the sword with my fingers.

"She can keep it, if she likes. I have more, and she does not seem to have any," Temurin said.

You held out the scimitar to Temurin, pommel toward her. She slipped it back into its sheath.

"You. Tall boy," you said, pointing to the guard who'd chided us before. "Go to the courtyard ahead of us. Let it be known that my mother's sword is to be prepared for me."

This order chafed him, but it did not stop him from taking off at a run.

Then you began walking.

* * *

THE HALLS RANG with the clacking of your wooden sandals, but not your voice. So many twists and turns. So many identical portraits of this emperor, or that emperor. How was one fat Hokkaran different from any other fat Hokkaran? Couldn't they dress differently, at least? But no. Each one wore the same Dragonscale crown. Each one sat on the matching Dragonscale throne. Each one was fat, each one was pale, each one had the same forced serenity painted onto his face.

How, I ask you, did you tell your ancestors apart?

To this day, I cannot navigate the palace without you. I do not know how anyone can live in such a place, with walls and ceilings and hallways of identical men staring at you. Cages are for animals, not people.

So it was to my great relief when we entered the courtyard—the opposite of the labyrinth you'd just led me through. Here was a forest in miniature. Here peonies in all the colors and patterns known to man blossomed on tree branches; here rows and rows of chrysanthemums swayed in the soft morning wind. A single tall, white tree grew in the center, almost as tall as the palace itself. Around it, a small pool of water glittered in the sunlight. At the northern end of the yard was a raised dais upon which your uncle and aunt sat. Everyone else picked a bench and staked their claim.

I took a deep breath of the fragrant air and greeted Grandmother Sky for the first time all day. But then I saw Kagemori waiting just in front of the great white tree, and my prayers died unspoken.

But you continued walking. And you stood three paces away from him, cloaked in your pride, armored in dignity.

A servant scurried by me—a young boy so nervous, he bumped into my knee on his way to the inner ring. In his hands he held a black lacquer box almost as big as he was. He finally sank to his knees next to you and opened the box.

Your mother's sword rested inside. The Daybreak blade, its sheath lined with solid gold and carved from finest ivory. An intricate sun on the cross guard, a crescent moon for a pommel. It was a thing of impractical beauty. How the Queen of Crows used it with any regularity baffled me. There was not so much as a single chip on the sheath.

You reached for it, and you took it in your hands, and I swear to you, I saw the cross guard flash. You stepped out of your wooden sandals and pushed them aside with one delicate toe, standing barefoot on the grass. Kagemori may've been taller, but you looked down your nose at him all the same.

The crier, too, was present, and it was he who sounded the gong. "O-Shizuka-shon, daughter of O-Itsuki-lor, challenges Kagemori-zul to a duel," he announced. "They meet with the blessings of the Son of Heaven. Let the first shedding of blood hail the victor."

Silence. Kagemori sank into a fighting stance and drew his sword—plain, unadorned, and antique in style.

You did not draw yours.

Indeed, even as he circled you, you did not draw your sword, nor did you change your posture.

Next to me, Temurin crossed her arms. "Rice-eaters and their rituals," she muttered.

I shushed her.

For you were a coiled spring. Any second now, he'd make the mistake of setting you off.

"Do you fear me, Shizuka-shan?" he asked. "Why do you not bare steel?"

"I do not need to, for the likes of you," you said. "And you will not goad me into attacking."

In the shadow of the great white tree, I saw him tug at the corners of his mouth, saw the disappointment on his face. What a quandary he faced: If he struck first and you countered him, this duel would be over in a single stroke.

Minutes passed. A quarter hour he circled you. A quarter hour you stood unmoving, your gold eyes fixing him with feline malice. Your breathing was shallow and unnoticeable.

Then he got tired of waiting.

Then he raised his sword high overhead. A bloodcurdling scream left his painted mouth. He ran toward you.

And then . . .

As a man lost in the sands signals to a passing caravan with a mirror, so you signaled your victory with the flashing of your blade. You drew your sword, slashed him clean across the face, and sheathed. One smooth motion too fast to follow with the naked eye, and it was over. Kagemori stopped. The sword fell from his hands and clattered to the ground. Red seeped from his wound like juice from a fresh-cut plum.

"You do not deserve to hold a sword," you said.

He screamed. "My face! You cut my face!" He clutched the gash as if it were a seam he could hold closed. A man in doctor's robes ran to his assistance, but Kagemori pushed him away, shambling toward you with one hand on his face. "You insolent brat!"

"Insult me again," you said, "and I will have your tongue. You've been defeated. Continue your aggression, and I will not be so kind to you a second time."

But still he lumbered for you. "My face," he muttered, over and over. "You took away my face!"

Guards leaped rows of chrysanthemums, surrounding him within seconds. A ring of pike blades pointed straight at his throat.

"Stop where you are!" shouted the captain. "You threaten the Imperial Family!"

"I threaten a puffed-up child," he snarled. "Can you not see what she's done to me?"

"What sort of a man enters a duel and expects to escape unharmed?" you said. As you spoke, your voice grew louder and louder. "A coward. A simpering coward. Your presence offends me!"

For a moment, you stared him down, one hand white knuckled, holding your mother's sword. I glanced toward your uncle—how could he abide this in silence?

And yet he sat on his dais and he watched, and he did nothing.

You spoke through teeth clenched tight. "Take him away."

Guards tied rope around his hands. Roughly they dragged him away, likely to throw him into the infamous Hokkaran prison system. In the south of Fujino, a fortress nearly the size of the palace loomed like a noose at the gallows.

In the days when your mother acted as the Emperor's Executioner, the prisons were always empty. After her death, they began to fill again—and I do not envy the thought of returning to them. Your uncle will throw anyone in the fortress, for any reason at all. With my own two eyes, I have seen a man hauled off in chains for having the audacity to call your uncle Iori. The name he was given at birth. The name he wore until he put on the Dragon Crown.

I have seen women arrested for stealing a handful of rice; I have seen hunters locked away for killing the wrong color stag.

Your uncle likes to say he is civilized—that your mother's death enlightened him, that he realized executioners were a base thing for an Emperor to have.

But there is nothing civilized about flinging someone into a dark room, with no windows, for the rest of their life. There is nothing civilized about letting them stew in their own excrement and beg for week-old bread.

But I am only an illiterate brute. What do I know of civility?

I watched him go. Already gossip flew from mouth to mouth to mouth; by nightfall, you would again be a legend. A girl of thirteen who struck down a grown man with a single stroke. Your mother's sword flashing in the light; her Daybreak blade come to life. More than one of them joked that you'd already slain a tiger, so a man was no trouble.

You stood proud in the face of it all. As sycophant after sycophant sang your praises, you nodded and smiled and thanked them in a distant way. For hours I stood by your side. When you needed a moment to yourself, you'd casually tap my leg with your sheath, and I would pretend I had something to say in private. And so we'd steal moments from the crowd.

"Bees," you muttered. "With their incessant buzzing. Why should a phoenix concern herself with the buzzing of bees?"

I had some idea. Though your uncle did not speak to you, he made a point of looking in your direction. Every quarter hour, a messenger jogged up to you and whispered something in your ear. You never reacted well to that.

"Too mouthy," you said to me after one such occasion. "Too unladylike. As if he has any right to define what a lady should be."

I pressed my lips together.

By the end of Sixth Bell, purple fingers crept across that

beautiful blue sky. Moon reaching for Sun. Courtiers began to make their excuses. Wives waiting in their rooms. Children who needed to be put to bed. Would they have the pleasure of your company, should they wish to call on you?

The answer, universally, was no. And you made no excuses when Seventh Bell rang. You walked right out of the garden, leaving a collection of awestruck faces behind you. Your guards followed; as did Temurin and I. And so you led us back to your rooms, where Temurin again waited outside.

When the door closed behind us, you let out a groan. "Shefali," you said, "I think I would rather live on the steppes than let those fools nip at my toes."

You sat before your mirror. With sharp motions, you removed the peacock feathers from your hair, removed the ornaments and the bells. These you set on your table. You yanked a cloth from its hook and wiped off your makeup. At least, you tried. Though you swiped only once, smearing blue and black and green across your painted-white face.

But you tossed the cloth at the wall anyway, rather than continue.

I sat on the bench next to you.

You held your head in your hands and slumped forward, as if your skull suddenly was very heavy.

"Meaningless," you mumbled. "Meaningless tripe. Our crops are blighted, our livestock die in droves. Our fishermen bring up hundreds of terrible, blackened things. Every day peasants gather outside the palace and beg to be heard. But instead, we let grown men harass thirteen-year-old girls. Instead, we parade about in our finest and do our best to ignore the problem. 'We will endure.' What tripe."

My throat hurt.

My people, too, had seen such things. Wolves that did not die when we shot them, that did not stagger. Dogs that laughed like men in the dark. Some of my clanmates' horses died overnight, and in the morning, only their heads remained. The rest of their once-proud bodies was reduced to . . .

It was like stew. Raw meat stew, left out in the sun to rot.

I cannot describe to you the anguish on my clanmate's face when he discovered his horses in such a state. For days he screamed at the sun. Foul blasphemies left his lips: How could Grandmother Sky allow this to happen? She saw all, did she not? She sheltered the souls of the fallen Qorin on her starry cloak—why did she not strike down the attacker with lightning?

Because there was no attacker.

Because dark things ride the winds at night, while we huddled near our fires and pretended we were safe.

Silence hung between us.

You reached for my hand. Yes, that was lightning, striking me dumb and deaf and blind. I was frozen in place by the slightest touch.

"Shefali," you said, "you and I will stop this, one day. We will go North, where the blackbloods go, and whatever it is we are meant to do, we will do. Together, Shefali, like two pine needles."

Your face smeared in half a dozen shades. Your hair not quite brushed.

Your eyes.

From our childhood, you'd been saying this. As we grew older, you said it with more and more conviction, as if you spoke of moving to Sur-Shar. Difficult, yes, but doable.

But you did not speak of moving across the Sands. You spoke

of finding your way North, where the Traitor dwelled, and if I knew you at all, you meant to challenge him. As if he could not simply squish you between his forefingers like overripe fruit.

But may the Sky slay me where I sit now if I did not believe it more and more each time.

I swallowed and squeezed your hand. Then I reached for the cloth you'd thrown away. I dipped it in a bowl of water on the desk and I wrung it dry.

I reached for your face.

You did not stop me. Instead, you closed your eyes and let me wash away your mask. When I was done, only Shizuka remained. Only the finest sword in the Empire; only the finest calligrapher.

Only the most . . .

I shook my head rather than fully voice that thought. You were my best friend. I could not allow myself to think such things about you. I could not allow my heart to hammer as it did; I could not allow myself to dream about touching you.

When you began speaking, I wanted to heave a sigh of relief. Something to listen to other than my own thoughts.

"My mother let me into a tournament, you know," you said. "The Challenge of the Sixteen Swords."

Held every eight years to commemorate the first Challenge of Sixteen. Being allowed to enter at all was a great honor. Each province was allowed only two participants. To think that Imperial Fujino sent a small girl as one of their champions!

I laughed. Oh, how I pitied anyone who crossed swords with you.

"For years I begged her, but all she ever did was speak to me of danger. My father pointed out the Challenge is to first blood, and healers would be nearby. He pleaded and pleaded. Finally my mother relented."

As I wiped the last of your lipstick away, you smiled like a knife.

"And, of course, of the Sixteen finest blades in Hokkaro, mine is the finest."

Ah, Shizuka, how I wish I could've seen it! How I wish I could've seen you strike down fifteen duelists—fifteen adults who prided themselves on their swordplay. Sometimes I imagine it. I've tracked down a few descriptions of that tournament, and had Otgar read them to me. You must tell me one day if you really lopped off Isshi Keichi's nose with just the point of your sword!

"Was she proud?" I asked.

Your amber eyes darted toward the shrine. Your mother's war mask stared back at you.

"She was," you said. "She called me a pompous show-off. But she was proud, I think. Before . . ." You licked your lips. "Before she left, she promised we'd begin lessons together."

Gods, but that hurt to hear. Again, I squeezed your hand.

And it was then I noticed you had a scar on your palm from that day in the woods, when we were eight. I touched it with my fingertips.

"Together," I said.

"Together," you said.

And you leaned your head against my shoulder, as if it were the most natural thing in the world. You slipped your arm around my waist. The smell of peonies met my nose. My lips went dry, and for a moment, I wondered what might be the right thing to do.

I pulled you closer, leaned my head against yours.

We held hands. Scars brushed together.

I decided that I did not care whether or not it was right, so long as I was doing it.

HOW WILL I TELL HER?

I could write to you forever about those heady days spent in Fujino. I could write of how silly I looked when you let me try on your dresses—how the billowing sleeves came just past my elbow, how none of your belts fit around my waist. I let you try on my deel. It was massive on you, pooling on the floor around your feet. You left the collar mostly undone.

I saw your collarbones, accents to the slender curve of your neck. I tried not to stare at them.

I was fascinated by you. By your motions, by your expressions, the smallest details of your life. In the mornings, you rose at Third Bell. After rising from the bed, you moved to your writing desk. In careful strokes, you wrote a line from one of your father's poems—first in Hokkaran, then in Qorin letters. We'd read it together, so that you understood the pronunciation and I understood how to read it.

We took tea together. On the second day, I realized you were not let out of your rooms unless you were going to court. You did not say it aloud. I suspect you did not want to admit defeat.

And so you spoke of anything and everything except your parents.

"My uncle despises me," you said one night.

I drummed my fingertips against the desk.

"He has not said this, but I know it to be true," you continued. "He picked these rooms for me. He summons me to court, but only after peasants have worn him thin.

"To him," you said, "I am nothing but a passing amusement. Someone to write his edicts, I suppose. But I have seen the jealousy festering behind his eyes. I am never invited to dinner, never allowed to greet our people."

As you spoke, you wrote. Another set of notices, from what little I could read. You took no joy in this. You stabbed your brush into the water.

"He hopes people do not think of me," you said. Brush met paper. You took a deep breath. A single, short, stroke.

"Three wives," you said. "Three wives, no children; no bastards running amok. Peasants call him the Limp Emperor."

It came together in my mind. Without any children, you were the only Hokkaran heir.

You were crown princess now.

Rocks against your window. You ignored them. The dark clouds on the horizon were somewhat harder to ignore. To the north of Hokkaro—toward the Ruined Lands—inky clouds marred Grandmother Sky's skin. It was just the way of things.

"I shall be a woman soon, of proper age, and then no one will cage me," you said.

Again, you spoke with certainty. But as your lips shaped the words, my heart forged them.

Cages were not meant for people.

TWO WEEKS AFTER I barreled into the palace in the dark of night, my mother followed in my footsteps. It was past Last Bell when we woke to clattering weapons outside the door. Qorin shouting reached my ears.

"Stand down, you Imperial dogs!" Temurin shouted. No one understood her, but she shouted all the same. When I opened the door, my mother stood outside. In her hand, a bared blade; on her face, a wolf's fury. Temurin stood back to back with her.

"Stand down!" you shouted from behind me. And because it was you who spoke, they listened.

With a snarl my mother, too, sheathed her sword. The gesture she made couldn't have meant anything nice.

And yet when she laid eyes on you, her whole manner changed. Waves of anger gave way to tides of sadness; bittersweet joy replaced red-hot wrath. My mother, Burqila Alshara, the Destroyer, the Terror of the Steppes, embraced you with a whimper.

I watched her run her fingers through your hair. She pressed her nose to each of your cheeks, took a breath of you. Then she perched her head atop yours and held you so tight, I wondered if you could breathe.

Temurin watched with lips parted. I hugged myself, a few steps away.

Because I saw what Temurin did not.

I saw my mother whispering in your ear. I saw her scarred lips moving. Frozen in awe, you were, your eyes carved from glittering ice, your skin turned to gooseflesh.

In the ages to come, drawings and woodcuts tried to imagine this scene. Most of them bear captions. It seems everyone has an idea what my mother said to you. A thousand purple promises; a hundred boisterous boasts. I've seen some that make a joke of it. Yes, some people make a joke of my mother breaking her vow of silence.

"I left the firepit alight!" I would like to see that writer try to lead an army without making a single sound. I would like to see him raise two children without speaking to them.

But the truth of the matter is this: My mother only ever spoke to your mother. The first time she broke her oath was during the Eightfold Trial, when one of the Generals imprisoned them together. As you well know, the most popular story goes that Shizuru kept cracking jokes about the prison needing more bamboo mats—the Minami clan being bamboo mat merchants at the time.

My mother looked at her and said, "If we live, I will buy your mats."

Shizuru told this story whenever she got the chance; I believe it to be true with my whole heart. To hear her tell it, the whole reason she never lost hope was that she had a hut full of mats to sell.

But Shizuru could not tell that story anymore.

And that was why my mother spoke to you.

In a minute it was over—this moment frozen in my mind. The two of you parted. Only then did Alshara embrace me and sniff my cheeks. But she did muss my hair.

Then she gestured that we should follow her.

You laughed.

"Alshara-mor," you said. "I have guards."

Among the many things in the chest pocket of her deel, my mother keeps a slate and chalk. She produced it now. In confident, if inelegant, Hokkaran strokes, she wrote. I couldn't read it, of course, but you've told me this story so many times, I thought I might return the favor.

I am Burqila Alshara. O-Shizuru entrusted me with the care of her daughter. If you doubt me, you are welcomed to try and stop me. I have killed in front of my children before.

She held it up so it was plain to read from behind you. You covered your mouth. Only my mother would be so blunt, so audacious.

Yet still she stared each of the guards down, fingering the hilt of her knife.

"So the stories are true!" said one of them. He was smiling. Sky rest his soul, he was smiling. "You use slate and chalk! What kind of a warlord does that?"

"Kai-tsao, don't be a fool," said another. As he spoke, his upper lip trembled. A certain smell fill the air. Acrid, warm, stale. The same smell that filled any ger in the morning.

Piss.

A dark trail trickled its way down the second guard's pants.

"When you broke down the Wall of Stone, did you write it a sweet love letter beforehand?"

You held your head in your hands. Temurin bit the back of her palm. I winced.

My mother never wastes time with elegance. Whenever she attacks someone, it is quick and brutal, vicious as a dog. This occasion was no different. With one hand, she slammed the guard called Kai-tsao against the wall and held him there. With the other, she drew her hunting knife. He wriggled, he tried to kick, but she only slammed him again. That's when she slid the knife between his lips. That's when she made a single cut. Then she dropped the knife, shoved her fingers into his mouth, and pulled.

A flopping pink tongue landed on the ground.

Alshara stepped on it.

The man screamed. It was less scream and more wet gurgle. The other guards looked away as Kai-tsao dropped to his knees and collected the pieces of his tongue.

My mother erased her words. She wrote a few new ones.

I am mute by choice. Now you are not. When you pray for your tongue to be regrown, you should write it a letter beforehand.

So it was that the guards parted like reeds in the wind before us. No one questioned us as we left. Perhaps because my mother was covered in blood. Perhaps because my mother was my mother, and also covered in blood. It is hard to say which frightened them more. Whatever the case, we were not stopped. Outside, our horses waited, saddled and ready.

All except yours.

You could not ride with me. Not then, not in front of my mother. Only husbands and wives rode the same horse. Despite the fluttering in my stomach when I looked at you, I could not have us riding together with others watching.

Alone, yes. You did not know what it meant. You would wrap your arms around my waist for steadiness. I could let you hold the reins, while I held the whip. Together we could ride.

But not in view of others.

So I offered you one of the spare horses I'd brought along and tried to wipe the idea from my mind. Later. Alone.

Since we did not have a ger, and the Daughter's warm breath

swept Hokkaro, we slept beneath the stars. My mother brought bedrolls, at least. You'd never slept in one before, and it took you some fumbling before you were able to open it. The first time I'd ever seen you fumble with anything at all. I laughed as I watched you, the heir to the Empire, slap your bedroll against the ground.

I came over and opened it for you.

Pouting, you turned a bit away. "I could've figured that out," you said.

I dragged my bedroll next to yours. Temurin, the guards, and my mother slept closer to the fire. We had here some small amount of privacy. As you eased into the bedroll, you shot a glance toward the others.

"Does your mother always do that?"

I looked over. Alshara sat on a log, fletching arrows.

"Only when needed," I said. She found fletching a relaxing activity, but she was not very good at it. Other clans presented her with gifted arrows so often, she used those instead. They flew straighter.

You rolled your eyes a bit. "Not that," you said. "I meant . . . When we were leaving Fujino. She tore out that man's tongue."

I tapped my fingers to my lips in thought. Had my mother torn out other tongues before this?

I shook my head.

"But she did it so casually," you said. "Without hesitation." Your voice was softer than usual, as if you were afraid my mother would hear us.

"Normally," I said, "she'd slit his throat. Or tear it out. Cut off an ear, nose. This is the first time she takes a tongue."

You pressed your lips together and nodded. "I've heard the stories about her," you said. "Is it true she killed her brothers?"

Again, I nodded. Qorin children all knew the story. Alshara once had six sisters and two brothers. This being before the Qorin united, it was still common to promise girls to other chiefs to curry favor. So it was with the two oldest sisters. My uncles bartered both of them away to rival clans.

But these were not pleasant times, and my aunts did not please their new husbands.

So their heads came back to us.

My uncles gnashed their teeth. To declare war, or not to declare war? We were smaller than either of the other clans. If we did attack—which of the two clans would be our target?

Each of my uncles had a different idea. For two months they argued, then four, then eight, and then a year flew by with no revenge. The two enemy clans raided us five times while my uncles deliberated. Five times. We were cold, hungry, and poor—yet they did nothing. Not even attack one of the weaker clans.

Alshara was the eldest of the remaining sisters. Grandmother was beginning to look for husbands for her, but it was not marriage that my mother sought in her heart of hearts. Food in her belly, boots that did not clap with every step, and her elder sisters put to rest—these were the things my mother wanted. But to get those things, she needed to control the clan. She could not seize power unless she was the eldest surviving child. It was a wall against Alshara's progress.

My mother has never been fond of walls.

Alshara's solution was brutal and simple. She took them out on a hunt, and when they were far from camp, she called for them to dismount.

She then ran them through, wrapped their bodies in felt, and dragged them back to camp.

This was the woman sitting on a log, fletching arrows.

"Did no one rebel against her?"

"At first," I said. "But they died."

You mulled this over. I imagine it must've been strange for you. After all, you'd known my mother only briefly before this. You could not speak with her. Whatever you knew stemmed from Shizuru's war stories, colored pink and gold with faded glory.

But here she was, the woman herself, the most feared person in all Hokkaro. Your mother's best friend. The woman who had adopted you.

Whatever your thoughts were, you kept them to yourself. If you were more tense around Alshara than most, no one called you out on it. Not even me.

My mother is terrifying at times, and I did not expect you to get accustomed to her overnight.

Yet you did.

Two months later, we arrived at the edge of the steppes. The Burqila clan welcomed us with open arms. My aunts threw another feast to celebrate my mother's return. I didn't see Otgar's boy among the revelers, but I did see her. The three of us sat by the fire and ate our stew. Otgar brimmed with happiness. She'd grown younger since I last saw her three months prior. No longer did she hold herself as if she had something to prove.

"Your mother," she said in Hokkaran, "sent the boy away."

"Did they mean to marry you?" you asked.

Otgar nodded.

You scoffed and shook your head. "You should have dueled him."

"We do not have duels," Otgar said. "A duel implies one person will walk away with their life at the end. We do not do that. If someone insults you, you either kill them or die trying."

You pursed your lips and glanced about the ger. "Should the Qorin be killing each other?" you asked. "My tutors tell me there is one of you alive today for every three that were alive before the wars."

It is just like you to bring up something your Hokkaran teachers taught you about Qorin in a conversation with Qorin.

Otgar rolled her eyes. "That is why we have so many children," she said. "So we can have spares."

I spat out my kumaq. You sat there gaping, reaching for something vaguely polite to say in response. Once, twice you opened your mouth and no words came out.

Then Otgar clapped you hard on the shoulder, and I thought you were going to leap out of your skin. "Do not worry, Barsatoq!" she said. "This is Qorin humor. You will get it soon. For instance!"

I braced myself. Qorin jokes are awful, Shizuka. They're horrible. I love them dearly, but they are awful, and I would never repeat them in your presence.

"Dashdelgar is out hunting!" Otgar began in a loud voice. All at once, my uncles and aunts ceased their talking and turned toward her. No Qorin in existence misses a joke. Especially not a Dashdelgar joke. He is our patron god of obfuscating stupidity. So what if it was being told in Hokkaran? Most of us understood Ricetongue, even if we did not speak it. Except Temurin. She said she'd learn it when Hokkarans learned Qorin, which was a fair point.

"But Dashdelgar hunts in winter, and he took with him only four arrows. After a whole day out in the cold, he fails to hit anything. So he fills his belly with kumaq and makes his way back to his ger."

You listened. Your brows scrunched like caterpillars above your eyes, but you listened.

"He finds his wife with another man—not his brother either!"

A chorus of laughs. You blinked at me.

"Qorin marriages are different," I whispered. "Sometimes brothers share wives."

You swallowed and licked your lips. I could hear you thinking that you were not in Hokkaro anymore.

"They do not notice him, but this is not out of the ordinary; Dashdelgar is a small man, and he shares his ger with his entire family. His wife and the other man keep right on going. Dashdelgar watches them, infuriated. But he sees that there is another skin of kumaq and so he drinks it."

I was going to have to explain a lot of things to you because of this joke. Hokkarans don't speak of lewd matters, but it is not uncommon for such things to happen in the ger, in full view of the adults.

"It is then Dashdelgar notices three important things. One: he is drunk. Two: the ger is empty, except for the couple. And, three: this is not his ger."

There it is. Everyone breaks down laughing. Even you spare a chuckle.

That first night passed with many such jokes. As time wore on, each of my aunts and uncles added their own Dashdelgar story.

Dashdelgar prepares for a ride to the desert, going through great trouble to buy a Surian donkey, only to find he did not fill his waterskin.

Dashdelgar goes hunting with his clanmates, swearing he will bring home the biggest game. His clanmates want nothing to do with him and abandon him. He stalks through the grass, sure he will find something eventually; he stays out all night. Then, when Grandmother Sky's silver eye hangs in the sky, he is surprised by a rabbit and wets himself.

If you ask a Kharsa who the most valuable member of her clan is, she may say it is her most skilled hunter. She keeps the clan fed, after all. Another might name their sanvaartain, who keeps the clan healthy. Still another would name the eldest person in the caravan, whose knowledge saved them from disaster.

Allow me to tell you a secret, Shizuka, as the daughter of the Kharsa-that-was-not.

The most valuable member of the clan is the person who tells the best stories around the fire.

You may think me silly, but listen: That hunter picked up her bow because she wanted to be like Tumenbayar. That sanvaartain idolized wily Batederne, and quotes her whenever she gets the chance.

And the caravan elder—how do you suppose they share all this knowledge rolling around in their brain?

They tell stories.

Before my mother insisted on commissioning an alphabet for us, this was how we learned of our world: sat around the fire, learning of Tumenbayar and Batumongke and Batederne. And I tell you, Shizuka, the Dashdelgar stories are every bit as important as the others.

Tumenbayar lives in the clouds, and the hooves of her horse bring thunder on dark nights. But we have all been Dashdelgar.

You'd never heard any stories about Tumenbayar, and no one told them that first night, but you strove to mimic her regardless.

In Hokkaro, you woke to practice calligraphy. Here on the steppes, you did not need to write anything. Here on the steppes, there was no one to tell you how dangerous, how foolish swordplay is.

In fact, my entire clan wanted to prove it to you.

You fought anyone and everyone. Young warriors with no braids in their hair. Old veterans with ropes sprouting from their heads. Temurin was one of your favorites; she did not care if she hurt you.

Not that she ever came close, but it was the thought that mattered.

Watching you fight my clanmates was watching oil float on water. Nothing touched you. Your opponents lunged; you melted away from them. They waited for you to strike, and you turned to stone. In the three years you stayed with us, only my mother hit you with any regularity, and that because she was fond of cheating.

A blacksmith stands at his forge. In his hands, a pair of tongs; at his side, a hunk of rough-hewn iron. When he lowers it into the inferno of the smelter, he does not see a hunk of iron. He sees a sword waiting to be born. And so he pulls the iron out once it glows white-hot, lays it on his anvil. With all the force he can muster, he hammers it into shape—and then he quenches it in water.

For months, you subjected yourself to the same routine. When you awoke, you'd see who wanted to test your mettle that day. One, two, three challengers; you didn't balk at being outnumbered, and the clan wanted to know how good a pampered Hokkaran girl could be. After you finished your first round of challenges, you'd demand that we go riding. When we finished riding, you demanded to practice wrestling.

It is hard to put into words the single-mindedness with which you pursued your training. I must stress this, Shizuka—you never turned down a challenger. When four warriors came to you, you fought them all at the same time, standing barefoot on the silver grass. Over the years, the number grew. You fought mounted Qorin, you asked my clanmates to shoot at you, you went in search of wolves. Anything to test your abilities.

So it was every morning, every afternoon, every night. Months wore into years. More than once, I caught you weeping in your bedroll at night. Whenever I caught you mumbling in your sleep, you were saying that maybe you could've saved your parents, if you'd gone with them, if you were strong enough.

I tried talking to you, Shizuka, but milking a stallion would've been easier. Either you thought I was babying you, or you said I could not understand the dedication required for Hokkaran swordplay, or . . .

Once, you snapped at me to "cease my incessant nagging."

That was worse than your hands around my throat.

But I could not abandon you, even during those dark years when you fought so hard to be abandoned. When we ate, I was at your side. When we hunted, when we rode. Though you sometimes ignored me, I was there. That has always been my purpose, Shizuka—to protect you from everything, including your own foolish self.

And foolish it was to practice sword forms outside. At night. In the steppes. But I was there all the same.

"Are you not worried about the cold?" you said one night.

"Are you?" I asked. For you did not have a deel yet—I was still working on making one—and you had no warm hat either. Your cheeks were the color of fresh fruit, your hands raw around the hilt of your mother's sword. "The ger has a fire."

"I am not done," you said. Indeed, as we spoke, you continued to move from form to form.

"You will freeze."

"I cannot freeze," you replied. "Imperial blood burns with heavenly fire."

I cocked a brow at you. You believed that the same way I believed a mare birthed me. Yet you did not stop your sword forms. One stroke led to another: a dance you seemed to be trapped in.

But the more I studied you, the more I was troubled. Your steps were short and shaky; your blade rattled in your hands. Your lips were cracked and pale; beads of sweat clung to your forehead.

I rose to my feet. "Shizuka?"

"I cannot freeze!" you repeated. Your next stroke would've gotten you killed on a battlefield. I went toward you.

Now that I was close, I could see how pale you were. My stomach twisted. Though you still tried to go through your forms, I wrapped my arms about your waist. Like trying to hold the sun in my arms.

"Let me go!" you shouted. "I am not done with my forms."

But we were sixteen then, and I was eighteen hands tall to your almost fifteen. I scooped you into my arms and took you inside.

A hummingbird could not hope to flap his wings faster than my heart fluttered in my chest. Alshara was already asleep, but woke at once when I kicked her rib lightly. And when she saw you . . . my mother's brown face turned the color of milky tea.

She yanked Otgar out of her bedroll and fired off a series of signs. I stood there, holding you. What were we going to do? Take you to the shaman. But healers never helped me—how could they help you, if your old theory was true? Who among men can heal a god?

So I sat by your side as fever twisted your protests. You kept raving about your blood. About your heritage. About the dawn pulsing through your veins.

"When the daylight comes," you said, "when the daylight comes, it will cleanse me, you will see. Scarlet runs gold. Brighter than ever."

Listening to you, I had to fight my tears. You did not make sense, Shizuka. How is sunlight going to cure your fever? Dawn cannot banish sickness. I clutched your hand; I rocked back and forth in the shaman's ger.

The sanvaartain took one look at you and shook her head. Like any sanvaartain interested in healing, she looked eighty. In reality, she could not have been older than Otgar.

"Burqila," she said, "if you asked me to journey into the center of the earth, where Grandfather sleeps—if you asked me to steal his belt and bring it to you, I would. But I cannot heal this girl."

My mother did not bother signing. She shattered a divining bowl instead. I recoiled from the sound, my head already throbbing with pain.

"Burqila is displeased with your answer," Otgar said, as if it needed saying. "You tell her you can reattach a man's severed arm, but you cannot cure a simple fever?"

The sanvaartain showed no fear in the presence of my mother. "I cannot," she said. "The girl is not mine to heal. Even if she were, this is no simple fever. Look at her eyes."

Glassy. You did not focus on anything; your eyes flittered

everywhere like shy birds. When you lay down like this, the skin of your face sank into your skull.

"This is her fourth day of fever," the shaman said, "that is the face of a girl who sees the Mother coming. Pray that she does not carry her home tonight."

How long had you been sick? How long had you hidden it from us?

Guilt tore into me. You could die. You'd driven yourself day and night, you'd fought and fought and fought. And I'd done nothing. I watched. I let you do it all, and now, here you were—your own ghost.

"And if the Mother does not come for her tonight?" Otgar asked.

"Then she will live. But only if she wakes in the morning," said the shaman.

After an hour of haranguing, the shaman admitted that water from the Rokhon might help your body rid itself of toxins. That did not make much sense to me; water is water, even if it is taken from a holy river. And what good would that do us? The Rokhon was a whole day's ride away. By the time someone made the trip and returned, you'd be better (because you were not going to die, could not die, would not die).

But things like logistics never stopped my mother. Especially not when her best friend's daughter lay on what seemed like her deathbed.

I glanced over my shoulder. Otgar and Alshara signed furiously at each other. I caught a few words here and there. "Madwoman," "insane," "impossible," from Otgar. "Must," "do not challenge," and "soon," from my mother. Eventually my mother stormed out of the ger.

"Burqila is riding to the Rokhon," Otgar said. "Because she seems to think roads are shorter for her than for anyone else."

The sanvaartain shook her head. "She's going to kill that liver mare of hers," she said. Nadsha—my mother's liver-colored mare, with a star, strip, and snip—was getting old. It was true she could likely not survive being driven so hard.

It is fortunate, then, that the Burqila clan possesses more than ten thousand horses.

"She will not take the liver mare," Otgar said. "Or if she does, they will not go alone. She will take a gelding, or a stallion, or a hot-blooded colt with something to prove. She would not risk the liver mare."

"Then she will run two good horses to death," said the sanvaartain. "For some Hokkaran girl. When has a rice-eater done anything like that? The only gift they've ever given us is plague."

Liquid flame shot through my veins. How dare she? While you lay in bed, fever robbing you of your strength—she insulted your people? As much as our Hokkaran wounds festered and turned to rot, now was not the time.

I rose to my feet and locked eyes with the sanvaartain. "Out," I snarled.

Otgar scowled. "I would listen, if I were you," she said.

Perhaps the sanvaartain was used to be snarled at. She did not move.

"This is my mother's ger," she said. "I am entitled to stay in my mother's ger at night."

Pain shot through my jaw, from clenching it too tight. No, I could not remove a woman from her own ger. Raiders might do such a thing, but never a clanmate. This woman was my blood in some small way. Making her leave the ger her mother built with her own two hands was the same as dragging her away from her mother's soul.

So instead, I picked you up in my arms. In thick fur pelts, I swaddled you. You muttered my name; I whispered that all would be well soon. And I carried you out of the sanvaartain's ger.

Otgar followed us. "Are you going to take her to your mother's?" she asked. "With our aunts and uncles, too?"

I had not thought this through, so I shrugged. When you shivered, I held you closer.

"Auntie Khadiyyaar's little one isn't old enough to be left alone yet," Otgar said. "If whatever Barsatoq has is contagious . . ."

My eyes lit up.

Otgar paused, holding up her hands to try to soothe my rage. "Cousin," she said. "Barsalai. Shefali. That girl might be the most self-absorbed person under the Eternal Sky, but she is important to you. And, if I'm being honest, she is almost as talented as she claims. But she is one person. You must think of the clan, Shefali. A Kharsa must put her clan first. You cannot keep her around the children."

Send the children away, then! Let them sit in their own ger! But . . . No, they would fall into the fire, and someone had to watch them.

I looked down at you, swaddled like a baby, pale in the moonlight. Gods, Shizuka, you looked so weak.

"My ger is empty."

What? Otgar had a ger? Auntie Zurganqaar stayed with us. Why did Otgar have a ger?

She shifted her weight. "I enjoy a bit of peace and quiet every now and again," she said. "I am a woman grown, I am allowed to begin my own ger if I want."

But Otgar was unmarried at twenty—itself an anomaly. And only married women began their own gers. What was my cousin up to? And how, exactly, had she gotten out of her marriage when that boy had already paid his bride-price? Yet I did not have the time or the wherewithal to question her. Instead, I followed as she led us to the very edge of the camp.

Otgar's ger was the one tree in autumn whose leaves fell before all the others. Small, with a frame half the size of a normal one, only the barest sheet of felt lined it. Once we stepped inside, we saw a few carpets draped from the supports in some effort to provide warmth. In the southern corner was a single bedroll, and in the center, the smallest fire pit it's possible to have in a ger. I felt as if I were not standing in a ger at all, but something in between a tent and the white felt palaces I am so used to.

"It is not much to look at," Otgar said, "or to sleep in. But it is mine, and tonight it is yours."

She stoked the smoldering coals that passed for a fire and laid out the bedroll. As I lowered you onto it, she tucked you in, rolling the sheets up to your chin. I took my place at your side.

"I must wait for Burqila to return," said Otgar. "I'd ask if everyone in your family is such a foolhardy, mule-stubborn pain, but we are cousins. I still say it's only your branch. But . . ."

She paused by the red door. Her pale eyes fell on you, sputtering meaningless syllables.

"May Grandmother Sky smile on her," she said. "No one deserves to suffer like that."

The door closed behind her.

And so we were alone, you and I.

I squeezed your hand. As the sands of Sur-Shar when baked beneath the sun, so was your flesh. The words that dropped from your lips were not Hokkaran or Qorin. They were the crack of fire consuming wood; the dull roar of flames igniting; the pop of boiling oil. Thick fog hid the brown-gold of your eyes.

I stared down at you and considered our life together. Our life apart, really. The first day we met, your hands locked around my throat, your face a demonic mask. All the letters you wrote me that I could not read; all the letters I made Otgar write to you. The stories you'd tell me of the goings-on at court. That afternoon beneath the tree, our blood mingling on an arrowhead.

I touched your cheek.

How I had longed to do this, Shizuka. Oh, I'd found reasons to touch you. I did take you out for rides, as I'd imagined when we first left. With perfect nonchalance, you touched the star-shaped blaze on my horse's forehead.

Perhaps you do not know this. My mare and I were born on the same day. You might be asking yourself how such a thing is possible, when we are now nearly thirty and I ride her still. Just as you and I are something more than human, my horse is something more than a horse. This was known from her birth. My mother's liver mare was her dam; her sire was a roan. Yet when she emerged, she was black as night, with the white star on her forehead.

In no way should such a union have yielded a black horse, or the gray she grew into. In cases like these, we say Grandfather Earth guided her birth. My mother hosted a grand feast to celebrate her dual fortune—an Earth-blessed horse, and a healthy young daughter.

You did not know that when you asked. At least you did not know it consciously. You could not talk to her as I did, could not speak the tongue of swaying wind.

I wondered if you were speaking your own version of that tongue. I wondered what you were saying.

I touched your lips while my own trembled. Dry, cracked, flaking. When I dreamed of this moment, I imagined how soft they'd be.

Yes, Shizuka. I imagined touching your lips, your cloud-soft skin. I had for at least two years. Other girls my age had boys paying their bride-prices already. When my mother asked if I wanted her to find someone, I shook my head.

I wanted you. Only you.

From the day we met, I've known this as my heart has known to beat. That it took me so long to recognize is my own great shame.

And I saw you there, a ghost of yourself. You still had so much to do, Shizuka. We were going to slay gods together. The Empire of Hokkaro needed you, too—you had to found your own dynasty, had to raise children, had to ascend to the Dragon Throne. Empress O-Shizuka you would be, and no one in the land would be permitted to write your name without dropping a stroke out of deference.

You could never be mine. Much as I wanted you, much as we were destined to spend our lives together, we could never be together the way I wanted us to.

I licked my lips.

A fever. That such a mundane thing would lay you so low . . .

"Shefali."

At the sound of my name, I jolted back to reality. The fog on your eyes had lifted.

"Shizuka?" I said. "Do you need anything?"

Weak as you were, you squeezed my hand. Again, fire burned

in your gaze, all the more bright against your pallid complexion. "Shefali," you said, tugging on my hand, "kiss me."

My mouth hung open. I drew back, a chill running up my spine. "Wh-what?"

You screwed your eyes shut and forced yourself to sit up. From somewhere within yourself, you found strength enough to pull me onto the bed. "I don't care how wrong it is," you said, almost shouting, "I am not going to die without kissing you at least once. Hurry up!"

How I wanted to! But what if this was just your fevered raving? What if, when you recovered (you had to recover) you regretted it? This could not be happening. You were going to be Empress one day. You could not want to be with me that way.

"We're both girls," I said.

You grabbed me by the flap of my deel. Mad with strength, you rolled us over. Hot tears fell on my chest and face.

"Did you hear me?" you roared. "I don't care! In all the lands of the Empire, I've only ever wanted to marry you. You fool Qorin! You do not hesitate to slay a tiger, but you hesitate to kiss a girl?"

I stared at you, your cheeks flushed red, your whole body trembling.

"Are you not a warrior?" you said. "Are you not a leader? Act decisively! Don't sit there and gawk at a dying woman!"

I sputtered. No words came to me.

But this was not the time for words, was it?

And so I wrapped my arms around you. So I held you in my arms as men hold women, as Grandfather Earth held Grandmother Sky. And as Tumenbayar loved Batumongke, as O-Shizuru loved O-Itsuki, so did I love you.

Yes, Shizuka. The sky is full of stars beyond number, each one representing a life. And yet in all those lives beyond number, in all those millions of years lived by those before us, in all their shared experience, none have loved so thoroughly as we.

When our lips met, the stars grew jealous of us. I cannot begin to tell you how it felt. How my whole body rang with the sound of temple bells.

When we parted, I could not remember how to breathe.

I stared at you, eyes wide, fear creeping back in. What if you had not liked it? I'd never kissed anyone before.

But you tugged me down toward you again. "Keep going," you said, "until I tell you to stop."

And so I did. Our mouths met again. You wasted no time slipping your tongue between my lips like a lick of flame. My hands traveled the wall of your spine. I touched your skin and felt the muscle hiding beneath, felt the bones that made you up. Your hands, too, wandered. With a calligrapher's grace, you danced across my rib cage and collarbones.

You became my air. Whenever we parted, you redoubled your efforts. You kissed me like a monsoon; you touched me like lightning. You tugged at my deel, too weak to take it off. Whatever doubts I had disappeared when I rid myself of my deel and pants. I paused with my hands on the brocade edges of your dress.

"Are you—?"

"Keep going."

When I slid off your clothing, I think I died for the first time— for no one can live through such a divine vision. For an eternity I sat up, gaping at your beauty before you tugged me back downward.

"Fool Qorin," you whispered into my ear. "I did not say stop."

And then your mouth pressed against my neck. Heat and pressure and pain against that tender skin made me moan. You smiled as you kept at it, knowing full well you'd leave a mark.

"Shizuka, everyone will see," I whimpered.

"Let them," you said. There would be no arguing.

Still, my hands kept traveling. I left the delicate road of your spine for something softer. Your breasts have always tantalized me, Shizuka; this you well know. Now that I was touching them for the first time, I hardly knew how to contain myself. I kneaded at them as my heart hammered in my chest, as warmth spread throughout me. Burning within me was the desire to be near to you, to burn in your flame, to show you just how much I'd wanted you all these years.

I took your delicate pink nipple in my mouth. As my tongue ran over it, you made the most wonderful sound—a half moan, half whimper. It only drove me on. You took fistfuls of my hair.

As best you could, you rocked your hips against my knee.

I continued worshipping your body. My mouth moved in unspoken prayers at your other breast, your throat, your collarbones. You threw your head back as I kissed you. How you purred, Shizuka! How I treasure that sound above all others still!

"Lie down," you said.

I did as I was told. And though you were sick, when you positioned yourself over me, I swear I was looking up at the Eternal Sky.

Gods, but the sight of that part of you. It, too, was beautiful—pink and glistening like an orchid slick with dew.

"Shizuka, are you sure?"

"Keep going!"

You fell forward and braced yourself with one shaky arm. With my hair still in your hand, you rode me—a canter at first, then a full gallop. Your wetness covered my mouth and jaw and chin, and I could not get enough of your taste. Again, I licked and suckled; again, I teased your opening. The louder you were, the harder I went.

"Don't . . . don't you dare stop. . . ."

I could feel you throbbing against my tongue. You tugged my hair so hard, I thought it would fall out; you squeezed my head so tight, I thought it would pop off my neck. When at last you went taut as a bowstring, you spoke my name like a prayer.

I was covered in you. Gods, the smell, Shizuka. How I wish I could smell you again. How I wish I could take a bit of your spirit into me again.

For a few moments, you lay on top of me, catching your breath. Perhaps you shouldn't be engaging in such strenuous activity in your state. But I could not say I regretted it. How could I ever regret being so close to you?

"Shizuka," I asked, "was that . . . did you feel . . . ?"

In response, you rolled over and smiled. If only for an instant, you looked like your old self. You were going to make it. You had to make it now.

But . . . well, there was another matter to attend to. My inner thighs were slick, and I would be lying if I said I wasn't desperate for you.

You clambered on top of me and bent to kiss me.

I turned away. "You shouldn't—"

"You're only a mess because of me," you said. "Let me kiss you."

Your kisses were more insistent than mine, and your hands more needy. You grabbed me as if you were going to die in the morning, because there was a very real chance you might. Your long nails left trails wherever they went; your flashing teeth nipped at my nipples and skin. You cupped my bottom and squeezed.

Our eyes met. Your fingers hovered a hairsbreadth away from my center, from the heat between my legs. My breath hitched; I needed you inside me more than I'd ever needed anything in my life.

"Shefali," you whispered.

I licked my lips. I was so eager, Shizuka. I was the bowstring now, waiting to be fired.

"Before I do this," you said, "you should know that I've loved you since we were children."

"I love you, too," I said.

And just like that, your fingertips rubbed against me. Pleasure sank into me like an arrow. I clutched you tight and rode your hand.

"Ready yourself," you said.

But how could I when I was so overwhelmed? Your fingers slid inside me and I moaned loud enough for all Sur-Shar to hear me. After that, I bit at your shoulder to try to keep quiet.

You thrust your fingers in and out of me, hooking them with each stroke. I moaned into your mouth as the pressure built up at the base of my spine. Soon I was going to explode like Dragon's Fire, soon I was going to burst, soon I was going to die in your arms and . . .

And then it all came to a glorious climax, to a small eternity of bliss.

When it was over, I leaned against you slick with sweat. We both needed a bit of time to catch our breaths—to process what we had just done. Women did not do this with other women. I couldn't think of anyone who'd done such a thing. And even if one of us were a man, we were unmarried. If your uncle tried to find you a husband now . . .

Yet I could not feel bad about it. If this was not how the gods intended us to live our lives, then I'd rather be executed at your side than never touch you again. Looking at you with your eyes so wide, panting, your chest flushed red, I thought this must be the point of it all.

You were the point.

And you were also the first to speak.

"I see your shy nature does not extend to the bedroom," you said.

We both laughed. We linked hands underneath the blanket, and I hid my face against your shoulder in mock embarrassment. We stayed that way for a while.

"Thank you," you whispered. "I've wanted to do that with you for some time."

"Since you saw Aunt Zurgaanqar and Uncle Ganzorig?" I asked.

One night you saw my uncle and aunt rutting. How red you got looking at them, how you stared and sputtered! That was the first time you'd ever seen anything of the sort, you said. No one in Hokkaro spoke of such things.

But here on the steppes, there is no privacy. What goes on between man and wife has long been known to me. Qorin girls are supposed to ease their shy husbands into it.

How amusing, then, that we should be together like this. Was I your shy husband? Or were you mine?

A blush came to your cheek, but you nodded. "I've always known I wanted to be with you," you said. "The same way a child knows who their parents are, so I knew you were the one for me. But I did not know what it meant until . . ."

I kissed you on the cheek. "You stared."

"I did," you said. "Because I wanted so badly to do the same with you."

You huddled against me. We had done the same now, and we could never go back.

No one could know.

If anyone found out about us, you would not inherit. And much as I loved you, the people of Hokkaro needed you . . . No, I cannot say they need you more. I need you more than any hundred thousand people put together. But they are the ones to whom you should turn your attention.

Do you pay attention to them now, in my absence?

I did not know what the future held that night. So I held your wasting frame in my arms, and I prayed to every god I knew that we'd wake together in the morning.

SURE ENOUGH, I woke before you. The first rosy fingers of dawn turned the blue sky violet. Bright morning stars flickered above our ger; the warm morning air washed against the white felt walls.

I looked down at you asleep against me, our feet entangled beneath the blankets. Already red crept back into your complexion; already you felt cooler. I squeezed you tight.

And under the sheets, you were naked. I had not been dreaming, after all.

But with the dawn came the return of reality. We could not be caught like this. I slipped out of the bedroll. In your sleep, you reached for me; as I stood, your fingers trailed through my hair.

It hurt my heart to leave you, but I, at least, had to be dressed.

Just as I tugged on my deel, I heard the clattering of hooves. I did my best to tuck you in tight.

A few seconds later, my mother threw open the red door. There were dark circles underneath her eyes, and a halo of frizz crowned her head. As a caged animal finally set free is wild and crazed, so was my mother's expression. In her hands was a dripping water-skin.

I tried to stop her, but she barreled straight for you.

"Mother—"

She knelt next to you, slipped one arm beneath your shoulders, and sat you up. When she saw that you were naked, she scowled at me.

My cheeks flushed. "She was cold," I mumbled.

My mother tilted her head. At times my mother's muteness is no obstacle to communication. I read her look easy as Qorin letters carved onto a cliff.

We will speak of this later.

I cleared my throat and averted my eyes as if I had not already seen you. As if I were the shy virgin I had been last night.

As she jostled you, you stirred, your eyes adjusting to the half light. My mother tipped the waterskin to your lips before you could protest; you choked as the water trickled down your throat.

"Burqila," you gasped, clutching your chest.

She slapped you hard on the back. Then, with unexpected tenderness, she took your temperature with her hand. A sigh of relief left her. She touched her fingers to her lips and held them to the sky in praise. I took the opportunity to drape the blankets around your shoulders.

Otgar came in not long after that—a good thing, too, as my mother had many questions for you.

"Did you lose a duel with your clothing?" Otgar teased.

"I won the duel with the fever, that is all that matters," you said. I must admire your aplomb; the question did not faze you in the slightest. Your princess's dignity shielded you from shame.

My mother interrupted us with a raised hand. Signing followed. Otgar let out a small laugh.

"Burqila says that if you allow yourself to get so sick again, she would treat with demons to revive you just so she can kill you again."

We called the sanvaartain in to check on you. She affirmed your health the same way one might declare a woman pregnant.

"Give thanks to Grandmother Sky," she said, "who shielded you from the Mother's grasping hands."

When we were eight, we faced a tiger. From it we received our names, and I received a scar. The image of it is still vivid in my mind—the way it sank low to the ground with its hindquarters raised. I remember its golden eyes and the proud, sagacious way it regarded me just before it attacked.

So, too, did you regard the sanvaartain. "I will thank no one save Shefali and Burqila," you said, "for they are the ones who aided me. If the gods wish for me to thank them, then they shall come into the ger to speak to me."

Skies darken over the Silver Steppes. It is the moment before a thunderstorm. Animals run for shelter; Qorin hurry to their gers, leaving bowls and cups to catch the rain. If anyone were outside, they would hear the perfect stillness in the air—the worried whisper of the grass.

So it was after you spoke. Otgar, my mother, and the sanvaartain all spat on the ground. Even I, who knew you so well, found myself staring blankly at you. Qorin and Hokkarans may hold different gods, but you challenged all of them to speak to you. A mortal.

But . . .

If the gods spoke to anyone, perhaps they would speak to us.

You did not wait for mortals to chide you. Instead, you wrapped yourself in your robes and got to your feet.

"Barsatoq," said Otgar, "has it occurred to you that you are daring the world to slay you?"

"I will dare and dare again," you said, "since I cannot die." You tied your robes closed and tucked your sword into your belt. "Not until I finish what I was meant to do."

And as you spoke, your eyes met mine. Our night together played out again in my mind, bringing a flush to my face I coughed to conceal.

"Let all the gods of man and beast face me, if they so wish," you continued. "I cannot be humbled by my equals."

Honey-sweet lips summoned thunder and lightning. When you opened the red door, light crowned you.

I did not know what to say. What is there to say to such a thing? Boasting was as natural to you as archery is to me, but you'd never insulted the gods like this before.

You stood silhouetted by the dawn in the doorway. I thought of the second time we met—when you stood like this at Oshiro's garden gates, cloaked in golden silk, a thousand flowers swaying behind you. Now there was only the tall silver grass and the Eternal Sky.

But the image was no less striking.

"Shefali," you called, "you are coming, yes?"

"She is not," cut in Otgar. Strange. My mother did not sign anything for her to translate. "We have much to discuss."

You wrinkled your nose. "You intend to leave me alone?"

I opened my mouth, but Otgar spoke first. Again. She had a knack for that. "Well, Barsatoq, if you are so comfortable threatening the gods, then being alone should be no problem."

I stood. My quiver, bow, and whip were within easy reach; I needed nothing else to survive. I walked to the red door.

"Shefali, your mother wants you to stay," Otgar said.

But I looked to you crowned with daylight's glory.

When I met my mother's and Otgar's gazes, I shook my head. I was sixteen. If I wanted to disobey my mother, I could. It did not matter that my mother happened to be the greatest fear of most Hokkarans—at the time, she was keeping me from the person I wanted to be with.

So I said nothing, only shook my head, and left out the red door. I did not look behind me as I left, but I imagine they were frustrated. They did not chase after me, however. Whatever words we were all going to share would wait until you and I returned from wherever we were going.

Come to think of it, I did not know where you were leading us.

But as we made our way through the camp, you laced your pinky through mine and I decided not to think on it too hard. Better to savor the moment. Better to savor the way the wind tousled your hair, the simple sight of you on the steppes. I cannot say you were ever truly at home there—more than once, you complained of the smell, or longed for a proper shower—but you were here among the rolling hills of my childhood. For that sight alone, I am forever grateful.

Watching you, it occurred to me you might not remember what happened the night before. Sometimes fever claims one's memories. And what if you didn't remember? What if you woke naked and confused?

As you approached your stocky red horse, I summoned my courage. I could not bear the thought of you not knowing.

"Shizuka," I ventured, "do you remember what happened?"

You turned from saddling your horse. Somewhere between mirth and embarrassment was the look you gave me. "Shefali," you said, "do not be silly. I could not forget . . . I could not forget such a night."

Relief left me in a long gasp. After a quick look around, I embraced you tight. You kissed the tip of my chin and pushed me away—more playful than condemning.

Then you squeezed my shoulder. "Which is why," you said, "we are leaving today."

THE EMPRESS

FOUR

The Empress of Hokkaro surrounds herself on all sides with splendor. The many-faced gods of Ikhtar, rendered in gold and ivory, guard the four corners of her room. Her gilded bed is larger than a peasant's hovel; its sheets made from silk dyed in a hundred different colors. Paintings and woodcuts adorn her walls; Surian carpets prevent her sacred feet from ever touching the ground. Even the robes clinging to her small frame are woven from gilt cloth. A single thread would beggar an entire village.

Yes, she is surrounded by a hundred splendors.

But not a single comfort, save for the far-off voice of her lover. Nothing but ink and paper to soothe the ache of loneliness. Nothing but words and memories.

With one gold-taloned hand, O-Shizuka rings the small bell by her desk. Before she can take another breath, a servant slides the door open and touches her forehead to the ground.

"Imperial Majesty," she says, "I am yours to command."

"Bring me a bottle of rice wine," says O-Shizuka. "Another."

Is that hesitation on the servant's part? For O-Shizuka swears the girl does not immediately skitter off to her task. Yes, there is a pause, minuscule in span. A beat. A hesitation.

A memory, perhaps, of the orders Lai Baozhai left with the staff. Of the dark times, before Baozhai stayed with her.

The girl knows better than to question the Daughter of Heaven, the Virgin Empress. With another bow, she is gone.

It is another ten minutes before the girl returns with a full bottle of wine. She slides open the door and sets it down, along with the Empress's cups. Then she slides the door shut. It's Seventh Bell now, and the Imperial Timekeeper is pacing the halls, reading from the Divine Mandates.

O-Shizuka sniffs. The room spins a bit. What use was there in such a tradition? Why remind everyone of gods who had clearly abandoned them? Two hundred years. Two hundred years since the Daughter-Made-Flesh last visited a temple. Having someone shout her family's words at the top of their lungs would do nothing to bring her back.

That was what the commoners failed to understand. None of their prayers were being heard, none except the ones Shizuka herself tried to ignore in the middle of the night. No—that was not right. She did not ignore them. Much as she wanted to. She listened, and if she thought it might be something she could help with—

It sounds so foolish to say she willed something to happen, but Shizuka can find no other words for it. She shuts her eyes and sends . . . sends *something* of herself out into the world.

Does it help? She isn't certain. All she ever hears are requests for crops to grow, or flowers to make it through the winter, or for a duel to go well. At times she does not hear the words, only feels the emotions tugging at the back of her mind like an upset child.

It is no wonder she drinks.

She tips another cup. Another. One more. It's gotten to the point where it takes this many, and she is faintly proud of herself, faintly ashamed.

And the alcohol starts to drown the memory replaying, like painted opera, at the back of her mind.

"Itsuki!" O-Shizuru sputtered, black blood flecked on her deathbed. "Where is Itsuki?"

Itsuki was dead. O-Shizuka explained that to her ten, twenty, thirty times. O-Shizuru either could not hear her or did not want to, but O-Itsuki was dead, and no one had found his body.

To this very day, no one had ever found the body of the Poet Prince. His funeral services were a farce, at best, performed with scrolls of his work instead of his body. O-Shizuka attended—but as drunk as she is, she cannot remember the details.

She is too focused on what her mother looked like lying in a dirty, stained blanket on a dirty, stained Imperial bed. Her mother's bone peeking out from the rotting, gray flesh where her arm used to be.

O-Shizuru, Queen of Crows, lying in agony on a soiled bed.

O-Shizuru, Shizuka's hero and namesake. O-Shizuru, who was imprisoned in her youth by a Demon General for eight days and emerged with his head. O-Shizuru, who should've been Empress if the world were anything like it should be; O-Shizuru, who always brought her daughter a new story whenever she returned home; O-Shizuru, quick with boasts and bawdy jokes and blades; O-Shizuru, who loved O-Itsuki more than even he, master of poetry and song, could ever convey.

O-Shizuru.

Her mother.

Lying in agony on a soiled bed.

By the end of the sixth cup, O-Shizuka, the Empress, Light of the Empire, Eternal Flame, Serene Phoenix, has forgotten all this anew.

But she has not forgotten what it was like to end her mother's life. She has not forgotten the terror, the despondency, the resignation, the realization that if she did nothing, her mother was going to rise as a blackblood within a day's time.

And it is a strange thing, to realize you are utterly alone. To realize you are not the person you've pretended to be, you are not the infallible, unreachable god you keep saying you are. To realize you are nothing but a child on the verge of adulthood; to realize there will never again be anyone in your life you can trust as completely as you've trusted your parents.

She was thirteen, at the time. The sole heir to the Imperial throne. No siblings, and her only cousins too far removed to inherit; only a single friend, one whom she'd not seen in years, and an uncle who saw O-Shizuka as an ominous loose end.

An uncle who knew what he was doing when he sent a forty-nine-year-old woman—mother—wife—to fight two dozen risen blackbloods. You send seventy soldiers to deal with that many. Seventy, if you live recklessly and do not care how many come back to you. One hundred eight would be preferable.

But her uncle sent only O-Shizuru.

It filled O-Shizuka with unspeakable rage to think of him. To think of what he'd done. There were no blood trails spattered on his hands, never, but he had done this all the same.

Yes, Shizuka remembers hovering over the trembling lump of flesh that was once her mother.

If only her mother were still herself, if only her mother could think clearly. That's the irony of it—if their positions were reversed, then the Queen of Crows wouldn't have hesitated. O-Shizuru never left room for doubt. She would have demanded that Shizuka give her a clean death.

So why was it so hard, then?

If O-Shizuka was going to be a warrior, she was going to have to take lives. And yet, looking at her mother she saw more than the present, mangled form. She saw O-Shizuru and O-Itsuki having tea together in the mornings, stealing kisses when they thought their daughter wouldn't notice. She saw O-Shizuru's stern face, heard her voice shouting to put the sword down and get back to the zither.

O-Shizuka has not forgotten what it was like to lift her mother's pillow. She has not forgotten how heavy it seemed, steeped with the weight of her childhood memories.

She has not forgotten her own grim determination: if she hadn't done it, then Uemura would have had to, and she could not bear to let her mother be killed by an outsider.

O-Shizuka has not forgotten how wrong it felt to hold the Daybreak blade. How her hands shook, disrupting the balance. The rattle of drawn metal as she pressed it against her mother's pallid neck.

It had to be her. This was the duty of a warrior. Of a future Empress. Of a loving daughter who would never have her mother's blessing on her wedding day, who would never again clamber into her parents' bed during a nightmare, who would never again make her mother proud.

O-Shizuka wept as she slit her mother's throat. She wept and she crumbled and she threw her arms around the corpse despite the danger her mother's blood posed. She stayed there for . . .

She cannot remember how long.

But she has not forgotten what happened afterwards. She has not forgotten her hatred, burning like a forge in her stomach, how she'd thought it could grow no larger—but it was merely the first blossom beneath a frost. Her uncle had done this. Her uncle had given the order. Her uncle, who then kept her locked in her chambers, except when he paraded her at court like a mare in search of a stud. And only in her own rooms was she permitted to wear mourning white.

O-Shizuka drains the last swallow from her cup.

When the time had come to seize her uncle's throne, she did not kill him. Yoshimoto—the Toad, the Limp Emperor—lived on private lands far, far away from Fujino. Let the souls of his ruined family, his tattered Empire haunt him. Let him toil in the fields. Let him see, from a distance, what his niece makes of the nation he could not salvage.

That will be his punishment, she thinks. The day that she returns with Shefali at her side, happy and healthy and thriving despite all his efforts to the contrary.

A sight her parents will never get to see, for they left not even bones to bury.

So she throws the bottle of rice wine against the wall. It shatters, sending shards flying through the air. By some miracle, none hit the Empress, at least not until she lies on the ground and weeps.

When sleep takes her, she is too drunk to notice.

In the morning, she awakes to a pounding headache. Whatever mess she's made has disappeared as if by magic. O-Shizuka winces.

She has a dim recollection of falling on the floor, and no memory of getting in bed.

Yet here she is, tucked in and comfortable in her sleeping gown.

The servants must've done it. Dimly, she thinks again that she must pay them more.

O-Shizuka forces herself to sit up. The room goes topsy-turvy for a moment, and she grabs her nightstand to steady herself. Hair falls like inky brushstrokes against her sleeping gown. The first few rays of the morning pierce through her blinds. She shields her eyes and sighs.

The scowl drops off her face the moment she sees Shefali's letter. She laughs, in fact. Shefali never had to deal with hangovers. Maybe it was that rancid milk she insisted on drinking. O-Shizuka can picture her now: sipping from a skin in the eastern side of the ger, wearing her brightly colored deel. She takes a deep gulp and chuckles in that quiet way. "Try some."

And Shizuka did, every time. And she forgot, every time, how much she hated kumaq. Shefali looked so happy drinking it, so it must be good, right?

O-Shizuka reaches for the manuscript. For her old friend, for her joy. She opens the pages, and her headache melts away.

THE MIDNIGHT MOON

"We are going back to Hokkaro," you had said, "to the Wall of Flowers, where we are needed."

At this, I put my hands on my hips and frowned. Even if we managed to avoid bandits, wolves, or worse, the Wall of Flowers was four months from Fujino. You could not just up and decide to ride that far. You could not do such a thing without careful planning. You could not do it without at the very least informing my mother of your intentions.

"Don't look at me like that," you said. "The Sun spoke to me this morning. Blackbloods creep—"

"The Sun?" I asked.

You frowned. I tried not to smile, but—you do have a cute frown, you know. "Yes," you said. "The Sun. Does it not speak to you?"

"Does it . . . what does it sound like?" I asked. Oh, you looked foul! But I did not mean to make you feel awkward. I really was only curious.

You pursed your lips. Your eyebrows reached for each other. "Music," you said. "All your favorite music, all playing at the same time, but . . . it does not sound jumbled. Whenever I hear her, my face gets warm. She makes me feel taller."

I rested my chin on my hand. "Just the Sun?"

"And the flowers, sometimes," you admitted.

That did not surprise me, after what you did when we were children. Whenever I see a flower, even now, I think of you. Sometimes I consider asking it how you are doing.

"It might not be the Sun for you," you had said then, "but still, there must be something. You've heard it, haven't you? It says to go North. Every few days, I hear it again—go North, where the blackbloods go, find your fortune there. This time it's the loudest it's ever been."

I frowned again. Yes, I had heard that voice on the wind. Less often than you had, it seemed. My mother always liked having me around when plotting our routes, for I knew which way north was without consulting a compass. My uncles used to spin me around until I was near vomiting, then ask me to point north.

I was always right.

My mother said I had a fine career ahead of me as a Qorin messenger, if I could not make ruling work.

But the flowers themselves turned to face you. You could change their color. Wherever your bare feet touched Earth, blossoms appeared, though it often took a few days.

And I'd never missed a shot in my life, my horse spoke to me, and I never returned from a hunt empty-handed. I'd killed a tiger at eight years old. When I was ten, a demon had spoken to me as if she knew me.

How long could we profit from these small miracles, Shizuka, without paying the price for them?

NORTH.

I was an arrow trembling against a bowstring, and you were pulling me back.

YOU TOOK MY hand in yours. How was it that I never noticed how tiny your hands were?

"If you do not want to come," you said, "then you may stay, and I will go alone. I feel this in my bones, Shefali, there is something for us beyond the flowers. If I must find it myself and bring it back for you, then I will—but I cannot sit here and watch my people suffer. If the blackbloods are going north to join his army, then we must stop them."

You met my eyes with your fierce determination, but behind it was . . . a depth of yearning. As if you were throwing yourself off a cliff and hoped that I would have rope for you to cling to. And no matter how foolish I thought your ideas were, I always did have a length of rope ready for both of us.

I sighed and pulled myself into the saddle. "We will gather our things first," I said.

Tension melted off you. You would never admit you were

afraid I was going to let you go alone, but your shoulders gave you away.

It took only an hour to gather the things we needed. Two or three days' worth of jerky and mare cheese. Two skins of kumaq. Two more empty waterskins. A single bedroll; we would be sharing now, and no one could stop us. One spare horse to carry our tent and camping equipment. No ger, since I had not started making my own yet.

People in camp asked us where we were going, you said we were going for a hunt—but my mother did not check on us.

We left that afternoon, and we spent that night lying together in the tent just past our usual grounds. Whatever awkwardness I felt that first night melted away on the second. Now with a better hold of yourself, now with more strength, you showed me all the ways you'd longed to touch me.

That first week was poetry. Before dawn I woke and hunted. When I returned, we broke our fast together. After that, we set out to do our day's riding. When we were done, we crossed swords, so that you would not lose your talents. That was the excuse you used. You always won, so I am not sure how your talents were at all tested against me. Maybe you wanted to smack me with a sword a bit. That was all right. I raced you back to camp each night, and not once did you win.

I tried to teach you how to talk to my horse. If you could talk to the Sun, you could talk to a horse. One was much farther away than the other.

"You must call her by name," I said.

"Your horse has a name?"

"Of course she does," I said. I rubbed her long face and kissed the blaze on her forehead. "Her name is Alsha."

At the sound of her name, my horse whickered. I whispered to her in the tongue of swaying grass: *This is Shizuka, you know her well, do not be so dramatic.*

You're calling me dramatic? she said back to me. *I have seen the way you act around her.*

"You named her after your mother?" you said. You, too, touched the blaze on her forehead.

She did not whicker when you touched her.

"She has always been named Alsha," I said. "As my mother's horse has always been Nadsha. A Kharsa's mare is always named after her mother."

You smirked. "Yet in sixteen years, I have never heard you say that out loud," you said. You ran your fingers through my horse's dark mane and toyed with her ear.

"Bad luck," I said, "for anyone but the rider to say her name."

To anyone else, my horse nickered just then. But to me she spoke, plain as day: *Shizuka may say it.*

I nodded, both to you and the mare.

"Well, Alsha," you said, "will you let me ride you?"

She stomped her right hoof twice. Grinning like a child, I helped you into the saddle. I handed you the whip and helped you get situated on the high Qorin seat.

Alsha danced with you. I know of no other way to put it—she trotted this way and that in complicated steps, showing off just how smart she was, how graceful. Thinking of that moment puts me in a state of peace.

After our sword lessons, and our races, and our archery practice, we settled in the tent and went about our business. We'd work on our strange little language together, or I'd sit on the northern side of the tent to finish your deel. Little use it would be to you now that we'd be leaving the steppes, but I both wanted you to have it and wanted to finish what I'd started.

You wrote letters. Some you wrote on my behalf, to my brother. Kenshiro read Qorin just as well as I could, yes—but having a letter written by O-Shizuka was a valuable present. I asked him when he planned on marrying that girl of his, and if we would be invited. I told him how our mother fared, and asked after our father. And though you warned me against it, I told him of our plans.

"It is just Kenshiro," I said. "We could trust him with our lives."

"You have not seen him in how many years?"

"Eight," I said, pouting.

"Eight years is plenty of time for a person to change," you said. Nonetheless, you inked your brush. "My uncle, for example. Eight years ago, one could hold a conversation with him. Now all he ever speaks about is siring an heir, or proving to the people that he is not so weak as he seems, or eradicating the Qorin for crimes you have not committed."

You wrinkled your nose. Your uncle's hatred of the Qorin was not a secret. Your grandfather, Yorihito, was the one who started the Qorin war in the first place. As the blackbloods and demons first began their return, Yorihito demanded their bodies be studied. When he realized what a plague it was—worse than anything the legends told us—he made his grand decision.

The study of blackblood bodies would continue. But it would be done by flinging the corpses over the Wall of Stone, into our camps.

And at the time, no one had seen a blackblood for at least four hundred years. Even the most wizened matrons remembered only the vaguest warnings. They did their best to pass these on to the rest of the clan. Do not touch them. Burn them on sight.

But you cannot stop the curiosity of children.

That is how it spread, Shizuka. Did you know? Children found the bodies lying out in the sun. They saw the black blood seeping out into the earth and they touched it—for it could not really be blood, could it? Perhaps paint, or ink, or sweet sap the Surians bring from the land of Pale People. And so they touched it. So they tasted it.

So they changed.

It did not take long to discover what the cause was, but that did not mean it was a problem easily solved. Qorin do not burn bodies, nor do we bury them. Our custom is to leave them out beneath the Eternal Sky. We read portents based on what happens— whether an animal eats the body, or it decays; if anything grows where the body once lay. This is one of our most sacred rites.

It was . . . difficult convincing the clan to burn their loved ones. We are a practical people, yes, but we take comfort where we can. All of us wish for the birds to come for us once we're gone; all of us wish to join the sky.

There were some who refused to be burned. Some who wandered farther and farther from the clan. North, they went. Always North. Hunters leaving in the middle of the night became a commonplace occurrence, second only to morning funeral pyres.

And when my mother learned of the source of this unspeakable evil—my mother, with a newly united Qorin people at her back— she promised to wreak vengeance upon the wall-sitters. The horde rode to Sur-Shar. When we returned from the land of a thousand spires, my mother blew a hole in the Wall of Stone and collected a scalp for every one of us who had died.

This was your grandfather's doing, Shizuka, though I know you've done your best to distance yourself from it.

Your uncle, on the other hand . . .

"Eight years," you said. "He used to send me gifts, eight years ago."

I did not want to think of the sort of gifts such a man might send you. I did not want to remember that you shared his blood.

We rode through Oshiro with little trouble. I know the roads there well. But given how long it'd been since my last visit—and given my province's mixed population—no one recognized me. Did they not remember what I looked like? Did they know who I was? Did they care? If my brother rode out in the open like this, he'd be mobbed.

Their adoration painted you in bright tones. You cloaked yourself in their attention; wrapped yourself in it; wore it as a mantle. Oh, you hated when they actually spoke to you—but you basked in their gazes. And though it was only you and I and the horses, you rode as if the entire Hokkaran army was at your back.

We stayed in warm homes when they were offered to us, inns when they were not. I preferred the inn rooms. Enclosed though they were, their walls provided some modicum of privacy. We could be together there, as we were meant to be.

It was during one of those nights I asked you what you thought would happen when we reached Shiseiki.

"We will find the blackbloods there and we will kill them," you said.

"Why?" I asked.

You turned in my arms. Inky black hair hung over your shoulders; your eyes shone in the dark like twin moons.

"Because we must show them," you said. You touched my face with one hand. "Because to them we are only girls, only mortals.

Because they doubt us. If we do this—if we strike down enemies grown men fear to name—then we take our first step. Then they shall see."

You say the Sun speaks to you, my love. You say she pours her golden words into your ears and sets you alight with purpose. I say that I do not need to speak to the Sun to know how that feels.

What little light there was in the room strove to illuminate you. "I will follow you," I said. "Wherever you lead."

You grabbed me by the ears and brought our lips together. "You had better," you said. "Whom else can I trust at my side?" More laughs left your plum-flavored lips. You spread your arms wide. "In all Hokkaro!" you said. "In all the world, only you and I are worthy!"

I did not know much about the world. I knew there was Hokkaro, large enough that it would take nearly a year to cross from east to west, and more than that from north to south. I knew that four Ages ago, Hokkaro consisted only of Fujino Province. Once, the eight provinces were four countries, until your ancestors saw fit to stitch them all together.

The steppes sat directly to the east of your great empire. Half a year's ride from east to west, a bit more than that from north to south. To the east of us is great Sur-Shar, a land whose eastern border I had not yet seen. Beyond Sur-Shar was Ikhtar, which I'd never seen at all. To the south of the steppes were the Golden Sands; beyond them I did not know. Somewhere lived the Pale People. There were many things about this world I did not know then.

But still something of what you said rang right to me. If there were other warriors in the world of our caliber, they had not made themselves known. We may not have been the strongest. But we were the strongest we knew.

So I followed you.

FOUR MONTHS, I followed you. Four months, we traveled great Hokkaro. From the cliffs of Tsukaido to the wide mouth of the Kirin River we traveled. Do you remember how pale I went when we had to take a boat across the river? The Rokhon is a quarter as wide at most. We pulled up to the riverbank and there was just so much water, all moving at once, like swaying grass except wetter and deeper and smellier. Like all the rain in the world held in one place.

So what if I vomited?

You would have, too, if you hadn't seen a river like that in your life.

And the boat! I spent the entire day in bed. No. I was not going to stand on some rickety wooden things held together by nails and goodwill. Why was this floating? What made it float? Why did it exist? These are all questions I asked myself as I emptied my stomach again and again into a pail by the bed.

"If we were in the Imperial barge," you said, "you would not feel so terrible. It is much larger and does not sway so often. We keep both singing girls and actual musicians on board; you can hear the music rise and fade with the water—"

I groaned. Facedown in the blankets, I waved at you to stop talking. "I think," I said, my already quiet voice muffled by the pillows, "the Traitor invented boats."

"We'll have to take one back . . . ," you teased.

At that point, we'd been on the gods-forsaken wood-chip pile for half a day. I wasn't even vomiting up food anymore. Only bile. The back of my throat burned. With every rock of the boat, I thought I was going to slide off the bed. Looking around sent the whole room spinning; I had no sense of balance. And there was nowhere I could go to escape it all.

"I would rather die," I said. And I was sure of this. I would rather die than suffer through riding a boat again.

When we made shore on the other side of the river, I fell onto the ground and kissed it. I swore to Grandmother Sky that I would never again abandon her husband. I didn't even care when my back screamed with pain as I leaped into the saddle. I was mounted again, off that boat, and I would never be stepping foot in one again.

So I told myself.

Four months, we traveled. Four months together without anyone watching over us. Four months with you. Four months of restful nights spent together, four months I could stay out in the sun, four months without hearing that awful sound in my head, four months without seeing the Not-You, four months . . .

I can hardly believe it is real, looking back on it.

I remember the night we arrived at the Wall of Flowers. I remember the sight of it—half-wilted and sagging in places. One thousand years ago, the Daughter made this wall herself, summoning it after the Traitor slew her Brother. It was said a single petal contained so much of her presence, it would cause an entire field to spring up, if planted. Desperate farmers tried to steal petals so often, an entire branch of the Imperial Guard was dedicated to the Wall.

A thousand years ago, the Daughter painted the Wall of Flowers in all the colors she knew. But time and sunlight and rain washed them away, and now we were left with pallid blossoms clinging to the vine like drunken vagrants clinging to railings.

I had never been one of those who dreamed of seeing the Wall, and I knew it would no longer be as the stories told. Not with things the way they were. Not with the constant cloud in the North, not with babies being stillborn more often than not, not with all the blighted fields we saw on the way here.

No, I was not expecting the Wall to be glorious.

But the sight of it still struck me hard in the gut.

We arrived in the middle of the night again. Upon seeing us, the guards here raised their spears and called for us to halt.

"Who approaches the Wall?"

"O-Shizuka, Imperial Niece," you said. Your voice was rough; we'd been traveling all day and you were saddle-sore. "Traveling with Barsalai Shefali Alsharyya, daughter of Oshiro Yuichi and Burqila Alshara."

Tired though you were, you sat straight in the saddle. Any second now, you must've thought, they'd explode in gratitude. They'd lead us to the barracks. You'd give them an inspiring speech. All of us would ride out with the dawn and trample black-bloods beneath our feet.

But that was not what happened.

Instead, the guards called for reinforcements.

Instead, ten men surrounded us. Instead, the lead guard spoke with borrowed authority.

"His Majesty the Son of Heaven has decreed no one will enter the border village," he says. "We are to detain you until His Serene Highness can send someone to retrieve you."

You reached for your sword. "My uncle," you said in a level voice, "is not here."

"The eyes of Heaven see all, O-Shizuka-shon," said the guard captain. The gold stitching on his armor distinguished him. Around his neck hung a bronze war mask carved in the shape of a snarling dog. "We cannot let you pass."

"You can," you said. "You simply choose not to."

You waved a hand toward the gathered spears. As if you pulled their strings, the guards took several steps back. I laughed, softly, at the magic of your station.

"All of you will stand down," you said. "Your captain and I are going to duel."

The captain clenched his jaw. No sword hung at his hip. His spear was his only weapon. Before the troubles began, such a thing would've been unheard of. All warriors carried swords back then, as symbols of their station. Only the very rich and the very arrogant did so now.

Which meant you carried two: your mother's Daybreak blade, and a short sword you kept just to show everyone how rich you were, how ready to duel. The last person to wear two swords in their belt was Minami Shiori.

You dismounted. I did, too, though I hated leaving my horse. A mounted Qorin is as much a threat as a naked blade.

"Do not look so frightened," you said to the guard captain. You smirked. I think you did this on purpose. You just looked so comfortable in your own skin—your confidence exuding from you like heady perfume. "It is only a duel to first blood."

"O-Shizuka-shon," said the captain, "my orders are strict. You are not to pass."

"It is the right of a Hokkaran warrior to challenge any other warrior to a duel," you said, "so that their swords may write their arguments. For one thousand years, this has been the way of things. I call you to duel in full view of your squadron."

The smile on your lips, Shizuka. You looked as if you and half a dozen of your handmaidens discovered him with his pants down on a cold day.

"If," you said, your voice dripping with condescension, "you need to name a champion to fight in your stead, you are free to do so. I am sure there is at least one among you brave enough to face me."

And indeed there were. Two or three of the guards called out—they'd be honored to duel you. But the guard captain's face turned to stone. For a moment, he looked down at his feet; then back up to you. He spun his spear in his hands.

"Very well," he said. "I see I cannot refuse you."

"Wise man," you said. "You cannot."

I crossed my arms and waited. The guards formed a loose circle around us. You kicked off your shoes. On your tiptoes you stood, a dancer waiting for the music to start. Beneath Grandmother Sky's dull gray eye, you sank into your favorite stance.

And you closed your eyes.

The guard captain circled you. He held his spear out in front of him. Reach, then, was his primary concern. As a cat pawing at a rat's den was he, cautiously feeling you out.

Two minutes, five, ten. He wasn't sure how to approach you, or if he even should. You were Imperial Blood, after all, and you stood with your eyes closed, waiting for his attack. What if you were trying to trick him?

"Captain," called one of the men, "did you not kill one of the enemy? Did you stare it to death?"

I covered my mouth to stifle a laugh. Soon others joined in the jeering. I expected you to smile, but you did not; your face remained impassive as the sun.

At last the captain saw waiting was doing him no good. With a great, reverberating cry, he thrust at you, the point of his spear leaping forward. A fearsome strike, truth be told. Were I a common Hokkaran soldier and he my commander, his fighting spirit would've emboldened me.

But I was not a common Hokkaran soldier, and neither were you.

And where his cry was a hammer on iron, yours was the roaring forge.

Two strokes it took you. With the first, you chopped his spear in half. Between strokes you floated forward, your footsteps light as rain, quick as falling. Then, the second stroke: a cut across the bottom of his chin.

The guard captain tore a piece of cloth from his coat and stanched his wound. He was a proud man, but he was not a dumb one. A duel cleanly fought and cleanly lost.

He cleared his throat. "Beneath the eyes of gods and men," he said, "I am defeated. Are you pleased with yourself, O-Shizuka-shon?"

"I am," you said. I took a rag from our bags and handed it to you, that you might clean your sword. "I came to help you, Captain."

His black eyes turned to coal. He looked to me, then back to you. "You brought a Qorin," he said. "You should have brought an army, and you brought a single Qorin instead."

Only I caught the stiffening of your spine at his comment. That is all right. Such a thing was only meant for me to see. For my part, I stood tall as I could, one hand on my horse.

Technically, you brought two Qorin with you.

"Her name is Barsalai Shefali," you said. "And she is an army, thank you."

I was not so sure I counted as an entire army. Four good archers, yes. But an entire army? You and your exaggerations.

You sheathed your sword. "It is between bells, Captain," you said. "We will retire for the evening. You shall provide us room and board."

"O-Shizuka-shon," he said through gritted teeth. "We have barracks here."

"Then you shall provide us rooms in the barracks. Private rooms. In the morning we will speak at length, and by nightfall your problem will be solved."

As if you were Tumenbayar herself. As if you could guarantee such things. The captain's doubt was plain to read. When he called for his men to lead us away, it was tinged with defeat, with bitterness.

"By nightfall," he echoed. "You will solve our problem by night-fall."

And yet you believed it. I knew you did with all your heart. As you lay in my arms that night, I could almost hear your thoughts. *We will kill them, we will slay them, we will be the heroes we were meant to be.*

And I believed in you.

I WOKE BEFORE YOU. No hunting to be had here—the Wall once played host to a variety of game, but I saw none. Instead, I rode around the camp. Even the soil was dark here, Shizuka, even the grass gray and dying. The Wall stretched for miles in either direction; I rode two miles east and back. In that time, I cannot remember seeing anything green, save the occasional petal on the Wall.

What I did see was decay.

What I did see were once-proud trees now blanched and hollow. What I did see were hovels and mansions alike abandoned, with only dust to inhabit them.

An old temple stood at the center of town. My curiosity drew me there. I am going to use that word, "curiosity," though I am no longer sure it was something so simple.

Inside the temple, a thick blanket of dust kept the relics warm. My footsteps summoned small, dusty tornadoes. My tongue stuck to the roof of my mouth. Something holy once shed its skin here. Remnants of divinity filled my lungs with every breath.

So did the smell of rot.

They say when your hairs stand on end, Grandmother Sky is calling you. She must've called very loudly then. I remember it— I tiptoed through the ruins, muttering prayers under my breath. I do not know what drove me on save . . .

I shall call it curiosity again.

When I saw him, I was standing near the upended offering bowl. Tattered prayer tags fluttered like dead moths in the wind. I heard him before I saw him, heard the soft whoosh of dust flying into the air.

"Steel-Eye."

That name again. The name that was, and yet was not, mine. I reached for my bow. Leaning against a jade statue of the Daughter was a man in ancient armor. A thick, curved sword hung at his hip, the sort of thing far heavier than it had any right to be. Black and violet, he wore, and a sinister black war mask. Fire pits sat where his eyes should be. I could see no trace of skin. At his neck and wrists and beneath his ears, there was no flesh at all. Only shadow.

"Steel-Eye," it rasped. It had a voice. It had a name, too, that popped into my mind without my asking. Leng. "Home at last. How does it feel?"

I fired. In a swirl of black vapor, it vanished. As I ran toward Alsha, I heard laughing.

"I will see you again," it said. The sound of his voice was a bitter taste in the back of my mouth. Something was wrong. Something was very wrong. The last time I'd seen someone like that, we'd been attacked. Leng was a demon, not a blackblood.

Was it not blackbloods you said we were going to kill?

When I came back to camp, you were already awake. The captain was in our room. Excitement and fear at once dulled my senses and heightened them. I was aware, for example, that you wore the deel I made you instead of your robes. But I did not know what the captain was saying as I burst in, and I did not care to listen.

"The temple," I gasped.

"You went to the temple?" said the captain. "You idiot! He lives there. Do you have some kind of death wish?"

"Watch your tongue, Captain, or I will liberate you of it," you said. Concern written on your expression, in characters only I could read. "Who lives in the temple?"

"The Old Commander," he said. "We do not know his name, or we would've bound him. Shadows in the shape of a man. He's swallowed good soldiers whole. I have seen him only once with my own eyes, and once is enough."

You listened to this. Your amber eyes met mine once more. I licked my lips.

A child is playing near the fire. The flames are warm and the night is cold. It reaches for the flickering flames in an attempt to keep warm. For just the smallest moment, the sensation feels pleasant. Refreshing, even. But then the burning starts, and the child scrambles away.

So it was for me. Afraid as I was, I could not deny the thrill of fighting such an enemy—I just wished I had you by my side to face him.

You rose. "I am going to the temple," you said. "You can come if you wish."

The captain shot to his feet. "As guard captain of the Wall of Flowers, I cannot allow you to do that," he said. "Given the Emperor's trouble, you are the only heir we have. If you go into that temple, you will die, O-Shizuka-shon, despite your great skill."

You laughed and shook your head. Laughed, Shizuka. I came in pale faced and slick with sweat—and here you were, laughing at the idea of your death. Had you ever seen a demon before making this plan?

"I will not," you said. "The gods will not allow me to be hurt today."

So you hadn't seen one, then.

Yet I would follow you still. Someone had to.

The captain gawked. "O-Shizuka-shon, I am sorry," he said, "but this I cannot allow. Your uncle would have me executed."

"'Cannot allow,'" you repeated with scorn. "Very well. I am sorry, Captain, but I cannot allow you to bar my path."

You struck him in the head with your short sword's hilt. He swayed, swayed, then fell over. I looked from him to you.

"Do not look at me like that," you said. "I am sorry. He is a good man, for all his stodginess. But we have important work to do, you and I."

Something shifted in my chest when you spoke. A weight, I think. To tell the truth, I did not feel myself that morning. I could not name the feeling exactly, but . . .

A shamed noble wakes before First Bell. He bathes in ritual water, with the herbs of death to give it scent. He cloaks himself in white. He sits in an empty room. Before him: a blank sheet of paper, a brush, an inkblock, a bowl of water. Whatever he has done in his life, he must condense into three lines of poetry. Grass on his knees, a kiss from his wife, blade meeting flesh.

After he leaves that room, he will commit public suicide.

I felt like that man.

Important work to be done.

"Armor," I said. If you were so insistent on facing Leng, then I would not let you do it in a deel.

"I do not—," you began to say, but you stopped when you saw the look I gave you.

The quartermaster provided us with one suit of armor for you. He did not offer one for me, and I did not think to take one. I did not intend to be close enough for the demon's blood to be a problem. I would pelt it with arrows. You'd give it the final killing stroke.

That was the way of things. I did not need armor, and I did not much think of it.

We went alone, the two of us, because you determined it would be more like a story that way.

"Only the two of us are necessary," you said. "We will bring back this demon's head, and that will forever bind these men to our service. How could they be disloyal after that?"

So we left. So we came to the empty temple. The sun hung just above its peaked roof. Our shadows were tall as trees when we dismounted.

"Careful," I whispered. "It disappears sometimes."

You walked with your sword drawn. I remember this; you never unsheathed first in duels. We made our way to the first cracked steps.

"My love," you said, as if you were a woman grown, and not sixteen years old, "we walk into the first chapter of our lives. Together."

You pressed your palm to mine. Our scars aligned. For a brief moment, I felt . . . light. Like the sun shining within me, as if I'd swallowed a star whole. The intensity of it staggered me.

It staggered you, too. You gave me a slow, shocked nod.

Together we walked into the temple.

You remember the stillness of the place. Temples are never still, no matter how hard they try to be bastions of peace. Whether it be the monks and priestesses going about their duties, the worshippers going about theirs, or the birds outside, drinking from the water fountains, temples are not still.

Yet here, books lay open on tables. Here, robes lay on the ground as if their owners had dissipated with the morning dew. Here, nothing lived, not even insects. Here, the sound of my heart was louder than war drums.

Where I'd seen only the statue of the Daughter earlier, together we saw the entire Heavenly Family. Gathered around the shrine they were: the Father holding his books; the Mother, a sickle in one hand and a baby basket in the other; the Son, clutching his own severed head; the Grandfather with his clock; the Grandmother, cloaked in clouds; the Sister, with her scrolls of regrets. All of them were missing limbs—more than the usual severed head and leg in the Son's case.

But only the Daughter was untouched. Only the Daughter stood tall and proud and joyful, with flowers in her hair and a wreath in her hand. Only her smile had not been ruined with a chisel. The dust feared her; she shone softly green in partial light.

You bowed to her as you walked past.

Looking back on it, I think that is what angered Leng. For it appeared in the darkness behind you, with that heavy sword hung high, poised to chop down on you like firewood. Crimson flames consumed the pits where its eyes should be.

I expected it to shout. Warriors throughout Hokkaro shout to show their spirit; Qorin do it to frighten people. But Leng made no sound as it brought its sword down.

"Shizuka!" I shouted.

With your sword, you parried its attack. You shouted so loud, I think you must have been trying to make up for its silence.

A sharp thrust countered its next stroke. How perfect your form was! Your old tutor would've died of joy had he seen it. It pierced Leng's lightly armored underarm.

And the demon laughed. "Virgin Empress," it said. "How honored I am to make your acquaintance."

I drew, fired, drew, fired. Arrows shot right through him and clattered against the stone ground.

Just what did we plan on doing if our weapons didn't work?

"We've been watching you grow," it said. It reached for you

with its off hand. Talons on its gauntlet gleamed. "How beautiful you are now. And more beautiful, you will be, when grown."

"Silence!" you said.

Another cut from you, this time aiming for its arm. Again, your sword went through it. Again, it laughed. Again, I loosed and loosed and loosed. Fear dampened the base of my neck. Nothing was hurting it. Nothing was hurting it and it just kept making that sound like rattling bones and what if this was it, what if you were wrong, what if we were going to die here——?

Cold metal around my throat. My feet lifting off the ground. The smell of day-old corpses left out in the sun. I gasped for breath but felt none coming; I kicked and kicked but didn't connect.

But I could see you, Shizuka. I could see the rage on your face, see your sword hand shake like a teacup in a storm.

"Steel-Eye, the adults are talking. Cease your interruptions."

And then . . .

Oh, you remember the sight better than I do.

It impaled me. I don't remember how it happened or where the blade pierced me, but I do remember my vision going white.

Then it dropped me.

I wish I could say I stood fast. I did not. I fell flat on the ground. Dust choked me. Blood gushed from me so quickly, I felt as if I'd jumped into ice water.

But I saw the flash of gold light, and I heard your voice.

"You come into the home of the gods and you presume to hurt my beloved?" you roared. "Leng! I name you! May your shadows be made flesh!"

How did you know that name? I'd never told you. To this day, Shizuka, I do not know how you did it——but I am grateful you did.

And it was then that Leng made a sound—a soft gasp. I forced myself to my knees. The room was spinning, but I did this anyway. I could see him: his skin like spoiled milk, see his plain black eyes.

"So you have learned that trick!" it shouted. "It will not save you, Empress!"

You came at it. Steel met steel. I struggled to my feet and reached for my blood-soaked bow. I could get a shot off, I think.

Draw, loose. Watch it soar.

Just as Leng raised its sword again, my arrow landed in his neck, near his shoulder. The swing was ruined.

I staggered forward. This was not so difficult. I could hardly feel anything anymore. Any second now, the world would cease to exist, but while it existed we were together, and while we were together we would fight.

Draw, loose. Another solid hit, this time piercing its hip. It screamed; you sliced off its hand. Gouts of black blood spattered across your armor. I thanked the gods we stopped and got it for you.

But Leng caught sight of me again, and the fury of a hundred lifetimes burned in its eyes. In its marrow-sucking voice, he snarled: "Steel-Eye, must you continue pestering me?"

In one hand it held that massive sword. And perhaps the loss of blood did not affect it as it affected me, because it charged toward me with all the ferocity of an animal. A wounded animal.

A tiger.

It started its slash, but never finished.

A thin gold line separated its head from its body.

Behind him, you stood with sword in hand; demon blood staining the Daybreak blade.

And for that small fraction of a second, you were so proud of yourself.

But then the demon's head came off, and it fell forward onto me. And it bled and bled and bled.

I screamed. I screamed and I tried to push it off me but it was so heavy, and then you came, and you screamed, and you pushed it off.

"Don't look down," you pleaded. "Promise me you won't look down."

But I didn't need to.

Because my wound burned like a hot brand rammed into my gut.

"Shizuka," I said. "Shizuka, the blood—"

You touched my cheek. I do not know if you could think of anything else to do; your other hand hovered over the wound. Over your shoulder, I saw the statue of the Daughter shining bright as emeralds.

"You will be fine!" you shouted. "Shefali, you will be fine, but I need you to stand. We are going to your horse. We are going to your horse and you will see a healer and you will be fine—"

I tried to stand. I managed it, barely, and vomited when I did. The burning spread out from my wound. Soon I could feel it: the blackblood, the corruption. The Traitor's evil flowing through my veins and multiplying. Anger, hatred, greed, jealousy—all these emotions swirled within me.

"Look at me!" you said. "Whatever is going on in that thick skull of yours—look at me!"

You kept shouting at me as you led me to my horse.

Except it was not my horse waiting outside. The guard captain and his men were there.

"O-Shizuka-shon!" he shouted. "Your clothes—"

Blood got on you, too, but Leng had not hurt you. "I am all right!" you said. "You insolent fool, you see her struggling and ask after me? Get us a healer!"

But there were no healers for four li in every direction. You knew this. You knew no one was going to be able to help me.

I knew it, too.

My thoughts raced like wild horses. Demon blood. Demon blood in my wound. I was going to die. This was it. In three days, if not sooner, you'd be standing in front of my funeral pyre. I thought of the man your mother killed. I thought of him lying in bed, I thought of the fear on his face, I thought of the panic.

I was going to die.

And suddenly I couldn't breathe.

Suddenly my lungs closed up on me; suddenly I felt as if I were not in my own body anymore. Like a bird looking down on this strange scene. "Die." That word, over and over. I was going to die at sixteen before I got my second braid. I was going to die without marrying you. I was going to die without seeing my brother ever again. I was going to leave you alone and . . .

Yes, I heard you calling.

But as the dark took me, I could not answer.

IT WAS NOT FOR THIS I PRAYED

Imagine you are underwater. Not something I like to imagine, of course, but I am not the one imagining it. You are.

Imagine you are floating in the water, completely submerged. Light filters down onto your face. The water's cold, horribly cold. Shadows play upon your eyelids; strange shapes and colors come into existence. You want to name them, but your mouth is frozen shut. You want to breathe, but you realize your lungs are heavy, realize your chest is full of water. The longer you float, the paler the light on your eyelids.

Imagine that, Shizuka. A peaceful way to die. I wish I could tell you it was like that.

But it was not.

Instead, I floated in a sea of flames. Instead, constant cackling, constant growling filled my ears. Rot and death and burning threatened to empty my stomach. Smoke made my eyes water and my lungs burn. Whenever I coughed, the foulest taste coated my tongue. Like swallowing funeral ashes, Shizuka. Like a ripe plum suddenly gone rotten.

I threw up often. I threw up more than I thought I could. Instead of food, thick, oily black filled the buckets you held out for me.

Worst of all, I could see, and sometimes hear—but I could never speak.

Yes, Shizuka, I saw everything. Through the suffering, I clung to the fuzzy sight of your face. As terrible as I felt—and "terrible" does not begin to cover the anguish I suffered in that bed—you looked worse.

I did not need to sleep, for instance. The fever kept me awake. Or the screaming did; it is hard to tell. But though I felt exhausted, I never felt tired.

I think you wanted to keep me company—to be there when I fell asleep and when I awoke. Insomnia disagreed with your plan. The first time you helped me vomit, you were yourself; the second time, your cheeks sank in a bit; the third time, I thought I must've been sick for five years—how else would you look so different? No, I did not see you sleep in the three days I lay in bed. Nor did I see you eat.

I saw your altercation with the guards. I will say I saw it, at any rate; I saw blurs more than anything. Did they try to take you away from me? For I saw the flash of your blade, and I saw crimson spraying out. Later, I saw flecks of brown-red on your cheeks.

"Come back to me," you said.

You held my hand. Did you wash me before you touched me? I hope you did. I hope you did not touch my marbled blood; I hope you kept yourself safe.

You hung your head. You still wore the butterfly ornaments from the day we went to the temple; their wings fluttered as you moved. In my haze, I swear I saw them fly right off your hair. They landed on my cheeks, turned black, and died.

"Come back to me," you said, and your honey-sweet voice cracked. "Shefali. Please, if you have ever loved me, come back."

I tried to open my mouth, Shizuka, I did. I tried to summon the strength to touch you, but even that was beyond me.

The demons laughed at me. "Look at Steel-Eye, laid so low!" they said. "Are you happy to join the family?"

The voices. The gravel, the rusty knife, the high squeal of a pig in heat. I heard them as if they were in the room with us. As you spoke, I saw them flickering in and out of existence. Shadows in full armor. A woman in robes with tentacles for arms and two mouths lined with needlepoint teeth. A man with a half-bare skull, the tendons and ligaments of his jaw holding on to bone. Laughing.

I forced myself to look away from them. You. Focus on you.

"Shefali," you said. You cupped my cheek. I coughed; you did not draw your hand back. Instead, you sat me up and held a rag to my mouth. You kissed the tips of my ears. I was limp in your arms; you turned me toward you, and my head lolled backwards. With one hand you held up my head just so you could speak to me properly. "You cannot leave me."

Again, I coughed; again, you reached for the rag.

"Listen to me," you said, halfway between angry and afraid. "I . . ."

So exhausted. So hot. So much pain. My blood burned, Shizuka; with every pump of my heart, it seared my veins. A scream welled up in my throat; I writhed because I could not free it.

You wrapped your arms around me and squeezed. "I'm here," you said. "I don't know what's going on behind those eyes of yours, but I'm here."

But I could not stop squirming like a dying serpent. Wet gurgles left me; black spilled from my mouth and trickled down my chin. Shaking. I was shaking, I think.

"Shefali, please," you said. You sniffed. I tried to look at your face, but my eyes did not listen to me; I couldn't focus on anything at all. "This is my fault. Oh, my love, this is my fault. . . .

"Come back," you whispered again, soft and desperate. "You are all I have left."

Fingers going through my hair.

"My mother is dead. My father . . . I hope he is dead, it is better that way."

Your hand in mine.

"My uncle does not care," you said. There it was, the crack in your voice, like porcelain shattering. "You are all I have."

For a moment, you went silent. Then you began to shake, too; then tears fell from your eyes.

"In all the Empire," you croaked, "beneath sky and stars, I swear it eight times—you are all I have."

I closed my eyes.

Fire in my lungs, fire in my veins, everything was burning.

When I opened them next, you loomed over me. Floating behind you were three severed heads, ghastly and dripping with gore. Toothless mouths cackling.

"Steel-Eye!" said one of them. "Did you know your mother lies with your cousin?"

"Steel-Eye!" said the other. "Your father complains about how dark you are! Perhaps if you were light as snow, he'd care about you."

The first one cackled. "Or if you could read!"

I growled at them.

But you recoiled, and guilt stabbed into me. For your lips quivered with unspoken fears, your cheeks were puffed and red from crying, and in your eyes my own anguish was reflected.

"Shefali," you said, your voice low. I could hardly hear you over the demon's cackling. "Barsalai Shefali Alsharyya, I call you now. Eight times I call you. Eight times I beg for you to return. On this, the fourth day of your sickness . . ."

You swallowed. You licked your cracked, swollen lips.

"On this, the fourth day of your sickness, you must be killed," you said.

A shout died on my lips: No, not yet.

But yours was the expression of a young woman who knows her children will not remember their father. Wrath and fury; sorrow and despair; all these mingled together.

You cupped my face and pulled me up toward you. "But I know you are still there, my bullheaded love," you said. "I know you are not dying!"

Spittle flew from your lips. "I have watched the blackblood take a life, and it looks nothing like this!"

So loud, so vehement were you that I thought you were going to slap me.

You did. I did not much feel it; do not let it weigh on your conscience.

"You swore to me we'd be together for all our lives!" you roared. "Are you a woman of your word, or are you a coward?"

Speak. I had to speak. Though I could not breathe, I had to find the wind to shape my words; though fire coursed through me instead of blood, I had to find the will to live.

Speak. Fight. Return.

Over and over I repeated this, over and over I tried to drown out the voices.

No one survives the blackblood. It is an awful disease; in three days, the victim is dead, and on the fourth, they rise as something different.

But I had not died, had I?

No, this could not be death. We were together and I refused to believe that you'd died, too. So I was alive. And if I was alive, then . . .

Then I had already lived longer than anyone else with this affliction.

My mother once attacked a Hokkaran border village. The first time she attacked, she was young and unlearned. While the Qorin made camp at night, the Hokkarans diverted a river toward them. Alshara had to leave in shame—for how could she attack them after such an incident?

But the next village she raided, she made sure to flood beforehand.

So it is with all Qorin. We take the things that defeat us. We use them. We master them.

And I resolved in that moment as you held me that I would do the same for the blackblood. I would not let it kill me. No. I had too much to do. I had a people to rule; I had to ride with you against the Traitor.

No disease would slay me.

I would take this weapon the Hokkarans used against my people, and I would welcome it into myself. I would strike fear into their hearts.

I would become something more than human.

I coughed. I coughed, and coughed again, black spewing out of my mouth. I sat up. With one hand I braced myself; with the other, I cleared the hair out of my face.

I opened my eyes, and there you sat on top of me. And as the dawn breaking over Gurkhan Khalsar, so was your smile.

"Shefali," you said, "you've returned to me."

I ached to kiss you. I could not—if my lips touched yours, they'd bring with them my affliction.

"I would not let it kill me," I said.

You wrapped your arms around me, and I smelled peonies. You pressed your lips to my forehead, and I swear to you the laughing stopped, if only for a moment.

"Good," you said. "I will not allow you to die. Royal decree."

And somehow, despite the color of the blood seeping from my wound, despite the pain and the fever, despite your exhaustion and mine, we laughed.

It did not last long. Knocking on the door roused us from our reverie.

"O-Shizuka-shon! You cannot keep us from entering!"

I looked toward the door. You'd piled all the furniture in the room in front of it. Whoever was on the other side was pounding so hard, everything rattled.

You bit your lip. "I could not let them near you," you said.

I nodded. I needed new bandages; you had no idea how to bandage to begin with, and could not touch me as I was. This was not our bed, and so I did not care what happened to it. I tore cloth from the sheets and set about bandaging myself.

"When I'm done," I said. You nodded. My head throbbed and throbbed. That awful taste was still in my mouth.

But I was alive, and that was all that mattered.

As I finished, you tossed me one of your robes. It was far too small for me—the sleeves ended half past my elbows, and it covered me to the knee only. To say nothing of the fact that you could never wear this again, and it must've cost you more than some villages produce in a year. We had other things to concern ourselves with.

Like what they would say when they saw me standing and breathing.

You helped me to my feet. Again, the doors rattled.

"O-Shizuka-shon, the Emperor's Champion is here to collect you. You will allow us entry, and you will allow us to remove the corpse from this room!"

You winced.

You tried to move the heavy desks and wardrobes you'd forced in front of the door. I think you must've put them there at night, and it must've taken you hours—you struggled against them now, your meager weight not enough to move them.

The wound in my side burned. All of me burned, and my limbs were wrought iron. But I wanted to help you. I grasped one of the desks by its leg and pulled. As easily as a child moves a toy cart, I moved that desk. It felt so light!

You stared at me. "Shefali?"

I cleared my throat again. Do not think about it. There was a reason for it. Probably just my greater size. And I have always been stronger than you. That was surely it.

But I moved the dressers, too, with hardly any effort, and the wardrobe taller than I was. Cold fear prickled the hairs on the back of my neck.

I was still myself. Of course I was. My body was not distorted. I was still Shefali.

You must have thought the same, for you squeezed my arm. "Do not worry, my love," you said. "You have not changed in your appearance."

And it was then that they burst open the doors. Two dozen armed guards just to retrieve you. Two dozen armed guards who stopped in their tracks when they saw me.

I met their eyes, each and every one of them. Some were afraid. Others angered. But that did not change the state of things.

I held up my hands, palms out, to show I was not going to hurt anyone.

You stepped in front of me. "Barsalai Shefali lives," you said.

The guard captain stepped forward. Slack-jawed, he stared at me. With the butt of his spear, he moved my head this way and that. I suffered this, though I know you rankled at it. I did not particularly feel like being impaled that day.

"Oshiro-sun," he said, despite my proper name being used not two moments before. "I saw your wound myself, three days ago. You have the blackblood. How is it you stand here before me? Have you risen?"

A voice in the back of my mind shouted that I should tear his heart out for questioning me. I closed my eyes long enough to banish it. My hand twitched. The guards fell into position as one.

I opened my eyes to find two dozen pikes leveled at my face.

"No," I said. "I didn't die."

"Impossible!" shouted the guard captain. "I saw it myself—"

"And now you see us standing here, Captain, and hear her words," you said. You stood between the two of us, your arms on your hips. "If Uemura-zul is here, then you may bring us to him. But you are not to restrain Barsalai in any way. Am I understood?"

"She's a demon!" shouted one of the men. "Look at her eyes!"

"Sir! We have to kill her, she's enspelled the Imperial Niece!"

I wanted so badly to roll my eyes. As if magic were real, beyond the simple things healers could do. As if we lived in the Age Long Gone, as if anyone had seen a fox woman or a phoenix or even a lion dog in centuries.

"She has not," you said. "I will offer you any proof you like."

You reached for your short sword and pricked your finger. A single ruby of blood flowed from the tip.

It looked delicious, like a cherry ready to be eaten and . . .

I am sorry, my love. My affliction is . . . it is like hearing your most base urges shouted back at you by an entire army. Things that would normally be fleeting distractions become horrible drones.

But if you have read this far, then you deserve to know what I thought, and when I thought it, and all the terrible things that came to mind. As I have wondered what went on behind your amber eyes, so you must've wondered what went on behind my green ones.

And so I say to you now that since my infection, blood has not looked the same. It has not tasted the same, either, on the few occasions I've been made to taste it. Gone is copper, gone is metal. Instead, it is sweet as the first fruits of spring.

I do not consume it. I will not reduce myself to such acts. But I have had to leave a room more than once.

At the time, this was not so familiar to me as it is now. I was sickened by myself. How could I think such a thing about you? About your blood?

What if this was how it started?

You smeared the blood in a lotus shape on your palm and named the Heavenly Family as you did. Your last petal was the Daughter's, and you kissed that one when you were done with it.

"I swear it to be true in blood and spirit, and if I am wrong, may I wilt where I stand. Barsalai has not bewitched me."

A moment of silence. I think they were waiting for you to wilt. Occasionally it has been known to happen with false oaths. Or at least it did, when the gods-in-flesh still roamed.

When you did not wilt, the party relaxed as much as they could when confronted with someone who is possibly a demon.

"Now, Captain," you said, crossing one arm across your chest and gesturing with the bloody one. "Lead us to Uemura-zul. And do be sure to introduce us properly."

The guard captain grit his teeth.

But he did lead us through the barracks; he did lead us out near the Wall. A large pavilion tent with Imperial flags stood not far away. Such tents have always puzzled me. The felt walls of a ger are more warm, more comfortable, than canvas could ever be. Why, then, do outlanders insist on canvas tents? A small tent is one thing. If only one or two people are traveling, a tent is preferable. But any tent large enough to fit four or more should be a ger.

This is a gross failing of your people, and I expect to see it rectified by the time I return. You have the power. Do not disappoint me.

The three of us stepped inside the Imperial tent. I tried not to reach for your hand. It was such a natural thing to do, Shizuka, like breathing, except I was not sure if I was breathing. I was sure that I needed to feel your skin on mine. Though we were only a handspan apart, I might as well have been in Ikhtar.

But we were not in Ikhtar, we were in Shiseiki, and we had a rice-eater to deal with. Uemura Kaito sat in front of a shallow desk. On it, a map of Shiseiki and the lands beyond the wall. He was younger than I expected; five years older than us at most. He kept his hair long, in the old style, tied into a topknot. The tip of his chin was prickly as a hedgehog. Bushy sideburns needed trimming. A thin scar ran from his ear to corner of his mouth. He wore deep green robes beneath gold-trimmed armor. One sword was tucked into his belt.

When we entered, he flashed us a friendly smile. The guard captain announced us. He used my Hokkaran name, of course. Uemura rose and bowed to you from the waist. For me, a short bow from the shoulder. He gestured to two mats for us to sit on.

"O-Shizuka-shon, it is always a pleasure to be near you," he said.

Sycophants disgusted you. I prepared myself for your cutting retort.

"Uemura-zul," you said, "you are courteous as ever, but we both know you did not come here simply to be near to me."

"Would that I did!" he said.

And something bitter rolled in my stomach. By your standards, that was outright inviting!

Wasn't it?

Laughter in my ears. *See how she looks at him, Steel-Eye? She has always admired his sword. . . .*

No. No, no, no. You were just being polite. Just saying hello. You were allowed to speak to other people, I did not own you, you were not a thing to be owned.

But what if?

I squeezed my eyes shut. Forced myself to take a breath.

"Oshiro-sun," he said, "I was told you were . . . injured."

Ah. So he did know I existed.

How to respond? How does one broach that subject? Yes, I was infected with a disease that kills its victims within three days before twisting them into abominations that must be slain lest they slaughter everything in sight. No, I don't feel like slaughtering everything in sight.

I met Uemura's eyes. Silently I nodded.

He tugged at his whiskers. "I was, in fact, told you contracted the blackblood."

"It is true, Uemura-zur. I saw her myself. She wears O-Shizuka-shon's clothing because her own was soaked in demon blood," said the guard captain.

Uemura rapped his fingers on the table. For some time he said nothing. "O-Shizuka-shon," he said. "What have you seen in this matter?"

Your parents did their best to instill in you something like decorum. You were not very good at it, but every now and again, if you tried, you could make your features blank as paper. You did so then.

"Barsalai Shefali was wounded fighting Leng," you said. The captain spat on the ground when you spoke the demon's name. "She now sits before you whole and unharmed. I fail to understand what is so confusing."

"You know well what is confusing," Uemura replied—but he kept his voice light. Friendly. Again, he turned to me. I think this is the most a Hokkaran noble has ever looked at me. "Oshiro-sun, baseless though this rumor may be, I kindly request you allow my healer to examine you. If only to assuage the fears of our guard captain, here."

I stiffened. Healers never liked being near me to begin with. What would they think now? Would they know? How I wanted to reach for your hand. Perhaps then your thoughts could've melded with mine, and we could've made a decision without having to speak to each other.

But I could not.

"Uemura-zul, you cannot be serious. Barsalai Shefali slew a demon four days ago, and you want to have her examined?"

He smiled and laughed. Oil on flame, that was.

"You laugh? Uemura-zul!" you said, rising to your feet. "How many demons have you slain? Or have you never ventured far enough away from my uncle's heels to see one?"

The smile died on his face. "O-Shizuka-shon," he said, his voice low as a stalking cat, "you insult me."

"Your presence insults me," you said.

And I admit I gaped a bit. Not five minutes ago, you were all pleasantries with him. The guard captain eyed me; he must have thought this was my influence on you.

Why not tear his throat out and be done with it?

Because that is not what civilized people do. That is not what I do.

"O-Shizuka-shon," said Uemura. "You will not speak to me in such a way. You are a young girl; your uncle worries for you. I am to bring you home safe. If that means restraining you, I shall not hesitate."

A string snapped between my ears.

I rose. "You will not," I said.

"What did you say?" he said. At this point, his hand fell to his sword. I did not want to hurt him. I did not. Ideally, no one would be hurt here, but . . .

But I could not let them take you away. I could not bear the thought of it.

I stood in front of you. "You will not," I repeated.

"Oshiro-sun," said Uemura. He rose to meet my eyes, or tried to. I had a hand and a half over him in height. "You understand I am the Emperor's Champion?"

I nodded.

"And still you bar my path?"

Again, I nodded.

"I could have you arrested," he said, though I cannot say with any malice. Simply a statement of fact. "You'd remain in the prisons here for years. Is that what you want?"

What I wanted was to hurt him. What I wanted was to strike him down and run off with you. The winds would lead us where we were needed.

Your foot brushed against mine. When I looked to you, your eyes spoke to me: *Stand aside, my love, if only for a moment.*

I did. Begrudgingly.

"The Son of Heaven does not worry about me," you said, your voice calmer and more level than I thought it would be. "He cares about his dynasty. I have the misfortune of being a part of it."

Guards spat on the ground; Uemura winced. May as well slight the Father himself.

"You have been tasked with returning me to the capital. I say to you that I will return, on my own terms, in eight years," you said. "And if you restrain me, you will have to get ahold of me first. Two dozen men you have waiting outside. I would fight them all at once and win."

You paused, daring him to correct you.

"That is why you have not asked me to duel," you continued. "Because you are well aware I would win."

Uemura crossed his arms. "You cannot expect that to work," he said. "O-Shizuka-shon, the Emperor himself sent me. I will not return to Fujino empty-handed because you told me to. Especially not when . . . when Oshiro-sun's health is in doubt."

"It is either you let us leave or I duel you," you said. "And you do not want to duel."

Being defeated by a sixteen-year-old girl would not be good for Uemura. Bad enough if he lost; the Champion was not supposed to lose. But to you? To a girl, to a young girl? No one would take him seriously again. Even if you were O-Shizuru's daughter.

He tugged at his whiskers. "You have insulted me," he said. "I cannot let you escape punishment for that."

You scoffed. "You insulted Barsalai Shefali," you said. "I do not know what you expected to receive in turn. She is too quiet to insult you herself, and so I spoke in her stead."

Uemura and you stared at each other. This was a different sort of duel. If he wanted, he could call for the guards to intervene. We'd have to fight them then. I did not trust myself in such a situation.

We could surrender to him. We could let him lead us back to Fujino, where your uncle would marry you off to whoever curried the most favor with him, and I would likely be put to death for my condition.

You could challenge him. You would win. I'd never seen him touch a sword, but I knew you would win.

Finally his posture relaxed. "If Oshiro-sun consents to an examination, then I will consent to your request," he said.

I grunted. So it was up to me, then. I thought of you. I thought of your reputation, I thought of your stake on the throne. If this came to blows, you might lose favor.

You looked to me, your brows knit with concern. "You do not have to," you whispered.

And then your face changed. Then your porcelain skin cracked; then your hair fell from your head in clumps; your tongue became a wriggling worm and maggots crawled out of your eyes.

"You could kill everyone in this room," you said.

Except it was not you. The awake part of my mind knew this, but there you were—there it was—staring me down and smiling with blackened teeth. My stomach turned inside out. I staggered backwards.

"Shefali?"

Was that your voice? Was that the Not-You's voice? Laughing, laughing, why couldn't they just leave me alone? People were going to see. I took a few deep, rattling breaths and tried to blink away the apparition. Gradually its face melted back into yours.

"Shefali, are you all right?"

You reached for me. You. The real you. Sweat trailed down my forehead. I licked my lips and stood, knowing the sort of scrutiny you'd get for letting me touch you.

"Doctors," I said.

For I no longer had the luxury of hiding it, and, more important, I needed to know if I would get worse. I needed to know if I would get bad enough that I might hurt you.

I REMEMBER EVERYTHING the doctors did, sharp as the knives they cut me with. As soon as I was taken into their rooms, the guards barred the doors, and no matter how much you shouted, they would not let you in.

Four of them piled on top of me. With great steel chains, they bound my hands and feet. One of them cut through my clothing, cut through that beautiful robe you'd lent me and tossed it to the floor like a pile of rags.

They called it an examination. They cut me over and over, to better collect my blood. They reopened my wound. They referred to me as "it," as "the demon." They heated a knife and held it against my skin to see if I felt pain. When I yelped and pulled away, they continued, for they had to see if I'd become a blackblood then and there, if my limbs would suddenly break and re-form into something great and terrible. The lead doctor pointed out my many scars, my height, the lean muscles of my arms. These things were "barbaric," he said. But he made certain to joke that I arrived in such a state and it had nothing to do with the demon's blood coursing within me.

Hokkarans hunt tigers. Trap tigers, I should say. They dig huge pits and cover them with leaves. When the tiger steps on it, it falls far enough down that it cannot easily leap back up. Hokkarans stand at the edge of the pit, firing arrows into the tiger until it dies.

Maybe the tiger we killed is haunting me in more ways than one. At least the hunters are smart enough to make sure the tiger does not leave the pit alive.

Yes, I was a wounded tiger when I loped out of that room, wounded and sick with hatred. They gaped at me in fear because they knew I could squash them between my fingers. With my bare hands, I could reach into their guts and tear out all the things that kept them alive. I could do these things and I could've escaped those bonds—but, Shizuka, Shizuka, I did not want them to take you back. I did not want to kill them.

No, that is a lie. I wanted to kill them.

But I did not want you associated with such an act. I did not want blood to soak your reputation; I did not want people to whisper about the company you kept. All I had to do was endure. A little pain, a lot of shame, and . . .

I should've killed them. I should've listened to the disembodied heads that watched as they cut into me. I should've slaughtered them.

Upon seeing me, your whole countenance twisted. The Mother herself feared you in that moment. Your delicate hands became talons; your doll-like features now were a war mask.

"What have you done?" you roared at the doctor.

"We gave Oshiro-sun a thorough examination," said the lead doctor.

Already I was not in my own body. Already I leaned against you for support and did not care who saw. But as the doctor spoke, I saw the Not-You standing behind him, cackling.

I whimpered.

"We have determined she is, indeed, infected with the blackblood; how she lives, we do not know. All blood drawn ran black as the Traitor's Heart, yet the subject seems docile enough. Certainly it did not—"

"You shall cease talking," you snarled. "You shall fall to your knees and you shall apologize for what you have done. You shall crawl, on elbows and knees, back to Uemura-zul's tent. You shall tell him what you have done, in detail. You shall tell him I have sent you in such a state. Go. Crawl. If you stop for a single moment, I will cut off your hands."

And as he sank to his knees, the Not-You sank with him. Its head twisted all the way around on its neck, like an owl's, so that it could stare at me.

I could not stand it, Shizuka. I turned away. I did not want to return to Uemura's tent, I did not want to look at it, I did not want to hear the awful voices in my mind. I wanted it all to stop. I longed for darkness; I longed for the silence of the steppes. Anything.

Anything that was not this pitiful excuse for an existence.

Did you glance down the hallway before you kneeled next to me? Did you check if anyone saw us? For you pressed your forehead to mine and you embraced me in the way lovers do.

"Shefali," you said, "do not worry. I am here now, my love; you are safe. I am sorry. If it . . . You have suffered so much on my account, and . . ."

And there comes a point when one has suffered so much in one day that one no longer feels, that one no longer exists. A snuffed candle leaving only a smoldering wick and smoke.

For me it was that moment. I could think of nothing to say. The word "suffering" meant nothing until I woke from my deathbed. Now it was everywhere. It was the air I breathed, it was the beating of my heart, it was my blood and my flesh and my bones.

We did not leave the Wall that day.

When we returned to our rooms, you held me close and whispered in my ear of better days. You told me of your garden and all the flowers you had. You recited to me from memory the letters we'd written to each other as children. You told me with such certainty, with such fire, that everything would be all right. That you would never let anyone hurt me again.

You kept whispering until you fell asleep, but I stayed awake.

* * *

THAT NIGHT—and most nights since—I lay awake, staring at the ceiling. Though I tried to calm myself enough to sleep, though I closed my eyes and prayed to all the gods for just a moment of peace, nothing came.

Only the Not-You. Only its taunting. Only its fungus-stained nail dragging down my cheek.

"Come with me, my love," it said. "Leave her behind. Kiss me, that you might taste true power."

I turned away and nuzzled closer to you.

Still I felt it there next to me. "Does it not bother you how you are treated?"

I shook my head.

"Does it not bother you, how she makes you suffer? How she swears to keep you safe but only hurts you?"

Bile in my mouth.

"Think of what you could do on your own, Steel-Eye. What you could do with me at your side. All you have to do is crush her throat. Simple as that. Hokkaro will crumble without an Empress to lead it. You and yours will overtake it. Never again will you struggle beneath their heels, Steel-Eye. You could do it."

I covered my ears, knowing it would not help.

Its wormy tongue lapped at my earlobe. "But you are weak, aren't you? You've always been weak. A coward. When was the last time you slew a man with your sword? I do not think you could do it. So you will weep in your bed like a child rather than do what needs to be done."

You woke to the sound of my weeping.

* * *

FOR MANY NIGHTS it was like that. I did not leave our rooms, and so you did not, either. Uemura called on you. You wrote him a polite—if dismissive—letter informing him you would not leave until I felt ready to travel. You mentioned, casually, that the doctors who "examined" me should be imprisoned. So they were.

Two weeks we stayed in Shiseiki. I slept twice in that time, and ate perhaps four times. I no longer felt hungry, no longer felt sleep calling to me. Only in the dark hours of the night did I leave the room. I left the barracks altogether, mounted my horse, and rode for a few hours.

What did I have to fear from the dark?

Demons? I was near enough to one.

Bandits? Let them come, I could throw them like toys.

Guards? I was a monster to them. A thing to be avoided.

So I split my time between you and my horse, the two most important women in the world. Alsha did not try any of her smart tricks. No, she cantered about as if I were a child. That was fine with me. I did not want to go too fast. I did not much want to do anything.

It was on one such nighttime ride that I saw campfires in the distance. I was out farther than the patrols went.

I found myself riding closer. If they were bandits, I could end them. I might welcome the distraction it'd bring to the demons haunting me. If they were not bandits, I could leave and bring back word of what I'd seen.

But the closer I came, the clearer it was: three bright white gers guarded by one dozen braided warriors.

My mother had finally found us.

OUR SLEEVES, WET WITH TEARS

I did not spend much time around your mother, and for this I will always feel some regret. O-Shizuru exists in stories as a dark woman, hands forever coated with blood, trailed always by crows. I know these stories cannot hope to capture her essence, just as the stories of my mother fail to capture hers.

But I remember distinctly the way she spoke about her position. Imperial Executioner. Whenever the subject came up, she would scoff. Once, I awoke in the middle of the night, after dreaming a dragon ate my leg, and I saw your mother sitting with a cup in one hand and a bottle in the other. Her gray-streaked hair was all a mess.

"I'm no executioner," she said. "Yoshimoto calls me that only so he can feel better about himself. I am either his butcher or his last resort." And here I remember she took a sip of her rice wine, which was always at her side. "Bandits or blackbloods. That's all

I ever fight. He never sends me after nobles, never has me act as anyone's second. Between the two, Shefali-lun—between things that were once people I liked, and people who turn to robbery to fill their bellies, I'd rather have . . ."

I never got to hear her answer. Your father emerged not long after that, and with gentle words convinced her that it was time for bed.

I have thought on that moment many times since then. Which is worse—to confront the dead you once knew, or to confront strangers you sympathize with? Whose blood is heavier?

I will tell you:

The worst thing in life is to face your family after you have shamed them. For the moment I spotted my mother's white felt ger, I knew that if I told her of my condition, I might as well be killing her.

I wished it'd been bandits instead. If bandits approached camp, I'd know precisely what to do: draw my bow and fire until no one remained. If guards caught me, then I would've raced them back to the barracks. They would have had no hope of catching me on my good Qorin mare.

But she was my mother. My mother, who hated boats as much as I did, and warned me as a child never to take one. My mother, who abhorred leaving the steppes for any reason, except to see your mother. From what I knew, she had not been to the Wall of Flowers since she traveled with O-Shizuru and the Sixteen Swords. What was initially a mission to clear out invading blackbloods became a lasting warning against confronting them.

Oh, our mothers slew one of the Traitor's Generals—for this, the entire Empire sang your mother's praises—but every one of the other Swords died in the effort. Fourteen of the most renowned warriors in Hokkaro, from all walks of life. General Kikomura fought alongside a cobbler from southern Fuyutsuki Province. The youngest daughter of silk merchants, a man with grand-children about to marry. All that mattered was their swordplay—and look where that got them. Whatever triumph our mothers felt was tempered by the loss of their companions.

No, my mother had not returned to Shiseiki since she spent eight days in a cave being tortured. Yet here she was; here was her ger with its banner flapping in the wind.

She did not know what had happened to me. I could not tell her. I could not. My affliction, so feared by my people, had not killed me. Instead, I felt myself becoming something else.

Should I run? I sat frozen in the saddle. Should I run from my own mother, rather than tell her what had happened? Should I rouse you from your slumber, and ask you what to do? What if our riders spotted me first—what then? What was I going to do, what was I going to say? As far as she knew, I'd run off on some bullheaded adventure. She could not know. She could not imag-ine the thoughts drifting through her daughter's mind, could not know how afraid I was to leave the room when I knew others would be near.

But I could no longer listen to the voices calling me a coward.

Before all this happened, I faced a tiger, and felt no fear. Before all this, I faced a demon. I was Tiger-Striped Shefali, not Shefali the Fearful. And if I could endure the pain of a slow death, I could endure the shame of returning to my mother's ger.

And so I rode toward the bright white gers. And so I dismounted. Temurin, standing outside my mother's ger, had to look twice to confirm it was me.

"Barsalai!" she called, and she reached for me, she tried to take me by the shoulder and embrace me. "Burqila has traveled long to find you."

I recoiled from her touch, not out of malice, but concern. Some small part of me worried even that contact would infect others.

Temurin stared at her four-fingered hand. A deep frown engraved itself onto her brown skin, her wrinkles only adding to it. Our most loyal guard was earning a crown of gray hairs for her service. I had not noticed them before I left; when did they appear?

"Barsalai, you do not want my greeting?"

I licked my lips. No, I did want her greeting. I wanted everyone's. But if she sniffed my cheek, she might smell the rot that hung around me like a cloud. I could not risk making her sick.

"Mother," I said.

"You are acting strangely," Temurin said, crossing her arms. "You will not let me smell you—how am I to know you are truly Barsalai? You might be a demon wearing her form."

I opened my hand, closed it. My fingers twitched. My nostrils flared. Why was I standing around, listening to this, when I could barrel through?

No. Those were not my thoughts.

Instead, I leaned forward and sniffed both Temurin's cheeks. She smelled of old leather and horses. Yes, that was Temurin as I remembered her. She took me by the shoulders, and I forced myself to relax. I cannot deny the fear that grasped me as she pressed her nose to my cheek. What if, what if? What if this simple act killed her?

When she pulled away, she wrinkled her nose. "You smell different," she said, "like too-sweet flowers."

I flinched.

"Mother," I said again, my voice more sharp this time.

She narrowed her grassy eyes at me. "All right," she said. "Barsatoq must be turning you into something more Hokkaran, I suppose. Go in. Burqila is sleeping. If it is you, she will not mind being awoken."

I opened the red door.

Four bedrolls laid out around the fire pit. No warm orange light filled the inside; the pit had long since turned to ash. Only the roof of the ger allowed any sort of brightness. At the center of the roof was a small opening to see the stars through. On full moon nights, this illuminated a ger nicely.

That night was not a full moon night.

And yet I saw perfectly in the dark. I stepped among the sleeping bodies of my family with ease. Scattered pots and pans, bows tucked under pillows, empty waterskins and bowls—I avoided all of them. I do not want to say that the room was not dark in my vision, for it was. But it was not . . . not so deep, I suppose. Ink in water.

I found my mother sleeping on the western side of the ger. I shook her awake. She shot up and immediately reached for the knife she kept beneath her pillow. She got as far as grabbing me by the hair and pressing it to my throat before she realized whom she was about to kill.

Her lips parted. A sound escaped them akin to a mouse's squeak. She dropped the knife and touched my face, cleared my hair away.

"Mother," I whispered.

She drew me close and sniffed my cheeks. She squeezed me so tight, my back cracked; she rocked with me back and forth.

My mother swore an oath of silence at sixteen. I was sixteen then as she embraced me, as the soft sounds of tears filled the tent like clashing swords.

I was sixteen when I heard my mother speak for the first time.

I thought I imagined it. Honestly, I did. The voices must be taunting me. It was not my mother. It could not be my mother.

Except this voice was not like the others. It was warm and sweet and rich, like spiced tea thick with honey.

"You're safe," she whispered.

My jaw dropped. I did not know what to say; I was not safe, but my mother was so worried, she had actually spoken and . . .

No. I would not tell her tonight. Instead, I let her hold me. I let her count my fingers and toes, as she had when I was a child, and check me for new scars. The wound Leng gave me had already healed by then; she saw no trace of it. Even the cuts the surgeons gave me had healed. To my mother's trained eyes, there was nothing wrong with me.

After a few minutes of this, she grabbed a pot and banged her knife against it until the entire ger sprang awake. The entire ger cursed, too, but I do not blame them. It was long past Last Bell; no one in their right mind is awake at such an hour. Otgar, her mother, her father, and another one of my aunts angrily rubbed their eyes.

"Burqila," Otgar murmured, "I swear by Grandmother Sky, you must be deaf as well as mute—"

She stopped upon seeing me. A grin spread across her wide, flat face. She pulled me into a hug so fast and so tight, I slammed right into her, but she was the one who staggered backwards.

"Cousin Needlenose!" she said, quickly sniffing my cheeks. "Did you get heavier, lugging all Barsatoq's things around?"

And it made me chuckle. After all these months, that is what Otgar said to me.

"Your laugh tells me it is true!" she said, slinging an arm around me.

My aunts and uncles gathered around and welcomed me home, despite the hour. We lit a fire. We drank kumaq together, and no one questioned where I'd been. No one questioned what I'd been up to.

No one questioned why I did not sleep.

In the morning, I excused myself from the revelries. I needed to return to you, and I wanted to do so before too many people were out. Otgar demanded to come along. After all, the last time I left camp alone, I ran off to the north to fight demons.

A man leaves home to fight for the Emperor. When he leaves, he is a young man, perhaps twenty-two. His wife is pregnant. He swears to her he will return before their son is named. For ten years, he serves. Only when he loses an arm does the Emperor discharge him. The man returns home, traveling through the Empire on his own. He dreams of what kind of boy his son has grown to be. He decides to spend his meager earnings on books and ink for his son. When he reaches his old house, he does not recognize the weathered woman on the porch as his wife, does not realize the young girl selling flowers at market is his daughter. His home is the same—but nothing else is.

So it was with me. Every time I saw myself I was surprised. No, that could not be my reflection. It had not changed. My features were as dark as ever, my nose just as thin, my lips just as full, my hair the same shade of flaxen blond. My eyes had not changed color—still tea-leaf green. How was that possible when my mind was so different? How was it possible, after what I had suffered?

I kept my thoughts to myself. Otgar did not know, and I was not going to tell her.

Lucky for me, she had other concerns.

"You've got some explaining to do, Needlenose," she said when we were out of earshot.

I stiffened. My cousin spoke in her usual jovial manner. On the surface, nothing was amiss. She had no reason to suspect me.

But that does not stop the demons whispering in my ears that she knows. That she is going to tell my mother. That she and my mother . . .

I swallowed. No. Demons lie.

"That's right," Otgar said. "You should be afraid. Did you think you could bed the heir to this gods-forsaken Empire in my ger and get away with it? My ger, that I made with my own two hands?"

Oh.

I coughed. My cheeks felt hot. I was so wrapped up in my own troubles, I'd not considered that.

I opened my mouth to say something apologetic. She slapped me hard on the shoulder. It did not hurt as much as she expected it to.

"You've always hunted dangerous game," Otgar said. "Always picked the most difficult path. But this time you've really outdone yourself. Are you aware what will happen if others find out?"

As if I had not had nightmares about your people finding out. But wait a moment.

"You are not angry?"

She scoffed, staring at me as if I'd asked a question with an obvious answer. After a few seconds of this, her disbelief only grew. "Barsalai," she said. "You truly did not notice?"

I frowned and shook my head. I did not know what game my cousin played at, but I did not much like it.

"Barsalai, your mother loved Naisuran."

"Obvious," I said. My mother only ever smiled in your mother's presence. Of course she loved her. They'd been through unimaginable pain together; their friendship was forged from heavenly steel.

Otgar palmed her face. She tugged at her gelding's reins and brought him to a stop.

I am sure you know by now that Qorin do not stop riding until they've reached their destination, or their camp for the night. It is very bad luck. So Otgar spat on the ground before she continued speaking.

"Barsalai," she said. "Crawl out of your lovesick cave for one moment and listen to what I am saying. Your mother loved Naisuran. Loved her."

"Obvious," I repeated. Anyone could see what good friends they were. The two of them used to exchange war stories though my mother never spoke. Shizuru never learned a word of Qorin, but she still knew what Alshara wrote or signed just from reading her body.

Otgar tugged at her hair. "Barsalai," she said, her voice curt. "Your mother wanted to bed Naisuran."

What?

No.

No, no, no. That could not . . . no. My mother had two children. My mother had never in my sixteen years brought a lover into the ger. Certainly she and my father did not speak, ever, but that did not mean they were unfaithful. I'd never seen my father with a lover either. No, I did not see him as often, but . . . it just could not be. Not my mother. Not Burqila Alshara.

"Why do you think," Otgar said, "I had to go fetch her after Naisuran died? Because she wanted to go on a trading trip?"

No, she was just mourning her only friend—it was not that out of the ordinary!

I must've been gaping. I cannot imagine the look on my face. You will have to imagine it. I'm certain you know it better than I do.

Otgar pinched her temples. She took a deep breath. "Your mother keeps a clipping of Naisuran's hair with her to this day," Otgar said. "She wears it beneath her deel, where no one will see. It is the only such favor she received."

As she spoke, her voice rose higher and higher.

"No matter what Burqila did, she could not win Naisuran over. Her many fearsome deeds, her prowess with a sword, her skill as a Kharsa, her beauty—none of these caught Naisuran's attention. A poet did. A poet, Shefali! A man who never saw a day of battle in his life, over Alshara!"

Alshara.

Otgar used my mother's birth name.

My tongue stuck to the roof of my mouth. This was not how one spoke about an aunt. The demon's words echoed between my ears: *Your mother lies with your cousin, Steel-Eye.*

Otgar's eyes went wide. She covered her mouth, as if to try to hold in the words she'd already spoken. "It . . . It is a very sad story," she mumbled. But she did not meet my eyes. "I only meant to say that you must be careful, Shefali. If her people find out, they will not be so accepting. Remember how her uncle hates us. He could have you executed."

I grunted. Though birds soared overhead, though the wind rustled tree branches, I heard only screaming. Laughing.

"You should trust us more, Steel-Eye!" they said.

I screwed my eyes shut. My cousin meant well, she did. I am

certain she set out to do nothing more than berate me, possibly congratulate me. But she did not know what was going on in my mind at the time. She could not have known what a storm would envelop me.

My mother loved your mother.

My mother wanted to bed your mother.

What did she think, then, of the two of us?

And why did Otgar use my mother's birth name?

We rode the rest of the way in silence. When we reached the barracks, the guards questioned me. Who was this other . . . woman? A pause there. They meant to say "barbarian," of course, but they did not know if Otgar spoke Hokkaran.

"Dorbentei Otgar Bayasaaq is my name," she said, sounding for all the world as if she were born and raised in Fujino. "I am Barsalai Shefali's cousin."

"True cousin?" said the guard.

"No," said Otgar. "False cousin. I was created from a vat of clay by my mother, who happened to be Burqila's sister."

The guards blinked.

"Yes!" snapped Otgar. "I am her true cousin!"

It was only after some muttering that they let us in. I had Otgar wait outside while I spoke to you. I found you pacing our rooms, racked with worry. You, too, held me tight; you covered my face in burning kisses; you smelled me; you whispered into my ear that you missed me. In your embrace, I felt human again. Something about your voice drowned out the chorus of insults.

"Fool Qorin," you said. "Leaving in the middle of the night. I thought . . ."

I squeezed your arm. I was here. That was the important thing.

"Did you get any rest?" you said.

Pain in my chest. You fell asleep so quickly, and so deeply, that you had not noticed I left most nights.

I did not want to lie to you. If I did, the demons would approve. Nothing they approved of was good. Beyond that, it is hard to look at you and lie. It is as if the truth shines from your eyes.

But all this was becoming so heavy. My mother and her feelings, whatever they were. Otgar's strange outburst.

The demon blood coursing through my veins.

I could not do this alone.

"No," I said. "I do not sleep anymore."

Your amber eyes widened; you paused. You looked as if someone had struck you. I regretted speaking—I hated seeing you like this, knowing that my state of existence brought you pain.

"Shefali," you said. You cupped my face. "My love. We will find some way to heal you, and we will leave this place soon. You and I will find some place all our own. We will find somewhere quiet, somewhere you can ride your horse, and I will be safe from the court's prying eyes. And we will find a way to heal you. This I swear."

The only way to cure me is to kill me, I think, but I did not say that to you then. For you were so full of hope. Gods, Shizuka, it is so hard to look at you sometimes. I feel as if my whole being bends to your will; as if I have no choice but to follow wherever you may lead. What a terrible thing, to love someone so completely! What awful joy!

"We should leave today," you said. "Before your mother arrives."

"She has," I said.

You winced. "Do you want to tell her?"

I shook my head. Truth be told, I was not sure I wanted to return. My mother keeping something so important from me for so many years left a bad taste in my mouth, and my stomach twisted at the thought of seeing her and Otgar in the same ger.

This was my family. This was my home. And yet it felt alien now, or the people did. As if I'd been living with strangers my whole life.

"Shefali," you said, "she will hear, one way or another. Would you not prefer she heard it from you?"

I'd prefer she never learn that her daughter found the sight of blood appetizing, but I knew that was unlikely.

I looked at my feet. "Shizuka," I said.

You instantly looked up, stopped pacing, and came near to me. "Yes?" you said. "Is something wrong? Did something happen? Say the word, and I will find whoever—"

"My mother is like me," I said. "With women."

You tilted your head, squinted. "Like us?" you said. "How are you sure?"

"Dorbentei," I said. "Dorbentei told me. She said—"

The words stuck in my throat. What I wanted to say: *She said Alshara loved your mother.* But what left me was a strangled sound, a whimper. I laid my head against your shoulder; you ran your fingers through my hair.

Perhaps you sensed I was not done speaking. You scratched my head and whispered to me that it would be all right, that you would wait as long as I needed.

But there was so much I wanted to say. My mother loved yours and never told me. My cousin speaks of my mother in terms too familiar; my thoughts weren't my own anymore; my mother didn't know what happened to me, and I did not want to tell her.

There was just so much going on.

Wet lips against my ear. The smell of soggy death.

"Why not leave?" it said. "You can distract that cousin of yours easily enough. Leave, Steel-Eye. Why face such foul people ever again, when you can do so much more on your own?"

I forced myself to swallow the razors in my throat, grabbed handfuls of your beautiful robes. My decision was made.

I would not be the person my demons wanted me to be. I would not run from these mounting problems.

I held you at arm's length. When I spoke, it was more clearly, more loudly. "She said my mother loved yours," I said.

You leaned in, cocked a brow, parted your lips. The sort of face one makes when they are sure they've misheard something. "As more than a friend?"

I nodded.

Fingers flew to lips. Your delicate brow furrowed in thought. "My mother loved my father," you said. "They did not stray. They could not tear their eyes from each other."

"Your mother did not love mine," I said.

Your shoulders slumped. You sat on the bed, head perched on your hand, the bells in your hair singing a bright song. "Do you remember, Shefali," you said, "when we were eight?"

"The tiger?"

"The feast," you said. "Or the next morning. You were in your ger at the time, and your mother, too. My mother got it in her hungover head to say good-bye to Burqila's mare."

I flinched. One did not touch a Kharsa's horse. Not unless one had a death wish, or . . . well, a husband could touch his wife's horse. No one would question that. But Shizuru's husband was a Hokkaran poet, not the Kharsaq.

"I told her it was a fool thing to do, since horses cannot speak.

She ignored me. I remember she touched that mare between the eyes, fed it a sweet, and told it to behave."

How on earth did no one see that? But, then, most of us were hungover that morning, and we left very early on.

"My father saw her do this, too," you said. "And this is the only time I can recall he ever raised his voice to her. 'Shizuru,' he said, 'you would not do that if you knew what it meant.'" You paused. "I do not know what it means."

"Married," I said.

At this, you spared a bitter smile. "Is that why you insisted we ride together?"

Ah, I'd been discovered. To hide my guilt, I kissed you.

"You could have just proposed and saved us all the time," you said.

We were thirteen then! You would not have said yes. In no way would you have said yes. Even if you had, that was entirely too young to enter a marriage.

Except I knew full well it would've given you three years to pay your bride-price, and you would've said yes without a moment's thought.

Your voice stayed warm as tea when you continued. "When my mother heard my father, when she heard his tone, she rounded on him. One finger in the air, like she was reprimanding me for breaking pottery. 'Itsuki,' she said, 'it means nothing, and will never mean anything, save that Alshara is my dearest friend.' My father said nothing to that, but the ride home was the quietest it has ever been, and my mother did not come to dinner that night. I thought it strange at the time."

Now it was you who leaned on me.

"I suppose it makes sense now."

We sat in the silence of our shared shock.

Then, as always, you spoke first. "I feel sorry for her," you said. "It is an awful thing, to long for someone you cannot have."

You did not look at me; instead, you focused on the box I kept my bow in, hanging from a hook across the room.

"Do not let it get to your head, Shefali," you said, "but I do not think I could ever live without you."

And yet on this very night, my Shizuka, you lie in the palace in rooms of your own choosing. On your grand bed covered in silk and flowers, you read this. Perhaps there is another woman at your side—I will not fault you if there is. It has been so many years, hasn't it? Of course there is someone else warming your bed. You have always been more physical than I am, have always longed to sink your teeth into the flesh of another. No, I cannot fault you.

If we were like any other Qorin couple, such things would be commonplace. We have a saying, you see—you can never have one horse. Your sprinter is not your packhorse is not your long-distance steed. How different would things be, then, if we were together? Would I be your packhorse, Shizuka—or your sprinter?

Tumenbayar herself had more than one husband—did you know? Batumongke was her favorite, but there were others.

One day, Ages ago, when there were only two hundred stars in the sky, Tumenbayar was riding her horse and exploring the northern steppes. She found a man half-buried in the dirt, with hair the color of leaves, handsome as a man can be. He called out to her for help, for he'd been stuck in that spot for years now.

Tumenbayar took pity on him—and on his good looks—and threw her pure-white rope around him. She hauled him up out of the ground. That was when she saw the man's bottom half was thick with gnarled roots, and his skin was rough as bark.

"I thought I might take you as my lover," she said, "but if I took you in my arms, you'd tie me to this barren place."

The man pleaded with her. He sang her songs sweet as the first blossom of spring. Poetry dropped from his lips as easily as dewdrops. Over and over he promised that he would not tie her to the north.

And so Tumenbayar indulged him, and she married him for a night—but before the morning light could find them, she mounted her mare and left him there.

The man was so distraught that he tore his hair out and threw it, and wherever it landed, new trees grew. Every morning he'd hobble a little bit farther south, closer to the steppes proper, and every morning, he'd pull his hair out.

So the northern forests came to be.

I wonder, my Shizuka—have you sprouted any forests for me? Though you know how I hate trees, I think I might enjoy wandering through yours.

I THINK WE would've kissed each other all that day and into the night if left to our own devices.

Otgar knocked on the door after perhaps five minutes. "Are you done in there, Barsalai?" she called in Qorin. "You are not going to make your cousin wait while you rut, are you?"

I grimaced. You did not need to speak Qorin to know when I was being summoned back. We pulled away; I fixed your hair as best I could, you smoothed my dress—another you'd lent to me. We'd not gone further than kissing, and we hadn't since my injury. Blackblood is a volatile thing—I could not bear the thought of infecting you.

But my cousin did not know that.

She did, however, know that I was not happy with her. If we had been engaged in such activities, then I would've done my best to be as loud as possible out of spite. But we were not, and so we prepared ourselves to leave.

"We will not tell your mother," you said, "but I think traveling with her would be wise. At least until we reach Xian-Lai."

Yes, that did sound like a good plan, though I was not sure how to behave around my own mother anymore. Was I going to speak to her about Otgar? About Shizuru? What would I say? What a strange conversation it would be. Either I had to wait for her to write her answer on her slate, or Otgar would translate.

And I was not so sure I wanted to see Otgar around my mother.

Only after a few seconds did it occur to me what you'd said. "Xian-Lai?" I said. "Kenshiro?"

You nodded. "As good a place as any to hide from the court."

The thought of seeing my brother, too, made me feel lighter. Ten years had passed since I last saw him. He was married now, and a magistrate, too. I wondered if he still spoke Qorin or if he'd forgotten it. He'd better start practicing.

We left the room, you and I, and we took our meager belongings with us. Otgar greeted you and said she was happy you were safe. She did not bring up our relationship, not with so many people near. But she did not bring it up on the ride to camp, either.

As we rode, we spoke of things that did not matter: the beauty of the Hokkaran countryside, the food, the lack of kumaq. I said nothing, and you as little as you could. Your eyes kept darting toward me.

When we arrived at camp, the feast had already started. There was nothing to do to get out of it. Qorin feasts involve everyone around them, whether they know it or not.

And so we sat on the eastern side of the ger, near to my mother and near to Otgar, and I watched Otgar speak for her, saw the way she looked at my mother, saw things that were not there. And when we danced around the fire later that night, I held on tighter to you than normal, and when you asked in hushed tones if I was all right, I told you that I would have to be.

Long after kumaq sent the toughest to their beds, I lay awake inside the ger. The scent of burning singed my nostrils. My stomach felt swollen and heavy, though I'd had only one cup of soup. You slept in my bedroll, curled up against me, and I counted the bumps of your spine to pass the time.

And so it became the pattern of our days. In the morning, we rose with the clan and broke our fast. We'd ride for a few hours after that, careful to keep from straining our horses. My mother chose to avoid towns when possible. I do not blame her for this; whenever we so much as used a main road, we were met with derision. It is strange how highway patrols never appeared when it was just you and I traveling—but when we traveled with the clan, they were everywhere.

"Who among you speaks Hokkaran?"

That is how it would start. And before Otgar could open her mouth, you'd go to the front of the caravan.

"I do," you'd say. "And I imagine I speak it better than you do. What seems to be the problem?"

The patrolmen were never comfortable with the sight of you.

When they spoke, they asked two questions, but voiced only the one.

"Where are you going?" they said out loud. Are you traveling of your own will?

"We are traveling south," you'd respond. "Is it suddenly illegal for a caravan to travel south on a public road?"

"Barsatoq, I think it might be illegal for Qorin," Otgar piped in. She rode next to my mother. Too close to my mother. Throughout our journey, I had done my best to avoid the two of them. With you near, it was an easy thing to do; we rode ahead of them, and I listened to your golden voice. But when we were all together in the ger at night, when I had to watch Otgar voice my mother's words, my stomach twisted.

"Forgive us our caution," said one of the guards. "We have had reports of bandits, given the Troubles."

And even though I go cross-eyed whenever I try to read it, I know that in Hokkaran a single character may have a hundred different meanings. A skilled poet bears this in mind when he writes. Your father, for instance, was famed for writing poems that could be read three different ways, and be beautiful in each one. Yet if your father tried to wrangle the many meanings of "Troubles," his head would spin. From crops withering overnight to bandits to stillborn babes—all things were Troubles in those days.

"You will find no bandits among us," you said.

"Do we have your word, Noble Lady?"

Our word, of course, was not good enough. They had to hear it from you. Even though they had not recognized you as the Imperial Niece, though they knew nothing of you, they valued your oath above ours.

"Yes," you said, exasperated. "You have my word. What is your name?"

"Kikomura Kouta, Honored Lady," he said.

"Very well, Kikomura-zun," you said. "To whom do you report?"

"Honored Shiseiki-tur," he said.

"Keichi, or Toji?" you asked. By now, Kikomura was shifting his weight on the balls of his feet. You were not using honorifics. That meant you stood above both Keichi, the son, and Toji, Lord of Shiseiki. He could not answer using their names—that would be a great offense. You'd put him in quite a position.

You sat, preening, on your saddle.

He bowed. "With respect, Honored Lady, it is the younger Shiseiki-tur I serve."

Impressive for a guardsman.

"You may return to Keichi-tun, and you may tell him O-Shizuka-shon gives her word she will not raid any villages," you said.

To say he turned the color of milk would do a disservice to milk. I have never in my life seen a man bow so low to the ground. Up and down, up and down, like a bamboo fountain, until his forehead was covered in dirt. My clan laughed. I almost did, too, but I felt a measure of sympathy for him. How was he supposed to know he was speaking to you? It was not as if you wore your name around your neck for all to see.

But after some time, you dismissed him, and we continued on our way.

Three, four times this happened. Guards stopped us. You, or sometimes Otgar, would explain that we were just passing through.

They'd ask for our word that we meant no harm. They'd leave, and we would grouse. One would think the highway guards would communicate a bit more; they'd save themselves an awful lot of trouble.

But no. Again and again, it happened.

So it was that the eighth time we were stopped along the road, we did not bother listening to the guardsman.

"We mean no harm, you have our word," you snapped. "We are simply traveling. Go. Do not trouble us further, or my family will hear of it."

This man did not recognize you either, but he recognized your sharp dismissal.

"Careful up ahead, Honored Lady," was all he said as he left.

It happened to be that we were three weeks into our journey by then. Keeping my secret was growing more difficult; I forced myself to eat at feasts only to succumb to nausea later. Temurin kept asking why I rode in the middle of the night. I was being watched at all times, though no one meant any harm by it.

My mother, too, behaved differently. Perhaps it is just that I saw her differently. No longer was she the fierce warlord, striking fear into Hokkaran and Qorin hearts alike. No, she was a woman who wore an old token of favor around her neck; a woman with wrinkles; a woman I no longer felt I knew.

Hunting was slim in that final week. I found only a few rabbits, nothing more, and I was the most skilled of the group. We were coming up near Imakane Village. You suggested we fetch some supplies.

"Supplies?" scoffed Otgar. "Barsatoq, we are people of the steppes. We survive. It is our one great talent."

"Do not be a prideful fool," you said, and I tried my best not to laugh at the irony. "We need meat, and grain, and good cloth. I am almost out of ink."

"What use is ink to us?" Otgar asked. But before you answered, my mother gestured. Otgar crossed her arms. "Burqila says you pay for things with your calligraphy. Is that true?"

"It is," you said. "My calligraphy is worth more than my uncle's money."

At times I think you are a peacock in the body of a woman.

Otgar mulled this over. My mother, again, gestured. They had their silent conversation.

"Burqila agrees with your idea," she said. "She says you, Barsalai, Temurin, and Qadangan can stop for supplies at the next village."

Imakane was not a large village. It was the sort of place that had only one market, if you could call it that—really one old man who traded with merchants along the road. As the four of us approached, we saw one small temple, roughly twenty homes, a statue of the Daughter, a smithy, and a bathhouse.

I learned later that Imakane is famous for its bathhouse. As it happens, it stands near a natural spring whose waters are said to cure any ill. Idle talk, of course—the waters did not heal me. But either way, they brought in travelers along the road to Fujino.

We entered the village, the four of us, and the first thing we noticed was how silent it was. People make noise no matter where they live—yet there was no one tending the smithy, no one leaving flowers for the Daughter, no priests muttering mantras over burning prayers.

At once, I was on edge. I reached for my bow; you wrapped your hand around your sword. Together we dismounted. With quick hand signs, I told Temurin and my cousin Qadangan to scout the village.

Sure enough, they saw no one.

We had options: We could have left. We could have checked the houses, one by one. We could have called out to see if anyone answered.

But you have never been one for choices. You had an idea in your head, and you went with it.

"That guardsman," you said, "told us to be careful. Bandits must've attacked."

Ever the detective, weren't you?

"We are going into the bathhouse," you said, and I translated to Qorin. "It is the largest building here. Temurin, Qadangan, you will wait near the exit. Barsalai and I shall enter through the front door."

Yes, that rather sounded like one of your plans.

After you spoke, you turned to me. In hushed Hokkaran, you continued. "If you are up to it," you said. "I will not fault you, my love, if you want to wait at the exit with the others."

You were asking me to walk into a bathhouse that may or may not be full of bandits. We wore no armor, and I had only my bow and hunting knife with me. The last time you asked me to do something so insane, I woke up with demon blood in my veins.

I suppose nothing can go worse than that.

"I will follow," I said, "wherever you lead."

And so we took our places. Temurin and Qadangan circled around back. With one hand on the pommel of your sword, you opened the door.

Beyond the door was the reception hall. A small table stood close to the ground before us. Steam coming up from the springs fogged up the room. The walls, I noticed, were covered with stalks of bamboo split down the middle, so that the whole area was a hazy green dream.

But there was no one there in the reception hall, no girl wearing a thick layer of white paint, no man in flowing robes.

I took a breath. The air smelled of ginger and . . . something else. My nostrils flared. Something else. Sweet, but salty at the same time.

We toed our way forward. Up ahead, the hall split into two paths, left and right. Each was labeled in Hokkaran.

"Men there, women here," you said, pointing. "Which would you prefer?"

"Together," I said.

"What if we are surrounded?"

"Then we are surrounded together," I repeated. I love you, Shizuka, but at times I wonder how you are still alive. Were you born with an intrinsic desire to run headfirst, alone, into danger?

As we moved farther down the hall, the first noises reached us. Screams. Human screams, not the shrill wailing in my mind. Men, women; both voices mingled together. Laughing, too—so loud and so long that at first I thought it was the demons. Soon we heard the words to go along with it.

"How does the water feel, Blacksmith-kol?"

It was a man's voice. Shortly after that, another man's voice cut into my ears—but this time it was a wet, desperate wail.

I nocked an arrow.

"Doesn't look like it's healing that stab wound of yours."

It was about then we reached the end of the hall, which opened up into one of the springs. We were far underground now—the ceiling above us was rough stone streaked with minerals. The spring itself lay in the middle, shaped close to a circle but not quite. It was deep enough for one person to sink in, and wide enough for five to float in.

I knew all this because five people floated in the spring, four of them already dead. Commoners. Two dead men, two dead women; one man still splashing. One of the women was younger than we were. She floated on her back, her guts spilling from a large wound in her stomach.

Standing around the springs were the bandits: shaggy, starved-looking men and women with yellow scarves tied around their necks. Behind them, lined against the wall, were the rest of the villagers, bound and gagged and watching in abject horror as their family members were killed.

One of the bandits—a tall, lanky man with unkempt hair and a bristling beard—stood closest to the spring. He speared the squirming man. Short, shallow thrusts, meant to wound but not kill. The blacksmith splashed so hard that the floor was slick now, covered in bloody water.

"Aren't your type supposed to be hale and hearty, Blacksmith-kol?" He raised his spear again.

I sent an arrow into his mouth. It punched right through the skin of his jaw and kept going, landing with a clatter near the back of the room.

All at once, the bandits drew their weapons. Spears for the most part—cheap and readily accessible—though I saw a few swords among their number. One dozen.

One dozen bandits, against the two of us.

"Who's playing the hero?" shouted a stout woman with a naginata.

"O-Shizuka!" you roared. And as you entered the room, two

of the bandits lunged at you. I remember distinctly your wooden sandals clattering against the ground; I remember you leaping up. You landed on the shaft of the spear with just enough time to cut the bandit's throat. Spraying blood coated you in deep, dark red.

As you landed, you made a second, overhand strike. The second bandit was too shaken by your first strike to react in time; you cut him deep down the middle.

And I watched.

I do not like to admit this, Shizuka, but I was slow in drawing my second arrow. For there you were, cloaked in ruby, sticky with red. There you were with the snarl of war on your perfect face. There you were, at the zenith of your glory.

I licked my lips. I remember this. I licked my lips as I fought off the sickening thought that I should lick you clean.

No. No, no, I was not one of them, that was not how I thought, those were not my thoughts—

I forced myself to raise my bow, to nock an arrow and pull back—

But I snapped it. I snapped my own bow by pulling on it too hard, too fast. Qorin bows are notoriously flexible; when not in use, we can fit them in hoops hanging on our saddles. And I just broke one.

My hands shook. Blood rushed through my veins, but it was not good blood, not red blood. I could feel my heart pumping waves of black against my ears. Suddenly my teeth hurt; my whole jaw felt like it was splitting in two. I clutched my face, screaming in agony.

In front of me, you danced with the bandits. With every stroke of your flashing blade, you felled one. Droplets of blood flew from the tip of your sword like ink from a brush.

But even you cannot account for everything. Like a bandit, half-bleeding to death, chucking a throwing knife at you with the last of their strength.

I saw it land in your side.

I saw you crumple.

And then . . . ah, my Shizuka, I am glad you were not awake to see this.

Here is what happened, as near as I can remember.

Everything stopped. This is not to say that the bandits stopped moving because you were hurt. They did not. But in that moment, time stood still as ice for me. There you were on the blood-soaked floor, your lips parted as if you were sleeping, a jagged knife jutting out from between your ribs. There you were: my other self, my walking soul.

Unspeakable fury boiled within me. So far gone was I that I did not think in words anymore, only emotions, only images.

The bandits shared a laugh at your expense.

They did not laugh when I roared.

If you are going to imagine this, you must imagine it correctly. This was not the roar of your voice, nor the roar of a fire, nor the roar of a general. This was the roar of a creature twice as large as any tiger, and three times as hungry. This was the roar of an inferno swallowing an entire town whole.

And after it left me, I licked my teeth. Sharp. When did they become sharp?

Fast, faster than their eyes could follow, I lunged forward. With one hand, I grabbed the bandit on the floor, the one who threw the knife. My grip was strong enough to crush his throat; my nails were talons now, and sank into his flesh.

I took this man I held by one hand and I threw him at the others.

They slammed against the wall. Four of them, I think; it is hard to keep track. But I can tell you I smelled their blood. I smelled their fear, sweet as nuts fixed in fat.

One threw a knife at me. It landed in my shoulder with a wet thunk. I did not feel it. I simply pulled it out and threw it back. A wail of pain asssured me it struck true.

I jumped forward again. I do not know what drove me to tear that man's throat out with my teeth, but that is what I did, and when his coppery blood filled my mouth, I swear to you I grinned. It is the sorry truth. His body sank beneath me, and I leaped to another before he fell. A panicked young man this time, scarcely older than we were, pleading, pleading . . . I do not remember what he was pleading for. Leniency, perhaps.

It fell on deaf ears.

I sank my claws into his stomach. He emptied his bowels, and the smell made my stomach churn but did not stop me. As he screamed, I tore his throat out, too, and I sank to the ground.

Four bandits stood, four struggled with the body of their companion. I stooped opposite them, blood and gore stuck in my pointed teeth; my shoulder wound weeping black.

Weapons clattered to the ground.

"You're a demon!" shouted one.

"Worse," I said.

One still held her spear. She made a thrust. I grabbed the shaft and pulled her toward me, and I impaled her with my arm. I flung her body away from me; the crack of her broken bones rang out against the cold rock ceiling.

With every breath I took, I felt more powerful. Not only could I taste their fear—I could savor it, too. I could let it wash over me and give me strength. And, yes, they cowered before me now. Yes, their pants were dark with their own urine. Yes, I was something dark and horrible and wicked.

But they had hurt you, and so dark and horrible and wicked I became.

When one tried to run, I picked him up and slammed him against the ground so hard, his head split.

And when a second tried to run, I grabbed him around the waist and broke him over my knee.

Two.

Two left.

I was laughing. I do not know when I started laughing, or what it is I found so funny, but I was laughing. Already the gore was drying on my hands into thick cakes. Everything was so bright, Shizuka. The blood, the gore, the off-white chunks of bone. For once, I did not hear the voices at all. I was free of them.

And gods above, it felt wonderful. As if I'd had blinders on all my life.

"W-We surrender," muttered one of them. He fell to his knees before me. The other soon followed suit. "B-blackblood-mor, we surrender, we did not know, we were hungry—"

"Hungry?" I repeated. I laughed. "You kill because you are hungry?"

"Our leader said we could get food this way—"

"Thirsty?" I asked.

"N-No, Blackblood-mor."

I grabbed the two of them by the back of the head. As easy as lifting children, I picked them up and took them to the spring.

"Shame," I said. Then I plunged their heads beneath the now-fetid water. "Drink."

And I held them there as they kicked. I held them there as they struggled. I held them there until their bodies finally stopped their insipid protesting and they fell limp in front of me, until the whole room was thick with the glimmering of departed souls.

The remaining villagers were watching me, but if I am honest, I did not care—I could still barely think. But I knew you were bleeding, and that I could not touch you without contaminating you.

And so I picked one of the villagers to untie. I removed her gag. She screamed.

"Pick her up," I snapped, pointing to you. "I won't hurt you."

But I could taste it again. Fear, sweet and potent. I felt as if I'd drunk an entire skin of kumaq in one sitting.

"Pick her up," I repeated. "I won't hurt you. I swear."

I met her eyes. She was a mother, I think—I could smell childbirth on her. That sounds strange. If I said I smelled the sweets she made for her children; if I said I smelled long nights awake stressing over a cradle—would that be less strange? Or more, perhaps? These images land on the back of my tongue and play on the back of my eyelids.

She scrambled to her feet and scooped you up.

"Follow," I said.

So it was that I left the Imakane bathhouse, blood caked so thick on my skin, I may as well have emerged from a mud pit. My teeth came to a point now; the veins on the back of my hand were visibly dark; and, though I could not see it, delicate black veins colored my eyes, too.

When Temurin and Qadangan saw me, they screamed. I suppose they thought I was a demon.

"Barsalai," I said, pointing to myself. "Barsatoq needs help."

For in that moment, I did not care what I had done. As long as

I brought you out of the bathhouse safe and alive, nothing else mattered.

It would not be until later, when you were bandaged and healing, when I had to explain to my mother what had happened, that I broke down weeping at this thing I'd become.

The more I try to remember this, the deeper a nail's driven into my skull. I returned to the ger. We returned, I think. Otgar covered her mouth when she saw us, spat on the ground. To my disgust, she moved in front of my mother.

"Disgust" is not the word. As if Burqila Alshara needed protection.

The dark bubbling within me simmered over. Their voices were the hiss of steam in my ear—hurt her, make her suffer, look what she has done to you!

"Whatever you are," Otgar said, "leave here now—"

I bared my teeth. Fangs, now. Each of them came to a point, so that when I smiled, I looked like a wild animal or worse. My nails grew so thick and dark, they reminded me of a hawk's claws.

I was keenly aware of many things in that moment: One, Otgar's heartbeat. Two, the vein on her temple pulsing to unseen drums. Three, the shaking of her sword. Four, the power coursing through me. Drunk. I was drunk on it, Shizuka, on the knowledge that no one could stand before me and live—

But Temurin's strained voice returned me to my own mind. "Dorbentei," she called, this woman who had fought with my mother in the Qorin wars, this woman who now sounded terrified. "Dorbentei, that is Barsalai. Something happened, she is not herself—"

"Barsalai?" Otgar called. And my mother shoved her out of the way so hard, she fell to the ground.

Burqila Alshara slew her brothers without a trace of regret. Burqila Alshara rode with one hundred men and women to Sur-Shar, and rode back with five hundred, despite not speaking a word of Surian. Burqila Alshara blew a hole in the Wall of Stone with Dragon's Fire. Burqila Alshara conquered half the Hokkaran Empire with five hundred men and two thousand horses.

Yet when she saw me—when she realized it was her own daughter standing there, painted black with arterial ink—she covered her mouth. Slack-jawed and pale she was, the agony of recognition writ large on her brow. With trembling hands, she made the only sign I recognized. The one she'd made with a beckoning wrist, with a sharp flick; the one she'd made look soft; the one she'd made to call me to dinner.

My name. No, not even that—the name she alone called me. Shefa. My name was among the few hand signs I knew; when we were alone, my mother would always leave off the last syllable. You did not know this name, and this now may well be the first you've ever seen it.

And I heard Temurin's soft weeping; I heard your labored breathing. I looked down at myself. At the claws I once called fingers. At my skin, thin as rice paper, trying to hide thick black eels. I looked to you, to my wound, weeping darkness.

"Mother," I said. "Mother, I'm sorry."

Was that my voice? I didn't sound like myself anymore; I was echoing in an open field. My knees knocked together as the weight of my actions came upon me, as I saw everything that had just happened with my own eyes and retched.

I'd torn a man's throat out with my teeth. I'd drowned people. I'd enjoyed it, all of it, the thrill and the power and the rush.

"Mother," I repeated as I sank to the ground.

"Mother," I repeated as she held me.

And then I wept like a child who'd wandered onto a battlefield.

Otgar took hold of you. While my mother rocked back and forth with me, she tended to your wound. All the while, she kept looking up toward my mother and me. With her free hand, my mother spoke.

"When?" came Otgar's voice.

"Two months ago," I muttered. "We were fighting a demon."

Rocking, rocking, rocking. What was I going to do? What was she going to do with this abomination she'd birthed? Was she going to kill me? She should kill me. If this was the way I was going to behave now, I needed to die. Better to put down a wild dog than let it loose. I'd almost attacked Otgar, of all people, and even as my mother held me, I had to fight the thoughts flooding my mind.

"Your blood," said Otgar. She could not say it without cracking.

I nodded, eyes shut tight.

"Shefali," Otgar said. "Shefali, what happened?"

In bits and pieces, I told them. We wanted to help. That was all. We went into that bathhouse thanks to your amber-colored idea of heroism. We went in to make sure the villagers were all right and then you were hurt and . . .

My mother held me for some time.

I spent the night alone, in my own tent. I refused to be near my family. I refused to be near anyone at all, lest that creature I'd become overpower me again. No one quite knew what to do. We untied the villagers, of course—Qadangan and Temurin did that before we left. They were safe.

But they were going to talk. You'd shouted your name when you entered. They knew who you were. And how many other Qorin did you travel with, Shizuka? Soon tales would spread. O-Shizuka travels with a demon, with a woman who tears out throats with her teeth.

What were we going to do about me?

That night, the Not-You came into my bedroll. That night, she wrapped her arms around me, and I did not have the will to fight her off. She stroked my face with decrepit hands. She breathed, and I smelled fungus, smelled death.

"Ah, Steel-Eye," she said. "Look at you. You are so much more beautiful now."

I buried my head in the pillows, but her nails dragged across the nape of my neck.

"With your teeth, perfect for biting," it said. "Your eyes that see so much. Yes, you are more beautiful now, and you will be more beautiful yet."

"I do not want to be," I said.

"Ahhh," it said, planting a rancid kiss on my shoulder. "Finally you have spoken to me, my love."

"Leave me," I said, pulling the pillows over my head.

It placed its hand on the small of my back and I thrashed, I spun, I punched and clawed. I screamed. It melted away from every blow like a flickering shadow. Like Leng, like Shao, like the thing I was becoming.

"Leave me! I do not want you!" I yelled, pressed up against the tarp, clutching my bedroll. "Haven't you bothered me enough? Haven't you . . . I do not want to be like you!"

The Not-You sat laughing at my misery. How cruel it is, Shizuka, to see a face so like yours in such a state. How cruel to have the one person you love above all others laughing at your pain.

Someone opened the tent flap. I braced myself for Otgar or

Temurin or my mother. Instead, it was you. The real you, bandaged and swaying. At the sight of your radiance, the Not-You dissipated.

I scrambled for you and embraced you.

"Shefali," you said, cupping my ear, "what is the matter, my love?"

"Your wound . . ."

You kissed me. A measure of my panic slipped away, as if you breathed it in. "It is a small thing," you said, "soon healed. Wounds do not bother us. Remember the tiger?"

I touched my own bandages. The skin beneath felt solid and whole. I frowned. With my knife, I cut through the gauze.

Sure enough, the gaping gash I'd gotten earlier that day was already healed. Only a faint line remained, a bit lighter than the rest of my skin. I tore off the bandages and tossed them to the edge of the tent, far from you.

You reached out to touch the skin, but I waved you away. No. Too risky. You could not touch me. Not yet. Not until I was sure that I wasn't contagious. You drew away only slightly.

"Shefali," you said, "I heard you screaming."

"Nothing," I said, wrapping my arms around my knees.

"Nothing," you repeated. You laid your head against my shoulder, the one that had not had a knife in it earlier. This I allowed, if only to feel your hair against my skin. "Awful lot of noise, for nothing."

I stared at a spot on the floor.

"Nothing," I said.

You sighed. "My love," you said, "I am yours, no matter the circumstances. You know this, yes?"

I flinched. "Do you know?" I asked. "About today?"

Your grip relaxed. Pensive was your gaze. You, too, had picked a spot on the floor to stare at. Perhaps the same spot.

"I do," you said. "And I am still here. We will find someone who can help you. You are Barsalai Shefali, you slew a tiger at eight, a demon at sixteen! This . . ." You gestured to the bandages soaked in black. "This is something to slay. We will face it. Together."

You shifted, so that you were in front of me, and you took my face in your hands. The tips of our noses touched. Your brown-gold eyes warmed my spirit.

"And no matter what happens, Shefali, I know who you really are," you said. You brushed your fingertips over my heart. "The person who killed those people was not you. I will have relief brought to the town. But you and I, we are going to Xian-Lai. We are going somewhere far away from prying eyes. Somewhere quiet, where the voices cannot rule you."

And then you chuckled.

"After all," you said, "I should be the only Empress on your mind."

We laced our fingers together. You cleared the hair from my face and kissed my forehead.

"What if I never get better?"

"You will," you said.

I do not know what imbues you with your confidence. I think I trust more in your decisiveness than in the sun rising every morning. I have never seen you falter, never seen you think anything over for more than a few seconds at a time.

At times your confidence is a terrible thing. It's what led us into Imakane bathhouse, what led us into the abandoned temple, what led us into that clearing in Fujino where the tiger found us. But it is also what makes your calligraphy so prized, why you are with-out equal as a swordsman. It is why I have always trusted you.

Of course I would get better. You will not allow anything else to happen.

And yet we sat in the tent near Imakane. There was blood be-neath my dark fingernails and flecks of bone in my hair.

"Together," you said. You lay in my lap. The thought occurred to me—it would be so easy to snap your neck. You knew what I'd done, and you lay there anyway.

But you fell asleep in my lap without a trace of fear.

On that day, stories began to spread. The Demon of the Steppes. The Living Blackblood. The Manslayer. We would not hear the first of these until we were in Xian-Lai. We would not know how the villagers perceived me.

For in their eyes, I was as terrible, as awesome, as frightful as the Mother in all her fury.

And yellow-scarved bandits, for the first time since your mother's death, kept watch all through the night, afraid that I would come for them.

In the morning, when dawn's fingers crept into the sky, Otgar came to the tent. Red pinpricks dotted her face, mostly below the eyes; her already full cheeks were puffier than usual.

"Barsalai, Barsatoq," she said. "Burqila wishes to speak with you."

I squeezed your hand. You shook the sleep out from your head and stood. When I thought you might fall—you'd lost a lot of blood the day before—I offered you my arm. Did you notice how I trembled?

The ger was only a few steps away, but we might as well have been walking to Gurkhan Khalsar. White felt was not so far from white snow. Kharsas retreated to both when they needed time to think. If mountains were made of felt, they'd be gers, I think.

When someone is summoned to Gurkhan Khalsar, it is a momentous thing. They must take the winding path around the mountain, not the one carved into it by Grandfather Earth. Half a day it takes to climb the mountain this way. Some fall. The path is narrow. The summons always comes in the middle of the night—stepping on the bones of your predecessors is a real danger. After all, no one can remove anything from the mountaintop. The whole of it is sacred, even the bodies of those who died climbing it.

No bones barred the path to my mother's ger. No real ones. But I swear to you, I saw them all the same. Faded deels and clumps of hair; off-white bones turned black with dirt and grime. I stared at my feet the entire time we walked, not out of nervousness, but out of fear. With each step, I hoped I would not hear crunching beneath my boot.

Yet I knew the bones were not there. In my mind, I knew they were not there, that they could not be real—what were Qorin corpses doing so far north? They'd not been here yesterday. No, I was seeing things again.

But Shizuka, it was so real to me. More than once, my boot met something hard, something that creaked when I put my weight on it. I jumped away, staring at the spot.

"Shefali," you'd whisper under your breath, "they are only shadows, my love. Walk in the light with me."

You took my hand.

In full view of Temurin and Qadangan, in full view of my aunt and uncle, in full view of Otgar, you took my hand.

I clung to it as we entered the ger.

My mother sat on the eastern side, on her makeshift throne. She wore a fine green deel, embroidered with golden triangles that almost shone against her deep brown skin. Emeralds glinted in her hair, too, as beads on the ends of her many braids. She was stooped low with her elbows on her knees, her head in her hands. When we entered, her mossy eyes flickered up.

I do not think I've seen her more pained.

Otgar stood at my mother's right. And there is a certain way people stand when they are . . .

I squeezed your hand.

My mother began signing.

"Barsalai Shefali Alsharyya," she said, through Otgar. "Barsatoq Shizuka Shizuraaq. You stand before Burqila Alshara Nadyyasar, Grand Leader of the Qorin, Breaker of Walls. You stand in her ger awaiting judgment."

I stiffened. This was a trial?

But, then, I deserved no less. If anyone else in the clan had done what I did, my mother would've put them down on the spot. This was her being gracious. This was her mercy. This was her sorrow.

"Yesterday, Barsalai slew ten people," my mother signed. "We know this, as we have counted the remains. Ten. Only one died to an arrow. Nine, then, Barsalai slew with her own two hands."

I hid the offending hands behind my back. My teeth felt awkward in my mouth now, as well—every time I moved my tongue, I risked cutting it open. My fingers, my teeth—alien parts that did not belong to me. Evidence of what I'd done.

"They were bandits, Burqila," you said. "They held an entire village prisoner. Barsalai did what I would've done, had I not been wounded."

My mother scowled. Her signing now was sharp and sudden.

"You would've drowned them? With your bare hands?" Otgar said. She could not keep herself composed. Her voice cracked; her shoulders shook. Still my mother signed. "Barsatoq, I knew your mother well, and I delivered you myself. If you had not been wounded, we'd have ten corpses with neat, slit throats. Not bits of bone and organ scattered across a floor."

"She was angered, Burqila," you protested. You knew better than to raise your voice—that would not help your case at all—but you spat flame nonetheless. "What would you have done if someone hurt my mother in front of you?"

My mother half rose from her seat. She raised her hand, then set it back down. Fury on her face, she finally shaped her trembling signs.

"It is not the same, Barsatoq. Do not presume. In Hokkaro, you may be an Empress, but this is my ger, and the whole of the world beneath Grandmother Sky is my empire," Otgar translated. "I love you dearly as my own blood—but you will not speak to me in such a fashion."

You scrunched your face in response to this. There was more you wanted to say, but you would not. For now, you would not.

A pause. My mother took an audibly deep breath. Then she continued.

"Barsalai," she said through Otgar. "I find myself conflicted. Killing bandits is not a problem. Foul people deserve what befalls them. But killing them as you did is not permissible; you've known this since your childhood. Yet . . . yet there are other things on your mind.

"I do not know the extent of your illness. I do not know if it is permanent. I do not know if you will suddenly die tomorrow, or if you will once more tear people apart because you are angry.

"You have done many things, my daughter, my blood. In your youth, you slew a tiger. You and your cousin sneaked out to fight a demon when you were only ten. So you sneaked out again, with Barsatoq, to do the same.   •

"You at sixteen slew this demon, too. You have allowed the people of Shiseiki to reclaim their temple, and that is a good and noble thing.

"But . . ."

Otgar stopped. My mother, too, stopped, making a fist near her forehead. She screwed her eyes shut.

"You are my daughter," Otgar creaked. "From birth I have been with you. I have kept you warm, I have fed you, on the steppes where these things have weight. I taught you to fire a bow, I taught you to read and write. At every turn, you've repaid me. If I am remembered for nothing in this world other than giving birth to you, I think I should be pleased.

"But there is a shade about you, Shefali. There is a cruel darkness that was not there yesterday. You are a Kharsa; you will not succumb. I know this to be true. In eight years' time, you will break your demons and ride them into battle.

"But until that day, I cannot . . ."

Again, a pause. Otgar turned toward my mother. I think she might've whispered something. I did not hear her. Then once more they turned.

"I cannot allow you to travel with our people," Otgar said, choking on the words. "I cannot claim you as my own. You are not my daughter when you do these things—you are the tiger's. And you will wear her name, not mine. Barsalyya Shefali Alshar you will be, until the day we are certain you can control your outbursts."

We Qorin were sired when Grandmother Sky lay with wolves.

Long have they envied us, for Grandmother Sky favors us over them in all things. We ride strong horses while they lope through the night; we hunt with bow and sword where they must use their teeth. But at our cores, we are the same.

Wolves do not travel alone, and neither do Qorin. You hear of lone Qorin in stories. A woman who murders her Kharsa might be cast out. A man who steals a mare from the Kharsaq's family, too, would be cast out. Deserters, killers, horse-thieves, and traitors. These are the people left to wander clanless.

And so my cousin's voice was a bow, and my mother's words the arrow. For the first time since my sickness, I ached, really ached; cold disbelief froze me in place. I tried to draw breath but could not.

Exile. She was exiling me. I was not going to see my family again; I was going to wander the world with only you at my side. Never again would I enjoy kumaq; never again would I dance around the fire to a sanvaartain's two-voiced songs.

Not even to be able to hear my true name . . .

"You cannot be serious," you said. "Shefali is your only daughter! And you abandon her when she needs you most!" Your voice was shrill, sharp, as if speaking such things cut your throat from the inside.

My mother rose. She met your eyes with unwavering determination. Her fingers moved in heady motions, like hammers striking nails.

"I do not abandon her," Otgar said. "I leave her with you. The two of you had plans to travel, did you not? Go. Travel. Return when you are yourself once more."

You stormed toward her. "How dare you," you said. "My mother would be—"

I squeezed your shoulder. That was not something you wanted to say. You did not want to start that fight, not with my mother, not with the woman who loved Shizuru as much as your father did. This was not a negotiation.

It was a trial, and I was guilty.

You turned toward me. I shook my head.

Otgar handed me a package: rough-spun cloth tied with twine. "This is your mother's parting gift," she said. "May it keep you safe from harm, Cousin."

And that was that. It was final.

Exile.

I embraced my mother.

She stroked my hair and pressed a kiss into it. It was a good embrace—warm, loving, and strong. Tears dropped onto my deel; I pretended they were not there. A Kharsa does not cry in public.

But then, my mother never assumed that title.

Otgar soon joined us, wrapping her arms as best she could around Alshara and me. "Be safe, Shefali," she said. "We will be waiting for your return."

No, they won't.

I squeezed them tighter.

They won't mourn you, Steel-Eye.

I bit into my tongue. No. I wanted to enjoy this moment while I could. I wanted to remember my mother's smell, remember Otgar's. For just two minutes, I wanted to forget what I'd learned.

Don't they smell alike?

Bile rising in the back of my throat. Within this warm embrace, I began to shake.

Otgar drew away first. She frowned. "Are you all right?"

But as she spoke, her face changed. A second mouth opened up;

a fat gray tongue the size of my arm rolled out of it. Slobber drenched her deel. Now her teeth came to a point as mine did.

"Are you all right?" she said with her first mouth.

"Thank the Sky you are leaving," said the second.

I freed myself of them, covered my ears with my hands.

"Shefali?" you said, but I was already going. Eyes closed. Do not open them. Opening them meant seeing things I knew weren't real.

No.

Better to pack up my tent, throw it onto my packhorse, and mount Alsha. Better to feel her heart thrumming between my legs, hear her nickering, better to strap myself into the saddle.

But as I neared the tent, you took me by the wrists. "Shefali," you said, "look at me."

But what if it wasn't you? What if the Not-You learned how to speak in your tone, what if I was still in my tent and this was all a nightmare?

By all the gods in the world, Shizuka, there is nothing worse than doubting your own senses.

"Look at me," you said again.

When my eyes remained fixed on the ground, you took my right hand, turned it upward. With your fingertip you traced the thick white scar on my palm. Nail dragged across skin. My palm tingled the longer you touched it.

I took a deep breath and focused on that, instead of the voices.

"Together," you whispered. "Come what may, we will always be together."

The words are so bitter to me now, Shizuka, that I fear they will burn the paper I write on. The scent of dried pine is nowhere to be found here.

Together.

We left not long after that. I could not bring myself to return to the ger and face my family after being so overcome. My mother did not get to sniff my cheek for one last time. We bundled our tent, our meager belongings, and we rode away from my mother's ger.

It was only once we were gone that I opened the package. Pangs of sorrow twisted my stomach. There, neatly folded, was the tiger-skin deel I'd made for my mother when I was eight. A small piece of parchment lay atop the deel, bearing my mother's neat Qorin handwriting.

Tiger stripes, for the woman who earned them.

I wore that deel all throughout our journey to Xian-Lai. In the cold of the winter, I wore it. When the last snows began to melt, I wore it. My mother wore it so long that it still smelled of her. In that way, I did not feel quite so abandoned. If I could smell her, then a piece of her soul traveled with me, after all.

IF IT WERE MY WISH TO PICK
THE WHITE ORCHID

Has anyone ever told you that you are awful at camping?

This is, I think, the first you've heard of it, and for that I apologize. You know my love for you is boundless; you know I would condemn the entire Heavenly Family if only you asked me. That is why I am telling you now, from several thousand li away, that you are terrible at camping.

Well—all right. Terrible is an overstatement. I have to remind myself that you spent most of your life cooped up in the Jade Palace, or within the walls of Fujino. That's no place to learn basic survival skills. My mother tried to teach you, and I think you might have tried to listen despite your arrogance (remember that I love you), but you were not yet up to Qorin standards when you left. Even when we were children it was like this. I would do all of the hunting, and the skinning, and set up the fire, and everything required for a comfortable existence. You set up the tent, you

kept the fire going, and I think you'd learned to tell poisonous berries from safe ones. By the time we were adults you'd learned a
little more: you could hunt small game, but not skin it; you could
start a fire without any of your godly tricks, but only on a sunny
day; you knew how to navigate, but only with a compass. By
Fujino standards you were a hardened ranger.

By Qorin standards, you'd passed the standard weeklong test
of not dying in the wilderness. My mother, exasperated at how
long it had taken you to reach that level, probably would have left
you to your own devices for an entire month if we'd stayed with
her. Little did she know you'd cheated the first time, anyway.

Whenever we passed a tree, if it was the sort that bore edible
fruit, you'd run your hands over its branches. Without fail, at least
one fruit would grow right there before our eyes. You'd pluck it
and toss it into my saddlebags (always mine), smirking at your little
display of divinity. Sometimes you didn't wait for us to see a tree—
if you were in the mood for a particular herb, you'd grab your
brush and paint the character for it on the ground. Over the course
of an hour the named herb sprouted from the ground ready for
harvesting. In this way you helped provide—your calligraphy was
valuable, yes, but so were the spices you conjured up from nothing.

Not that many people wanted to trade with us.

"We wish we could," said one farmer. "But the Yellow Scarves
are passing through, looking for a Hokkaran noble and a Qorin
girl."

All through the side roads, we heard this. It gave us reason
enough not to try the main roads; what if a patrol stopped us? If
common farmers knew we were wanted, then I shuddered to think
of guards. The good ones would avoid us. Corrupt ones might well
try to take us in for the bounty.

Two weeks in—two weeks of sleeping in a tent, two weeks bathing in streams when we found them, two weeks of stringy rabbit and hard rice—you were fading.

I remember the morning I returned with one lonely hare hanging from my belt. I sat down by the fire to skin it. You practiced sword forms near the tent. When you saw me cut into the rabbit, you could not hide the disappointment on your face.

I stifled a flare of anger. Venison. You wanted venison. Had I seen a single deer roaming the tall emerald forests, we'd have venison. I spent all night and the better part of the morning stalking through the woods.

This rabbit was all I had to show for it.

"Shizuka," I said.

You turned mid-stroke to face me and the fire. You did not stop your forms; of course you did not.

"Shefali?"

"My catch displeases you," I said, biting into a rough spot on the rabbit's neck. I hated my new teeth—I had scratches all over my tongue—but they did have uses. Hard to cut this angle without ruining the meat. Far easier to bite it.

And I got a taste of the raw meat that way, as well.

My comment made you stop. Your lips parted; you tucked in your chin. Your brows inched closer together. "I never said that."

"No," I said. I turned the rabbit upside down and began peeling off its skin. When you get the right slices in, skin sloughs off easy. It's almost soothing. "You did not say it."

In response, you sheathed your sword. You stood right in front of me with your hands on your hips. I glanced up at you and twisted off the rabbit's head.

"If I did not say it," you said, "why are you so certain? I've had rabbit every meal for two weeks. Why should today's serving of rabbit upset me more than the others?"

My mind was flint; your words were steel.

I strung up the rabbit from the spit, wiped my hands on my deel, and turned to you. "Because you are spoiled."

To say that you gaped at me would be putting it mildly. Your lips formed an O, your ear met your shoulder. But your hands did not leave your hips, and the shock on your face soon gave way to anger.

"Spoiled?" you repeated. "Shefali, we have eaten rabbit every day—"

"You've eaten it every day," I said.

"No," you said, pointing a finger at me. "Do not make this—Of course you have not eaten it, you are not well! I am the one who has to put up with it."

There is a certain kind of thrill that comes to you in the heat of battle. Blood pounds in your ears like war drums, and you can almost taste your own heartbeat. Steel meets steel, makes your bones sing. Colors split into shades you cannot name. Everything comes into focus; every beat of a moth's wings is a lifetime.

So it was arguing with you. I hated upsetting you, but there was a part of me that . . . it was like burning a wound.

"Would you prefer having blackblood?" I said.

You scowled. "You know I would not," you said. "I cannot imagine how you suffer, my love, and I have done all I can to help you bear the weight. But is it so wrong of me to want something different to eat every now and again?"

I waved my hand toward the trees around us. "Go," I said. And it was like nocking an arrow, like drawing back the string. "Find a deer."

Everyone laughed.

No, no. The demons laughed.

You flinched. Fury crossed you like a bird's shadow; you turned away from me for a moment.

Victory washed over me. I could almost feel everyone patting me on the back. I'd won; you had nothing to say. I'd won and—

"This is not like you," you said. When you faced me again, two wet spots were on your lapel, and your amber eyes glistened. "Shefali, this is not like you."

Oh.

All of a sudden, my chest hurt.

I hung my head. "I . . . I did not . . ."

You sat on my lap. Rabbit's blood smeared onto your fine robes. In your hands, you took my head, and you held me close to your chest.

"I do not want to lose you," you said. "Sometimes it's as if you aren't there at all. As if someone else is looking out from your eyes."

Sky's thunder, I didn't mean to—

No. That was the worst part. I did mean to hurt you; that was why I said those things, why I acted the way I had.

"I'm here," I said into your chest. "Me. Shefali."

You held fast to me. And you said nothing, but I felt your tears falling on my head.

I will not lie and say things got better after that. I will not lie to you, who lived it, and say I changed my ways in that moment. For the rest of the day, we sat far away from each other. You spared me the occasional pained glance—no more.

I tried to think of something to say. If I just found the right combination of words—wouldn't that fix everything? I wondered what your father did in situations like this. As a poet, he'd know the words needed. He'd know how to write them, which characters to use, how to hold his brush.

I was no poet. I could not read the characters of your name. You told me once, what they meant—how your mother chose your name but your father chose the characters. When we stayed in the palace, you held my hand as I went through the strokes.

"The first character," you said, "my father did not have much choice in. All Minami women share it. This means 'quiet.' "

You lifted the brush, and my hand, and continued.

"But this one," you continued, "is the character for 'excellence.' My father thought it fitting that I was born with a reputation for it."

We wrote your name again and again, yet I still could not recognize it if I tried. How was I going to put together the words I needed?

I watched you. I could not read Hokkaran, but I could read the slump of your shoulders, the creases of your lips. At the end of the day when you went to bed, you did not wait to see if I was coming with you.

So no. I did not voice how afraid I was of losing you. I would rather lose my right arm, Shizuka; I would rather lose my tongue. In that moment, I thought I'd rather lose an eye than lose you.

I spoke none of this.

But I did try to find you different food.

So it was I saddled Alsha and rode out down the side road after you'd gone to bed. There was a village not far from where we camped. When I arrived, it was just after Last Bell. Only drunkards, vagabonds, singing girls, sellswords, and minstrels stayed out at this hour. I was not overly concerned. If someone foolish

attempted to rob me, they'd find no cash seals or heavy coins—
only a knife and unresolved anger.

Yet even these ne'er-do-wells spared an envious glance for me
as I rode through town at night. Qorin horses are a fair sight larger
than most Hokkaran steeds. Coupled with a likewise tall, dark-
skinned rider, and I cannot say I blame them. You have always
called me handsome, after all.

A throaty voice called to me. "Graymare-sur!"

I saw no other grays, save for a dappled silver gelding at rest in
the stables. The woman was calling me, then. I admit I spared a
small smile—calling an unknown Qorin by describing their horse
is, perhaps, the most diplomatic thing a Hokkaran can do. "Horse-
lover," "brute," "no-home," these things I am deaf to. These notes
blur together.

But Graymare, and Graymare-sur at that—these were new.

A woman stood on the veranda of one of the larger buildings.
By its open door and the thick scent of smoke coming from it, it
must be the village winehouse. She was not the only one standing
outside: two other girls in bright robes flirted with men in armor
a few steps away. But this girl was the only one looking at me.

I will describe her for you, since you have pictured her often,
I am certain. Jealousy is as cutting as any knife—you might as
well know what she looked like, I think, if you are going to hate
her from a distance.

Like you, she was not tall—though I think she is a bit taller than
you are. Where your hair is ink, hers was like charred wood: more
dark brown than black. Round was her face, small and dainty her
lips. She wore a two-layer green robe, with the first layer leaving
her shoulders bare. There was only one ornament in her hair, a
modest enameled orchid. Twenty-four, perhaps—not much older.

But she had a warm face, a welcoming face, like an old friend you've only just now met.

She waved toward me with the fan in her hand. "Graymare-sur, do you seek company tonight?"

Blood rushed to my cheeks. My first instinct was to say yes, to comment on the delicate silver stroke of her collarbone, to invite her somewhere private and—

I will not anger you, Shizuka. You know in those days the basest thoughts sprang to mind first. Rest assured, I thought of you asleep and banished the more lascivious thoughts.

Well.

No.

I cannot say that I banished them. I am honest with you in all things, and though it pains me, I must be honest when it comes to this woman. The way she smiled at me lit me up. Her skin was so smooth that I wondered how it would feel against mine. What were her hands like? For she would not have your duelist's calluses.

It had been some time since I was treated so kindly by a Hokkaran. And I did have questions. Where to find food, for instance. I did not have any money, no, but perhaps a singing girl might know where to go when times are tough and stomachs are turning.

So I rode up to the winehouse. In one motion I dismounted.

"Stay put," I said to Alsha in the tongue of swaying grass.

You're the one doing the wandering, she said back to me.

That horse. At times I think the other Qorin are lucky that they cannot hear their horses truly speak to them. I've never met a horse who wasn't fond of sarcasm. They're worse than scholars.

I shook my head at Alsha. "Don't make me tie you," I said.

You wouldn't dare, she said. And she was right, of course. With one word I told Alsha to stay put. I did not tie her to a post, as you might think I would. If anyone tried to steal her, I felt great pity for them, for soon they'd be lying on the street with several crushed bones.

The woman looked at my horse. As a child hearing tales of phoenixes and dragons gapes in excitement, so did she gape at Alsha. "Forgive me!" she said when I walked to her. "She's the most beautiful mare I've ever seen, even among those my Qorin mentors had."

Finally, someone who wasn't hateful. Though it did set me wondering what a singing girl could learn from Qorin women. Hunting? Riding? She didn't look like she did much of either.

It might please you to know that in smiling, I bared my pointed teeth, and the other girls on the veranda skittered inside.

But the one I was speaking to stayed. She opened her fan. I smelled jasmine.

"May I touch her?" she asked.

I shook my head. She was satisfied with this, and gave a small nod.

"Ah, understandable!" she said. "One cannot write the Son of Heaven's name, one cannot touch that horse. All things divine are beyond mortal reach."

Your voice is a lantern: bright and commanding. Hers is a campfire, warm and inviting, clinging to your clothes long after she has left.

I said nothing to this, for I could think of nothing to say. My experience dealing with attractive women, at that point, began and ended with you.

"You're a quiet one," she teased. With the tip of her fan, she touched my shoulder. "But I can make you sing, if you're willing. Why don't you come for a walk with me?"

She was not afraid to touch me. She'd seen my teeth, and they did not faze her—still she looked at me with eyes like ripe figs.

I do not know what came over me. But I can tell you it was warm as the first breeze of summer.

When I offered an earnest, if close-lipped, smile, she took my arm. She wore wooden sandals shorter than yours, and so her steps were a bit longer. I slowed my pace a great deal to keep up with her. One never thinks of how long one's legs are until walking with someone shorter.

I thought of how to approach this. Should I ask right out if she knew where I might find some food for free? Should I listen to whatever she was going to say? For on her lips were unborn conversations.

One thing was for certain. I had to make it clear my intentions were not romantic. I had a goddess descendant waiting for me in a tent at camp, and I had to return to her soon. As pretty as this girl was, I could not allow myself to listen to my urges.

But those urges were doing their best to get my attention. She had a way of moving, you see. Deliberate and confident, as if she knew I could not keep my eyes off her. The more I watched her swaying hips, the more I imagined—

No. No, I could not. So what if Kharsas often took more than one lover? I was content with you.

As I opened my mouth to tell her I did not want those services, she opened hers and spoke.

"Do not be afraid," she said, "but I know who you are."

We'd come to a stop behind what I assumed to be an inn. Besides the two small horses in the stable, we had no company. I think that is what she was looking for. Yet still I searched, still I tried to see if she'd set me up for an ambush. I reached for a bow that was not there, fumbled for my knife. What if they were coming for me, the Yellow—?

"Shh, shh, shh, do not fear," she said. "It's only you and me. I've told no one. I swear to you eight times, I mean you no harm."

Was she serious? Her brow, her gaze, even her posture—all colored with sincerity. She held her hands up as she spoke. They were larger than yours, but softer, too, and—

I didn't have time.

One more glance around.

I took a breath. "You know?"

"Ah, you speak!" she said. She touched my chin. She wore a nervous smile and I wondered how often a singing girl smiles in such a way. "I was worried your condition affected your speaking. My brother, he told me you spoke at Imakane—"

"Brother?" I said.

She nodded. "My brother, Kato, he worked at the bathhouse," she said. Now the words came tumbling out of her, and she could not stop herself from speaking. "When the Yellow Scarves attacked, he started praying to the Mother for a quick death. He told me some of the things he saw and . . ."

She took my hands in hers. She did not hesitate at all—she took my hands, with their talons, and cupped them between her palms. Then she touched her forehead to our joined palms.

"Thank you," she said. "Eight times, I thank you. If you had not been there, Kato would've been tortured like the rest."

Her voice cracked. Now tears poured from her sweet plum eyes, ruining the makeup she'd taken so long to apply. I stood there, unsure of what to do. Surely she could not be serious. Moved to tears, grateful for what I'd done? Touching me, knowing what color my blood ran?

I did not know this woman two hours ago.

Why was she so moved?

"The Yellow Scarves have been rampaging through Shiseiki for years now," she said. "They come, two dozen, three dozen at a time, into the winehouse. They drink more than any ox I've ever met, talk more than any hen, and stink worse than pigs. Do they pay? Of course not. On a good day, they don't kill anyone. That is payment, to them."

And it occurred to me then what her line of work was. It occurred to me who would have the most coin in a town like this. Even before she continued, my heart ached for her.

"Then they bluster into our rooms, throw coin at us . . ."

She shook her head.

"No one stands up to them. The guards are too afraid. Foolish youths run off to join them every day; how else is anyone supposed to make a living, when the Yellow Scarves take it all?"

She squeezed my hands tight. There was such pain on her face, Shizuka. How long had the commoners been dealing with this? How long had she been dealing with it?

"Only you," she said. "They call you the Demon of the Steppes, but you're holy as a shrine maiden to me. You saved my brother. You made the Yellow Scarves fear again."

I thought I must be dreaming, or else the demons must've figured out a way to make me live through illusions. A Hokkaran girl, a pretty Hokkaran singing girl, was thanking me for the monstrous display that made my own mother exile me. I was holy to her.

And I believed it. There is a certain way a person looks at you when the light of admiration shines within them. I'm certain you see it every day, Shizuka.

But for me?

For me, that might've been the first time.

"Please," she said, bowing to me. "Tell me your name, that I might thank my ancestors for sending you to me."

I licked my lips.

When we were children, you said we were gods. It was in that moment, with a woman I'd never met holding my hands and saying such things, that I began to believe you.

"Barsalyya Shefali Alshar," I said. I didn't like the way that name tasted on my tongue. Tiger's daughter. My mother's name, unadorned, abandoning me. It was a good thing Hokkarans know nothing of Qorin naming conventions, or—

"Alshar?" she said, a note of sympathy in her voice. "That was not always your name, was it? Come. Let us hear it, your real name. The one you earned."

Barsalyya was the name I'd earned. The pox I wore for what I'd done.

But . . . for a little while, I wanted to pretend.

"Barsalai Shefali Alsharyya," I said. How did she know Alshar was not a proper mother's name?"

She bowed again. "Barsalai-sur, I will light prayers for you every night of my life," she said.

I stood awestruck. My mouth hung open. For once, everything was silent. No chorus of demonic voices. No laughter. No screaming, no crying.

Only the girl standing before me with a tear-streaked face, swearing she'd light prayers on her altar for me.

"Thank you," I muttered. "I am honored."

"No, no," she said. "I am the honored one. So honored, I've forgotten to give you my name. If it pleases you, Barsalai-sur, you can call me Ren."

"Just Barsalai," I said. Yes, Barsalai, the tiger-killer and not the monster.

Ren. I can see you shaking your head as you read this, Shizuka, wondering who on earth names their child after such a flower. I will tell you: she herself picked the name. This she told me later, when we were—

But I suppose I am getting to that part.

"Barsalai, then," she said. How nice it sounded to hear it. She had the best Qorin accent I'd ever heard from a foreigner. "Is there anything I can do for you? If you want company—"

I shook my head. I flushed red, but I shook my head all the same.

"She is waiting, back at camp," I stammered. "I . . . She needs food."

Ren laughed. I imagine it's the exact sound a flower would make laughing; it hung in the air like perfume. "Food?" she said. "Is that all?"

I scratched at my head. That tone.

"Is my fruit not tempting enough?" she teased.

I consider myself lucky in that we never experienced this phase of courtship. Not once did I have to maintain my composure while you whispered something so . . . while you whispered anything like that into my ear. I am not a woman built to flirt. I can string a bow blindfolded, with one hand. I can skin almost any animal you put in front of me.

I cannot flirt.

"It is . . . I . . . You are sweet as plum wine, and beautiful as your name," I said, each word more tremulous than the last. "But

I love another dearly, and my condition . . . I would not want to hurt you, or her, or anyone. I cannot. My heart is hers, I cannot."

She covered her mouth with her fan. More heady laughs left her. I palmed my face to hide my shame. Thank Grandmother Sky we met so young, Shizuka; if we had had to court each other, you never would've picked me.

"Very well," said Ren. "You are shy as a virgin, Barsalai! But if food is what you want, I will provide. Return in the morning with your packhorse, and I will give you all the food you can carry."

"No rabbit," I said. "Hates rabbit."

"How could anyone hate rabbit?" she muttered. "She cannot be so wonderful as you say, if she hates rabbit."

I could not help myself—I laughed. That was the voice of a woman who'd grown up having rabbit as an occasional treat. That was the voice of a woman who knew hunger.

But I had to defend your honor. "She is," I said.

She quirked a brow. Then, more clearly: "No rabbit, then. But I have good rice, and salmon; eggs, chickens, and milk; quail and soft bread."

When I was younger, my family would tell stories about singing girls around the fire. We do not really have them, as a culture. If a man wishes to sleep with a woman who is not his wife, then who cares, so long as his wife and her husband are not home? If, later, that man should decide he wants to seriously court that woman, he presents her husband with a bottle of kumaq wrapped in wolfskins.

I suppose I've upset you with this part of the story already. But it is important. And I will remind you, Shizuka, that I never strayed from you in those days. I may have been raised Qorin, but I have

Hokkaran blood in me, too. And sometimes it is good to stop moving. Some people are worth stopping for.

At any rate, my family told stories about singing girls, for some of them had never met one. Surely, a woman who can have others pay her for a bedding must be beautiful beyond compare. Surely, she must walk draped in gold; surely her fingers glitter with precious stones. We call them Altanai. "Golden ones."

I'd seen singing girls before. I knew the stories about Altanai weren't true. But hearing Ren list off the food she could give us, I almost believed them.

"You may have all this and more, Barsalai. Anything you wish from my home is yours. But in return, I must ask you a favor."

I crossed my arms and nodded.

"Two li to the east of here is a river. You must've crossed it, coming up here. If you follow it to the northwest, where it meets the grand lake, you will find a cave. That is where the Yellow Scarves have hidden away."

"You want them dead?" I said. I did not know how many there were. What a grand thing to ask a person, as a favor!

"I do," she said, "but more important, I want my father's war mask. You won't miss it—it's a laughing fox, very ornate. If you retrieve it for me, Barsalai, you will have my eternal devotion. Whatever you need of me, I will provide."

Whatever I needed. She knew exactly what she was saying when she used those words.

"How many bandits?" I asked.

"Twice twenty," she said. "But that cave is where they sleep. You can find them at night, and kill them without a fight."

Forty of them—you Hokkarans hate saying "four."

I could do it. I did not have a bow, but I did have a knife and my hands and my teeth. You had your sword. That was all we needed. Forty bandits. We could do it, if we went at night and killed them in their sleep.

You would not want to do it that way, though; I knew this in my bones. You'd want to walk in and challenge their leader. Unwise. Bandits are not beholden to dueling laws.

But I could find some plan that would be safer, something that would still challenge you.

I could be the hero Ren seemed to think I was.

"I will do it," I said. "I will bring the mask to you."

She bowed in thanks. "Good," she said. "Then you should return to the one lucky enough to claim you. I am certain you are tired."

"I do not tire," I said. But I bowed to her, too, and when I mounted Alsha, I felt lighter than I had in weeks.

"My home is easy to find," she called. "Look for the stables. I own five mares and one stallion."

Hmm. Awful lot of horses for a Hokkaran woman.

You found me in the morning skinning the rabbit. When you emerged from the tent, you did your best to smile, as if everything were forgotten. You even came and sat next to me while I worked. As I cut into the little creature, you grew a bit paler. I remember, you scrunched your face, and that line across your nose came into being again.

You crossed your legs. "You will need a bow soon," you said. "Perhaps we can buy one in the next town. It must be difficult to hunt with only a knife."

In response, I wiggled my bloody hand. Sharp black nails gleamed in the sun. "Ten knives," I said.

"Small knives," you countered. Ah, there it was—a knowing smirk, a flicker of flame in your voice. "You cannot throw those."

"I could cut them off," I said.

You pursed your lips. "Do not dream of it. Your fingers are national treasures."

"They'd grow back," I said. I wiggled them again, this time right at your face.

You laughed and skittered away. "Barsalai Shefali, don't you dare!"

Barsalai and Barsatoq—like two pine needles.

I grinned. Only when you broke down laughing, only when I was tickling you and you flailed like a four-year-old, did I stop. Our faces hot with joy, we held each other there, by the campfire. I lay on your chest, your fingers tracing strands of my hair. I listened to your heart beating, like hooves on dry ground.

"Shizuka," I said.

"Yes, my love?"

"I went to the village last night," I said.

You quirked a brow. "Did you?" you said. "Did you find any-thing?"

"I know where the bandits are," I said.

And at this, you sat up. Your amber eyes sparkled. "Their hide-out?" you said. "Do you know how many? Can we reach them before nightfall?"

I have always found it amusing when you leap at battles most would run from. At that moment, for instance, you already reached for your sword. We were alone in the woods, hours away from the bandits—but you were ready to slay them.

"Forty," I said, "up the river."

"Forty," you repeated, never one for superstition. You rubbed your chin. "Difficult, but possible. Come. Let us plan. If we rid Shiseiki of these bandits, then the people will welcome us with open arms."

We sat by the camp and drew pictures in the dirt. Our biggest obstacle, as you saw it, was being surrounded. If we could face them in small groups, we'd be victorious. Five, seven each; this was manageable. But how were we going to cut a group of forty into eight groups of five?

For this you had an answer.

We'd set eight fires.

I did not want to harm the forest. Fires spread quickly near dry tinder like this. Nearby villages might be harmed, to say nothing of the damage to the animals living in it.

"We have no time to divert the river," you said. "That would be the thing to do—but two people and one admirable mare alone cannot do it. What else would draw them out?"

"I could," I said.

You shook your head. "No, Shefali," you said. "That is dumb and foolhardy, even by my standards. I forbid it."

"We cannot light the fires," I said.

"And we cannot use the river. What else, then, can we do?"

"I could kill things," I said. "Throw them in. Be frightening. I am good at frightening now."

Good at killing, good at scaring, good at hunting on all fours like an animal. I was good at many things—but nothing I'd liked before.

"Shefali," you said, "you are good for more than that."

I bit my tongue. You stared at your drawing in the dirt.

"We might as well ride," you said. "The closer we come, the more likely it is we'll see something we can use. It is a fool's errand to make maps of a place we've never seen."

That was all you had to say on the subject. Dejected, I climbed onto Alsha.

She's right, you know, Alsha said to me. *You are a fine rider, and you have excellent taste in sweets.*

"You'd say so," I muttered.

The ride to the bandit camp took us the better part of a day. Though I had demon blood coursing through my veins, though I could tear a man asunder with my bare hands, the sound of the river made me clutch my reins. So much water nearby, all rushing forward at once. If I waded in, I knew the waters would swallow me whole.

By the time we first spotted the Yellow Scarves, the Moon had begun her nightly ascent. Two guards stood on the riverbank. I spotted them before you did. With a raised hand, I stopped our advance and pointed them out.

A sharp metal tone hung in the air as you drew your sword. No. That would not work.

You wrinkled your nose, pointed at them with the tip of your sword.

I shook my head. I dismounted and came close enough to you to whisper. "Stay here," I said. "I'll follow them."

You scowled. "Why?" you protested. "It is better to kill them now, so that we do not have to deal with them later."

"Others would notice," I said. Part of me bristled at this—I did not question your fool decisions; why were you questioning my sound ones? "Better to track, for now."

You glanced at the patrol. For the most part, they avoided the road, weaving between the birch trees. One had a bow, the other a pike. How a bandit ended up with a bow is beyond me, but I resolved to take it from him regardless. With a bow in my hands, I'd feel more like my old self.

After some moments of pouting, you sheathed your sword. "Very well," you said. "See if there is another way into the cave."

As I left, I gave you a quick kiss on the lips. It did not remove the frown from your face. Resentment was a serpent coiled around my throat.

After all I'd done for you, after all I'd given up, you could not be bothered to smile?

"Return safely," you said. But I was not sure I wanted to.

I set out to follow the patrol. When I was out of your sight, I kicked off my boots. Bare feet were quieter, and I did not need to worry about stepping on something sharp. I wasn't sure I'd feel it if I did.

I loped through the darkness. Wet dirt stuck to my soles with every step. I opened my mouth and tasted the forest—the sharp tang of metal, savory earth, salty sweat, and sweet, sweet fear. My pulse quickened. Fear. Unmistakable in taste.

Were they afraid someone would spot them?

Were they afraid of me?

Oh, it was a foolish thought, self-centered as could be. But it was a sweet one, too, sweet as the poison assassins make from apple seeds. The closer I came, the easier it was to hear their hushed conversation.

"It's an exaggeration," said the man with the bow. "You think one woman did all that? One woman tore twelve men apart? Keichi is telling stories again."

My tongue lolled out of my mouth, but I found myself smiling.

If only you could taste it, Shizuka, perhaps then you would understand—it is better than chilled plum wine, better than kumaq.

Step out of the shadows, they whispered. *Let them see you. Hear them scream.*

Spittle hit the ground. Somehow in my fear-drunk haze, I'd started drooling. I shook my head. No. There was work to be done.

I wiped my mouth on my sleeve and followed them. Twenty, thirty minutes I followed. Our little hiding spot by the river lay near the end of their patrol. Soon, they came up on the cave. It was about as wide across as three horses standing nose to tail, though it did not look like much. Like the earth was yawning. More of a pit than a cave, really. From what I could see, it was a steep walk underground. Two more bandits kept watch here. They wore tattered cloth armor; notched swords hung at their hips.

The two I followed nodded solemnly to the guards. They exchanged some words I did not allow myself to hear. If the demons heard it, they'd encourage me to kill. It was not quite time for that.

So I kept my distance and waited. Eventually, after another ten minutes or so, the guards traded places. The ones formerly standing at the gates began a patrol. I trailed them, too, until finally I came upon our hiding spot.

At first you did not see me. You stood on the edge of the water, looking out, in the direction of the capital. One cannot see Fujino from such a great distance away, but one can see the mountains separating it from Shiseiki. You had the look of a sailor's wife waiting for her lover.

I called your name.

You jolted, drawing your sword in one motion as you turned. "You are a fool to attack me!"

You slashed at me faster than most can follow. But I am not most, and I jumped to the right before blade met flesh. I held up my hands, did my best to stand straight. Like a person, I thought. I must be a person. Must be human.

"Shizuka," I said, "it's me."

I cannot tell which was more dominant then, for you. Was it the pain of knowing you'd almost hurt me, or was it shock that you had not recognized me?

Either way, you stood, staggered, staring at me as if I were a stranger.

"Am I different?" I asked. For that thought was ice on the back of my neck. My teeth changed in a moment; what if something else had?

"My love," you said. "Dear one, your eyes . . ."

I touched them. They felt like eyes. So I went to the river and I knelt there, and I looked at myself.

As a paper lantern glows orange, so did my eyes glow green.

I frowned. Most of the changes to my body had been useful, until now. If the Traitor's blood was going to shape me in his image, he could at least focus on improving me. Glowing eyes did nothing. In fact, I'd be easier to spot in the dark now.

I closed my eyes and sighed. "It could be worse," I said.

You touched my face, your touch delicate as a flower petal. I remember how wide your eyes were. "Does it hurt?" you asked. "They look like they are burning."

"Everything hurts, Shizuka," I said. "This hurts only a little."

I pointed toward the cave, eager for something else to talk about. "Two guards by it, two on patrol," I said.

Whatever you thought about the changes, you said nothing. You looked down for a moment, licked your lips, and joined me in planning. Together we came up with something halfway between your burning the forest down and Ren's idea of killing them in their sleep.

For the next twenty minutes, we collected pine branches. I bundled them up and tied them together with rope from my saddlebags. Then we waited for the patrols to come around again.

Dispatching them was a simple matter; I will not dwell on it here. When they came near enough to us, I threw my knife at one, and you cut the other down as he moved to investigate the body. I took one of the notched swords—I really wanted the bow the man by the cave had, but this would do for now. With the patrol dead, we had only a few minutes to make our way to the cave. I slung the pine branches over my shoulder and led the way.

When we caught sight of the cave mouth, you drew your sword again. We crept around through the birch and pine, out of sight, until we were behind the guards. I set down the bundle.

Then we killed them, and I took the one man's bow and quiver.

It is as simple as that, and I am loath to give this any more detail. This was not a great, glorious fight. This was stabbing men in the dark. It would've been beneath you had it not been for such a noble cause.

We propped the bodies up with two of the branches and tied them up with rope. Then I fished flint and steel from my deel and got to work setting the remaining branches alight.

Only when the fire was truly raging, only when the burning branches birthed clouds of white smoke, did we continue.

I dropped the bundle into the cave. We stood on either side and waited.

A handful of Yellow Scarves bolted out with stinging eyes, shouting and disoriented. You did not bother announcing yourself. For each cut you made, another bandit fell, simple and solemn as that. This was not something to celebrate. This was not glorious.

I nocked an arrow; I loosed. I tried to isolate what I was doing to the motions. Drawing, loosing. I stared at the arrows and not at their targets. Maybe then I wouldn't focus so much on the color of their blood, on their fear like wine, on the glimmers like crushed gems as their souls left their bodies.

I thought if I didn't see it, nothing would happen.

But I tasted it. Their blood. Their souls, rich and shimmering. Their confusion, their anger. And the one taste hovering above them all.

Imagine your father journeyed to Ikhtar, and brought you back some of their famed desserts. You must have had some by now, but I shall tell you of them anyway. They are moist, thick, jelly treats, rolled in sugar. Putting one in your mouth is like tasting joy itself. Imagine he brought these for you when you were only a child, and you ate them all in one night. The memory of them stays with you. Longing amplifies a delicious taste to something heavenly. By the time you are grown, you crave them more than any other, and no Hokkaran sweet can compare.

It is like that, Shizuka. It is like that.

So when I opened my mouth and let my tongue loll in the air to get a better taste, and you noticed me, you stared.

"Shefali?" you said. "Are you all right?"

There was one thing you did not notice.

I never put my boots back on.

What a small thing to forget. What an insignificant thing. Nowadays, forgetting my boots would not trouble me. I have more control, you see.

But I was sixteen then, newly changed, and smoke seared my nose. Bandits are fond of drinking; I think one of them fell into the fire. Burning flesh has such a distinct smell, Shizuka, so hard to ignore. My stomach churned, and my lips grew moist in anticipation.

Yes, I could hear it now: they were screaming for help. Someone fell in the flames. When I took a deep breath of the darkening smoke, I smelled him. I took in a bit of his soul, and I savored it as one savors finely charred meat.

Burning flesh. Bones snapping as you stepped on the fallen. Rubies in the air. It was all so heady, Shizuka, it was all so unreal.

I took a yearning step toward you, and I happened to step directly into a corpse's wound. Still-warm organs growing cold; bone holding me in place.

Burning flesh.

Cherry-sweet blood.

If I had worn my boots, I think, and not felt that corpse's innards, I would not have had such a reaction.

But there were four men left when my jaw unhinged.

The bow fell from my hands. I lurched forward. A howl pealed from my mouth, a sound I had no idea I could make. I do not know how high I jumped, but I tell you, it felt like flying.

Horror dawned on my victim's face when I landed on him. His companions did not stay to watch. When I turned to laugh at them, to mock them, I saw only their backs as they ran into the woods.

"Do you see them?" I said into the bandit's ear. Spittle dripped onto his collarbones. "They're smarter than you are."

With my feet on his shoulders, I took a handful of his hair. He tried to push me off, but my grip was iron, my grip was death itself.

I twisted at the hips until I heard a wet crack. The bandit crumpled. I jumped on top of his body, on my hands and knees. Red. I could see it beneath his skin; I could see it in rivers and lakes and streams. So close. Gods, it was so close and so bright.

Saliva dripped from my mouth onto the man's broken neck. Yes. Yes, this is what I was made for, this moment before teeth met flesh.

Except someone stopped me.

Someone grabbed me by my braid and yanked.

I turned. Whoever interrupted me, whoever interrupted what they could not understand, would have to die as well. That was the way of things. There were mortals, there were gods, there were demons.

And then there was me.

The Not-You stood before me, baring blackened teeth, pointing at me with fingers so rotted, they were more bone than meat.

"You're misbehaving," it said, and as it advanced on me, maggots squirmed from its left eye. Soon they were bursting out through its iris. "This is not how I trained you, Steel-Eye!"

A crack of wrath. I beat my chest and roared, heedless of which bandits remained. "Trained me?" I said. "You do not train me!"

It took another step forward, its sickly gray tongue peeking out from between its lips. By now the maggots had devoured its left eye. The smile on its face was a twisted mirror of yours; all arrogance, all brash certainty.

"You are my dog," it said. "You always have been. Why else do you follow, nipping at my heels, like a lost puppy?"

It shoved a finger into my chest.

"When I want someone dead, I say so, and there you are."

It shoved me again.

"I give you orders. You carry them out. You get hurt and I get the credit."

It cupped my face, squeezed in my cheeks.

"That is how our relationship works, Steel-Eye. How it has always worked. I am the Virgin Empress. You are the bitch."

I grabbed it by the throat.

In an instant, we were on the ground. Beneath my hands, I felt bone and sinew. If I squeezed hard enough, I could end this. I could pop off the thing's head and never be bothered by it again.

Kill. Kill, kill, kill, the only thing I'm good at, the only thing I have ever truly been good at. Kill it. Kill it and find freedom, find peace.

So I squeezed and squeezed and squeezed, snarling all the while. Blood drained from the thing's face. As I choked it, it turned blue, it struggled beneath me, it slapped and kicked and punched.

But when its right palm struck me, so, too, did reality.

I was choking you. Your pomegranate lips turned pale as bird's eggs, your veins like rivers on the map of your skin. The look on your face, Shizuka. The anguish, the pain, the fear. You were so small and so delicate; my hands so large and monstrous and . . .

And I'd nearly killed you.

"Shefali?" you croaked. "Shefali, have you . . . have you returned?"

My jaw hung slack now, not in hunger, not in thirst, but in shame. It hit me hard as any hammer, winded me, left me hollow and broken. Prying my hands away from you felt like . . . they must've been someone else's hands. Must have been. My own hands would never hurt you.

Let go. Let go.

When I finally pried them off your throat, my hands were frozen in place, sore and aching. Try as I might, I could not will them to relax.

I stared at you, stared at my hands. Shaking. I was shaking. You massaged your throat and tried to sit up. I moved to help you, but . . . but I couldn't bring myself to touch you.

"It's all right," you said. "That wasn't you."

But it was not all right. And it was me.

No.

I needed to disappear. You'd be better off without me.

I shot to my feet. A faint glimmer of bronze caught my eye; the laughing fox mask Ren had asked for was strapped to a corpse's face. I looked from it to you.

You were scrambling up. "Shefali?"

"It was me. I did it, Shizuka, it was me," I said. "And I have to die."

And I grabbed the mask, turned my back to you, and ran to my horse fast as I could. I knew you could not hope to follow. I knew you'd try anyway.

But I hoped you'd let me go. I hoped you'd let me just die, as I deserved. What else was I good for, what else could I do?

As I rode through the woods, I thought of how I'd do it.

Traditional Hokkaran suicides are too painful, even for someone like me. Kneeling before a crowd and disemboweling myself? No. I could not and would not. The first stroke alone wouldn't be enough to kill me, and by then I'd . . . I'd change again.

No. It had to be something quick. Something that would not leave behind a body. A pyre. Yes, a pyre was ideal. All I had to do was gather kindling, purchase some oil to speed things, tie myself to a pole, and light it all up. Holy flame could cleanse me if nothing else could. When everything was done, a gentle breeze would carry my ashes to the sky, where they belonged. By the time you found me, there'd be nothing left to mourn over, and you could continue your life as if I'd never been in it.

Once, my people looked on me with admiration. My mother would never want her deel back now, would she? Tiger-Striped Shefali, who won her first braid at eight years of age. Tiger-Striped Shefali, who never missed with bow or with knife. The future Grand Kharsa of all the Qorin. The girl who would lead whatever was left of our people to glory again.

But she was gone now. In her place was the tiger's daughter, wearing her skin and clothes.

Once, you said we were gods.

What a bitter thought.

On most nights, when I see my mare, a sense of calm washes over me. During my travels, I've turned to her for comfort more than once. There is an old Qorin trick for anxiety—stand with your head up toward the sky. Touch your horse's flank with your right hand, and your own heart with your left. Listen to her breathe; feel her heart beat. Try to match hers.

It's said that Tumenbayar herself taught us this. She could speak to her horse, too, though she had to be touching her to do it. Every few generations, someone will claim to have the same ability I do—people pretend to be part of Tumenbayar's clan all the time.

But Qorin value deeds, not words. Anyone who says such a thing is soon put to the test, and my mother has never taken kindly to liars.

I've never told her about this ability of mine. The thought of being tested in front my entire family, in front of the whole clan, was enough to break me out in hives. Bad enough I never missed a shot. Otgar already took bets on whether or not I'd be able to hit a bird a hundred horselengths away, blindfolded.

I always did.

If she knew I could talk to my mare—I hesitated to imagine what she'd come up with.

I'd never have the chance to see now.

But still I stood there with my head up toward the sky and my right hand on Alsha's flank. I could not fool her; she knew my intentions.

You are leaving Shizuka behind?

"I must," I said. "She is better off this way."

Alsha stomped her front hoof. *And I am better off with three legs,* she said. Of course she was not going to understand. As much as I spoke to her, she was still just a horse.

"Will you take me, or not?" I said.

Alsha whickered. *Better I take you than you go alone,* she said.

Well. At least she wasn't trying to talk me out of it. I suppose my horse can see sense sometimes. It must be because she is a good Qorin mare. Hotheaded, stubborn, yes; but protective as can be.

I tied the war mask around my neck. It would be my last duty in this world, my last good deed.

Besides killing myself.

If you called after me, I did not hear you. I tried not to think of you at all beyond how much better off you'd be a year from now. What you felt now was a temporary pain. What you felt now was weakness leaving the body. Fire put to a wound. That's all I was. A gaping wound on your chest leaking thick black blood.

You'd heal. You always healed.

I made plans. I'd tell Ren what you looked like, so that when you came into town looking for me, she could provide you with whatever you wanted. Food. A place to stay. Company, perhaps. You deserved better company than me, deserved someone who would not wrap their hands around your throat and—

The one thing I'd ask for, the one thing I had to ask for, was oil. Otherwise, the fire wouldn't burn hot enough. What was I going to do with Alsha? I'd leave her to you. Yes. I'd tell Ren to keep everyone away from my horse except you. Alsha liked you.

It took only a few minutes for me to settle the minutiae of my life. My brother, my father, my mother—they would find ways to cope. My mother could name Otgar the Grand Kharsa. Clearly, she favored her. It would not be so difficult. Kenshiro was a recently married man; he'd name a child after me if he was feeling gracious.

My father would not mourn.

By the time I arrived at the village, it was the start of Second Bell. If I was stared at two nights ago (had it been so short a time?), then I was gaped at now. I'd not bothered wiping the blood off my feet or pants or deel. I did not see the point. Why bother hiding it anymore? I was a monster. I met the eyes of those who stared, nodded to them. They looked away quickly. Ren was standing in the same place, near the winehouse. When she saw me, she started, but she was kind enough to cover it with her fan. She ran toward me.

"Barsalai!" she called. "Is that . . . Is that the mask, around your neck?"

I offered the mask to Ren.

She took it from me gingerly. I watched as she held it above her head, so that the light of the sun shone down through the eyeholes.

It is a rare thing to see perfect joy on a person's face. I saw it then. Tears sprang to her eyes; she clutched the mask close to her chest. For a long while, she held it there. A soft smile contrasted against her damp cheeks.

What was I to say? I was glad to have helped her. But I did not want to continue existing if it meant I was going to hurt you again.

She tugged my hand. "Come," she said. "Come, you must let me thank you."

I drew back my hand and shook my head. "I need oil," I said.

Ren furrowed her brow. Two lines appeared at the corners of her small mouth. "What happened to food?" she asked. "Yesterday you asked for food. Today, oil. Why?"

I did not meet her gaze. "I need oil."

"What for?" she asked.

I could run. I could get the oil somewhere else.

But I had no money.

I grunted.

"Barsalai," she said. There was a quiet pleading in her voice. She took my hand and pressed it to her cheek. "Please come with me. My home is not far. I will tell you the story of the war mask, and I will see that you have your oil—but, please. Come with me."

I glanced around. Two sellswords watched us. They were concerned for Ren, I think. Part of me was happy she had people looking out for her, but most of me did not want to be bothered.

Yet when she looked at me, I felt the faintest memory of being a hero. Of Tiger-Striped Shefali.

So I sighed and dismounted, and I followed her to her home. It was the largest in the village, as it happened. On the way in, I caught sight of the stables. Yes, she did indeed have six horses: two red dun mares, one bay roan mare, a chestnut mare, a beautiful seal bay mare, and a dapple gray stallion. The seal bay and dapple gray intrigued me; I'd never seen horses of those colors outside the steppes, and these were all stocky Hokkaran workhorses.

Where had she gotten them?

Inside, a serving girl greeted me with a cheery face despite what I looked like, despite the blood I tracked into the house. Ren led me upstairs. The fact that she had an upstairs at all spoke well of her status. There are Ikhthian nobles who dream of having furnishings as beautiful as the ones I saw that day. Fine silk divans, gauzy curtains swaying gently in the nighttime air; plums of incense smoke imparting intoxicating scents. This was the sort of home even you would take pride in.

So the oil had to be around here somewhere. She had lanterns, after all, and if she could keep lanterns burning, certainly she could keep me burning.

She led us to her bedroom, and I saw no lanterns there. Only candles shining with dim orange light. What if she wasn't going to give it to me? What if I had to find it somewhere else? What if I had to break into someone's home and steal it? Was I capable of such a thing?

The whole room smelled of flowers. They almost drowned out the scent of sex, the scent of burning.

I was in a singing girl's bedchamber at Second Bell while you ran through the woods, trying to find me.

"Take a seat anywhere you would like," she said.

I did not sit. I stood and crossed my arms. Ren was fiddling with something in the corner of her room, something on a shelf. When she finally turned, I realized what it was: a small portable shrine, similar to the one you had. Two little statues—one of the Grandmother and one of the Daughter—held unburnt prayer tags. The foxhead sat between them. Grandmother and Daughter—Ren had to have been born in either a first year or an eighth year, then. Eight years older than me, or eight years older than you.

Was that why I liked her so much? I did not think much of Hokkaran astrology, but the coincidence stuck out like a bone in thin stew. One of those idols was her birth year, and one was her chosen patron.

Which was which?

"This mask belonged to my father," she said. "He fought in the Qorin war against Sur-Shar, and when that was done, he went to the Wall to help send the blackbloods back."

She touched the edges of the mask as if she were touching her father's face. When she looked to me, she wiped away another tear.

"That was why, when Kato told me what you had done, I was so impressed," she said.

A knock at the door. The serving girl came in just long enough to set a tray down on a nightstand. On it, a bottle of plum wine and two small cups. Ren sniffled, but that did not stop her reaching for the wine. She held her billowing sleeve back as she poured into the cups. Her bare wrist was pale as her namesake, small and delicate and—

Like yours. Like your small hands beating at my face, trying to get me to stop hurting you and—

"Barsalai?" Ren was speaking to me.

I'd closed my eyes to shut out the image of you. Now I opened them and found that she, too, looked wounded.

She slid over the cup of wine. "Drink," she said. "You look like a woman who needs it."

I was a woman who needed oil. Not alcohol. But I did not have much to counter that with. It'd been some time since I last had plum wine, at any rate. I sighed and tipped the cup to my lips. It tasted like dirt, which didn't much surprise me. Foolish of me to hope it'd be any different.

"Barsalai," she said, tutting softly. "Something wears on you."

She reached for me; I drew away. No. No one could touch me. I did not deserve such sympathy, nor the wine that I continued to drink. This entire situation was preposterous.

Ren must've realized her doting was getting her nowhere. She finished her cup and set it down. Then she held up the mask again. "Do you know how many years my father wore this?"

I studied it. Whoever cast it did a fine job—the fox's whiskers stood out now after at least a century—but nicks and scratches betrayed its age.

"Many," I said.

Ren nodded. "Twenty years," she said. "He stopped only when he lost his left eye."

My head hurt when she said that—a sudden, sharp pain, like an arrow in my skull. I rubbed my eyes to deal with it, but it was gone within a few seconds.

"I was ten, I think, when that happened. Kato was five. All of us moved back to Imakane, where my father was born. With the money the Son of Heaven provided him, he bought a plot of land." A fond smile crossed her face. "Would you believe I was a country girl?"

I shook my head. This village was not Fujino, but Ren made it seem bigger just by being in it.

"I was," she said. "I've always wanted to go to the capital, but back then it was just an idle dream. My father thought he had two sons in those days. Perhaps he sought to marry me off to some other farmer's daughter."

I LET OUT a soft sound as it all fell into place. So that was why she kept so many horses! Like the healers of my people, she was a sanvaartain. With the proper medicines, she could change her body into one that suited her. Now her Qorin mentors made sense.

"I think I would have gone already, if the Yellow Scarves hadn't attacked us. But they did. They were hungry, they claimed, and ours was the only farm that bore crop that season. So they took everything, torched the land, and killed my parents."

She said it softly, quieter than a whisper. I fought the urge to touch her shoulder. I wanted to comfort her somehow. I know what it is like to lose family. I know what it is like to be alone.

But my hands were no longer meant for comforting. The moment I reached out, I caught sight of my talons and drew back. No.

"I've been here, trying to earn enough so that Kato and I can move to Fujino together," she said.

Silence followed. Oil. Ask her for the oil. A great pyre I'd light, and she'd see it here from her balcony and know that I was free. Oil.

But Ren stood from the bed. Without her wooden sandals, she was smaller than I thought. I could see her pulse as she came closer. One, two, one two—I could see it. I bit my lip and resolved to look at her hands, and only her hands.

Except I saw her pulse there, too.

Urges. Half of me screamed to pin her against the wall and tear out her throat. The other half still wanted to pin her to the wall, still wanted to press my teeth to her neck—but that was different. Singing girl. I could make her do more than sing, if she wanted me.

But neither of those things were me, neither of those were *my* thoughts, so why was it that I kept thinking them? Why did I keep hearing them over and over when all I wanted to do was die?

I pressed myself flat against the wall.

"Barsalai," she said. "Did something happen at the cave?"

Did something happen at the cave? she asked, as if I wanted to speak about this at all with someone I barely knew. Yes, something happened at the cave. I proved I'm a worthless human being.

Save that I was no longer human.

I massaged my temples. Biting my lip, I nodded.

"I thought as much," she said. "That is why you want oil today, and not food."

Again I nodded. Just give me the oil. Just give me the oil and let me jump into the fire; better that than live and continue hurting you.

"Was she hurt?" Ren asked. "The woman you wanted to buy food for."

I was a waterskin, pierced by an arrow. Something within me just . . . just burst. And before I knew what was happening, I was on the floor of a singing girl's home in tears.

"I did it," I kept repeating. "I hurt her, I almost killed her and I couldn't stop. . . ."

Clutching my knees, I was clutching my knees, rocking back and forth. Horrible, weepy moans left me. At times I'd tug at my hair or rake my cheeks. Ren sat in front of me, whispering words

I did not quite understand in the haze of my depression. I remember her saying she was going to hold me, I remember that. I remember how she struggled to fit her arms around me because of our disparate sizes. I remember how much she looked like you: small, dark, delicate, like a porcelain doll I'd nearly shattered.

I let her hold me. I let her hold me because I knew I was never going to let you do it again. Not with what had happened.

I do not know how long I was weeping, only that by the time I was done, my voice was hoarse and my eyes ached. It was only then that I began to hear what Ren was saying.

"You must keep going, Barsalai," she said. "For all those who cannot."

"Why?" I snapped. "Why bother?"

At this she pursed her lips. "Because we need hope," she said.

I hung my head. Hope. As if I could provide such a thing.

Ren stood, all at once, and reached for the shrine. "You are the only one who has ever helped us," she said. "Really helped us. The guards sit on their haunches and complain of danger; the captains on the Wall don't pay attention to commoners. Only you helped us. Only you have lived, where everyone else has died."

I wished I were dead, too. I looked up at her and frowned.

"There will be other villages," she said. "Other singing girls who need help. There will be soldiers, once afraid of the black-blood, who remember that you've conquered it. Barsalai, you must keep going."

"I hurt her," I said.

"Does she live?" asked Ren.

I nodded. Yes, I'd seen you get up. You were alive, thank the gods.

"Then you have to see her again," she said, "if only to apologize."

Ren sat near me again. With shaking hands, she offered me her father's mask. "Here," she said. "Wear it and remember: You are a hero in Shiseiki."

I stared at it, stared at her.

"Take it," she said.

"It was your father's," I said.

She nodded slowly. She touched the fox's muzzle one last time. "It was," she said. "But he cannot wear it now. So I think it is right for you to have it."

I stared at the mask.

Yes, it was a fine piece of craftsmanship. Every hair on the fox's muzzle ached to be petted. Wrinkles around its eyes suggested mischievous mirth. Ren was being humble about her father. Only officers receive war masks of this quality. Such a thing could easily fetch five hundred ryo at market. More, if the buyer, like my brother, delighted in historical artifacts. That was more than enough to leave this village. It was enough to *feed* a village.

Yet here she was, offering it to a woman she'd known for all of a day.

I shook my head. "I cannot," I said.

Ren pursed her lips. "Barsalai, please," she said. "It is the only thing of value I can give you."

"Why?" I asked, meeting her gaze. Why give me anything at all? I'd only asked for oil.

Yet she did not waver. There was so much about her that reminded me of you, Shizuka—a different version of you. For she, too, was small as a yearling, but coltish and stubborn. I saw in her eyes and the set of her dainty feet that she was not going to let me win.

"You know the story of Minami Shiori and the fox woman?" she asked. Of course I did. I'd only heard you tell it forty times.

One day, while walking through the woods, a distraught woman came running up to your ancestor. The woman, dressed in finery, claimed that she was part of the Son of Heaven's caravan. Bandits had just attacked. The guard captain was among the slain. She needed someone to fight back, and Minami Shiori was the first person she saw holding a sword.

Instantly Shiori was suspicious. Fine though the woman's robes were, they were also old—the sort of thing a grandmother might wear.

"My lady," said Shiori, "you understand, the gods are at war—these are troubling times. Swear on the Eight that the Son of Heaven is truly in danger, and I will go."

At this the woman faltered. She hemmed and hawed and tried to find a way out of it. Just as Shiori was about to draw her blade, the woman spoke.

"I swear to you on the Eight," she said, "that the Son of Heaven is truly in danger, and I will truly take you to his side."

It is well known no one can break an Eightfold Oath. So Shiori followed the woman without reservation. Sure enough, she did come upon the Son of Heaven tied to a tree. Sure enough, his entire coterie lay as corpses around him, with holes where their hearts should've been.

It was then that the woman rounded on Shiori. She'd kept her word, for she'd brought her back to an endangered Emperor. But that was where the oath ended. As she fixed Shiori with her heart-piercing glare, she was sure of her victory.

But Minami Shiori knew the instant she laid eyes on the Emperor what had happened. She drew her blade and sheath, then held her sheath before her face.

"Will you not put your weapons down?" cooed the fox woman. "I mean you no harm."

"You mean to kill me," she said, "and bewitch the Emperor besides. No, I shall not put my sword down."

She crept closer, staring at the fox woman's feet to judge distance. Fox paws peeked out from beneath the hem of her robes.

"But must you kill me, my darling?" said the fox woman. "For I have loved you long from afar, and I know all the secrets of your body. Come to me, lie with me, and I will make you strong enough to conquer Hokkaro."

Shiori took another step forward, and another, and another. Eventually she did drop her sword and sheath—but she never looked directly at the creature. It wrapped its arms around her, pulled her in close—

And it was then that Shiori struck. She pulled a knife from inside her sleeve and slipped it between the fox woman's ribs. After the creature crumpled to the ground, she cut off one of its nine tails, and dabbed the blood on the Emperor's lips. This broke the fox woman's spell.

That is not a very good telling of the story. I am certain that, reading this, you are shaking your head, lamenting some part I've forgotten. I know Shiori says something before she stabs the fox woman in your version. I do not know what it is. Something full of bravado, probably. I will let you fill in that detail now, as you are reading.

"I don't know much about your condition," Ren had continued, "or how it affects you. But I do know you are more of a hero than Minami-zuo was. All she had to do was resist a fox woman. Dif-

ficult, but it is something anyone might do if they put their mind
to it."

She paused and touched my face. I do not want you to think
it was an amorous sort of touch; it was not. Concern, pity,
sympathy—these things dominated her features. If she'd wanted
to bed me, she would have made it clear, Shizuka; this was nothing more than comfort.

"What you fight is much worse. It is not a fox woman, standing
in front of you. It's in your blood," she said. Her hand hovered
over my heart, but she did not touch it. Already she was treading
on broken ice. If she touched my heart, she'd fall into the frozen
water. "Barsalai, I cannot know how you suffer. But you must keep
fighting her, this fox woman in your veins. Your Empress is help-
less until it is slain. If you give in, she, too, will wither and die."

I find it strange, to this day, that she chose a story about Minami
Shiori to make her point. Why not one about Emperor Yone, or
the Gray Master? Or Yusuke the Brawler?

Why choose a story about one of your ancestors saving another?

Something about this struck me. At times, Shizuka, life is like
watching pine needles falling into poems.

And you and I, well . . .

"Take the mask, Barsalai," she said. "Mock your temptations.
Do not let them rule you. Your Empress needs you."

I looked down at the laughing fox.

I thought of you in the woods alone, with no idea how to hunt
and less idea how to make a camp. No—that wasn't right. You
knew how to make a camp, didn't you? My mother sent you out a
day's ride from the clan once, on your own, so that you'd learn how
to set up a tent and hunt for your own food. She left you there for
a whole week before she allowed me to go to you. I was terrified

that you'd be lost or hungry, but there you were hale as ever. You'd coaxed a birch tree from the ground and slung a blanket over its lowest branch in lieu of a real tent. Your campfire was badly made, and by all rights should not have lasted an hour, let alone however long you'd been keeping it. Next to the fire was a pot full of berries not native to the steppes. On second glance many of the same berries grew on the birch tree, somehow, though they don't normally bear fruit. You had a single marmot cooking on a spit above the flames. You had not bothered to skin it. Did the smell of burning fur not bother you?

"Cheater," I said.

You laughed. "To survive is Qorin, isn't it?" you said. "Your mother said I should use all the tools available to me."

You and I both knew she hadn't meant divine tools.

But you and I both knew that I wasn't going to tell her.

Now, even as the memory hurt me, it brought me comfort. You could hunt. Not well, but you could. You had my tent. If an animal approached you, then you had your sword. When it came to survival you'd get by, as you always did.

But what about *you?* About *us?* I tried to kill you and then left without saying anything at all. That would shatter the hardest of hearts.

And so I put on the mask.

Ren's smile was one of teary-eyed relief. She threw her arms around me and held me tight for a few beats. "Barsalai," she said, "you may have whatever you wish from my home. If you . . . If you still want the oil . . ."

I shook my head. "Food," I said. "I will return in the morning for it."

Together we rose. She gave a short bow. "Good," she said. "I shall watch for your mare. And, Barsalai?"

I turned, one hand on the sliding screen.

"I hope I will see you again."

There is a certain pain one feels at times. Not from a wound, but from the anticipation of the wound. In that instant before blade meets flesh, already you can imagine what the cut will be like. Your mind hurts you before the metal does.

That moment, I think, was an arrow soaring toward me.

"I do, too," I said.

I rode into the forest like a crack of thunder. Our camp didn't take long to reach. When I arrived, I saw only our tent, only the trappings we'd left behind. I did not see you. I did not see your stout red gelding. I swallowed the worry rising in my throat and closed my eyes.

I have known you all my life, Shizuka. I have played with you in the gardens of Fujino; I have slaved over letters written in a language I could barely read, I have shared a bed with you, I have held you at the moment of your small death. Part of a person's soul is in their scent: I have half of yours, and you have half of mine.

On some level, I knew this. So when I took a deep breath of the forest air, I knew what I was looking for. Your scent. Your steel peony scent.

I caught a glimmer of it to the east. I urged Alsha in that direction, standing in the saddle to get a better view of things. The scent of you grew stronger and stronger. But there was another smell, too, just as floral.

At last, I spotted familiar felt. There was my tent, flung over a low hanging branch. Bright white lilies surrounded it, lilies I'd only seen in the Imperial Gardens. At the center of the flowers, just in front of the tent, you sat with your arms around your knees. Twigs and petals alike were entangled in your now-messy hair; your cheeks were puffy and your eyes were red from all the tears.

But it was you.

"Shizuka!"

When you turned and saw me, your eyes went dawn-bright, your mouth hung open. "Shefali!" you cried. You ran to me. The flowers parted for you.

I jumped off Alsha and met you halfway, and you slammed into me with as much force as your small body could muster. I staggered backwards a step or two as you squeezed me tighter than ever before.

I kissed your forehead, kissed your hair, took deep breaths of your soul. I counted all your fingers, checked you for injury. You were fine. Thank the gods, you were fine. Weeping, but fine.

The gasps that left you reminded me of a mewling kitten. Tears rained down from your eyes; snot dripped from your button nose. You beat my chest with your tiny fists.

"Idiot!" you said amid the weeping. "Running off like that, after saying what you did . . ."

"I'm sorry," I whispered. Gods, but you kept crying and crying—you gasped for breath. "But you need to breathe, Shizuka."

You kept beating at me, raking your nails down my deel. "I didn't know where you were, Shefali, you left me alone and—"

You gulped in a deep breath. When you next opened your mouth, only syllables came out, not real words. Still you beat at me. Breathe, I said, and I remembered to do it so you'd have something to emulate. In, out, in, out.

Suddenly you grabbed fistfuls of my deel and buried your head in its roomy chest pocket. You slipped one hand inside, laid your palm flat against my heart.

"Shefali," you whimpered. "Shefali, I didn't know how . . . how hard it was for you."

Was I worth all those tears, was I truly worth them?

Bruises circled your throat where my hands had been. I touched one now.

You shook your head. "Don't," you said, "don't dwell on that."

"But—"

"Don't!" you snapped. A sob left you. You caressed my cheek with your head still buried against my chest. Do not dwell on it. Do not dwell on nearly killing you.

Your eyes were red as the peonies you so treasured. "Listen to me," you said, your fingers trailing over my lips. "Heart of my heart, listen well. Today will be the first and last time you hurt me."

I brought my brows together. You sniffed once and drew away just enough for us to look at each other eye to eye. Or as close to that as we could get, considering the height difference.

You stood proud as ever, straight backed, with your head held high. Salt trails, bloodshot eyes—these were the remnants of your previous mood. But you'd cast it aside like sullied armor.

You'd become the Empress again.

"When we were three," you said, "we met for the first time. I saw you and I felt something horrible in my bones, something awful and great. Even as a child, I knew that I could never be free of you. And, young as I was, I rankled at that idea. So, I lashed out. I tried to rid myself of you. I tried to kill you."

You paused, your regal mask dropping for an instant. You looked at your feet.

"I do not think you remember this, and you are better for it."

I did not want to tell you that I did remember. You had not yet finished speaking, and I knew interrupting you would stifle the courage you'd mustered.

"I have spent years atoning for that," you said. "I hold you dear as air, dear as light, dear as flame and earth. All my life I've . . . I've endeavored to show you how I feel. And I may not be my father, I may not be a poet, I may not make the flowers weep— but my actions, I hope, have spoken as loud as thunder."

You bit your lip.

"Yet when I look back on them, I see constant missteps," you continued. "You would not bear tiger stripes on your shoulder if I hadn't insisted on camping out. And—"

You drew a deep, sharp breath.

"And if the blackblood has driven you to such violent acts, it is only because I encouraged us to go into the temple. This yoke you wear, I have placed upon you."

You could not have known. You could not have known we'd be bested, or that I would be infected. It was not your fault, Shizuka; you sought only to fulfill the destiny you so longed for. You would've gone with or without me.

If the price of keeping you safe is this walking damnation, then I do not mind. As long as you are safe, my Shizuka. As long as you are safe.

"Shizuka—"

"Beloved, I am not done," you said. "This curse in your blood is not an enemy I can cut down—but it is something you can fight. And I will help you in whatever ways I can, insignificant though they may be. Whatever it takes to master this beast, Shefali. We will track down monks and sages. We will visit butchers together. I will hold you back and watch with you as the animals are slaughtered, that you might learn self-control. I will stand before you with an outstretched hand, my love, and if the time should ever come when you succumb—"

You swallowed.

"—then I shall be there to free you of your suffering," you said, your voice cracking. Tears streamed anew down your face. "This I swear to you. No longer will we take comfort in hollow platitudes. It is time we took the field."

You held yourself with renewed purpose. I stared at you, unable to think of words. How was I to thank you?

I drew you close and kissed you quick, and beneath our canvas tent we shed our clothing together for the first time in months.

THE EMPRESS

FIVE

The Empress of Hokkaro sends for a singing girl.

She's done this before. Eight years is a long time to sleep in an empty bed. Yes, as much as she loves Shefali—and she loves her beyond measure—she has shared herself with others. Not often, and never the same girl twice. But it has happened nonetheless.

Here is how it went: The Empress would send one of her servants to the brothel, and they'd return with someone tall and dark and silent. O-Shizuka would ask her name. That was the extent of the conversation the two of them would have. In the morning, she'd pay her handsomely and send her on her way and that was that.

O-Shizuka's heart is stitched together with the hope that she'll see Shefali again. Sometimes she needed to add a bit more thread. That was all.

But this time is different. This time, she sends her servant out with specific instructions.

"Find the brothel with the stables out front," she says. "The one run by a woman from Shiseiki Province. Enter it, and return with the madam, or do not return at all. No other will do. I don't care how beautiful they are or what charms they possess—I seek only the madam."

She knows the name of this particular pleasure house, of course. Everyone does. The Imperial Gardens. It is a gesture of Shizuka's magnanimity that she allows it to exist when it so clearly insults her.

Her servant swallows. The madam is notorious throughout Hokkaro. If Shizuka represents divinity, then the madam represents the underworld. She is in every plume of Sister's Gift; she is in every dark alley. She is an unexpected knife to the gut; she is your most precious secret spoken on the lips of a stranger.

Yes—Shizuka has dealt with her before. But never like this.

And then she waits.

And so the thoughts come.

She's seen the place before. It's not far from the palace. Oh, not too close, of course. But as close as they could conceivably get. Courtiers and warriors alike favor it; they say it's the only brothel in Fujino where you and your horse can both get a good rubdown.

O-Shizuka chuckles, alone, at the joke. It distracts her from the fires of jealousy for a fleeting moment. Then the thoughts return.

Madam Ren held Shefali. Madam Ren comforted her. The queen of the Hokkaran underworld, the woman who rules all the things Shizuka cannot be seen to touch—she is the one who comforted Shefali in her darkest moment. The thought of it— a common singing girl laid hands on the love of O-Shizuka's life! The thought of it—

Nearly infuriates her, but not quite.

She tries to get angry. She tries to fume and throw her silent fit over it, but so many years have passed since then, and O-Shizuka herself is no storied saint. Shefali kept emphasizing they never went to bed.

No, it's not worth getting upset about. That's what O-Shizuka tells herself as she waits. Somehow, it doesn't get rid of the acrid taste in the back of her mouth.

But she waits, regardless, for her servant to return. It's Seventh Bell when she does.

"Your Imperial Majesty, I've returned with the . . . ah . . . businesswoman you requested."

That was a polite way of saying it. Sometimes, thought the Empress, she did not hate her servants.

"She may enter."

And so she does.

The woman prostrates herself. She wears a lilac-colored robe, with a scandalous red one visible underneath. As much as O-Shizuka hates to admit it, she is lovely—lustrous dark hair tucked expertly into a flowering shape; painted pink lips and striking cheekbones. She has the look of a woman who knows something private about you, something that at once amuses her and makes you close friends.

The sight of her is so appealing, in fact, that it at once sours O-Shizuka's mood.

"You are called Ren," she says, her tone turning a simple statement into an interrogation. She circles the woman but does not bid her to rise.

"I am," the older woman says. "I am honored by your presence, O Phoenix Queen." Her voice is throaty and rich, like unsweetened tea.

O-Shizuka sniffs. "You will tell me all you know of Barsalyya Shefali."

Ren does not respond as fast as O-Shizuka would like. More reason to dislike her. O-Shizuka cannot shake the feeling that when the woman does open her mouth, she'll spout some nonsense poetry. As if Barsalyya Shefali can be contained within nonsense poetry! No. No one knows her the way O-Shizuka does.

But then Ren speaks. "Barsalai Shefali does not speak much, but every word that leaves her is worth eighty pages of poetry," she says. "A starry sky of heroes await her, for she is as brave, honest, and as kind a woman as I have ever met. She is handsome as a carving, with warm skin that aches to be touched; she is tall, and her legs bow under the weight of the false accusations she carries with her."

O-Shizuka clears her throat. She said Barsalai, did she?

She tells herself that she has grown past challenging people to duels, and she thinks now of the boy who will forever bear the weight of losing to her. O-Shizuka thinks that she is beyond jealousy, but only because she would not want Shefali to be furious with her. Jealousy. The more she thinks on it, the guiltier O-Shizuka feels. How dare she be so hypocritical? How dare she be jealous of Shefali, when she's done far worse herself?

"You speak as if you know her well," O-Shizuka says. "Did she share your bed, Ren? This great and mighty hero, did you ply your trade with her? Perhaps you do not know her as well as you think."

Ren touches her forehead to the ground again. "Regrettably, I did not," Ren says. "Barsalai Shefali's heart is stolen by another, whom she loves as purely as moonlight. In another life, I think. In another life, I would be honored to—"

"Stop," O-Shizuka almost shouts. She raises one hand to cut Ren off and pinches her nose with the other. "I cannot listen to this anymore."

Purely as moonlight. Yes, that was right, wasn't it? Shefali's love for her was the purest in the Empire, and here was Shizuka . . .

"My sincere apologies, Imperial Majesty," says Ren. And damn it all, she does sound sympathetic. "I knew her lover was a noble, but I had no idea it was the Empress."

"I was not Empress at the time," says O-Shizuka. Tantamount to blasphemy, if anyone else heard. Shizuka is too tired to care about that. The Empress is always the Empress, from the moment she is born. When she takes the throne, she simply assumes the title. "But, yes, I am Barsalyya's great love. And you were intimate with her, though you did not share a bed."

It is some time before Ren next speaks. She does not rise, does not level her eyes with the Empress's, does not so much as raise her forehead from the floor. Yet when she speaks, each word is a caress, each syllable a touch, each delicate sound the hush of bodies moving beneath silk.

"Your Majesty," she says. "You should know how Barsalai spoke of you. On all other subjects, she was a lake, but when I asked about you in the smallest way, she became a river. I may have been intimate with her for that moment, Your Majesty, I may have helped her through a dark time—but you have always been her light. She would never dream of casting you aside."

These words are wind beneath O-Shizuka's heart. The image is clear to her: There is Shefali, huddled in some brothel, dimples showing on her cheeks. In her quiet voice, she speaks of the time Shizuka stared at two Qorin mid coitus, of the blush that flushed royal cheeks. Flickering lantern lights ring green eyes with orange; she's smiling so hard, it makes Shizuka's jaw hurt in sympathy.

O-Shizuka touches her chest.

She knows this is just an image. From what Shefali wrote, she knows there were probably tears trailing down her love's face, snot dribbling from her nose, black veins on her eyes.

But she clings to the idea that Shefali was happy, for she has so few happy memories left.

Will she still be so happy, Shizuka wonders, when she returns? When she realizes?

She licks her lips. "Ren," she says, "I called you here because of a letter Barsalai wrote to me. When she was so far gone—when I could not reach her—she found comfort with you."

A pause. These words taste so bitter on her tongue, and they have not yet been birthed. Yet she must speak them.

She must slay the jealous girl inside herself. She must slay her own guilt.

"I do not know if you are aware," she says, "but Barsalyya thought of ending her life. Your intervention saved her. And so I must thank you. You may rise."

Ren does. She is careful to keep her gaze on O-Shizuka's feet, but she rises quickly and with pride, as one would expect from a woman of her position.

O-Shizuka reaches for a sealed letter on her desk. She hands it to the madam. Ren places it in her lap without opening it. Good. She knows how disrespectful it would be to open it without O-Shizuka's consent.

"A year and a half ago, one of my least favorite courtiers ceased pestering me," she says. "He was never fool enough to say anything obvious, but I believe he doubted me. Even after Shiseiki, he doubted me. And one day, he just—"

She holds up her hands, makes a gesture like sprinkling water on plants.

"I was curious about this, and so I sent my spymaster to investigate. The man moved to the countryside in Fuyutsuki Province. He lives as a beggar now, in a hovel near the rice paddies. No one knows his name. I wondered what impoverished him so. My spymaster informed me.

"It seems the man had a taste for singing girls," continues O-Shizuka. "A specific taste. He liked women who bore childbirth scars. And when he summoned them, he would cut them along their lower bellies and stick his fingers in the wound, and he would send them back with triple pay."

Ren flinches.

O-Shizuka does not. "The last brothel he visited was yours. Only hours later, he left Fujino in the dark of night, with nothing save what he could carry on his back."

Now Ren's eyes flicker up toward the Empress's.

O-Shizuka offers her a small smile. "I do not know how you did it. I do not want to know. But it was admirable all the same," she says. "You are a woman who deals in flesh and secrets, in more ways than one. Do not think the Phoenix Throne is blind to this."

"Your Majesty," says Ren, her voice suddenly unsure. "Are you asking me to cease business?"

"No," says O-Shizuka. "In your hands is an Imperial Writ of Pardon. Whatever business you are conducting—whatever secrets you trade in, whatever lives you take in the night—is yours to deal with. You have done well to make it to Fujino, but if the time comes when you find you've made a false step, that pardon will free you from prosecution. You need only produce it."

Ren stares back at her. "You do not want a cut?"

"I am not requiring one," O-Shizuka says. "If you want to negotiate, that is a separate thing. But this is a gift, from me to you. From one woman to another."

And the singing girl touches her forehead to the floor before rising again, clutching the red envelope in shaking hands. "Your Imperial Majesty," she says, "I do not think I've ever received a more thoughtful gift."

At this, O-Shizuka laughs. "You are an excellent liar! Was the return of your father's war mask less thoughtful?" O-Shizuka says. She waves. "This is paper and ink. Only my position makes it powerful; only my position makes it thoughtful. Anyone could make you a forgery of it. But that war mask was the only one of its kind, and I can tell you Barsalai kept it with her when she left. Do not flatter me."

The madam clears her throat, a vain attempt to hide a blushing smile. Did she not know that Shefali kept the mask? "Be that as it may," she says, "this one is genuine."

"It is," agrees O-Shizuka. Strange. Something's changed in the woman before her. She is still as warm and inviting as morning tea, but . . . it's as if someone slipped poison into it. Not that Ren is hostile. No. But she is more dangerous now.

"Your Imperial Majesty," Ren says. "If you would like to arrange for either of my services again—"

O-Shizuka raises a hand. "I am interested only in your spies, and I am not interested in discussing them at present. I summoned you here to thank you. This I have done. You may now return to your home. In two days' time, then you may return—when I have finished Barsalai's letter. But not a moment before then."

And Ren touches her forehead to the floor. "Thank you, Your Majesty," she says. "May the Eight return Barsalai to you in two days."

When Ren leaves, she is grinning.

It must be the pardon. O-Shizuka wonders if she's made a mistake, doing that. But Shefali spoke so highly of her, and Shefali has always been an excellent judge of character.

She returns to her reading.

LET ME REMEMBER ONLY THIS

The journey from southern Shiseiki to Xian-Lai takes the better part of five months, for Xian-Lai lies to the southeast of Fujino. Though our trip from the steppes to the North was largely uneventful once we reached the Empire. For obvious reasons, our trip to my brother's new holdings was different in method.

We stopped at temples whenever we could, in search of answers about my condition. Not many temples, since the Troubles, boasted a full staff. Before things took this turn, there were eight priests in each village.

But as we rode past villages . . . now we struggled to find even one.

I can sympathize with them. Who can keep their faith when the gods withdraw signs of their favor? When the Daughter's Everblossoms wilt beneath her watchful gaze; when daggers placed at the Son's feet rust within days?

It used to be that a different member of the Family would visit every eight years. That is how Hokkarans predict a child's fortunes. The year of one's birth combined with the day and the week and the month formed a prophecy, or so we are told.

You, naturally, were born on the day, the week, the month dedicated to the Daughter. Even the minutes and hours lined up. I can't tell you how often priests commented on this. How commoners commented on it. Everyone did, really, and more than one story about you being the Daughter reborn was making the rounds in teahouses.

And I was born one month after you were. And it so happened that my dates aligned, too, with those of the Grandmother, but no one ever praised me for it.

That was just fine. I praised her on my own. So it was with all Qorin. This notion of going to temple is distinctly Not Qorin. Who needs a temple, when the Sky herself stretches out above you, eternal? We do not burn prayer tags, Shizuka; we do not build shrines in her honor. Grandmother Sky is happy to listen to us when we pray to her, and Grandfather Sky is happy to drink any milk we pour onto him.

But it had been so long since one of the Heavenly Family visited during their year! Not even the most devout, who prayed every day for the slightest glimpse, had seen them.

Your uncle summoned the High Priests to convene in Fujino that summer—the summer of our seventeenth year. This made finding priests doubly difficult: those who remained faithful in the face of adversity were on the way to Fujino.

That said, we met a few along the way. You had no trouble flagging down religious caravans when you saw them, and less trouble gaining an audience when you did so. A quick word, a few strokes of ink, that was all it took to establish your identity. I found I got fewer stares if I wore the fox mask, which was all the better for me.

The trouble always began when I entered the caravan, sometimes before I took the mask off. Without fail, the priest seized up against the wall and recoiled from me. Daughter, Mother, Father, Son—it did not matter to whom they were dedicated.

"You wear the Traitor's Crown!" they'd say.

"Do not stand near me!"

"You are unclean!"

Tiring. It was all so tiring. Every time they protested like this, the demons I carried protested right back. It is a trying thing to let a demon's vile insults fall on deaf ears, but you and I spent a great deal of time practicing for it. Clearing one's mind is an important part of dueling, and as the finest duelist in the Empire, you made it your duty to teach me.

So I did as you'd said. I imagined my mind as a pool of water, and my thoughts as ripples. I focused on the image—focused on calming the water—and in doing so tuned out the voices. It was not an easy thing to do. I failed more often than I succeeded.

But I was failing less as time went on.

Still, we found no aid.

In all the history of the Heavenly Empire, has there ever been a case like mine? The Traitor slew his nephew Ages ago; if someone lived with the blackblood, there would be a record. Certainly we have stories of other heroes. Brave men and women who slew demons with hardly a thought. Tumenbayar and Batumongke, your ancestor Minami Shiori, Brave Yasaru and Foolhardy Mitsuo.

Yet I can think of no hero whose jaw unhinges in the heat of battle. None who craved blood, or tasted fear. None who wandered the nights sleepless, tireless, unrelenting. None who are quite as strong as I am, or as fast.

I am an anomaly.

But that is all right. I would not wish my condition upon anyone else, anywhere in time. Let me deal with it. I have already for so many years.

Regardless of the answers we didn't find, we were still on the run. Your family did not know where you were, and we could not return to the clan. That left us with one option.

We sent word ahead to my brother.

During a stay at an inn in Kaikumura, we wrote him a long letter. Not half so long as this one, no. Not even a quarter as long. But it was long enough. We told him we were coming to stay with him, if he would have us; we told him our mother had banished us; we promised to explain once we arrived in Xian-Lai. And, to ensure it was he who read it and replied and not my father, I wrote it entirely in Qorin.

A return letter found us somewhere in the Southern Provinces, where they still spoke Xian and had Xian names and wore different clothing. I have never been skilled when it comes to history, Shizuka. I cannot remember which village it was, and at times I can't remember all the provinces. The only reason I knew of Xian-Lai so well was because my brother was there.

Though, thinking about it, this did mean I'd have to become more familiar with Xian customs. His wife was Xianese. It was only now that this occurred to me, now that we were going through land more foreign to me than the Northern Provinces.

But regardless of my confusion, the letter found us. I tore it open as soon as we received it. You leaned over my shoulder, as if by

staring at the letters, you'd somehow be able to understand them.
Did you expect it to be written phonetically, the way we write
things? The way I've written this?

No, it was in Qorin, and reading it made me feel warm. I could
almost remember what Kenshiro's voice sounded like. Almost.

> *To the Tiger-Striped Princess:*
>
> *It pains me, Little Sister, to hear that you've had trouble
> with our mother. My home is ever open to you, and I am sure
> Baozhai will be more than happy to meet Shizuka-shan.
> I suppose I should write "O-Shizuka-shon," but it doesn't
> feel right to refer to her in such a way. Did you know,
> Shefali-lun, I changed the future Empress's bedclothes?*
>
> *Do not tell her I said that.*
>
> *At any rate, I eagerly await your arrival. Our father has
> gone to Fujino for the Grand Audience the Son of Heaven
> has called for. I escaped only by virtue of being a newly
> married man. You could not have picked a better time to
> visit; our garden is in full bloom. We will prepare a feast for
> you. A small one, I remember how you dislike crowds.*
>
> *But you do like horses, and archery, and wrestling. I will
> see to it that we have a little tournament of our own. No
> more than twenty entrants, I promise. But it will be nice to
> watch a few Hokkaran and Xianese lords lose a race, don't
> you think?*
>
> *Sister, it's been so long since we've last met that you might
> just be taller than I am. It sounds like life has been unkind to
> you of late, and I know you may think of me as a distant sort
> of relation—more a cousin than a sibling. But it is important
> to me that you keep this in your heart: No matter what the*

world may think of half-breeds like us, we will always have
each other.

But I will always have the last sweet, and you cannot stop
me from taking it.

With love,

Halaagmod Kenshiro Alsharyya

I read that letter about as many times as I used to read yours,
back when that was our only method of communication. You asked
me to read it out loud—it made me so excited, after all—and sure
enough, you protested Kenshiro's teasing.

"He is only five years older!" you said, pacing around the room
with your arms crossed. "How dare he. How dare he. There's no
way he can remember!"

I kept chuckling, for my brother has always had an excellent
memory.

"He touched the Imperial Cheeks," I said.

You stopped midstep, your amber eyes going small and fiery.
"Don't you join him!" you protested. "I'll hear none of that 'Imperial Cheeks' nonsense from you."

At this point, I could no longer contain my laughter. I doubled
over in bed, wiping the tears away. You were just so upset about
it, Shizuka! As if no one in the world ever changed your under-
clothes except for your mother. Do you realize there are probably
dozens of serving women who did the same?

And yet you'd given me an opportunity I could not ignore.

"I've examined them," I said. "Thoroughly."

You threw a pillow at me, but it was worth it.

That was the tone for most of our traveling, Shizuka, was it not?

In public, we were the Imperial Niece and her dear friend, that Qorin girl. In private, we were equals; in private, we could be ourselves. We spent our nights tangled up in each other's limbs.

And, yes, there was quite a bit of learning to do. Not just the things you taught me about stilling my mind (though we spent hours every morning meditating to that end) but also about my own body. About my limits, and what I could do.

As you promised, we visited butchers. They were always so surprised to see you. Did you want their finest cuts, did you want the tenderest steak you'd ever tasted? Might you bless their slaughterhouse with the Blood of Heaven? It was a little exciting, I admit, to see a butcher try to wipe himself clean in the presence of royalty. You'd offer a smile and a written blessing if the butcher would let us assist in the slaughterhouse.

And without fail, they'd protest.

"I will not have the Peacock Princess standing by as pigs are gutted, no, I won't! Not in my slaughterhouse!"

"How am I to bless it if I never step foot in it?" you'd say.

So it started. After a bit of back and forth, you'd earn our passage. Sometimes it came down to pointing out that as the Imperial Niece, you technically owned the entire Empire. Sometimes you just had to write a silly note for the butcher's daughter or wife. Sometimes you wrote up cash seals right then and there. Conditions varied.

But our work never did.

We'd go in with the butcher. He'd start his work. You stood next to me, observed as he slit the pig's throat or the cow's or twisted the chicken's head off.

Some days were more difficult than others. Some days I let out the most guttural growl, my jaw hanging open, my sharp teeth bared. You'd touch the back of my neck. In a firm voice, you'd whisper to me: "Shefali, stay here. Stay in your own mind."

If it was a good day, we would assist the butcher. The first time we did this, I was shocked to see you join me. Her Imperial Highness, the Crown Princess of Hokkaro, tying back her sleeves and her hair in a common slaughterhouse.

"What needs to be done?" you'd ask. If you bothered asking. For the most part, you watched the butcher do it once. That was all you needed. With brush, knife, and sword, you have always been an artist—your cuts were clean as your mother's, and the butcher was always impressed.

Mine, on the other hand . . .

I've been a hunter all my life. Skinning an animal and preparing it for consumption were not new to me. Yet, somehow, the paring knife felt clumsy now. Would it not be easier to use my talons, or my teeth? I'd get a better feel of the meat that way. Maybe taste it a bit and—

This was why we went to these butchers to start with.

So I struggled at first, and on occasion you caught me sinking my nails into pork or duck. But you always reached out for me. You always touched the base of my neck.

"You can do this, Shefali," you'd say. "It is only blood and flesh."

And so it was.

The longer we traveled, the more things you'd try to help me with. If a peddler traveled with charms supposedly from Sur-Shar, you'd buy every single one. We stopped at every holy site we could along the way. Springs, forests, even a pit supposedly inhabited by an ornery rock god. We did not see the rock god, but you did nearly fall in, looking for him. I caught your sleeve and pulled you back up again.

But that was what it was like, traveling to Xian-Lai with you. Long days and long nights. Afternoons spent in local markets, me wearing my fox mask and you with a rice farmer's hat you insisted flattered you. It did not flatter you, of course, but it made you happy, and that was the same thing. In the evenings, we'd set up camp, and I'd try to cook whatever I'd hunted that morning with varying levels of success. I don't know how Uncle Ganzorig makes his stews so appetizing, but I can be sure it does not run in my blood.

As we ate, I'd ask you about Xian-Lai, though you'd never been. About what the Xianese nobility are like, and how they might view someone like me.

"You are only half Hokkaran," you said with a smirk. "So I imagine they'll like you much more than they like me."

"Why?" I asked.

"You do not represent two hundred years of oppression," you said. "They were independent, before my ancestor Emperor Yoshinaga sent General Iseri to conquer them. Ages of their own traditions and customs—and we forced them to embrace ours. Yoshinaga wasted ink telling our people we were superior to the Xianese. In reality, he only wanted control of their ports. And, perhaps, oranges. My family has a regrettable love of citrus fruit."

"Citrus?"

"You will see," you said, smiling. "If I don't eat them all first."

As we came closer to my brother's holdings, I found myself sitting up at night in bed.

Moving clears my mind; it always has, and I find still it a useful habit. But in those days, I was so focused on what my brother would think of my condition that I was paralyzed.

Staying in one place leads to a stagnant soul and mind. You see only one patch of the sky, one patch of stars, and never witness Grandmother Sky's true glory. Demons, too, find you more easily when you stay in one place.

I think the last is somewhat unique to me. Ghosts are an exception. Ghosts will haunt you to the ends of the Earth if you've upset them, even if it has been actual decades since you did so, and you've tried to repent, but . . .

Continuing.

In our room not far from Xian-Lai's capital, the Not-You found me again. It formed from the shadows in the far corner, like smoke solidifying into a human form. Our previous encounter left it with thick bruises around its neck. A festering pit gaped back at me where its left eye once was. It did not stand, did not beckon me. It merely sat in the corner and stared at me.

Seeing it tore at old wounds. I hissed, bared my teeth, my nostrils flaring.

"Leave," I said.

Bones rattling in a cup—that was the sound it made. "You cannot be rid of me, my love," it said. "I am not a stain on your prized deel."

I thought of waking you, for you slept curled at my side with your thumb between your lips. Who was I, though, to ruin such perfect slumber? No. I would be all right. This thing was not real. One hand on the bare skin of your heavenly hip would be enough to ground me.

"Why are you here?"

Now it craned its awful neck at me. A thick black tongue darted out from rotted lips. "To warn you," it said. "Your brother will lie to you, Steel-Eye."

At this, my fury threatened to bubble over. I squeezed your skin; you groaned in your sleep. Sad as it sounds, I clung to that noise. I forced myself to remember the consequences of losing control.

"You're the liar," I said.

Its head lolled to the side, ear to shoulder. The matted clumps of black that served as its hair swayed just enough for me to catch sight of its right ear.

Your uncle is in possession of a dog, a monstrous red thing half his size at the shoulder. I want to say it is more fur than dog, but I've been tackled by it once before and can attest to the creature's strength. Regardless, there is so much fluff, it is difficult to make out the thing's features. All except for its ears. To prevent infection, its ears are cropped to resemble a horse's.

So it was with the Not-You's ear, or what was left of it. A twisted nub of flesh poked out from the side of its head; about the top third of a normal ear. Seeing it sent a chill straight to my gut. I covered my mouth.

Why, I wondered, did this disfigurement upset me more than the rest?

That is the trouble with telling you the story this way. You know why it upset me. Yet I must continue to tell the tale, for I have gone too far now to abandon it.

The Not-You fixed me with a piercing look. "Am I?" it said. "Steel-Eye, I alone have never lied to you, and I never will. How could I lie to my own precious blood?"

"You sicken me," I said. I kept one hand on your hip; the other moved to my stomach. This lurching . . . I wanted to throw up, but I hadn't eaten anything in a week.

"An upset stomach is a small price to pay for the power I've given you," it said. "And you will continue to grow stronger. How beautiful you will be, when you finally meet Him."

Not worth getting angered over. Not worth striking it. Not worth giving in to that rage. But gods, how I wanted to hurt it.

"I will leave you, Steel-Eye," it said, "for you will not hear reason. But when the conquering one comes, when you most need him, remember what I said. He will lie."

As it spoke, it began to lose substance. Again it was smoke, though this time it dissipated in the wind. The word "lie" hung in the air like a ringing gong.

I slipped beneath the sheets and let my fingers climb the ladder of your spine. When I reached the top, I kissed the nape of your neck.

Only then did you turn toward me. Your eyes fluttered open, weary with sleep; but your hands cupped my face. "My love?" you said. "Is everything all right?"

Tomorrow we'd see my brother. Tomorrow I would know what his wife was like, what his new holdings were like. Tomorrow I'd have to tell him what happened in Shiseiki. The Not-You spoke of lies and dark futures.

But in that moment, it was just you and I in an inn room, away from the prying eyes we'd soon have to avoid. You and I, alone and naked, huddled together beneath the sheets. When our skin meets, when our hearts beat so close together, when we are so tangled up in each other that we cannot tell ourselves apart: this is the most sacred time.

Yes, Shizuka, as I stroked your face and wiped drool from the corner of your mouth, it was a holy thing.

"Yes," I said.

And I pressed my lips to yours, speaking silent prayers. I held you until you fell asleep, and then I kept vigil for you. Against what? I did not know. But I was not going to let anything ruin your hallowed slumber.

In the morning we readied to travel. Half a day, it took us, but it felt like more in that heat. Oshiro in the summer was, at best, a little warm. The steppes were hotter. But the Southern Provinces? Sweat trickled down the back of my neck. My deel was damp in an hour. There was a thickness to the air here, like breathing underwater.

Maybe it was all the vegetation. Xian-Lai was green as far as the eye could see. And not a Hokkaran green either, bright and bracing. This was a dark color, near black in places. Where Fujino boasted tall trees and mountains, here the trees weren't much taller than a man might be, and everything was . . . wet.

Yes, after two hours of riding, it rained. And I do not mean to say it rained a little, as it does on the steppes. This was not a fine mist, nor was it the gentle pitter-patter we enjoyed in Oshiro.

I felt as if I, personally, had upset Grandmother Sky. There is no other way to explain the amount of water she poured down on us that day. Had she burst open the largest cloud she could find? Was she attempting to water her garden, and instead, she watered the earth itself? Was she filling her rice pot with water?

I do not know, Shizuka, I do not know. But there is no reason any place should ever experience that much rain. It got in everything. Even inside my saddlebags! My deel, already wet, flopped against my skin like old leather. You were doing your best to guide your horse with your knees and hold my old deel above your head to keep the rain out. It wasn't working very well on either count.

By the time we spotted the Bronze Palace, I'd seen enough water to last ten lifetimes. I was swaying in the saddle from the frustration of it all. We didn't see rain for months on the steppes, and now I knew why! The damned Southern Provinces hoarded it!

But then I caught sight of it.

The Burqila clan banner, hanging from the outside of the palace.

And my whole body shook with laughter. I pointed it out to you, and you grinned, too.

"Go," you said. "Greet your brother, my love. He must have missed you dearly."

I glanced over toward the palace, then back to you. I jerked my head in the direction of the banner.

You offered a warm smile. "I will be right behind you," you said, "but if you arrive first, he can properly greet you. If I arrive at the same time, he will be forced to follow protocol. It is better this way."

I wanted to kiss you, but there were guards outside the gates. So, instead, I kissed the scar on my right palm.

You flushed a bit.

And then I was gone, kicking Alsha into a full gallop. Gods, Shizuka, I was so happy to see him again! My brother, eight years gone, my brother, who helped me make my first bow!

I decided that if I was going to be the one to enter the Bronze Palace first, then I would make a show of it. First, I grabbed a strap from my saddle. This I tied around the horn in a loop. Then, just as I caught sight of a tall man with sandy hair who must be my brother, I swung myself off the saddle. My back was against Alsha's flank, my legs extended out in the air, my head closer to the ground than most riders are ever willing to go.

An explosion of applause and whistles made my heart sing

Was it a bit of overkill to perform such a trick?

Perhaps.

But I had to show my excitement somehow.

And when I dismounted, I ran to my brother.

I ran to him as if nothing had changed. As if I were still eight, and he was still fourteen, and we'd never been apart at all. Yes, he was taller now, but so was I. And so what if he wore his sandy hair in a Hokkaran topknot? His skin and eyes had stayed the same.

He squeezed me so tight, I could not breathe, and then he sniffed my cheeks in turn. "Little Sister," he said in Qorin. "Welcome home."

I stood on tiptoes to better sniff Kenshiro's cheeks.

Excitement buoyed me so that I forgot about my condition, until that moment. Then the rush of scents mixing together reminded me of what it was I'd become. Rich perfumes; something bright and sharp; parchment and . . .

Fear, beneath it all. A corrupting sweetness that turned everything else to rot.

Why was he afraid?

Cold dripped down my spine. He was afraid. My brother was afraid, and I didn't know why and—

He squeezed me tighter before holding me at arm's length. No trace of trepidation showed on his face. Indeed, it was as wide and warm as ever. My father's nose looked natural on him, a complement to his high cheekbones. His eyes, too, were more Hokkaran than Qorin.

It's a common joke that no one can tell when a Qorin opens their eyes, since they are so narrow. I do not understand why this is so common. Hokkaran eyes are narrow, too; no one here on the Sands has eyes like yours or mine. No Surians I've met, either. And the Pale Man I met had eyes like a frightened deer.

So no, I do not understand why Hokkarans make such a grand deal of it. It's not as if we can't see. I cannot tell you how many times I've been asked this outside the steppes. With every repetition, it grows more and more grating.

Yes, I can see. I can even see out of . . .

I'm losing myself again.

Kenshiro was happy to see me—that's where I was. At least, he was acting happy to see me. But I could smell the fear on him, though when he was grinning from ear to ear.

"Shefali-lun," he said, "you're so pretty! The boys must be beating their way to you."

Oh.

Of all the things for him to say, I expected that least. He did not know about you and me. I'd gotten so used to being with you that I'd forgotten.

I shifted from foot to foot and looked at my boots. A blush rose to my cheek. I did my best to try to fight it; blushing only made me look bruised. I ended up hiding my face against the crook of my shoulder.

Kenshiro laughed. "See! I knew it to be true. Well, do not worry. They shall not reach you here. The Bronze Army will be more than enough to keep suitors away," he said.

I continued shifting from foot to foot, wishing for you to return. Whatever pomp and circumstance accompanied your arrival would be a welcome distraction from all this.

Someone spoke up, someone with a soft voice. I glanced over. For the first time, I noticed there was a woman standing next to

Kenshiro. Taller than you, though not by much, she wore Xianese-style clothes. That is to say, one loose-fitting plum dress with impossibly large sleeves and a short green jacket over it, with even more impossibly large sleeves. I envied the cut of it—Hokkaran dresses were so narrow they afforded little movement; Baozhai's dress at least allowed her to walk like a normal person. The jacket's high collar came just beneath her jaw and closed with two elaborate clasps I could see from a great distance away. It gave her the look of a flower on a stem.

Yes, I think a flower is a good comparison. Not a peony, or a chrysanthemum, or any of the ones you favor. No, she was a stem of lavender, straight-backed and fragrant.

Kenshiro took her arm and brought her closer. If he was grinning before, he was beaming now. "Shefali-lun," he said, "this is my heart of hearts, Lady Lai Baozhai."

Instead of the full bow favored by Hokkaran courtiers, she bent at the shoulder and touched her lips. "I am eight times honored to meet you, Lady Alsharyya," she said. I winced at the name, but she did not know any better. And then her polite smile became something more genuine. "To be honest, I have always wanted a younger sister. I have so many older ones."

And this time, there was no fighting the flush on my cheeks. She thought of me as a sister? We'd never met. But . . . well, if my brother liked her enough to marry her, then she must not be so bad. She hadn't commented on my appearance or my color yet. As far as I was concerned, she was doing a fine job of being a sibling.

I did my best to mimic her half bow. When I rose, I also attempted a warm smile that did not bare any teeth. I think I succeeded only in pulling my lips back.

I tried to think of something to say. It is not every day one meets a new sibling for the first time. A momentous occasion like this warranted something sage and profound.

"Thank you," I said.

That would have to do.

Horns sounding behind us tore away our attention. The forty guards gathered in the courtyard bowed their heads at the same moment.

I turned.

You sat on your red gelding, riding in through the gates. You robbed breath from my lungs—but you always do, Shizuka.

"Presenting the Eight-Times-Honored Imperial Niece!" shouted the crier. He'd not announced me. I did not hold it against him. "May she live long as her storied ancestors! Look how her Heavenly blood paints her cheeks red! Witness her regal bearing, her unmatched beauty! We of Xian-Lai are blessed to be in your presence, Highness!"

You fought to keep that imperious look on your face. It was a battle you lost. Halfway through the crier's diatribe, you cracked a wry smile. It's a miracle you did not roll your eyes.

I covered my own mouth to hide my teeth; I couldn't help but smile at the sight of you.

But I did somehow manage to forget that one is supposed to prostrate themselves in the presence of royalty. Only when you gestured at me did I remember, and I hoped that no one caught sight of me standing as you entered.

I'm sure someone did anyway.

I listened for the sound of your feet hitting the ground. Your golden voice soon followed.

"My two feet have touched your land, thus you are twice blessed," you said. "Approach. I bid you speak your name, Lord of Xian-Lai, and speak your lineage. In speaking to me, you are again twice blessed."

I'd never seen you do this before. Had things changed because you were heir now? Or simply because you'd gotten older?

"May it please Your Imperial Majesty," Kenshiro said, "I, Oshiro Kenshiro, son of Yuichi and Burqila Alshara, am Lord of Xian-lai."

I love my brother, but I do think it's foolish he had to go through all of this and not his wife. He was Lord of Oshiro, without a doubt, but his claim to Xian-Lai came only through marriage. Was it not more fitting to let the actual heir to the Province take care of all of this?

But I am only a simple barbarian, and what do I know of politics?

You raised your right hand and waved him forward. "Come," you said, "Oshiro-tun. Kiss my feet, and be twice blessed; kiss my hands, and be eight times blessed."

It is a strange thing to see someone you love become something else. I'm certain you know what that is like, for you have seen me in my states.

What I witnessed that day was not horrible. I do not dread its memory; nor do I think you've gone through some irreparable change.

But it was uncanny all the same to see the face I so loved become so distant. Even your flaming tongue was cold now. You hardly sounded like yourself.

I watched as Kenshiro kissed your feet and your hands in turn, and I imagined what you would look like on the Dragon Throne.

Is it a comfortable throne, Shizuka? You have no wife to stand at your side. Do you wear the Dragon Crown, or the Phoenix one I so admired as a child? And if it is the Phoenix Crown—do you touch the places where the feathers used to be, and think of me?

Once this strange ritual was complete, you allowed yourself to return to the Shizuka I knew.

Kenshiro got to his feet with a monklike smile. "O-Shizu—"

"Husband," Baozhai cut in. She tilted her head toward him as a silent reminder.

Kenshiro cleared his throat. "Ah, yes!" he said. "You must forgive my terrible manners, Lady of Ink."

I cocked a brow.

You chuckled. "So it is true, then, Lady Baozhai?" she said. "Your people do not name the Imperial Family?"

"And yours never write your name fully," Baozhai said. "We do not speak your name for the same reason. It is an old custom."

"I see," you said. You raised a brow as your lips curled into a smirk. "Was it you, Oshiro-Lao? Did you pick the name?"

Kenshiro shook his head. "Oh, no," he said. "I could never be so poetic. It was my wife's doing."

Baozhai, for her part, preened at the attention. She shot her husband a coquettish glance, then gave you another half bow. "I felt it fitting," she said. "Scholars even here in Xian-Lai mimic your hand. If you would prefer something different . . ."

"No," you said. " 'Lady of Ink' is acceptable."

Baozhai's relief was visible in her slightly slumping shoulders; in the breath she let out all at once. "Thank you, Lady of Ink."

Baozhai wasted no time, and no expense.

An hour, at most, was all it took to prepare the feast. In that time, she offered us a change of clothing and took us on a tour of the Bronze Palace. Here were some soldiers her ancestors were buried with, here were some portraits of them, here was a massive garden twice the size of yours at Fujino, here was a bridge over the garden's private river. Everywhere we went, a young girl followed throwing jasmine in front of us. Two men carried umbrellas behind us. I kept trying to avoid mine, or at least get him to put the umbrella down.

"The sun is bad for your complexion, Lady Alsharyya!" he protested.

"Why?" I asked.

"It makes you dark—"

Such foolishness did not dignify a response. All I did was point at my own skin, at its loamy brown color, and keep walking.

To her credit, Baozhai apologized for this incident later, during the feast. And what a feast it was! Do you remember, Shizuka, how every single plate was either gold or porcelain or both? Whole ducks, exotic fish, hearty soups, bowls of rice larger than some toddlers! There was so much food!

And the smell of it all. Gods, there were so many smells, it made me dizzy. Imagine twenty, thirty different courtiers screaming at you to pay attention to them. You, of course, have no interest in hearing them speak, and I had no interest in eating the food.

But it was nice to look at, and I felt bad for Baozhai.

She kept pushing more portions toward me. "Lady Alsharyya," she said. I was going to have to correct her eventually, but . . . "Is the duck not to your liking? We don't have kumaq, but I think there might be horsemeat on the table somewhere."

"Sorry," I mumbled. "Not hungry."

"Not hungry?" said Kenshiro. "You've been riding all day!"

"This must be why you are so skinny," Baozhai said. "Is she always like this?"

My brother shook his head. "When she was a child, she'd eat anything we put in front of her," he said.

As a young girl looks for her parents when she is asked to answer a question, so I looked to you.

"Barsalyya-sur is recovering from a long illness," you said. "Her appetite has sadly withered."

Wrinkles appeared near Kenshiro's eyes; I do not think he believed you.

"Lady Alsharyya!" Baozhai exclaimed, one hand rising to her mouth. "I did not know! Forgive me. If you like, I have healers—"

"They will not be necessary," you said. "Lady Baozhai, you must tell me about your dress. . . ."

So we made our way through the dinner. For the most part, conversation was pleasant, and you liked the food enough to have second servings. You were served from separate bowls, separate utensils. If you wanted duck, there was one just for you; if you wanted soup, there was a whole pot bearing the Imperial Seal. You did not come close to finishing all of it. I later discovered that whatever you did not eat was burned.

Can you imagine, Shizuka? People could've eaten that. But the Xianese ascribe a certain level of holiness to their royal family. Hokkarans do, too; if their legends are to be believed, your veins hold heavenly blood. Yet I have never seen Hokkarans throw away food simply because you touched it.

I wondered why Baozhai was extending this courtesy to you. If the custom applied to the Xianese royal family, then it should apply only to Baozhai, Kenshiro, and myself. You were not a relative by blood or marriage. Baozhai, who would've been sovereign ruler of a nation if not for your grandfather, should have hated you.

But she did not. And here she was, lavishing you with courtesy and respect.

It gladdened my heart, Shizuka. The two of you struck it off from the first instant you met. Listening to you talk of various dressmakers and novels and perfumes—for the first time in my memory, you were enjoying yourself with someone besides me.

So, yes, it was strange that Baozhai went through all that trouble in your behalf—but it was a pleasant surprise.

But after the servants began gathering our trays and we said our good nights, Kenshiro asked us to come out onto the veranda.

"I've some plum wine," he said, "fit for the Little Empress herself!"

And, yes, he smiled—yes, there was a twinkle in his eyes—but I could smell the suspicion on him like smoke.

"It's been some time since I had plum wine," you said.

We were going to have to tell him sooner or later.

We trudged outside. I trudged. You glided, as always. I do not think it is possible for you to move without elegance.

"What if he hates me?" I mouthed as we walked.

You could not touch me in public, but you softened your features toward me in the way lovers do. "He won't," you whispered.

The three of us stood outside on the veranda overlooking the gardens. "Gardens" seems too small a word. It was more . . . it was as if all of Hokkaro existed in microcosm here. Large trees grew in miniature; mountains were replicated with thick slabs of rock. Dense shrubbery mimicked the forests around Fujino. Someone even built a miniature Jade Palace.

The weather was balmy that night. Lightning bugs flickered in and out of existence. Night clouds veiled Grandmother Sky's starry gown. Everything was dark and lovely and fragrant.

Why was Xian-Lai not the Imperial Seat? I liked it far better than Fujino.

Maybe it was all the rain.

"You've done well for yourself, Kenshiro-lao," you said. You leaned on the railing. With a wave, you dismissed the guards he'd brought with us. "Lord of Xian-Lai. And your wife certainly knows how to welcome guests."

"She's excited to meet you, O-Shizuka-shon," he said. "I was nervous, given the tension between Xian-Lai and Fujino, but I had the feeling you two would get along. The hope, really. Perhaps it helped that I talked you up a bit."

"It did," you said. "I've never had such a pleasant reception in all the Empire."

Kenshiro offered a small smile. "I will tell her you said this," he said. "She will hold the words forever dear to her."

I watched the two of you talk. Soon. Soon. Until I had to speak, I'd watch the lightning bugs. We never had them on the steppes; they were one of the few things about Oshiro I missed.

"Shefali-lun, O-Shizuka-shon said you were sick. Is that true?"

A steadying breath. A nod.

He broke eye contact for a moment. "And our mother is not speaking to you."

Another nod. I did not want to do this. Couldn't I let you do it? No, Kenshiro was my brother, my last remaining family. Besides my father. Though I am not certain if he considers me family at all.

So I held open my hand, and you gave me your short sword.

I drew the blade across my fingers.

I'm not sure which was more unnerving to the two of you: that I did this with such ease, or that I did not flinch at all from the pain.

In the weak light, it was hard to see my blood's true color; I stepped toward one of the hanging lanterns.

Kenshiro's brown skin went pale. "She . . . Shefali-lun, your blood is . . ."

I could not bear to look at him. I stood there with my palm raised, blood dripping down my wrist.

"You should know," you said, "that your sister slew a demon with me. If it weren't for her, I would not be standing here today. But . . ."

You swallowed.

"She has paid the price for her unwavering devotion," you said, and the words simmered in your throat.

My knees shook and my empty stomach threatened to turn inside out. No doubt Kenshiro looked on me with disgust now. Any second, he'd call the guards back and have me escorted out of the palace.

But when I opened my eyes, he was rushing toward me with arms outstretched. He scooped me up into an embrace tight enough to knock the wind from me. I froze, unsure of how to react. Surely he did not mean to do this? Surely he meant to strike me?

No. He held me as his chest shook with weeping, as his tears landed on my shoulders. "My baby sister," he said. "Eight gods, you're the bravest girl I know."

"Kenshiro?" My whole face felt hot, and suddenly there were knives in my throat.

When Kenshiro released me, he was wiping away tears. "Does it hurt, Shefali?" he asked. "Do you need anything? If it exists, we'll find it—"

"It . . ." I swallowed. It hurt constantly, but the pain was a fact of life now. I couldn't escape it. "It doesn't hurt."

"Has it changed you?" he asked. "You're acting like the same sister I've always known, and you've brought Shizuka-shan. You must be the same, yes?"

You spoke then, holding yourself tight. "Your sister," you said, "is fighting demons we cannot see. Sometimes they . . ." You touched your throat. "They cloud her judgment. But she is learning. Growing. She will master them soon."

Kenshiro paced about the veranda.

Snot trickled out of my nose. I tried to swallow. No, my throat was too dry, and the knife was still there.

"Is this why you did not eat?"

"I don't need to," I creaked.

"Not at all?" he said. "What happens if you do eat? I do not want you to force yourself, Shefali, but people might notice. We must come up with something to say to them if you cannot eat at all."

"Ash," I said. "Tastes like ash."

Which was true. The few times I'd attempted eating, everything tasted burnt. Everything except raw meat and blood. Kenshiro did not need to know that yet.

He rubbed at his chin and nodded. "Is it the same when you drink?" he asked.

I nodded.

"She no longer sleeps, either," you chimed in. "An hour or two at most each week."

At this, Kenshiro quirked a brow. His dark green eyes moved from you, to me, to you. "Were you often forced to share rooms while traveling, O-Shizuka-shon?"

For once in your life, you were caught off guard. You opened your mouth, shook your head, and raised your hands all at once. "I, ah, well—"

"One tent," I cut in. "No money."

Kenshiro kept his eyes on you, but nodded. "I see," he said. "Yes, I suppose you girls didn't want to identify yourselves either, isn't that right?"

This pause was enough for you to get your footing again. "Exactly right," you said. "If it was known we were traveling, I imagine we would've dealt with far more bandits."

You sounded confident. So confident, in fact, that it was clear to anyone who knew you that you were lying. When you said things, they came into being; you did not need to be so firm about it.

Kenshiro nodded once. Something in his face changed, but then it was gone. If he was beginning to wonder about us, there were larger things to worry about. "Shefali," he said, "you are a smart girl, I know you have already seen healers. Does anyone know what is happening to you?"

"No," I said.

You raised your hand, stretched it out toward me, and—

Drew it back, once you realized how you'd already aroused suspicion. This charade already hurt me. I did not like this; I did not like having to pretend I did not love you. Especially in front of my brother, of all people. It was not fair. If you were male, my father would be falling over his own feet to get us married.

Why was it so different because we're both women? Traveling through Xian-Lai, we noticed for the first time men leaning close together, cooing into each other's ears. Women walked hand in hand out in the streets, and no one batted an eye.

Why was it so important to your uncle, to my father?

So many other things about Xian-Lai enraptured me. Whenever we saw commoners, they were kind to me, and did not gawk at me or my skin or my hair. No one here spoke a word of Qorin, but that was all right; we spoke hobbled Hokkaran together. In Xian-Lai, I was invited to tea whenever I went out riding. In Xian-Lai, they used Qorin messengers instead of Hokkaran ones. In Xian-Lai, my difference was something I could take pride in.

I loved the music. I loved the people. And though I could not taste the food, I could smell it, and it was sumptuous enough that way for me to enjoy.

I did not want to leave this place. Not for a while. If I could not be on the steppes, then Xian-Lai was not so bad.

"Shefali," my brother said, "you may stay as long as you like. Whatever comforts you need, I will find for you. I don't know how your . . . condition affects you, but rest assured, you are still my baby sister." He embraced me again.

It was not the reaction I was expecting, but it was what you expected. Whenever we spoke of this moment—of what might happen when my brother learned what happened—you were optimistic.

"He will still love you," you said.

"My mother exiled me," I said.

You propped yourself up and kissed my forehead. "Because she is a harsh ruler, Shefali, with an image to maintain and people to keep safe. Your brother has not seen you in years, and I'm certain that has worn on him. He will be overjoyed to see you again, no matter the circumstances."

I didn't believe you at the time. How could anyone look on me and still see a child of eight? Yet here we were, and Kenshiro loved me as much now as he had then.

Over the next few days, we got to work on the details. Kenshiro made all his guards swear an Eightfold Oath not to speak of my sleeping habits. Lady Baozhai served me only the smallest portions at meals—a mouthful, no more. Enough to avoid being impolite in public. A notice circulated around the palace kitchens. I was on a restricted diet, Baozhai said, due to a wounded tongue, which also explained my quietness.

And as much as I wanted to avoid attention, Kenshiro had already sent out invitations for the small tournament he promised me. Magistrates from throughout the Southern Provinces promised to attend. He could hardly uninvite them now.

But we had the benefit of knowing when they'd arrive, and knowing when the tournament would be. Six months from our arrival, to allow the magistrates time to travel. Six months to figure out how I'd get through such an arduous social engagement without baring my teeth or eating more than a mouthful. If I was confined to my quarters at night, that was not so terrible, but the thought of eating too much turned my stomach.

Besides, I was not going to stay in my own quarters. Not for more than a few minutes at a time.

In the northeast corner of the garden was a plum tree. Beneath its leaves like butterflies we spent our mornings. Thanks to its distance from the garden entrance, not many people bothered to visit it. Remote, peaceful, the sounds of nature swirling around us: it was the perfect place for meditation. Sometimes, different kinds of meditation.

You spent whatever time you could in the gardens. It soothed you, I think, to spend time near the plum tree. In its clearing, you practiced swordplay and calligraphy alike. On the rare occasions a visitor asked to see you, you met with them there.

You kept saying I needed a hobby.

"One that does not involve taking life," you said. "Something creative, to soothe your mind."

"Hunting," I said.

"Is taking the lives of animals," you pointed out. You touched my nose with your brush. Ink stained my skin. You laughed. "Something without any killing."

At the time, I could not fathom what you meant. I did plenty of worthwhile things. Like hunting, and riding, and wrestling. All good Qorin ways to spend one's time. I did not have your talent for calligraphy, and I've never had a good hand for drawing. Kenshiro could play the shamisen, but I could not tell one note from another. If I was not hunting, riding, or wrestling, what was I supposed to be doing?

I found the answer in a roundabout sort of way. Because I broke Kenshiro's bow while out riding, I decided to make a new one for him. From finding good solid bamboo to tracking down a stag for its horns and sinew, I found the whole process a welcome distraction. My idle hours were spent working on the bow, and I could not spare many thoughts at all while I was doing it.

The bow I made for Kenshiro was not the most perfect. I forgot to find him a birch wrapping. In the Xianese rain, it would not last an entire season; the whole thing would come apart when exposed to moisture.

So I made him another. This time I tried making it all out of one piece of wood, which led to many, many snapped bows. After a week's worth of terrible attempts, I found a shape that stayed put. Of course, that shape was more Hokkaran than Qorin, but at least it would not come apart in the rain. And it was not quite so large as a Hokkaran bow. Somewhere in the middle, then, like we were.

I found it took less time to make a bow from a single piece of wood, so long as I knew what I was doing. One day was all it took there. For Qorin bows, it could take up to a week, since I had to put all the parts together first, and subject them to the right amount of stress at the right angle and . . .

Well, if I'm being honest, the Hokkaran bow is much easier to make, and I'm somewhat ashamed it took me so long to get the hang of it. There are so many more variables with the Qorin kind. My problem was that I kept trying to make the Hokkaran bow short, and it did not have the power it needed.

But once I realized I had to make it larger, things got much simpler.

Every now and again, I'd see one of Kenshiro's men carrying around a bow I'd made with my own two hands. It felt good to create something. You were right about that.

But eventually I had to make a bow for myself, one strong enough that I would not break it. Not something I could do alone, since I was less than a novice. I told Kenshiro about my plans, and he invited a local bowyer to help me. Since all of Xian-Lai by now knew I had a damaged tongue, I could not speak to the man. Kenshiro had to do all the talking at our introduction.

"My sister," he said, "enjoys making bows in her spare time. She wishes to make something more difficult: a Qorin-style bow so strong, no man can draw it. Will you help her?"

The bowyer wrinkled his nose at me. Did I smell?

"A bow no man can draw," he said. "Why do you want to do this thing, child?"

Child. I was seventeen, yet still a child. I grimaced; Kenshiro deftly stepped in.

"Remember, my friend, you speak to Lady Shefali, my little sister. She may be a child, but we don't like to remind her of it," he said.

The bowyer huffed. "That does not explain why she wants such a bow."

Kenshiro grinned. He had an answer ready. "Only the man who can draw it will be able to marry her," he said.

At this, the bowyer chuckled. He reached to clap me on the shoulder, then thought better of it. "To work, then," he said. "Can't have any weak-armed Hokkaran boys stealing you away."

Two months, it took us, for we could not use birch and bamboo and normal horn. Oh no. We purchased an exotic sort of horn from a merchant recently returned from Ikhtar; we used yew, and not birch. Bamboo was still present, though in smaller amounts, and the bow received a double coating of birch bark to save it from water. For the string, we used bear sinew. Bear sinew. I had to hunt the bear myself, Shizuka; do you have any idea how hard it is to hunt a bear on one's own?

Oh, do not look at me like that! It is still hard in my condition!

The bowyer complained constantly. "This does not feel right," he'd say when we added in the sinew. "There's too much; it's going to be far too stiff. Ah, but I suppose that is the point. . . ."

It was difficult for him to make something useless on purpose, I think.

Regardless, the end result was, and still is, the most beautiful bow I've ever seen. When it was done, we passed it around the barracks. Not a single soul could budge the string.

Kenshiro clapped when he heard. "Good," he said, "then I shall not have to marry you to any of them, Shefali-lun. Could you imagine how upset O-Shizuka-shon would be, to lose her closest friend?"

Except the way he said it . . . He knew. He had to have known, Shizuka. I blushed and cleared my throat.

We resolved to test the bow that night. Baozhai came along to see. The four of us stood in the barracks. Kenshiro dismissed the watchmen for an hour or so—enough time for us to have some practice.

I hefted the thing. It's heavy, for a bow. At normal shooting distance I stood, far enough away that the target was a bit hard to see.

I took a breath. I no longer had the ring I'd need to draw this bow the normal way. Then again, I didn't feel much pain anymore; what did it matter if the string cut my fingers?

I drew. It was not easy, but it was not so hard as everyone made it look. Baozhai applauded the second I pulled the string a bit back. I decided to see how long I could hold it at full draw. A long while, it seemed; my shoulder ached and my old scar tugged at my skin, but it was nothing I could not ignore.

Then, the final test.

I loosed.

The arrow moved about as fast as your sword does. I did not see it fly; I only saw the target fall over from the force.

Kenshiro whistled.

"Did it go straight through?" you asked.

I walked over to it, fighting the smile on my lips. Yes, yes, the arrow had gone straight through the target. Only the back third— the fletching, and a bit more—stuck out from the fence. The rest stuck out from the other side.

Kenshiro jogged over. "Look at that!" he said. "Shefali, you must let me try to draw that thing."

"Absolutely not!" called Baozhai.

"What?" teased my brother. He gestured for me to hand him the bow, and I did. My face hurt from smiling. This was going to be good. Kenshiro could barely draw a normal Qorin bow. Oh, sure, he was older now, but as you came over, I stood next to you and cackled.

"Does he want to lose a finger?" you said.

"I certainly hope not," said Baozhai. "My husband is in need of all his fingers."

You shot her a sidelong glance and smirked. "Is he, now?"

Baozhai hid her reddening face behind her fan. I cleared my throat. You winked at me. That did not lessen my secondhand embarrassment.

By then, Kenshiro was waving at us. Each of us drew in a quick, anticipatory breath. He closed his fist around the string and . . .

It did not move. He tugged and tugged, but the string did not budge. Soon he began grunting. Then he dug his foot into the ground until there was a small hole. One end of the bow went in. With his legs spread into a triangle, he grabbed the string. This time, all the muscles in his body went into it.

And still, it did not move.

"You're so strong," Baozhai called.

"Thank you, my love!" said Kenshiro. At last, he stopped trying. A great gasp left him; beads of sweat trickled down his brow. "I am the strongest man in Xian, you know."

I picked up the bow and fired another shot.

All through the night, I tested it. The normal range of a Qorin bow is five hundred spans. Most arrows fired from such a distance tend to nick their targets, at best.

Mine was a clean pierce.

We tried seven hundred. We tried eight hundred. Around eight hundred fifty, it seemed, was the bow's upper limit.

After an hour or so, you and Baozhai retreated to your chambers. Both of you were tired, you said.

"From doing all the work," Baozhai specified.

"Ah, that's fair enough," Kenshiro said. "Shefali-lun and I will enjoy the manly Qorin practice of archery ourselves."

"I think Lady Barsalyya is the only one doing any archery," you said. "Do not hurt yourselves."

My brother and I stood together in the barracks and watched our lovers retire. I remember well the look on his face: his soft features, his distant gaze, his smile innocent as a child's. It looked silly, I thought.

But I knew I looked the same when I thought of you.

Kenshiro sighed.

"They're great, aren't they?" he said.

I could still see you in your peacock robes. Baozhai gifted you a Xianese-style jacket, with a high collar, lined with even more peacock feathers, twinkling under the starlight.

You'd be waiting for me to return. You wouldn't sleep until you saw me again, for you had to know I was safe.

How strange. The Imperial Niece needed a security blanket.

It's a job I've always been happy to fulfill.

"Yes," I said. "They are."

Despite Kenshiro's boasting, he did not stay up much longer after that. An hour, at most. Just before Last Bell, I led Kenshiro back to his rooms. His arms were so sore, he couldn't move the screen doors on his own.

I slipped into our bed. Just as I expected, you were awake. You took me in your arms and held me close. In your porcelain embrace, I forgot myself. I covered my hands in the ink of your hair;

I drank the wine of your plum lips. When we were spent, I held you near to me.

"Shefali," you said, "let's be like them one day."

"You cannot nag me so much," I said.

Laughter like bells. "You are right," you said. "I'll nag you more."

Ah, Shizuka, I could write for years about the kiss you gave me then. It was the barest thing, the lightest caress of your lips against my chin—but even that is more potent than a thousand poems. In the twenty Ages of Hokkaro's history, we have loved each other. Before the Qorin began telling stories, we swore our eternal devotion. Before Grandmother Sky yearned for Grandfather Earth—yes, even before then, our souls entwined together.

How I miss you.

Gods above, how I miss you.

It grows more and more difficult to write this. Yet I have come this far, and I must continue, no matter the pain. In reading this, you've remembered our time together. You must remember these perfumed days. You must remember our life in the Bronze Palace, free of worries and cares, and you must hold those memories as dear as I held you.

As you hold whoever it is that lies with you tonight.

For six months, we prepared for the tournament. For six months, we delayed our fears. My condition bettered somewhat, with the relaxing atmosphere and my newfound hobby. I was with my family again. With you. I ache to think of that half year; how could I have been so foolish? How could I have let those days slip between my fingers like milk?

If we are gods, as you say, then I command you to take us back.

Take us back to the miniature palace in the garden. Take us back to the plum tree.

Take me back into your arms.

Take me back to the night of the eighth of Shu-zen, before the first Imperial messenger arrived. Before he offered you a scroll sealed with your uncle's signature. Before your uncle came for us at all.

Before the day we lost everything.

THE AUTUMN TIME HAS COME

When you received it, you were in the drawing room, playing go with Baozhai. You were losing, which surprised absolutely no one, but you were losing more graciously than usual. A cup of plum wine sat near your hand on the table. Baozhai teased you about your reckless tactics; you teased her for being so cautious. In the other corner of the room, Kenshiro tried to teach me to play a simple melody on the shamisen.

It was a hazy, warm moment, shattered utterly when the Imperial Courier joined us. He didn't bother greeting Kenshiro and Baozhai; he went straight to you and prostrated himself.

"Your Imperial Highness," he said. "The Son of Heaven sends you this."

All the comfort drained away from you. "My uncle?" you said. Your eyes fell on the scroll, on its seal. "You came all the way from Fujino? How did you find me?"

The messenger kept his eyes on the ground. "Highness," he said, "I was sent from the Son of Heaven's caravan. When I left, he was two days from Xian-Lai. He will be arriving tomorrow."

You could do little to hide your shock. I went to your side immediately, positioning myself so that no one could see you shaking.

"Tomorrow?" you repeated. "You jest. The Son of Heaven right outside our walls, and no one noticed?"

"Highness, His Majesty ordered any who saw him to silence. He wished to speak with you personally, and has sent this letter in advance."

You twisted toward Kenshiro. "Are your guards blind?" you snapped.

Kenshiro flinched.

You pressed your lips together and sighed. "I . . . did not mean to be so rude, Oshiro-lao."

Kenshiro, shoulders slumped, nodded. "Considering the circumstances, anger is an acceptable response," he said. "I am sorry, Lady of Ink, that you did not have more time to prepare."

"You," you said, waving to the messenger. "Wait for my response outside. When it is ready, you will be summoned."

"The Son of Heaven requested I stay at your side."

"The Son of Heaven," you said, "is not present. You will wait outside."

The messenger was not allowed to look you in the eyes, but he did stare at your feet in confusion. Either he could obey the (absent) Emperor's orders and upset you, or he could listen to you and risk the Emperor's ire. Technically, your uncle outranked you, and he was the only person living who did. In practice, you were the demonslayer, your calligraphy adorned official documents, your father's poetry was read by lovers everywhere, your mother's techniques obsessively studied by expert swordsmen.

Your uncle had the throne, but you had the people's hearts.

The messenger stood and left.

You pried open the scroll. Next to you, I leaned in and squinted at the paper. Strokes wiggled in my vision, moving from one character to another. The more I looked, the more I got a headache.

But you blazed through it, and when you were done, you threw it clean across the room. The scroll crashed against a lacquer screen. Both clattered to the ground.

"Lady of Ink!" Kenshiro said.

"Shizuka, what's wrong?"

You covered your face with your hands. I tried to hold you, but you collapsed toward your own knees.

"My uncle," you seethed, "thinks he can rule me."

"Is he recalling you to the palace?" Kenshiro asked. "You are nearly grown; your birthday is in two months, is it not? You can stay—"

"If it were that pedestrian, then I would not be so upset," you snapped. You drew in a deep breath and pressed your fingertips to your temples. A storm swirled behind your eyes. "My uncle has made an Imperial Declaration: Any man who bests me in a duel is entitled to my hand in marriage."

Six months, I'd avoided the bitter rage of my illness. Six months, I'd gone without thinking of killing anyone.

But the snarl that left my lips then was inhuman. You, Kenshiro, and Baozhai all paled to hear it. My jaw ached from clenching my teeth so tight; trails of drool left the corners of my mouth.

You touched my wrist. "Shefali," you whispered, "no one will beat me. Please, do not worry."

I smelled the deceit as it left your mouth, but I knew you were only trying to keep me in my own mind. I thought again of the still pool of water.

"Lady of Ink, I am sorry," Kenshiro said. "I . . . this is my fault."

All at once, we turned toward him. Alarm bells rang in my mind: *He will lie he will lie he will lie.*

"What do you mean?" you said. Your voice cracked. "Kenshiro-lun, what do you mean this is your fault?"

Kenshiro sniffled. His shoulders slumped, and the whites of his eyes went damp and red. Despite his great height, he shrank to a child. Baozhai reached for his wrist, but he shook his head.

"The Son of Heaven sent me word that he was coming," he said.

"What?" you said. "You knew?"

He will lie.

Kenshiro fell to his knees before you, forehead to the ground. "He said that if I did not keep you here, he would take my and Baozhai's titles. I'm sorry, Shizuka-lun—"

"Don't you 'lun' me," you snapped. "How dare you? You knew he was coming, and you didn't warn me?"

The veins at your temple throbbed, as did the one by the base of your throat. I saw them, I smelled your rage, your fury.

I heard the voices laughing in my head. *You see now, Steel-Eye?*

"I didn't want Baozhai to lose her ancestral palace—"

"You did not consult me," said Baozhai. "Kenshiro, we could have found something to do. . . ."

My brother stayed there, his forehead against the ground. His big hands shook. I smelled the salt of tears coming off him, but . . .

I could not help how furious I was. He knew. My brother knew this was going to happen, and he lied to us, he lied to us—

"This is not beyond saving, Lady," said Baozhai. "My husband's indiscretion aside. You have enough time to leave."

You shook your head, exasperated, furious. "Then you'd lose your title for certain," you hissed. "I know how important that is to your husband."

"I didn't know he was going to try to marry you off," Kenshiro said, but no one was listening to him. Even Baozhai wore anger and shock. "I didn't realize."

So he was a storied scholar, but he could not realize your uncle's intent? When had Yoshimoto ever tried to do anything good? Of course he meant to marry you away from his throne. Gods, how it hurt to think of. Qorin are nothing without our families—but my mother had disowned me, and now my brother sold us out to the Emperor.

"Lady Barsalyya," Baozhai said. "Your, ah, your jaw . . ."

It was unhinged again. I snapped it back into place. With every blink, I saw my brother's and sister's and your dying forms. The laughing started up again.

"Steel-Eye, Steel-Eye, you're going to lose her soon! Steel-Eye, Steel-Eye, marching toward your doom!"

Children chanting with decayed tongues danced in circles around you. *Do not look at them, do not look at them, they are not real. The more you look at them, the more they revel in the attention, the more they grow, the stronger they get.*

I pressed my palms into my eyes.

"Is there any way out of it?" Baozhai asked. "Could you not declare your intentions for a particular man, one you trust?"

"The only courtiers I ever trusted," you said, "have been dead for almost six years. Whom would I marry? Uemura-zul? He ordered surgeons to cut Shefali open. Ikkimura-zul, Aiko-zul,

Toji-zul? None of the Cardinal Generals are worthy of me. And do not get me started on that dog, Nozawa."

You got to your feet.

"There is nothing to be done," you said, "except to beat every single man with a sword who enters your doors tomorrow."

"Lady of Ink," Kenshiro said, still on the ground, "you must believe me—"

"I believe you've made the most foolish decision of your life, Oshiro Kenshiro. I believe I am furious with you, and I believe that I will not speak to you until I am ready to do so. Leave my presence. Baozhai, you may stay."

Your tone—Shizuka, it was as if you spoke to a demon and not a man, not a man you'd known most of your life. When Kenshiro slunk away like a kicked dog, you watched him go without a word.

I ached. Gods, how I ached. What should I do? Go after him, when he'd betrayed us? Stay with you?

I squeezed my eyes shut. I would stay. You were the only family I had left.

"Lady of Ink," said Baozhai. "I cannot begin to apologize enough. He never consulted me—"

"I know," you said. "You wouldn't dream of doing such a thing."

Baozhai half-bowed to you again. In half a year at the palace, I'd never seen her so distressed. "If you need anything at all, I will provide it. There are ways out of the palace, ways only the Royal Family knows of, that I would be happy to show you."

You slunk backwards. Your jaw was tense and your temple throbbed every few heartbeats; I could see the headache brewing already.

"I cannot spend my life running away," you said. "This day . . . It was always going to come, one way or another."

You dragged yourself to the writing desk. As stressed as you were, the lines on your face smoothed when you held a brush in hand. Ink met paper. You wrote off something short, only a few characters in length, and sealed it.

"Two days to prepare for an Imperial visit," you said. Writing soothed you—your tone was more wry than furious. "Any lord in the Empire would pale at such a prospect."

In better times, Baozhai might have laughed at that. Things being what they were she only pressed her lips into the ghost of a smile—but I knew from her posture she appreciated the levity. "With all due respect, Lady," she said, "I do not run from challenges, either. The Bronze Palace will be ready."

She was right, of course. Baozhai is one of a precious handful of women who makes things true by saying them aloud. Just as I always believed you when it came to our future, when it came to swords and ink, I always believed Baozhai when it came to the palace. The flurry of servants preparing for the visit was chaotic, at first, but only as bees flitting about their hives are chaotic to anyone but a bee.

We had two days to prepare for the tournament proper, but less for the early arrivals. Some lords like to impose upon others for as long as they possibly can. This is true for my people, as well. During the Festival of Manly Arts, there is always one chief who arrives four days too early so his people can have their fill of candied horsemeat.

After you sent your letter back with the messenger, only two hours passed before the first Xianese lord arrived. His name was Lord Shu, ruler of Xian-Shu, which lay on the western coast. Baozhai was not concerned with impressing him; I overheard her lamenting the dilapidated state of his own holdings at dinner once.

The Bronze Palace on its own was spledid enough to humble him. His retinue consisted of his wife, young daughter, and two adult sons.

Both of whom were fool enough to challenge you. Foolish of them. You were already upset, and you needed something to do to let off steam.

Shu Huhai, the elder son, went first. In place of the straight sword favored by most Hokkarans, he used a club nearly as tall as you were. The thing was thick as my forearm and plated in steel. I've no idea where he found it or where he got the idea it would be useful in battle. It weighed as much as a child.

Shu Huhai stood tall enough that you had to crane your neck to look at him, and broad as two Hokkarans across. When he entered the dueling ring, he grunted and growled, and rolled his head from side to side like an animal.

"You do not wear any armor, Lady of Ink!" he shouted. "Have your servants fetch some for you, you will need it!"

"I will not," you said.

And, yes, you stood in that same peacock dress. Your delicate, bare feet met the fresh-tilled ground. If it were not for the sheath in your hand, you would not look like a warrior at all.

"You fight me in your court frippery?" Shu Huhai said.

"I will have you know this dress was made for me by the finest tailor in Xian, and given to me by one of my best friends," you said. "But, yes, I shall fight you in it. And I will win, without a single feather hitting the ground."

"Very well," said Shu Huhai. "You face your defeat bravely, and I admire that in a woman."

It was predictable of him to heft up his club. For his first strike, he twisted at the hips just to get enough momentum going. An amateur move. Hips and shoulders give away a strike before it's made. To be so graceless and brazen . . . well, it made your job very easy.

For the club was so heavy that it took him a moment to lift it, and in that moment, you ran toward him on his off side. With a flash of your blade, blood spurted from beneath his arm. By the time he'd staggered back into his stance, he'd already lost, and you were flicking his blood off your mother's sword.

He stomped away as loud as he stomped in.

"You face defeat with cowardice!" you called out with a grin. "I admire a man who knows his place!"

Your second duel that day was with Shu Guang, the younger son. He was tall as his brother, though not so broad. Our age, I think.

When he entered the dueling ring, he had the sense to bow to you. "Lady of Ink," he said. "I am honored to face you today."

"You will be just as honored when you leave, Lord Shu," you said. "Let us make this quick."

And quick it was. Shu Guang fought with a straight sword. Not so thin as the Hokkaran one—this was a tapered thing, thin at the hilt and broad at the tip, made for slashing rather than piercing. Apparently no one informed him of this, as his opening stroke was a thrust for your stomach. You parried it with your sheath and knocked him in the nose with your pommel.

I admit I laughed watching it. You broke the poor boy's nose for first blood. He was, by far, the most approachable of all the suitors that came for you that day—and you broke his nose.

Shizuka, my darling Shizuka, I wonder at times how you have not broken my nose. But then again, you have tried to kill me.

But on that day, when your first two duels were done, I stood at your side.

"How many more can there be?" you said. "If they are all so unskilled, I can duel fifty. But if they are not . . ."

"Eighty," I said. "Challenging."

I said it warmly, to try to distract you from the gravity of the situation. You have always preferred a challenging fight, but you do not often meet someone who can offer you one.

Your smile was so slight, it might've been a trick of the light.

"Shefali," you said. You entwined your pinky with mine. Such a small gesture—but if any of the lords present saw, it'd mean rumors. "What if I lose?"

I looked down at you. You hold yourself with such dignity that I forget how small you are. You are a phoenix crammed into a woman's body; you are fire shaped into flesh; you are the sky at sunrise; how is it that you are so small?

But before you are any of those things, you are a woman. And you were a girl then, not yet eighteen. An orphan in expensive clothing; a girl facing the threat of a marriage she did not want.

I had to keep you safe from all this.

Yet there was nothing I could do. Only stand at your side and cheer you on as the duels kept coming, one after another. Besides Lord Shu's sons, there were ten more on that first day. Twenty on the second. None of them posed you any real threat; you dispatched them all with a single stroke each.

One-Stroke Shizuka, they began to call you when they thought no one was listening. I've heard that name even here.

Yet despite the ease with which you fought, the stress wore on you. Whenever someone arrived, you'd have to perform a different version of the Eightfold Blessing, accept whatever gifts they offered, and keep a smile on your face, knowing they'd come only to conquer you. To own you. To brand you like a wayward mare.

I stood at your side through all of it. You could not touch me, you could not hold me, but you spoke of me whenever you could.

"This is my dearest friend, Barsalyya Shefali," you'd say. "You have not greeted her; is it customary in Xian to ignore demon-slayers?"

I never knew how to react when you did this. How to stand. Was I supposed to straighten my back and shoulders, bring my legs together like a good Hokkaran girl? Was I to remain bow-legged and silent, your dark shadow?

All I knew was that you needed me. So I forced a close-lipped smile when the dignitaries butchered my name. I nodded when they thanked me for my service, not knowing what that service might be.

You sang my praises and I hummed along. I knew the melody, but not the words.

It was Fifth Bell. Kenshiro and Baozhai were showing the lords of Xian-Lun and Xian-Qin around the Bronze Palace; we had a few moments to ourselves.

Tugging my sleeve, you took me into a spare room and slid the screen closed. "Shefali," you said, your voice quivering. "Shefali, there are so many people here. I saw Ikkimura and his wife. If the Eastern Conqueror is here, then West, North, and South are, too."

I loved my brother dearly, but I still hadn't said a word to him. Only a dozen or so people, he'd said. A small little tournament to welcome me home, just a way to race around nobles.

If he had only told us what your uncle was threatening, we could've done something about it. Could we not have? Oh, it is a fool's errand to dwell on such things, but I spend so many nights wondering what would have happened differently. Perhaps we could have met your uncle at court. Perhaps *he* would not have been there, then. But we would have crossed paths eventually.

Kenshiro, for his part, did not impose his presence on us. What he'd done was beyond mending in one day, or two, or three. If we made it through the tournament without issue, then you might take your first steps toward forgiveness.

But as things stood—no, we would not talk to him.

But you and I were together then, in a room away from all the commotion, from all the difficult emotions. And I had not seen you so terrified in years.

"Shizuka," I said. From side to side, we swayed. "We will be fine."

"Nozawa is here," you said. "I know he is. I have yet to see him, but I can feel his filth."

There are some men who look at a woman as if they're already holding a knife to her throat. There are men whose eyes are wandering, unwanted hands. There are men who by their posture alone can make a woman feel violated. Nozawa Kagemori was the king of those men. Thinking of the years we'd spent apart—the years he spent near you, when you were a young girl— made my stomach churn.

"You have me," I said.

You pinched my cheeks with none of your customary enthusiasm, as if the motion alone would cheer you. The ghost of a smile appeared on your lips. "I do," you said. "But, Shefali, what if I must duel him?"

"You'll win," I said.

Silence.

Silence?

Gods, I ached to see you like this.

So I took your right hand, and I held it up to the light. An old arrowhead scar stood out in a patina against your pale skin. I traced it before placing my palm over yours. Scar met scar.

Like swallowing a star.

"We are gods," I said. "Gods do not lose."

When your eyes met mine, a thousand lifetimes passed between us.

Until someone came running to the door and knelt outside.

"Your Imperial Highness, His Majesty the Son of Heaven has arrived and demands your presence."

"Come with me," you said. "I can't do this without you."

We made our way out of the palace. Baozhai insisted that the tournament take place two li off the palace grounds; even the Emperor could not sway the Bronze Lady's insistence. And, to be fair, it was a much nicer setup than we would have had inside the palace. Guards lined the whole path, bowing their heads to you as you went. Though I followed only eight steps behind, they stood upright after I passed. Every eighth guard bore an Imperial banner: entwined dragon and phoenix. The arena itself was a large square with one of the four gentleman trees at each corner. Young musicians stood in the shadow of the trees. Girls played zither and Sister's strings; a boy played the drums. Holy incense swirled gray poetry onto the wind.

And at the center of it all—his litter set up nearest to the plum tree—was your uncle. He was as fat as I remembered. Sunlight highlighted the greasy sweat on his face. His lips reminded me of overripe fruit.

At his side, three wives. The elder was the one I'd seen all those years ago in Fujino, my father's first love. To my surprise, she still wore the Phoenix Crown—yet all the housings were empty. It was little more than a bronze circlet without the feathers. Perhaps it was their lack that made her seem stark now, and I wondered if my father still found her beautiful. Where her husband was round and wet, she was dry and thin. Not slender. Thin.

The other two wives I'd not seen before. Neither was older than us. One had a pair of striking green eyes that spoke of Qorin heritage; the other was a Surian beauty with smooth, obsidian skin, whose brown hair hung in a hundred small braids. Back home, only my mother wore so many braids; in Sur-Shar, many is the norm.

That was the first time I'd ever seen a Surian in the flesh. If your calligraphy sprang to life, it would look rather like her.

We came to a stop before the Emperor. In all of Hokkaro, you are the only one who is not required to prostrate herself before the Emperor. Instead, you gave him as small a nod as you could manage.

And you did not wait for him to speak.

"Uncle," you said. The eldest wife swallowed her own tongue in shock. "Your retinue is marvelous, of course, and your robe exquisitely tailored. Your wives thrice bless you with their beauty, wit, and charm. Your calligraphy has improved from the last time you sent me a letter. Life has been kind to you."

To this day, I marvel at how you managed to insult him and praise him at the same time. Where was the frightened girl from a few moments ago? In her place was a woman crafted from jade and steel and silk.

Yes, you stood unblinking, and when your uncle rose to his feet, you did not flinch.

"Shizuka," he said, "were you not the daughter of our brother, we'd have you executed."

And I admit that I had to stifle a growl when he said this. I bit into the back of my palm to hide it.

But it did not bother you. For all you spoke of being afraid, it did not bother you.

"Uncle," you said, "with all due respect, that would leave only ghosts to sit on the throne after you. And my grandfather detested ghosts."

I scanned the attendees. Uemura, in golden armor, hovered near the Imperial litter. The four direction generals were, I assumed, the four men standing behind the makeshift throne. Kenshiro was pale as my—

My father.

My father was on the Emperor's right, standing next to Kenshiro. When I was young, I thought he was tall. I saw then that he was not; he came only up to Kenshiro's shoulders. What little hair he'd clung to in his youth had all fallen out.

I shook my head. I had not seen my father since . . . I could not remember. So what if he was here? He would not speak to me. He would not acknowledge me.

I owed him no more than what he gave me.

"We see we've arrived as the Grandfather wills," said your uncle. "This willful nature—your mother's shadow—cannot be permitted to continue. You shall find a husband here. You shall marry him, before the tournament is over, and you shall resume a quiet life in Fujino."

You wore the scrutiny of the court as a cloak, and it only suited your proud beauty.

"Uncle," you said, "my husband is the man who can best me in combat. When you first tried to marry me off at thirteen, that is what I told you. I say it again now before two hundred witnesses. You cannot force a phoenix to wear a falcon's hood."

I've seen this moment rendered in ink, in wood, in stone, in paint. Artists are fond of drawing a phoenix landing on your shoulder as you speak. The closest I've come to seeing myself in these illustrations is one woodcut from the point of view of someone near the ground. It is not quite my vantage point, but it has all the important things. You, mainly.

I bought it.

You know what happened after you spoke. Everyone in the room lost eight years of their life from shock. The Emperor's youngest wife, the one with the green eyes, smiled like an enlightened priestess.

"If you insist on living your life by the sword, then so be it," he said. "The tournament begins now. Your first true opponent is Uemura Kaito, as worthy a man as we have ever met. Take your places and begin."

You clenched your jaw. Uemura turned toward the Emperor and said something in a quiet voice. Whatever it was, it did not change the outcome.

At last, those of us of lower standing were permitted to rise. I took my place on your side of the arena as you took yours in the center. You and Uemura exchanged bows, but not words. Before you assumed your stance, you searched for me in the crowd.

I held up my right hand.

You touched your palm in return.

Then the duel began. Uemura's blade was chased in gold and

emeralds. It glittered when he drew it. The sword, coupled with his ornate armor, made him look like the legendary General Iseri.

"O-Shizuka-shon," he said. "It is an honor to face you."

You did not wait for niceties. Bare feet against the ground—you moved like wind through grass, like a courtier's cutting remark. Uemura parried your thrust with uncanny speed. While you were off center, he lashed out with a slash up your front.

And I have known you to do ridiculous things, Shizuka, but before that day, I'd never seen you parry with the palm of your off hand. Swatted, really, "swatted" is the word—as if tempered steel amounted to little more than a mosquito bite. Uemura's brows rose in shock. He staggered backwards and tried to regain his stance. By then, you had enough room to thrust again. Uemura kept backing away, and you kept advancing. Strike after strike, clash after clash. Your swords rang like sharp bells.

"Her mother must be proud of her."

That wasn't Kenshiro's voice.

When I looked to the source, I saw my father. Oshiro Yuichi, bald, with a delicate gray beard, stood chin height next to me.

"O-Shizuru would've finished this in one stroke," he said, "yet I do think she'd be proud."

What was I to say? Why? Why was he here? Did he think I languished without attention from him? A child does not need a father; a child needs parents. My uncles, my cousins, your father—they raised me far more than Yuichi did.

I focused on the fight. For now, Uemura kept up with you. Parry, block, step away. For now.

But you were relentless. Just watching you made my shoulders and arms burn. Stroke after stroke! How you kept it going, I do not know; you do not have my affliction and the stamina it imparts. Uemura's arms shook every time he parried.

"Is your mother proud of you, Daughter?"

I twitched. He had no place asking me that.

"Father, have you nothing else to say to Shefali?" Kenshiro said. He had no right to join this conversation, either. The two of them put together made me want to run—but you needed me here, you needed me watching.

"I have no words of tenderness for barbarians, Kenshiro," Yuichi said.

Grab his throat. No, don't. He's my father. I cannot just grab his throat and squeeze and *squeeze until he turns blue, until his eyes pop, until his tongue lolls out of his*—

"My mother is not a barbarian," Kenshiro said. "Father, if you must say things like that, don't say them in front of us."

As if there were an "us." Kenshiro was always my father's favorite. My existence was an inconvenience to Yuichi at best.

I bit into my fingers to keep from biting into him. Focus on the fight. Ignore him. For years, I've ignored him; that moment was no different. Let him and Kenshiro bicker. I needed to know you were all right.

And you were.

You were, in fact, about to make the final stroke. Uemura slapped at your slash in a halfhearted attempt to parry, but it wasn't enough. Your next thrust pierced his chin. Dark red dripped onto shining gold. Uemura tried to hold in his own blood; rubies dropping through his fingers.

Despite myself, I took in the scent. Salt and copper, metal and flesh. The things people are made of.

You held out your hand. I tossed you a rag to clean your sword with; in one swift wipe, you finished and dropped it to the ground.

"Uemura-zun," you said, "I will not be marrying you today."

He had one hand on his wound as he bowed to you. "No," he said. "You will not."

More blood fell when he spoke. Drip, drip, drip.

A surgeon hurried toward him with tools in tow. With another bow, he departed.

Hokkarans do not believe in applause. It is too open a display of emotion. Here in Sur-Shar, it is different. Complete strangers embrace as lifelong friends. Before you can conduct business with someone, you must have tea with them.

I have had so much tea, Shizuka, and I hate every cup. Leaves in water. How foolish. Why waste water? I can't taste it, and still they insist . . .

I lose myself.

Hokkarans do not applaud, but as Uemura stepped away, I heard clapping.

And, indeed, when you turned toward me, you wore a wide grin.

"Oshiro-tur," you said as you approached. "It's been some time since I saw you last. Your daughter has grown into a demonslayer, you know."

My father bowed at the shoulders. "Is that so?" he said. "Is that so."

That was all.

"O-Shizuka-shon," said Kenshiro. "That was beautifully done! I'm certain I'll see prints of it before long."

You ignored this. No—you did not just ignore it. You turned away from him and did not dignify him with a greeting.

Your eyes flickered over to mine. We did not need words. We did not need to touch. Just catching your eyes was enough. With a glance, you caressed my cheek; with a look, you pressed your lips to mine.

So the terror on your face was clear the second that man opened his mouth.

"Shizuka-shan."

A voice like cracking bones. A smell, familiar and rotten, that soured my stomach. The taste of him on the back of my tongue like spoiled kumaq. Nozawa Kagemori was behind me. Blackened teeth now sixteen years out of fashion. He wore them anyway, wore them still. His skin was clammy and slick. In the center of his head was a massive bald spot. And there was the scar, of course. The scar you'd given him. It was an angry raised line across the bridge of his nose. He'd never been handsome, but that scar dashed any chances he may have had for a wife.

Except for the tournament.

And oh, Shizuka, how you flinched at the sight of him, how you paled! How the voices within me sang at the sight of him, how they reveled!

"Kagemori-yon," you said, mustering outward calm like a summer pond. "How did you escape your kennel?"

If wolves smiled, they'd resemble him. There was nothing natural in that smile, nothing human. I squinted. What was that going on, with his shadow? It moved slower than he did, didn't it?

Voices. Screaming. Laughter. *So close, Steel-Eye, so close!*

Don't listen to them, don't let yourself be thrown off the scent. Now, more than ever, it was important I kept you safe.

But the sight of him made my blood boil.

"My master let me out," Kagemori said. "He let me go on a little walk."

Now he took a step closer. Yes, his shadow was definitely slower than the rest of him. No longer was he wearing coarse fabric; this was soft silk. And was that thread-of-gold at the borders? The only people permitted to wear thread-of-gold . . .

"You made quite a mess in Shiseiki, Shizuka-shan. Leaving it undefended like that," he said. "It is lucky I was around to clean things up. Your uncle thought so, too."

"What are you talking about?" you said. "As if you know your pommel from your point."

"I know my sword perfectly well," he returned. A dark pink tongue darted out to lick his cracked lips. "Well enough to slay a few blackbloods you were polite enough to leave behind."

"O-Shizuka-shon," my father chimed in. "You are speaking to Nozawa Kagemori, Commander of the Wall of Flowers."

You sneered. "My uncle really is mad, isn't he?" you said.

"Nozawa-zul is bringing honor back to his family name, much the way your mother did," said my father. "A fiendslayer and a demonslayer make a fine match."

I hissed. My father covered his mouth and glared at me in response; Kagemori only shook his head.

"Shizuka-shan," he said, "your dog is ill-trained."

"Barsalyya Shefali has done more in one year to better the lives of the Hokkaran people than you have in your entire existence," you snapped. "Insult me, if you like; your tongue's always been braver than your sword arm. But if you speak one more ill word against her, I swear to all the gods above, I will tear your grandfather's soul out of you with my teeth."

Whatever fear Kagemori struck into you was consumed by the fires of your anger. Your shouting attracted the attention of the other courtiers. Whispers, like cinders, sparked a commotion. Some wondered how you dared; some wondered how he dared.

But all were eager for the next fight.

I think you were eager for an excuse to end him.

First blood can mean anything in your hands. For respectful opponents, you are happy to leave them with a scratch. When they were not? When they had a reputation for making the serving girls at an inn we stayed at uncomfortable?

First blood meant a severed hand, then.

When it came to Nozawa Kagemori, first blood might mean a slit throat, or even decapitation. I found myself hoping it did.

"Your lips are sweet as cherries, Shizuka-shan," said Kagemori. "Even when they speak such sour words."

Was that voice human? For it sounded so much like mine, so much like the ones I heard in my head . . .

You drew your sword in a flash of light. "You've come to claim me, haven't you? Draw your sword, then. Draw your sword and let all of Hokkaro see what sort of man you are."

Have you ever missed a step, Shizuka? Climbing down on a set of stairs—have you missed a step? The fear that shoots through you, the chill, the tightening of your chest: I felt it then.

And when I watched the two of you walk to the arena, my stomach sank to my ankles. Cold sweat trickled down my forehead; my mouth went dry.

"Don't worry, Shefali," Kenshiro said to me. I hated Nozawa more than I hated him at the moment—but only barely. "Nozawa-zul has never been known for a duelist."

The two of you took your places.

Some noble's wife approached us. From the corner of my eye, I saw a blooming flower painted in red between her brows, in Xianese fashion.

She bowed to my father and smiled. "Oshiro-tur," she said. "You must be so proud of O-Shizuka-shon. Such a shame, what happened to her parents—but she has grown into a fine young woman."

And my father beamed with pride, as if he were the one who raised you.

"She has," he said, "and it's as I always told her father over tea: The only thing she is lacking is a good husband. Today, she will be complete."

"She already is," I said. The words left me without my thinking them. I was trying hard to ignore him, Shizuka. My father has always been this sort of man. Whenever you stayed with us in Oshiro, he'd throw feasts just to be seen with you. When your birthday came, you'd always find a new set of robes from him.

I do not think he has ever gotten me anything.

I am happier for it. To receive a present from such a loathsome, simpering sycophant would be more insult than joy.

The noble's wife raised a brow at me. "Who is this?" she said.

"Oshiro Shefali," said my father.

"Your daughter? But she is so dark. . . ."

I walked away, before I let my anger get the better of me. I wanted no part of noble conversations.

Already, the duel had begun. I paced around the edges of the dark circle of dirt. You stood at the east. Kagemori stood on the west. You cast a shadow toward him. He'd drawn his blade, and you had not.

"Shizuka-shan," he called, "if you surrender, this will be less painful."

"You know nothing of pain," you said. "Allow me to teach you!" And with that, you charged at him. One of your viper-quick lunges, to start with.

Kagemori moved away and parried. "I know pain," he said, pointing to his face, to the scar you gave him. "What a great teacher you were, Shizuka-shan."

Again, a charge; again, a thrust. This time he countered your thrust with his own. You quickly jumped back.

"I've learned so much because of you," he said.

And he lunged with such speed, it was hard to follow him. Where was his blade? I couldn't see in the swirl of silk.

But you did. I heard steel against steel. Flashes of gold against gray. I balled my hands into fists.

The two of you parted. There was a tear in your robe, in the sleeve. You were unharmed, but it was the closest anyone ever came to hurting you.

And . . .

Shizuka, it hurts to write things like this. But I must. Even these painful memories are ours, aren't they? Even these painful memories are a comfort to me, so far from your arms.

You were so scared.

No one likes to talk about it when they bring up this duel. In all the retellings I've heard, you keep boasting and taunting him.

But that isn't what happened.

Anyone else who watched would say you stood tall, but I saw your toes curl. I saw doubt's ghost possess you.

And my heart was in a vise.

"For all your talk," said Kagemori, "in the end, you are just an orphan with her mother's sword."

For a moment, you froze. You opened your mouth, but nothing came out. Nothing save wordless growls.

Kagemori walked closer to you, drew his finger across his ruined face. "Look at what you did to me," he said. "Do you think your mother would be proud of such behavior?"

"Silence!" you screamed.

"Do you think your father would write poetry about you, when you cut a man across the face because he dared to long for you?"

"I was a child!" you said. Your voice cracked. "I was thirteen! You had no right to speak to me in such a way, you had no right—"

"If I had no right," Kagemori said, "then prove it."

You charged again, like some fool recruit, like some ten-year-old playing with a wooden sword. There was no grace. No elegance. It was not you.

And you were easily parried, easily riposted, easily . . .

Easily cut by the man you hated most.

Two-thirds of your right ear hung uselessly from a thin flap of skin. The cut that severed it continued across your face, crossing over the bridge of your nose and nearly hitting your eye. It was an awful thing, a foul cut that wept the second it was created.

You screamed. I do not blame you, Shizuka, but you screamed and held your ear.

"My face!" you said. "My ear!"

Everything from your cheeks down was red, red, red. You kept screaming, Shizuka, and you fell to your knees clutching your face in agony and he . . .

Screams, gasps from the onlookers. Imperial Guards gripped their spears with white knuckles, waiting for the order to take him in.

Even your uncle stood. Even he looked to Kagemori in horror. How dare he hurt a member of the Imperial Family in such a way? He had the chance to give you a small, harmless injury—and he severed your ear.

But he laughed. Nozawa Kagemori laughed, and I roared.

Pain. Gods, it hurt. My jaw snapped and grew. Fangs pushed their way up through my gums. Crimson clouds swirled before me. Snapping bones; a sudden push.

Was I getting bigger?

I do not know. To this day, Shizuka, I do not know what I looked like at that moment. Some fearsome thing far from the girl you grew up with. Those crude talons were not the fingers that ran down your back at night. That jagged-toothed mouth was not meant for kissing.

No, I'd become something great and shadowy and awful.

And I was livid.

I did not see in the normal way. When you see a thing, you use your eyes. Demons do not. The best way I can describe it is to say that I was imagining people. My sense of smell was so acute, I could smell everyone, everything. A guard's rancid armpits, a savory roll tucked into a noble's pocket for later, the perfume of a rich singing girl clinging to a warrior's sweat.

Sweet fear. Bitter anger, stuck in my throat with every breath. Ten. Ten, twelve? Maybe twelve. Hard to tell. Fear. Fear everywhere. Breathe deeper. You. You, find you, must find you, if I didn't know which one was you, I might hurt you—

Deep breaths, Steel-Eye. I needed time to think, time to orient myself, but I could not make myself stop. It was as if I were locked within a puppet, watching someone else tug my strings. Only the most primal, shallow thoughts remained.

All around me, the clatter of steel, of wood. Boots on the hard ground. Dust in my nostrils, then in my lungs.

"Blackblood!"

"Beast!"

"Demon!"

Me, they were talking about me, and yet—not me, not Shefali. Steel-Eye.

Yes, that was my name, wasn't it? It had always *been* my name, though there were years I'd never acknowledged it. Steel-Eye. The woman you loved was someone different.

Howls. Screaming. I let the sound peal from my throat, louder than all of them combined. They wanted something to fear? All right. Steel-Eye was horrifying, wasn't she?

Yes, she was. I smelled sticky, stale urine; fear fear fear.

How intoxicating it was, to know how much they feared me! At last, I was giving them a reason!

But—

Was that really how I felt? How *Shefali* felt? Or was it only Steel-Eye?

Speak. I had to force myself to speak. Remember the still water, remember who I was, remember you standing in front of the butcher's desk, cutting meat so I'd have company.

"Leave!"

The others were still here. Easy to forget them when my own thoughts were so disturbing. I saw them staring back at me. I saw them bringing the story of this moment back to their families, to their loved ones. I saw myself through their eyes, but it was not I, it was not—

Had that been my voice? Had I said "leave"?

Fists meeting dirt. My fists? They had to be; I knew all those scars. Why didn't it hurt? I felt pain, but not much. Someone was laughing laughing laughing, screaming, screaming, and with a dull horror, I realized—

That *was* my voice.

Visions of the guards before me. I smelled their histories, smelled their souls, and my mind built some sort of image to match. Little girls with wooden swords. Old men with canes. Boys wearing girl clothes, before they knew they were boys.

"Kill it!" they shouted.

"No, don't!"

Your voice. That was your voice!

A whistling spear flew toward me. I raised my hand, let it through; pain does not matter, to survive is Qorin. My bones shook, my flesh split—but the shaft was still there. I tore it out. Black blood coated the wood; I broke it and threw it away before it infected someone.

There were more coming.

I ducked down, closer to the ground. Instinct drove me. I ran forward. Charged through them. How easy it was! What if I rammed them against the wall, what if I bit into them, what if—?

They were so soft!

No, I couldn't kill them. That was not me. That was not Shefali thinking. But I could not stop—the bodies slammed into my back

and I reared up and roared as loud as I could. Maybe they'd run.
I hoped they did. If they ran, they'd be safe from me.

But he wasn't.

Closer. I could smell you, smell him.

Smell the thing inside him.

That is the thing about how demons see the world, Shizuka. We
do not much care for your physical appearance. We learn everything we need to know about you, everything that ever was or
would be about you, from smelling you.

Part of a person's soul is in their scent.

And where Kagemori stood, I smelled rot. If Grandfather Earth
yawned and freed two dozen corpses from his grasp, it would smell
the way Kagemori did. Ash and cinders. Wet stones. Mold. Dark,
dark, dark.

Kailon.

I saw the demon so clearly, I wondered how I'd ever missed it.
Not tall. A small thing, young and untested. Knee-high. Large
nose taking up most of its face. Two teeth jutting out from its lower
lip like tusks, on either side of its drooping nose.

Young. Untested. But a demon nonetheless, a creature lovingly
crafted by the Traitor's own hands to wreak his vengeance upon
the world. One of his children.

And he'd been wearing Kagemori's skin this entire time.

I was not lucid then. I would've wondered when it happened.
What had driven him to this? There are stories of it; you spoke of
them around the fires we once shared. Minami Shiori was said to
have loved a man before she left for her wanderings, only to discover when she returned that he'd given up his body to a demon
for the promise of her safe return.

Demons can do many things. We are everywhere. We do not

exist as you do, bound to one time and place. We are constantly flowing from here to then, from now to there. And there are few creatures with the temerity to approach a demon.

Yes, it is a thing peasant wives do when their husbands leave for war. If a demon keeps the man safe for a specified time, it's entitled to possess the wife. It never ends well. Without fail, the demon will kill the husband the second it is free of the bargain.

Nozawa Kagemori sold his body.

But he did not sell it to a very powerful demon. He sold it to a child wearing its father's britches.

And the trouble with wearing a human body is you're trapped in the current time and place. If someone kills you . . .

I lurched in front of you. Gods, how I longed to be near you. The smell of you! You were gold and dawn and warmth. I could not see you, Shizuka, not the way I saw the others. I saw only a silhouette blazing bright.

But I stood before you nonetheless, and I raked my chest and roared at the invader. "Kailon!"

Ripples. In my mind's eye, the true image of him flickered into Kagemori's body. Yes, bind him. Bind him to that flesh. If I just reached forward . . .

He was skittering like a frightened bug.

"Steel-Eye, I'd heard stories, but I didn't know, I didn't know—"

I didn't have to listen to him. I grabbed for him.

No, it jumped, he jumped, where did he go? Deep breaths. There. To the right, no, above, no—

There were feet on my shoulders, hands on my face. It craned over me, a wave of scent and emotion. Fury. Fear. Panic. Was this its only chance, to cling to me like a child clinging to its mother?

Claws raking against my skin; burning trails where its nails had been. Pain. Pain. I stumbled forward, stumbled back, trying to shake him off. He held on, dug his claws in deeper, took a handful of my hair.

No. Stronger. I was stronger. I felt it in my veins, Shizuka, with every beat of my heart.

I reached overhead—grab it, grab him by the neck—

Blinding pain, a dagger rammed into my skull. No—talons. Its filthy talons digging into my eye like a knife into a ripe plum.

My eye. A piece of me gone, forever; a piece of me staining this demon's hand.

DIDN'T MATTER. Just a bit of pain. It wouldn't stop me. Not right now, at least.

I throttled him with one hand. With the other, I got a good grip on his scalp, a good hold, as fine as any hunter could ask for. And then?

Then I pulled.

MUSCLES RESISTED BUT eventually gave in. Skin tore. Its head came off with a wet sound that thrilled me. Hot blood cascading over my body, a waterfall of ink. I threw the head to the ground.

But its face. Its face, Shizuka, staring back up at me!

I couldn't stop myself. I fell to the ground and I bashed that head in, bashed it as hard as I could, bashed it until its bones were a fine paste and its brains were thin as leaves of seaweed and—

* * *

"SHEFALI!"

Someone grabbed my back. You.

"Don't touch me," I snarled. Blood, I was covered in it, black as pitch. I couldn't let you come near me in such a state or you'd get sick. Instead, I rolled away from the demon's head and curled up on my side, like an injured wolf.

You came creeping toward me. Bright, so bright. I covered myself. When I blinked, I could almost see your lovely face.

Darker.

Colder.

Something wet on my face, dragging along my cheekbone. When I touched it, it was . . .

It was what was left of my eyeball.

And that is the last thing I remember.

IF I COULD, I'D COME TO YOU

When I next opened my eyes—ah, I must switch to "eye," now—I found you sitting in front of me. I could not make out where we were, but it was not the arena. A great pounding ache in my head dulled what sight remained. As long as I saw you, and you were safe, nothing else mattered.

But as you came into focus, I saw your bandages. One strip ran across the bridge of your nose. A thick patch of cotton covered a gash beneath your eye. And the entire right side of your head was covered, probably to support what was left of your ear.

A sheet of paper distracted you. You scowled at it as hard as you could in spite of all the wrapping on your face.

"Shizuka," I said, "are you well?"

As soon as you heard my voice, your whole manner changed. In an instant, you went from a scowl to a euphoric smile.

"Shefali!" you said. You squeezed me tight. I felt your heart against my chest, and it was then I realized I wasn't in my deel. Instead, I was in a set of loose Hokkaran robes. "My love, how are you feeling? How is your head? Have . . . Have they been troubling you?"

I ached. I licked my cracked lips, pressed my fingers to my temples. Think. Did the demons speak to me during that span, however long it was?

No.

No, they didn't.

What happened? Think. Go out into the fog of memory with a lantern. Kailon cut you, I tore his head off, and . . .

Oh. That was right.

Slowly, hesitantly, I reached up and touched my fingers to my left eye. To where it had been.

"Shefali," you said, wincing, "please. Dear one, you have returned to me; we are together; let us not worry about our injuries."

"Show me," I said.

"My love," you said, "you are still my living poem. Don't trouble yourself with the mirror."

I forced myself upright. Dizzy. One hand on the bed, the other on your shoulder. On my left, only darkness; I had to turn my head if I wanted to see. That was the last thing I wanted to do.

There it was. The mirror. Couldn't see much from this distance, but it hung in the northern corner of the room. I took a deep breath and stepped out of bed. Besides the dizziness and the headache, I felt all right. Well. Not completely all right. I felt as if I'd lost a fight, yes, and as though there was something wet on the left side of my face.

One foot in front of the other. The mirror came closer and closer.

"Shefali—"

"Have to see."

There. That ashen creature in the mirror, with the pale brown skin, must be me. Once, my hair was the color of fresh wheat. The limp strands against my forehead were as white as Alsha's mane. The robes I wore had opened as I walked. If I wanted to, I could trace the dark veins now visible on my neck and temples.

But I was more concerned with my eye. Thick white bandages covered it. With my claws, it took little effort to peel it all off.

It was gone.

There was nothing left, nothing at all, of my left eye. That side of my face looked sunken in. Before this, I didn't realize just how much space an eye took up; when closed, it was obvious it was missing.

I pried my eyelid open. Gray-black flesh stared back at me, wet and glistening.

You were at my side within four steps, perhaps five. Wordlessly you held me.

"My bow," I said. "How am I going to shoot my bow?"

"You have two good hands, my love," you whispered. "And I have never known you to miss a shot, not even when your cousin blindfolded you."

"I can't aim," I said. And I kept trying to turn my head, to see all the room at once, as if I had both eyes. I couldn't shake the feeling that there was something on my face, and if I just shook it off, then all that darkness would go away.

It didn't.

"And you could not aim then!" you said. "Shefali, my dearest one—you are the first to survive the blackblood. You will not be the first one-eyed archer."

I touched my forehead to yours. At least you were safe, I told myself. At least Nozawa would never come near you again. I'd done that much. But . . .

But I traced your bandages and wondered. What if I had been just a bit more perceptive?

"Shefali," you said, "we do not have much time——"

"Highness, I hear speaking," came a voice from the other side of the screen. When I turned, I saw a guard's silhouette. "Is the prisoner awake?"

"One moment," you called back. "Just one moment more."

"O-Shizuka-shon, you are not to be left alone with her," said the guard. He turned, slid open the screen.

But it was not a guard; it was Uemura, and he eyed me with suspicion.

You stood in front of me with your arms spread, as if your tiny size would dissuade him from arresting me.

"Uemura-zul," you said, "she does not know what's going on. Let me inform her. Only a few more minutes."

"If you have anything else to say to her, the Emperor decrees you must say it in my presence," he said. Then he shook his head and sighed. "I am sorry, Barsalai-sun, but we can no longer trust you."

I wrinkled my nose. "I didn't hurt anyone."

"You killed General Nozawa Kagemori, who watches the north," Uemura said.

"No humans," I clarified.

He frowned. "Barsalai-sun," he said, "you changed. This form you wear now is not the true one, is it?"

Was I no longer considered human? I stared down at the backs of my hands. I was still made of flesh. My heart still beat beneath my breast, I still breathed, I still loved you.

I sniffed, and in so doing caught a whiff of Uemura. Shame and guilt stuck to the roof of my mouth like horse fat. Something else, too. Sweet, but a bit sour, like one of those fruits that look creamy on the inside when you split them open. But I only smelled that when he . . .

When he looked at you.

Let him look, I told myself. Let him look.

"I'm human enough," I said.

"How dare you speak to her like that, Kaito-zun?" you said. "She alone recognized Nozawa for what he was, and you're asking if she's human?"

Uemura let out a breath. "It doesn't matter, in the end," he said. "You're to come with me." He reached for his belt and fetched a pair of manacles.

I raised a brow.

"I know they are not much," he says, "but you are to wear them, regardless. The Emperor is strict on that point."

You argued. As an eagle must drop turtles on the heads of bald men, so must you argue. Ten, fifteen minutes passed, but Uemura would not budge. I had to be manacled.

I didn't mind that much. It was more amusing than insulting.

As we made our way through the halls, I made my tallies.

In my favor: I had not killed anyone except a demon. I'd acted out to keep you safe. My father and brother held favor at court. You loved me, for some reason, and still did, knowing what manner of creature I am.

Against me: The Emperor hates Qorin. I carry a fatal disease that will infect anyone who comes into contact with my blood. I became something else. I tore a man's head off in broad daylight. I tore through several more men back in Imakane.

With every step, my feet felt heavier.

Your uncle was the least popular Emperor in years, despite his efforts to the contrary. At forty-six, with no children, he was already a subject for ridicule. Unlike his father, Emperor Yorihito the Builder, who built eight academies in each of the eight provinces, your uncle had done nothing to better the Empire. When the Empire's crops were blighted in the fields, his response was to increase his gardening budget, send a few guards out to proclaim all was well, and continue about his business. He hadn't reclaimed any of the land beyond the Wall of Flowers, hadn't done anything about its decline, hadn't consulted the gods he was supposedly related to about their disappearance.

He was not a poet, like his brother. Not a man of science and technology, like his father. Not a conqueror, like his grandfather. He was . . .

He was not much at all.

But here he had an opportunity. No one would bat an eye if he had me killed. In fact, there might be celebrations. Killing a blackblood is a heroic thing, and has been since they first emerged. Killing a demon is more impressive still.

Killing a girl who contracted the disease and lived?

A little trickier. But given my display and Uemura's comments, I don't think I'm counted as human anymore by Hokkaran reckoning.

So killing me would bring great honor to whoever did it. And your uncle was a man desperately in need of honor.

I kept following Uemura. Though I knew I'd likely die at the end of it, I followed Uemura. I tried to force myself to be afraid, or to worry. Instead, I kept looking at you. What would happen if Uemura executed me before the Emperor? What would happen to you? I could see you, in my mind, throwing yourself on top of me just before the fatal stroke.

If it was going to happen, I hoped he would have me executed far away from you. I did not want your final memory of me to be my severed head hitting the ground. Ren's words rang in my mind. I could not leave the Empress tied to a tree.

But what other option did I have? What was I going to do if he made that decision and I disagreed? Kill the Emperor and Uemura, then plant you on the Dragon Throne and pretend nothing amiss happened?

I did not want to die, but I saw no way to escape my rapidly approaching fate.

"Uemura-zun," you said, "the shrine is just up ahead. May we stop to pray?"

Strange. I've never known you to pray of your own volition. In your mind, you were a god, and you did not need to pray to yourself to get things done.

"O-Shizuka-shon," said Uemura, "I have strict orders to escort the prisoner to the reception hall as soon as she awakens."

"You've not sent word ahead," you pointed out. "We can take as long as we like. Besides, Uemura-zun; we do not know what will happen once we walk through those doors. A small blessing alone would ease my mind."

You were up to something.

"Ask for the Grandmother's guidance," I added, because I have always gone along with your plans.

Uemura studied us each for a few moments. "O-Shizuka-shon," he said, "I shall allow this, but you must give me your word that you will not try to escape."

You touched your fingers to your lips eight times. "I swear it by the Heavenly Family," you said, "I will not try to escape, and neither will Barsalai-sun. We simply wish to speak to the priest."

"Very well," said Uemura. "As a favor to you, O-Shizuka-shon."

He approached me with a hunter's caution, the key to my manacles held up in one hand so that I knew what he was doing. I admit I flinched at his touch anyway. For some reason he thought it would be best to undo the left manacle first; some small part of me feared he was going to slip a knife between my ribs.

But he wouldn't dare do such a thing. Not with you standing right next to him.

You offered a warm smile. "Thank you," you said.

We stepped into the shrine as I massaged my aching wrists. It was Xianese style and not Hokkaran. The whole room was crusted with gold and jade; portraits of your uncle hung on the walls. Ahead of us, on the shrine itself, were eight golden statues of the Heavenly Family. A single priest was tending cones of incense that hung in each of the four corners of the room.

The scent, to me, was overpowering, and I covered my nose and mouth with my hand. But you wasted no time. We did not have much, I suppose.

"Priest," you said, "do you know who I am?"

At this, the priest turned to greet you. He gave a reserved bow, his hands extended in front of him, Xianese style. "I do not," he said, "but all are welcome in the Family's home. Have you come for guidance?"

"No," you said. "My name is O-Shizuka, called by your people the Lady of Ink. I am the heir to the Dragon Throne. I did not come here for guidance. I came here for a marriage."

"What?" I had to have misheard you. There was no way you just said what I heard you say.

"Shefali," you said, "would you have any objection to marrying me?"

"No," I said, "of course not, but . . ."

The priest's brows were so far up his head, they may've been hiding beneath his cap. "Two women?"

You nodded. "Is that a problem? Before my people adopted yours, such marriages were common in Xianese society."

The priest tugged at his whiskers. While he mulled it over, I stared at you. Marriage. You decided somewhere along that short walk that we absolutely had to get married right this instant. We'd never discussed this before, since it seemed so impossible. May as well discuss fire raining down from the sky. Who in Hokkaro would marry two women?

But we were not in Hokkaro.

"No such marriages have been performed for a hundred years," the priest said. "Your ancestors have tried very hard to eradicate the practice. As I recall, they said it was akin to people marrying their horses."

You cleared your throat. "My ancestors," you said, "were godsforsaken fools, I see. But still I must request this. It is not against the Heavenly Mandates—and think what a message it would send to the other Hokkaran nobles. Think what a statement it would make for your people."

My heart felt as if it were going to jump out of my throat and land on the floor. As the priest hemmed and hawed and tugged at his whiskers, the impossible seemed within my grasp. Within our grasp.

"And what of your heirs?" he said. "Tensions are already high, Lady, concerning succession. What will happen when you produce no heirs?"

The question offended you, but your answer came so quick I knew you'd considered the possibility he'd ask it. "You presume much. If Shefali and I can find no suitable father for a child, then I will name my youngest niece or nephew."

I was too gobsmacked by the situation to bring it up at the time, Shizuka, but you should know sanvaartains have a method for creating fatherless children. We call them urjilinbaal. I do not blame you for being ignorant of it; sanvaartains keep their secrets close to their chests. They figured it out not long after the war—with so many dead it was imperative we find some way to grow our population. Urjilinbaal allowed infertile women and sanvaartains themselves to give birth if they so chose.

We had options. Have options, if this is a thing you've considered. But at the time we were still young, and you were still trying to convince the priest to marry us at all.

"Please," you said. "I do not normally make requests; I command. But in this case, I must ask you, sincerely, from my heart—do this. Marry us. I do not care what I must do to compensate you. When I become Empress, you can move to Fujino, if you like, and lead the priesthood there. If you have family, I will have them looked after; they will never want. If you have daughters, I'd be happy to have one join my handmaidens. Whatever you like, Priest. But I must have this marriage."

As you spoke, your voice cracked. You took my hand.

"I promise you, you will never marry any two people more in love than we are," you said.

The priest stepped closer. He walked around the two of us, look-

ing us over from head to toe. "Are you not the woman who be-
headed Commander Nozawa?" he said to me. "They say you tore
his head off with your bare hands."

I pressed my lips together. "Yes," I said. "I did."

"She was protecting me," you said. "You shouldn't hold it
against her—"

"I don't," said the priest. "That pig waited outside my daughter's
bedroom each night, staring at her. I will marry the two of you.
Allow me a moment to get the wine ready."

He wandered off into one of the other rooms. In that private
moment, when we were betrothed, I took you in my arms. Your
cheeks went pink beneath your bandages.

"Shizuka," I said. "Shizuka, we're getting married."

When you kissed me, your lips spoke a hundred vows. I forgot
that Uemura was standing outside. I forgot about your uncle, about
Nozawa. Even my missing eye didn't bother me then.

Somehow, within minutes, I was going to marry you.

"My love," you said, tracing my brows with your fingertips, "I
only wish we could have had a proper ceremony. But I want to
keep you safe, and my uncle cannot harm a member of the Imperial Family. One day, I promise, we will have a real ceremony. You
can ride in on your horse and try to break a sheep's neck like your
cousin did and—"

I laughed so hard, tears came to my eyes, which had the unfortunate side effect of making my wound sting. Somehow you'd remembered the most important Qorin tradition: asking the groom
to break a cooked sheep's neck in two, and hiding a piece of iron
in the neck so it could not be done. How you remembered this, I
do not know. We saw only one wedding together on the steppes.
Had you been researching this?

I cupped your cheek. "Shizuka," I said, "my Shizuka. So long as we are married, I don't care how it happens."

We kissed again, and you touched my nose.

"Well, you might not care," you said. "But I do. And we are going to have a real wedding one day, I swear it."

I chuckled, and would've kissed you again, but the priest returned with two cups of wine. He set them down before us, spoke words of purification, and we began.

We held them with trembling hands. He led us through the ritual, of which I knew next to nothing. We sipped once from the cup to honor the Heavenly Family; once for the Emperor, which I drank in honor of my mother's status and not your uncle's; once for each of our parents. The wine was warm and pleasantly spiced, but nothing compared to the sweet scents you were giving off.

It was time for the final two sips. The priest handed me a scroll, and bade me read from it.

It was written entirely in Hokkaran.

I froze. As I squinted, the characters only got fuzzier and fuzzier; they all looked the same to me. My lips trembled. I could not read my own wedding vows. You were just talking about a real wedding, in front of people. If I could not read my vows before only you and a priest, how could I read them in front of other people?

"I . . ." I mumbled. My hands, too, began to shake.

You leaned toward me and pointed to the first few characters. "Before the Heavenly Family, and our ancestors, we make a vow," you whispered, slow enough that I could follow along and repeat after you. Soon, our voices became one.

"We, Barsalyya Shefali Alshar and O-Shizuka, are overjoyed to proclaim our love, and bind our souls beneath the eyes of the

Mother. Eight times we have sworn to love and respect each other for the rest of our lives. Eight times, we will strive to bring our families prosperity. We swear to remain true to our marriage, for the rest of eternity."

And we had no rings to exchange, no gifts to offer the gods. Instead, you plucked one of the ornaments from your hair, and I gave one of the beads I wore in my braid. Rings would have to wait, but that was fine.

For when our lips next met, soaked with rice wine, they met as the lips of a married couple.

"Thank you," you said to the priest, wiping away your tears. "You cannot know what you have done for us. When I am Empress, come to Fujino. You will live as a prince."

The priest bowed to us. "It is an honor and a pleasure to unite lovers, and to upset the Emperor," he said. "May the gods smile on you."

You took my arm. We kissed again, before the door. Once we left, we'd have to pretend none of this happened, until the moment was right.

"You might lose your throne," I said.

"It would be worth it, to keep you safe," you said. "But my uncle cannot disown me. For two thousand years, only my ancestors have sat on the throne. He has no other choice."

I pressed my lips to yours and hoped you were right.

When we exited, Uemura was scowling outside. "How much guidance did you need?" he said.

"My uncle may well have her executed," you said. You meant for it to be sharp, but your joy softened the blow. "Barsalyya is nervous."

I should have been nervous. But instead, I was fighting the urge to grin. How long could I keep this secret? I wanted to shout it from the rooftops.

Uemura sighed. "Very well," he said. "I suppose you are right. I hope you have made your peace, Barsalyya-sun."

I gave him a short bow. He closed the manacles on my wrists again and led us forward.

When the doors of the reception hall opened before me, I faced the Emperor's glistening face for a half second before I knelt. I wanted to see if murder hid behind his amber eyes. When he saw me, he flinched; his fingers twitched on his throne.

I hadn't covered my eye. Maybe that was what unsettled him. I find it amusing you weren't bothered at all by it during our wedding. You didn't mention it. Your uncle, however, smelled like he was about to retch.

"The Imperial Niece, Slayer of Demons and Tigers, Daughter of the Queen of Crows and the Poet Prince, has arrived! The Bronze Palace welcomes the Lady of Ink!"

The gathered courtiers bowed in deference to you. As Uemura led me to the Emperor's feet and forced me to kneel, I caught sight of my family. Kenshiro, Baozhai, and my father all stood clustered together to our right. My father's face was unreadable; Kenshiro wore guilty sympathy; Baozhai's bloodshot eyes told her story.

If only they knew, Shizuka. If only they knew what we'd just done. Even my father would be smiling then, I was sure of it.

We were married. Lady and wife. The Emperor could not harm me.

"Your Imperial Majesty," said Uemura. "I have brought the prisoner to you for judgment."

"Prisoner," said the Emperor. "Three days ago, we bore witness to your crimes with our own eyes. We saw you burst out of your skin and shift into one of the Traitor's spawn. We saw you shrug off a spear to the arm, and saw the black blood that spurted forth from your wound. We saw you tear a man's head off with only your hands."

Burst out of my skin? I swallowed. What did I look like, Shizuka, in that moment? Was it so different?

"You are a murderer," said your uncle. "Stories have reached our ears of a massacre in Imakane, and we now believe you to be the killer. The blood of countless men stains your hands. And that is to say nothing of your present state. How are we to know if you are as human as you appear, when the former General Nozawa, who was so dear to us, was a demon?"

A pause.

He was going to announce my execution. I felt it in my bones. Any moment now, you'd have to announce what we had done, and hope the court accepted it. If they did not, then the both of us might face punishment.

I had to trust you.

"We cannot be sure of you, Prisoner. Despite your esteemed father, we cannot be sure of you. While you may not outwardly bear the signs of corruption, your blood runs black as ink, and we have seen the damage you can do in a rage.

"It is for these reasons we have decided you must be put to—"

"You shall decide no such thing!"

You shouted this, standing in front of me. As one, the eyes of the crowd settled on you. I could not help but smile. I watched you, standing before me in your bright red robe, golden phoenix ornaments in your hair.

I watched you rail against Heaven itself.

"You, who have sat upon your pretty throne and spent Imperial money on younger and younger wives! Uncle, what have you done to fight off the Northern Darkness?" you roared. "When have you left your palaces? When have you walked among the people and seen how they suffer? You command me to write notices for them, ignorant of the fact that most of them cannot read. You! You think yourself just enough to judge?"

As an older brother gapes when struck by his younger brother, so did the entirety of the court gape at you.

"I say to you," you said, turning toward the others. "I say to all of you that Barsalyya Shefali Alshar has done more to serve the people of Hokkaro than the Son of Heaven himself. Never have I met anyone so skilled yet so humble; never have I met anyone more worthy of my trust. Barsalyya Shefali personally rid Shiseiki of demons and bandits both."

As you spoke, you gesticulated, your sleeves swirling about you like wings. You paced the reception hall, catching everyone's eyes at least once, burning in voice and passion.

"Uncle, if you are so holy, if you are so righteous, why did you not notice Nozawa was a demon?" you said. Now you came to stand in front of him. Now you stared him down with your slashing eyes. "From the moment I saw him, at the age of ten, I told you there was something the matter with him. What did you do? You sent him on valuable missions. You elevated him, held him as a glowing jewel in your breast. He wore the gold thread. You encouraged him to duel for my hand today. How dare you? That jewel you wore so proudly was a serpent's scale, his venom running through your blood. You, who cannot produce an heir, would've condemned your brother's daughter to an infernal marriage. And you seek to have Barsalyya Shefali executed for succeeding where you failed?"

I felt as if the heavens themselves struck me on the spot. As if I were watching the birth of a star.

"I will not stand for it," you said. "I, O-Shizuka, daughter of O-Itsuki and O-Shizuru, descendant of Minami Shiori, trueborn blood of Yamai and the eight hundred Emperors, forbid you from killing her. If you insist, then you must kill me as well. That is the only solution. I will not let you kill her."

Silence. A heavy sort of silence, not the kind one finds in an empty room. This is the sort of silence you find only when large groups come together and all wait for something to happen. Silence, thickened with anticipation.

At last, the Emperor spoke.

"Were you not our brother's daughter," he said, "know that you would've been executed for your willful words. How dare you, child? How dare you insult us so brazenly? How dare you say to the Son of Heaven that he cannot do something? We say the prisoner is to be executed, and we further declare that the prisoner will be drowned, for your insolence."

And you met his eyes the whole time he spoke, unbowed and unswayed.

"I dare because it is in my blood," you said, "and because I know something you do not. You cannot kill Barsalyya Shefali, for you cannot have any member of the Imperial Family executed, unless they have conspired against the throne—and she has not. That is the first of our laws, and we hold it before us now."

Thrumming. Buzzing in the air, whispering waves, hooves against ground. I half stood just to get a better look at the Emperor's glowering face. I thought steam was going to shoot from his ears, he was so red.

"Shizuka," he said, "you are an arrogant brat, but you have

never been an idiot. We have not adopted the prisoner. How could she be a member of our family?"

And at this, you grinned. "Because, Uncle," you said, "Barsalyya Shefali is our wife."

Gasps rang out through the reception hall. Cries of "What?" and "How?" I figured it was a good time to stand, considering we'd already flouted protocol and etiquette.

In full view of the court, you took my hand. "We married her not an hour ago, in the Bronze Palace's shrine, in accordance to the right of their province," you said. "You may ask the priest. We are married."

I spared a glance for my father, who was so white, you might mistake him for paper, his eyes bulging out of his head. Kenshiro and Baozhai wore broad grins.

The rest of the crowd had not yet made up their minds.

But your uncle? He was furious. A ripe strawberry could not hope to be redder. He shambled to his feet and pointed at you. "What is the meaning of this?" he roared. "Women do not marry other women, and the Imperial Family does not marry horsewives."

"We could make the meaning plainer only by public indecency, Uncle," you said. "And she is not a horsewife; she is, if anything, a peacock's wife."

Someone in the court dared to laugh. A brave individual, it has to be said. I fought off a smile myself. Peacock Princess, indeed.

On the one hand, the relief of not having to hide anymore washed over me like the first rain of the season. On the other, we were playing a dangerous game. Technically, we had not yet consummated the marriage. If your uncle realized, he could declare the marriage void, and kill me anyway.

But would he, in front of so many people?

Would he, when no one was shouting in outrage?

Would he do such a thing to you, knowing you'd one day wrest power from him, one day you'd have absolute command?

Two hundred eyes bearing down on me. I couldn't see half of them, but I felt the weight of their judgments. A one-eyed Qorin girl, one who tore off a man's head three days ago. That's what they saw. By that measure, I was not worthy of you.

"O-Shizuka-shon," said Uemura. "Is it possible you've been corrupted? The prisoner is a blackblood, we don't know what powers they might have."

How dare he? After he'd subjected me to his doctors, after he'd let me go, knowing what I was? Tones of panic in his voice; regret and shame in his scent. Perhaps he was trying to make up for letting us speak to the priest.

I grew tired of being silent.

"My name is Barsalyya," I said. "I killed a tiger for that name. I have killed three demons since. How many have you killed?"

He clenched his jaw, and suddenly his young face was fraught with wrinkles. "Uemura-zun, that is preposterous, and you know it," you added. "You ask if we are corrupted? Very well."

With that, you tore off your bandages and held them high as you could. The sight of your wounded face dropped me into cold water. The cut was so deep, Shizuka, and you held your hair up so your mangled ear was visible.

You dropped the bandages and touched your fingertips to your face. They came away coated in dark red. Then you leaned over. Using your blood as ink, you wrote on the floor in your blessed hand.

"Is that plain enough for you to read?" Shizuka said. It wasn't plain enough for me; I was grateful you continued. "For anyone who cannot see it: I am human as I have ever been, sound of mind and body. I've known I was going to marry Barsalyya Shefali since we were children."

"Yuichi!" cried the Emperor.

My father snapped to attention, bowing before hurrying to the Emperor's side. I thought I saw him trembling.

"Yuichi, tell your mongrel daughter what she has done is illegal."

My father has always had a fondness for Hokkaran law. He has scrolls and scrolls of old court procedures in his personal library. And, though I can blame him for being absent, for never caring for me the way he cared for my brother, I can never say he was unfair. Other lords often wrote to him for advice.

Legal knowledge—as well as a great deal of brownnosing— was what endeared my father to the Emperor. And now he was being called on to use it against me.

My father did not answer immediately. This alone made your uncle fume. My father stood there, staring at the two of us. At our linked hands, my missing eye, your scarred face.

It is strange, seeing your own features in someone else. I've never thought that I looked much like him. But in that moment, my father wrinkled his nose, and Needlenose Shefali stared back at me.

"Your Imperial Majesty," he said, "it is not illegal."

"What?" said your uncle.

"By the letter of the law, it is not. The Heavenly Mandates make no specifications about who may enter a marriage, only that they must occur before any woman gives birth," he said. "The Mandates tell us how a marriage is to be performed; they do not define it."

I thought he smiled at me. It may have been a trick of the light, but I choose to believe it was real.

"If a priest has performed the proper rites, then, yes, Majesty, they are married," he said.

A thorny ball in my throat. Was he going to bring up consummation?

The moment passed. He did not. I stared at the man in front of me, who owed me nothing, who had testified in our behalf.

My father.

The Emperor gnashed his teeth. For a long while, he said nothing and sulked on his throne. One of his wives, the eldest one, whispered something in his ear. But his lovely dark Surian wife clapped.

"Congratulations!" she said in accented Hokkaran. "In Sur-Shar, this would be a marriage most blessed! No silly old law in the way. Loudly, I would sing for your wedding march!"

Despite your wound, your smiling face was bright as dawn. "Thank you, Aunt," you said.

"Do not thank her," snapped the Emperor. "You think you are clever, Shizuka. You have lived a spoiled life. You are so accustomed to getting your way, you would flout tradition and integrity both. Lying with a savage. Your parents, if they lived, would be ashamed of you."

At this your face changed. You sneered, baring your teeth in the process. The angry red slash across your nose was like a tiger's stripe. "My parents," you said, "would be happy we married for love, the way they did. You'd do well to remember that Burqila Alshara was my mother's dearest friend. Did you not know your own sister-in-law, Uncle?"

He huffed. "We did," he said. "And we know how concerned

she'd be for your safety. Very well. If you want to sully your bed with a savage, you may. But it must face the consequences of its actions. A man is dead, torn apart; ink flows where blood should be. Do not think to proceed free from judgment because it is now an Imperial."

Oh.

So long as it was not death. I could do anything, so long as it was not death. My thoughts turned to my horse. What would I do if they killed Alsha? That, too, was unthinkable for me. I've been riding her since my mother strapped me into the saddle when I was three. She was my horse, my Earth-Mare, given to me by the Grandfather himself.

So long as it was not death. So long as they did not kill my horse, or kill me, I told myself, I could face anything with my head held high. I was your wife. Somehow we were married and you had not lost your throne.

What was the worst your fool uncle could do?

"For the crime of killing Nozawa Kagemori, for perpetrating the massacre at Imakane Village, for the corruption of its blood and the danger it represents, we sentence the prisoner to exile. It is to leave our kingdom at once."

Laughter. I whirled, snarling, trying to see who would dare laugh at me in such a moment. Only the demons. All the humans in the room covered their mouths in shock.

And there was you. Your jaw hung open, your eyes slick with unshed tears.

"You . . . you can't," you said to your uncle, your fire leaving you.

"We can," he said. "Because she is of our blood, we must provide a condition for her return. But we may exile her, and we have decided that is the most just course of action."

Exile.

True exile.

Already I could not speak to my own clan, already I was doomed to wander as a lone Qorin if I returned to the steppes. But if I could not stay in Hokkaro with you, what did I have?

I'd taken a spear to the chest. I clung to you with shaking hands. I had to leave immediately, he said, I could not spend the night with you, I could not worship you as you'd dreamed.

Shaking.

A life without you, without being able to hold you in my arms. A life waking to the rising sun; a pale imitation of you. An empty bed, a hollow in my chest. Silence where your laughter should be; cold where you once kept me warm.

Life without you.

It was happening so fast, Shizuka, I could not wrap my mind around it, I could not process it all. I'd had you. For one glorious hour, you were my wife, and everyone knew, and nothing could hurt us, but . . .

I wish he would've just killed me instead.

"Uncle," you said, "she was protecting me. The man she killed was a demon—"

"We have heard you say this," the Emperor said, "and it does not change our mind. The prisoner is exiled, until the day it returns with a phoenix feather. That is our condition. Men, take it away."

Guards took me by the shoulders. Two, three, four, all pulling me back.

You reached for me. Your small hands took fistfuls of my robes. Tears streaked down your face, contorted in agony. "Shefali!"

"Shizuka!"

Fight? Should I fight against them? I could kill them, all of them, I could scoop you up in my arms and we could run away together and . . .

And you'd give up everything you ever knew. Your throne, Hokkaro, the lavish life you've grown so accustomed to.

Oh, Shizuka, my light, my sun, my wife! How it pained me in that moment, as we pulled farther and farther away. You kept reaching for me. You screamed at the top of your lungs for the guards to stop, but they would not listen, they did not care.

"Shefali!" you shouted. "Shefali, we have to be together again!"

"I'll find the feather!" I promised. What other choice did I have? Oh, no one had seen a live phoenix in a hundred years, but I'd find one. If it meant getting back to you, I'd track down the gods themselves. "Wait for me, Shizuka, and we'll be two pine needles! I love you—!"

Just as the doors shut, I saw you fall.

"Until the stars go out," you said, "I'll love you!"

That was the last I saw of you.

THE REST OF it floats in a haze. Guards took me to my rooms and allowed me to gather my things. I took one of your robes and claimed it was mine just so I'd have something of yours to keep. They took me to the stables, set me on my horse, and began the ride.

Three months I rode with them. For three months, I said not a word. Everything I did had to be supervised. Making water? One of them stood next to me and watched. When they ate, they insisted I did, too; when I refused, they forced open my mouth and made me swallow. My nighttime rides became a thing of memory. One of them was always awake, always watching.

I wept, Shizuka. I wept for you every night. So what if I'd lost an eye? An eye is not an essential thing. I was born with two; I can live with one.

But a person can have only one soul, and you are mine. Without you near me . . .

I cannot put words to the pain. To the emptiness, to the longing. For every time I thought of my missing eye, I thought of you ten times. Your quiet snoring, the sound of you sucking your thumb and the small wet spot by your mouth. Whenever the guards decided on a campsite for the evening, I thought I heard you puffing.

"No, you fool Qorin," I imagined you saying. "We cannot camp here. Our tent would be in direct sunlight. Do you intend to bake us?"

The guards never spoke. They never complained about the tent or the bedroll or being out in the wilderness or the rain. They never encouraged me to hunt. (Indeed, they carried my bow in its case the whole way to the border.)

Every day it was the same: Rise. Mount. Ride until they told me to stop. Sit in my tent at night, unable to rest. Rise. Mount. Ride.

It was a cruel mockery of the Qorin way of life. Without hunting, without the occasional feast, without kumaq, the monotony of it all set in.

And it never rained on the steppes. That was another thing. You will be happy to know it does not rain very much in Sur-Shar either, and whenever it does, everyone acts as if the Daughter's own tears are falling from the sky.

Yes, it was only three months by the main roads from Xian-Lai to the southeastern border at Tatsuoka. This being so far south that it was wet and rainy and hot all the time, the Wall of Stone did not impede our progress. No. When we reached the border village, it looked like any other.

Except that half the people there had lighter hair and eyes, and darker skin. I do not know if the guards guided me to a town of mixed-bloods on purpose. I like to think they did, to offer me some small comfort during my final day in Hokkaro.

And it was there, at Tatsuoka, that my brother met me late at night. I still remember hooves beating against the ground at the unholy ring of First Bell. Some guard had seen something, I thought; a robber or a group of bandits. Nothing that concerned me. I continued lying in bed, pretending to be asleep, and did not give it a second thought.

But moments later, the door slid open. I shot awake and reached for the sword the guards had confiscated.

"State your name!" they shouted as I got to my feet.

"Oshiro Kenshiro, Lord of Xian-Lai!"

My brother? I sniffed the air. Yes, that was he. What was he doing in Tatsuoka? How had he gotten here so fast?

When they opened the door, I saw: My brother's riding clothes were worn right through, baring his bruised thighs. Dirt painted him black and covered his hair in grit. He had to lean on one of the guards, for he could not stand on his own power.

And in spite of all that, in spite of the pain he must have been in, Kenshiro lit up when he saw me. "Shefali-lun," he said. "Shefali-lun, thank Grandmother Sky, I am not too late."

"The prisoner is under our protection, Your Worship," said one of them. The leader, I think. He was short and thin, with a wispy mustache and beard. What he lacked in stature he made up for in posture and tone. He had the look of a wire about to snap. "We are under strict orders to keep her isolated."

"I've been isolated," I said.

Kenshiro nodded. "She will be out of your hair tomorrow, Captain Hu," he said. He knew the guard by name. That was Kenshiro. "Please, I rode a horse to death—"

"You what?" I gasped. "Kenshiro!"

He winced. "Shefali-lun, I'm sorry; there was no other way to reach you in time. The birds came for her. She is in the stars now."

"You let the birds have her?" I said. "Kenshiro, you did not use her meat, or her milk, or . . . you just left her there for the birds?"

My voice cracked. How could he do such a thing? How could he ride a horse to death, just to reach me faster? And how could he leave a corpse out there to rot? Yes, when it came to humans, that was what one did. But with horses, they are far too valuable to leave uncovered. If a horse dies in your care, you must make use of its body, or you are disrespecting everything it ever gave you.

Dogs are left out for the birds.

But never horses.

Without thinking, I'd switched to Qorin. Hu ordered us to switch back to Hokkaran, but I couldn't find the words. My brother ran a horse to death. If this had happened out on the steppes, my mother would have had him flogged. How could he?

Kenshiro shrank four sizes. He pressed a forehead to his hand

and stepped closer to me. He bowed low. "Shefali," he said, "I'm sorry. I didn't know, I thought . . ."

"You'll find her, when you go back," I said, "and you'll make a grave marker for her, as she deserves."

Silently he nodded. I wiped my tears on my sleeve. After all this time, three months under armed guard, I'd been so happy to see him, despite his foolish betrayal. The death of a horse turned the whole thing sour.

I turned from him.

He rose and touched my shoulder. I batted him away.

"Shefali," he said, "Baozhai sent you a gift and a letter."

That made no sense. Baozhai, nice as she was, wouldn't command Kenshiro to ride so hard to send me a present. I looked over my shoulder. Kenshiro held a small parcel in one hand, and a letter in the other. Neither bore Baozhai's too-delicate calligraphy.

Instead, it was the fine, confident hand you'd become so well known for. Kenshiro held it up only long enough for me to see it; then he quickly flipped both over and shoved them into my hands.

"Baby sister," he said. "I'm sorry we have to part like this. I'm sorry for all the things I've done, no matter the intention behind them. They say the more wives a man has, the more troubles— pity me, for I make such mistakes and I've only Baozhai to speak of. You'll return, I know you shall. Until that day, we'll all keep you in our thoughts. You were always meant for great things. Bring back that feather. Show them a half-blood is twice as good."

He knew better than to hold me at that moment. Looking back on it, I wish I had reached for him.

But, no, my brother sniffed my cheeks, and I sniffed his, and as he left, he paused at the door. "Remember," he said, "your wife is waiting."

I stuffed the letter and the parcel into my bags. Hu wouldn't let me read them now. When we crossed the border, I thought, then I would allow myself this last interaction with you.

It was a long few days, Shizuka. Longer than my time alone in the ger when I was ten. Longer than the three days I lay dying in bed, with you weeping at my side. In my deel pocket was a letter you'd written; perhaps the last words we'd share for years. I wanted to know what they might be, but at the same time—when I was done with the letter, would I ever hear your voice again?

The real you?

Yet I could not wait. The moment we passed the border, that letter started to burn against my chest.

So it was that I opened the parcel with shaking hands on horseback. I found a note hiding beneath the delicate red paper. Hokkaran, written phonetically in the Qorin alphabet.

> *Shefali, my dearest love,*
>
> *I shall not hope that this finds you in good health, for I know it will. You are my unstoppable rider, my soaring arrow—you cannot help but keep going forward. In time, you shall loop around and find your way back to my arms, where you belong. Of this I am sure.*
>
> *When we were children and I sent you my first letter, I asked you what sort of flowers you liked. I wanted so badly to be friends with you. You may not know this, but I used to drive our messengers half-mad, asking if you'd written back. I asked you about flowers because I have always loved them, and I planned to plant more of whichever was your favorite. That way I could keep something you liked near me at all times. I'd be closer to you, I thought.*

I want you to know I kept the flowers you sent me from Gurkhan Khalsar. I didn't plant them. You see, when it came down to it—when you gave me something of yours—I thought it was so sacred and so wonderful that I couldn't bring myself to do anything but hoard it.

I have kept everything you've ever given me, no matter how small.

So now, I send you something to hold on to.

Enclosed in this box is what remains of my short sword. Dueling has gotten me nowhere in the end. What good have I done for you, or for my country, by dueling?

No. If I am going to have to spend time away from you, then I will spend that time bettering Hokkaro.

May you wear this well, my love, my dearest one.

Return to your wife. She is waiting.

Ever yours,

O-Shizuka

I must've read it eight by eight times. Even now I write it from memory. Oh, do not think I lost it, Shizuka. I keep it in the chest pocket of my deel, safe from sand and weather. Sometimes I press it against my nose to try to inhale what's left of your scent. Whatever bits of your soul hide amid filaments of parchment, I treasure them.

But I was on horseback then, riding to lands I did not understand. When I was done reading your letter (over and over), I opened the simple red box that came with it.

I don't know where you got the idea for it. You'll tell me when we next meet, won't you? You could've just sent me the sword. Yet that would not do, and you had to make a grand gesture of it.

So you had the sword melted and reforged into a prosthetic

eye. One that bore an engraved peony where its iris should be, no less. When I saw, it I laughed. It was so like you to be ridiculous like this. The first time I popped it into my socket, it was so cold, I couldn't keep it there for long.

Now, well . . .

It is warm. As warm as the rest of me. And, this may sound strange, Shizuka, but I swear to you I can see through it. Not well. Everything on that side is fuzzy and distant, but I can see out of a steel eye all the same. Prince Debelo has a mirror he has let me use on occasion; would you believe there are veins on that steel eye now?

I tell you, when I return, I worry you will not recognize me. I hope beyond hope that you do.

But there is one letter left. A letter that sent me from the Golden Sands, where I began to write this, to the towering bazaars of Sur-Shar, and Prince Debelo's Endless Palace. Four years that journey took, and another two to ingratiate myself to him.

We leave tomorrow for what he calls "the Shadow's Mouth." You and I think of it as the Mother's Womb, where all souls return after death. Yes, Shizuka, he claims to have pinpointed an entrance to it. It is my hope I'll find a phoenix hiding there, waiting to be reborn.

The letter was from Empress Consort Aberash. You transcribed it into Qorin for me. This one I was forced to turn in to Prince Debelo as proof of my identity, so I do not have it with me. You'll forgive me if some of the words are wrong.

> *Barsalyya,*
> *My husband has exiled you from family and love, as if*
> *you stole his trade secrets and not merely killed a man who*

*deserved killing. He has not exiled you from my family,
however, for he did not think that far ahead.*

*My brother, Debelo, is Merchant Prince of Salom; if
anyone knows where to find a firebird, it is he. Since childhood, he's loved them; now that he has the wealth to track
one down, it is all he can talk about.*

*Here is what you shall do: Go to the Golden Sands, and
find a rabbit with horns. Take it to Salom (it is the capital,
if you don't know), and present it to Debelo. Show him this
letter.*

*I can't excuse my husband's actions, and I can't reverse his
decisions, but in this way, I can ease your trouble. Consider it
a wedding present from your new family.*

> *Your Aunt,*
> *Aberash*

And so that brings me here, Shizuka.

As I finish this letter, I am sitting in my rooms within the Endless Palace. My bed is so large, you would be jealous, and carved
from dark wood native to Sur-Shar. It is a good bed, a fine one,
but I am happy to leave it. I do not do much sleeping, and so it
taunts me with its size. I think over and over of what it would be
like to lie with you here. The cloth is soft as clouds.

But I think your skin is softer.

Tomorrow, I leave for the Shadow's Mouth, where the Mother
welcomes all her lost souls. Tomorrow, I leave for the underworld.
Years it has taken us to gather a team. Two Pale Women, a fox
woman, and a girl with an arm carved from stone that she uses as
easily as I use my eye. Debelo picked each of us for a specific reason, though he will not elaborate to me.

And there is Otgar.

Yes, my cousin is with me. That is a story for another time, I fear; if I do not return, then surely she will. Rest assured, she's been of great service to me. On top of speaking Surian, she is fluent in coins and commerce. The preposterous amount of money we've made here will serve us well on the journey back, I'm sure.

If we make it back.

I think that is why I am ending the letter here. Why I have waited so long to complete it. I may die soon, if I am still capable of it. If I do, then you must have something to remember me by. Something you can keep close to you. And I know I have wasted time and space and ink and paper on this letter, but if you keep any part of it, keep this:

From the day Grandmother Sky first dreamed of the Earth, I have loved you. From the time wolves and men lived together in harmony, I have loved you. Certain as frost gives way to moss, certain as the stars, I love you. And though I ride at sunrise to unmapped darkness, I will let my love for you light the way.

For on the steppes of my mind, you are a bright campfire, and I will always find my way back to your side.

Always.

THE EMPRESS

SIX

The Empress of Hokkaro rises from her bed in a storm of red silk. In her haste to leave, she does not bother fetching her outer robes; as she bolts down her Imperial corridors, her nightgown threatens to open. Like bees dropping pollen, the hundred thousand servants of the Jade Palace cease what they are doing. At once they turn their backs; at once they kneel.

"Messenger!" she shouts. "I need a messenger!"

A young man near the end of the hall bows. "Imperial Majesty, I live to serve!"

"Go to the brothel where the Merchant Prince is staying. Summon him and his retinue."

Throughout history, scholars of all stripes have agreed on one thing: It is unwise to question an absolute sovereign. It is especially stupid to do so when—as in Hokkaro—that sovereign rules by divine mandate. If O-Shizuka wanted, she could have the entire staff executed. All it would take was a simple word to the guards to kill every single person in that hallway. Easy as breathing.

The palace staff is conscious of this. O-Shizuka has a fiery temper, it is true—but she has yet to have anyone killed. In this, as in all things, she improves upon her uncle Yoshimoto. Not a week passed on his watch without an execution. It reminded people, he said, of the divine order.

O-Shizuka does not kill servants who displease her. She dismisses them. If they greatly displease her, or if they commit a crime, she metes out judgment as she sees fit. Few say she is kind—she has not been kind since Ink-on-Water—but none say she is unfair. In her three reigning years, she's lopped off ten ears, ten right hands and ten left hands; she's made perverts leave her presence stark naked and blooded; she's had the tongues of would-be blackmailers served to them on platters.

O-Shizuka does not kill her servants. But she is not kind to criminals.

Knowing this—knowing her reputation for swift justice, knowing that he exists solely at her whim—the young man speaks up. "Imperial Majesty, Fire of the Heavens, it is Last Bell," he says. "If the Merchant Prince is awake, he is surely entangled with the entertainment—"

"You were not asked for your opinion," O-Shizuka says, and the young man recoils as if he's been cut. "I do not care if you have to pull him out of her yourself. You shall bring him and his retinue to me, immediately."

The young man touches his forehead to the ground and leaves.

The Empress arrives in the throne room. Her guards turn their backs to shield her modesty; she has not yet stopped to think about it. No, as she sinks onto the Phoenix Throne, only one thing is on her mind.

She is an idiot. For the past two days, she's isolated herself to read Shefali's letter. For the past two days, she's insisted on refusing all audiences, even that of the Merchant Prince of Sur-Shar. Prince Debelo.

The very same Debelo Shefali was traveling with two years ago, when she departed for the Mother's Womb. The very same Debelo who sheltered her, whom she spoke of as a friend, has been here in Fujino for two days.

She wants to scream. Can it be possible? Can it be that Shefali has been in this city for so long, and O-Shizuka has not felt her near? Have they been apart so long?

Though the brothel is not far, the messenger seems to take an eternity. Eighty gold and jade pillars cast eighty flickering shadows by torchlight, each one a false promise. Her mind shapes them into tall, bowlegged silhouettes.

Why has he not yet returned? Does it take so long to round up a Merchant Prince and fifty retainers? Does it take so long to pay singing girls? What if they were attacked? What if, when they arrive, Shefali is not with them?

What will she say then? What excuse will she give to the prince?

No. Too many thoughts, too many things she does not want to take care of at the moment.

Except that if she left—if she walked the streets of Fujino after Last Bell in her nightgown—she'd be there by now. She'd know. She'd be wrapped in Shefali's warm embrace. Why hadn't she gone on her own? This waiting is agony, like an arrowhead digging into muscle. She tries to remind herself that she cannot leave the palace whenever she wants. Dark swords hide everywhere, and if she dies now, then there will be no one to follow her.

Shizuka tries to tell herself this, but she knows full well she would slay anyone who crossed her.

But the thing is done already. And there sits the Empress of Hokkaro on the Phoenix Throne, in her nightgown. If any of the guards turned, they'd catch sight of her sacred collarbones, her delicate ankles, her pearl toenails. Each lock of unbound hair is a brushstroke against her pale skin.

Yes, if the guards turned now, they'd see O-Shizuka glowing. She's been known to do it on occasion. It is a soft glow, no brighter than a candle, but it wraps around her like a cloak. No one dares mention it to her. No one mentions the Empress's mangled ear; of course no one mentions how she sometimes becomes a paper lantern.

It is their little secret. Their confirmation that, for all her temper and her arrogance, O-Shizuka's blood runs gold with divinity. For they have all seen it: when she is angry, it takes sharp shapes; when she is excited, the aura stands on end.

But it is there. And it is especially visible now, in the dark, the most visible it has ever been.

The Empress is glowing.

After no more than an hour's time, the messenger returns. He scrambles through the great doors alone and falls to his knees.

"The others?" asks O-Shizuka.

"They are following, Imperial Majesty," he says. "One of them carries a phoenix feather!"

O-Shizuka rises.

The air tastes different. Like milk, she thinks. Like fermented milk and horses. Like the cutting cold winds of the steppes.

Her heart drops to her knees, her breath leaves her for some distant land. She runs. Bare feet meet cold tile. Yes, she can feel it now—the painful thrumming in her chest, her lungs burning, her whole being vibrating at once.

And when O-Shizuka throws open the doors to the palace, when she gazes upon the expansive courtyard and gardens her ancestors built, she has eyes only for one.

Bare feet against stone.

First Bell rings inside the palace. The sky above is rich with stars, each one the soul of an honorable person, each one looking on in envy as the two lovers are reunited.

For, yes, there is Barsalyya Shefali, wearing her tiger-striped deel. Strapped to her back is the bow no man can fire. Her left eye is a steel peony covered in filmy black. Hanging from a cord around her neck is the laughing fox mask. An iridescent phoenix feather is tucked behind her ear, though the feather pales in comparison to the laughing green of Shefali's right eye.

And, yes, she has changed a bit. Her full cheeks are hollowing out; her warm brown skin is turning charcoal gray. Pointed ears peek out beneath her now dull blond hair. And when she sees O-Shizuka, when she smiles wide as the Wall of Stone, her teeth are all pointed.

But it is Shefali all the same.

O-Shizuka runs into her wife's embrace.

The rest can wait.

Turn the page for more

in the world of

THE TIGER'S
DAUGHTER

An early found remnant of the unfinished memoir

by the Poet Prince, O-Itsuki

CREATURE OF BEAUTY,
CREATURE OF TRUTH

If in twenty years I die, with Minami Shizuru at my side, then I wish for two things to be made known to the whole Empire.

First: I died happy.

Second: I tried to talk her out of it.

How easily she unravels me. In the fierce brilliance of her presence, even my finest poetry is the work of a lovesick novice. Worse! All these years I thought I wrote of brightly burning flame, when in truth I was writing only of the shadows cast by her absence, as yet unknown to me.

It is my great sorrow that I heard of Minami Shizuru for the first time during the Qorin war. Ah, but at what use my laments? The gods themselves cannot change the past to suit them; I am a fool for dwelling. There must be a reason I only heard of her then.

I can tell you exactly where I was the first time I heard her name—three hundred li from Fujino, nestled deep within the rolling hills of Hanjeon. My brother and I were on our way to Oshiro under order from my honored father. He, in all his Imperial pragmatism, knew the people would care for us more if they saw us at the front lines.

Iori could not contain his excitement. My brother, the Crown Prince, insisted on wearing his solid gold show armor and Dragon helm at all times. Briefings in the war tent were no exception.

There are lengths even I will not go to for aesthetic's sake. That helmet blinded the wearer to anything except that which was directly ahead of him. Supposedly this was meant to be a metaphor—the Emperor looked only to the future.

And though there is a time and place for metaphor, war is not it. Of course, I should not have expected anything different from Iori, who spent the majority of his time sparring with anyone who would have him. He was so inflated with his own glory that he didn't realize he won only because his opponents allowed him to.

I stood to the right of my brother whenever I could, so that I would not have to look on his excited face whenever the reports of battle came in.

On that day we were the highest ranking officers present, thanks to our prestigious birth and the fact that all real commanders had already been sent to Oshiro. General Kobayashi of the East had been among them, and so she'd sent us one of her captains—a man named Sato—to inform us of the situation and keep us from charging headlong into danger. He wore unadorned armor and the sword at his hip had come straight off the armory racks; the war mask hanging from its cord around his neck was a bog-standard wolf.

In short, Sato was the exact opposite of my brother, and I loved him for it.

A map lay spread out before us. A dozen or so figurines stood atop it, gathered in a half circle near Oshiro Castle, facing out toward the Wall of Stone. The invading Qorin forces were represented by little wooden cubes. There weren't many of them, but they were positioned all over the province. Past the Wall of Stone there were far more cubes, clustered close together near the hole.

"Tell us the truth of it, old man! How will we turn the tide?" said Iori. He picked up the dragon figurine that represented us and used it to push the nearest cube—situated at the border with Hanjeon—off the table. "That is where their leader is, isn't it? That is why we're attacking from this angle?"

Captain Sato, to his credit, did not react to this foolish display. "Their leader is here," he said, tapping a square much closer to the palace. "That was one of their smaller forces, your Imperial Highness."

"How many months can we maintain the siege?" I asked. I knew Oshiro Genichi only in passing, but I knew his son Yuichi well. He'd come to Fujino to study law, at great cost to his father. He was no warrior. I wondered how he felt, surrounded on all sides by attackers who would not listen to any of his elegant arguments.

"Half a year, given current conditions, your Highness. Assuming General Watanabe's emergency barricades hold and the bulk of their forces do not breach the Wall," said Captain Sato. He did not address whether or not the Qorin had any more explosives. "However . . ."

He pushed one of the figurines north of the castle toward a cache of wooden cubes.

"Captain Araya is attempting to liberate the river and surrounding areas."

"Then we must go north!" said Iori, banging on the table.

"We will provide reinforcements to him, and break the siege of Oshiro!"

Captain Sato's brow twitched. "Your Imperial Highness," he said, "I'm certain you know far more people than I will meet in my entire life, among them Captain Araya's father—but the Captain I speak of now is his daughter. Her unit is quite far removed from this one. To join with her we would have to march through much of Fuyutsuki; it is more efficient to flank the enemy from the south."

Iori grimaced. Not yet on the battlefield and his pride was already wounded.

"Besides," said Captain Sato, "the Minami family is with Captain Araya."

The name instantly conjured clouds of legend in my mind. "The Minami family? Is there a fox woman among the Qorin?" Ikuhara Ryuji, one of my childhood mentors, wrote a fine poem about Minami Shiori's famous rescue of First Emperor Yamai. Most people remembered it for its use of an all-new meter, but I remembered the confrontation at its climax. In all the Empire only Minami Shiori has ever resisted the charms of a fox woman.

"No one's seen a fox woman in centuries," sneered my brother.

It was a silly thing to say. Toy dragons should not question old soldiers. I regretted my words immediately.

But it was then that Captain Sato finally let out something like a laugh.

"Even if the enemy had a squad full of demons, I would not worry. Minami Shizuru would cut right through them."

Yes—her. Captain Sato said her name as if he were a small boy bragging about the strength of his father. This hardened veteran spoke of her in such a way!

Hearing her name soon became a familiar song. Captain Araya broke the siege of Oshiro within the week, and all reports sang the praises of Minami Shizuru. A woman too poor to afford a proper horse—she rode a mule—had unseated expert Qorin riders. A woman who wore smelly armor at least two generations old continued to fight in spite of her injuries, fiercer than ever. A woman who had the unbelievable audacity to feed crows whenever she encountered them, thinking of it only as a good luck charm. Crows! Most refused to go near those ominous birds, and yet she often started her mornings seeking them out with her excess rations.

But my favorite thing about her was that she didn't want to be there any more than I did. My father had forcibly enlisted her and all of her siblings. He'd called on their oath of fealty, knowing full well that they had nothing else to offer save their own service. A single soldier's paltry salary would have been a blessing to them, let alone six.

How could they refuse?

Alas, half the other Minami children had already fallen. Eldest brother Goro was found facedown on the field with six arrows in his back. Masaru, the middle brother, sustained a nasty leg wound while riding in the cavalry, which soon soured his blood. Only her brother Keichi, youngest of the Minami boys, survived to accompany her that day.

If Shizuru was a beacon, Keichi was only a paper lantern. Lack of charisma was his plague. He lacked the heroic bearing that made Shizuru so popular, and lacked the braggadocio that made her controversial. No one could remember any details about him.

Indeed, when Shizuru asked who among the army would stay with her after Captain Araya had called for a retreat, Keichi was the first to answer. Everyone agreed on that, yet not a soul could remember what he said.

And yet I could not imagine vouching for Iori in such a way.

My own brother proved my misgivings during our first battle, a smallish skirmish two days after Captain Araya broke the siege. Again he insisted on that ostentatious armor, despite the arrows flying through the air and screams of the dying all around us.

One of those arrows landed in his side—and then it was his voice screaming, a memory from our childhood tuned to the present. Bright gold is no bulwark against sharp stone and wood.

It took five heartbeats for me to realize anything had gone wrong. I had heard the sound, the wet thunk next to me, but I did not really believe we could be hurt, not until I saw Iori swaying in his saddle.

My mouth went dry.

We were in the center of a storm, the two of us—thundering hooves, whistling arrows cracking against shields, swords crashing against armor. None of this was real. None of it could be. I was the Poet Prince, second to the crown, playing war games with my brother.

Iori, wan and glassy-eyed, rivers of red spilling from his veins over the famed Imperial Gold.

I must be Minami Keichi, I thought, though he is no Shizuru.

And so I rode to him, and I pulled him onto my saddle, and I broke off the arrow shaft with my bare hands. Then I wrapped his arms around me as best I could and galloped back to camp.

I will remember, always, the fallen in my path. Men and women I'd sat with around a fire now lay at my feet gasping for breath.

More than one grabbed at my horse as I ran past, or shouted for me to stop. Some rasped my name.

There is nothing—nothing—so haunting as the look in a dying man's eyes when he realizes you are not going to save him; when he realizes you will not even give him the dignity of his final drink of water. Here he has fallen. Without eight coins for the Mother, here he will stay, his spirit forever bound to the field of rot. How many centuries would it be before someone found his forsaken bones and gave him the proper rites?

By the time I reached the surgeon's tent I was trembling like the last leaf of spring in autumn. As soon as the surgeons took my brother away, I emptied my stomach.

And that was the first battle. There were two more before we reached the front, but my brother's injury precluded him from fighting. Iori spent those weeks recovering.

I do not think it's shameful of me to say I was too afraid to return to the front lines. I was not born to be a soldier. Instead, I spent my time at my brother's side, bleeding out my fears onto whatever scraps of paper I could find. Mind—it was not good writing. But I was trying, at least.

"Why did we get stuck with these cowards?" Iori complained. "If we had the Minami woman with us, we'd already be at the White Palace."

Her name sounded wrong on his tongue, as if it were a foreign word he'd not yet mastered and not the name of the Empire's oldest vassal family.

"And if you were Yusuke the Brawler, you could do it yourself. The Gods have their plan, Iori; we are here and she is elsewhere, doing important work."

He glared at me over his shoulder. Iori and I both have amber-colored eyes, but his are darker—meant for glaring and sneering. "We are the princes of the whole Empire. What could be more important than doing our bidding?"

I could not hide my frustration with him. "We may be princes, but she is the Queen of Crows."

Inspiration struck me as the arrow had struck Iori. Though I was seated I staggered, swaying under the weight of this new idea—the image of Minami Shizuru walking in the Mother's shadow, a crown of black feathers on her proud brow. My hand began writing though the lines were not yet fully formed in my mind. For the first time in what felt like an eternity I was alight with passion.

This, I thought, was going to be different from anything I'd written before. These lines would be spare and unflinching. Instead of toying with meter as I so often did, here I would pray at its altar; instead of dwelling on the beauty of nature, I would turn my lens toward the frantic chaos of war—

And the woman who cut through it the way her sword cut through flesh.

Iori, of course, did not share my vision.

"I don't know why I bother talking to you about anything important," he said.

I paid him no mind. The poem was already forming. Within it I would find my solace, my comfort. Even if the Qorin pillaged this camp, then so long as this poem survived, I would live on.

Two weeks after that last battle—the very day I finished the first full version of the poem—we received word that the war was over. Oshiro Yuichi—son of Genichi and future lord of the province—was to be given in marriage to the Qorin warleader Burqila.

Bringing Oshiro and the steppes together in such a way would help smooth relations, was the thinking, and no one could say Yuichi was an unsuitable husband. Even then he was known for his essays on legal matters; more than once he'd been called on to tutor my brother. Who could reject a lord, a scholar, and a friend to the crown? By Hokkaran standards, Burqila's marriage was enviable indeed.

But she would, of course, have to pay a price for it. No woman could be both the Lady of Oshiro and the Grand Kharsa. Thus, she would renounce the latter title. All of the Qorin remaining in Oshiro would return to the steppes within a week. Her firstborn child would be born in the Empire, to be raised by Oshiro Yuichi— yet there was a mutual promise in that arrangement at least. After all, just as no Qorin would dare to attack a child of Burqila Alshara, no Hokkaran child would dare to attack their own mother. For the next three generations, all of Burqila's lineage would be both Qorin and Hokkaran for all rights and purposes and thus free from Hokkaro's conquering grasp.

It was a wise deal on both accounts—but especially on Burqila Alshara's. That was the trick of it, the trick of her—she was as canny as any courtier. If Qorin was her first language, and Hokkaran her second, then negotiation was surely her third. This was the woman who somehow persuaded the Merchant-Prince of Sur-Shar to provide her with wagons full of Dragon's Fire; this was the woman who established a system of messengers much faster than our own; this was the woman who sought out engineers as eagerly as she sought out soldiers. She knew precisely what she was doing, and this deal was emblematic of her forward-thinking nature. Burqila knew the limits of her people, and could read the currents of war. My father was going to throw army after army at her, and she had only three thousand within the Wall. Better to surrender now than risk losing so many.

And so as her people returned to the steppes, she stayed behind in Oshiro with her new husband—a man she did not know and certainly did not care for. Still, it was a fate she accepted without reservation, so long as her people were safe. Anything to keep the peace.

But it was an uneasy peace, at best. Many of the returning soldiers felt there was unfinished business between them and the Qorin—debts that could only be paid in blood. Though no one called for an invasion of the steppes, they found other ways to release their tension.

While I was sitting in a teahouse in the city I myself witnessed the end result: five former soldiers came over to a darker-skinned man and spat out all sorts of vitriol. As far as they were concerned he was spying for the enemy, his mother was a horse, and he needed to return to his own country. Now, this man wore Hokkaran clothes, and he was drinking Hokkaran tea in the Hokkaran capital. He had brown eyes, not green; dark hair, not light. In short there was nothing Qorin about him except for the color of his skin.

But that was enough for these men.

The man for the most part ignored his harassers. He sat by his table with a young woman in Xianese clothing. She squirmed in her seat, leaning over every so often and whispering to him.

The moment one of the soldiers grabbed him I knew I couldn't just sit idly by. I commanded my bodyguard to break up the fight—but to my horror half the teahouse was in support of the soldiers. The only solution was to shut the whole thing down until the city guard picked up the rowdy soldiers. I stayed the whole time. If I was present—and all those involved knew I was present—then the situation would not escalate again to the physical.

But there are many ways to hurt a person, and though I endeavor to do the best I can, I am only one man—and a far removed one, at that. What did I know, really, about the sort of struggle displaced Qorin were going through? I'd never gone hungry a day in my life. Few people so much as disliked me. How could I know?

More importantly—how could I help?

I attempted to bring the issue to my father's attention, but it was no use. Any Qorin blood made Hokkaro weaker in his eyes. My brother agreed with him. It was no use arguing with them.

And so I decided I did not need them. My poetry has won me friends in many circles. I called upon those connections, then, forming a covert network within Fujino. There were roughly three hundred Qorin within the province per the last census. A large number, certainly, but only a small percentage of Fujino's many-thousand residents. We would only need to cast a small net.

Lawyers were our first targets. Whenever a Qorin—or someone mistaken for one—was arrested on trumped-up charges, an exceptionally expensive attorney would materialize out of thin air to defend them. Sometimes all those allegations fell away the moment our lawyers turned up. Sometimes they didn't. Either way, our clients had the best defense I could afford.

Next, doctors and surgeons. No healers, as despite reports to the contrary, the Imperial Treasury has its limits. Still, a good doctor could serve an entire community—and it was their attention I sought. Some physicians in Fujino refused to serve anyone darker than sackcloth, and my father had done little to discourage them. So, whenever I heard tell of someone doing this, I added another doctor to my own payroll, and promptly sent them over.

Food, too, was important. Thankfully it was also both the cheapest to acquire and the easiest to distribute. All it took in that case was a network that ran from the Imperial kitchen out onto the streets and into eager hands.

I do not want to sound as if I fixed the problem single-handedly. I did not, and surely all of my efforts would have been in vain if not for the contribution of hundreds of others. Doing my best to help brought me comfort, and gave me something to focus on besides the war. I asked for nothing more than this.

In my other hours, I chained myself to the page, rewriting and editing "Queen of Crows." More than anything, I tried to convey the senselessness of the Qorin war—the despondency. I told the entire story as plainly as I could. Seven hundred lines of spare metaphor and cold truth.

By the time I released the thing, it had drained me of all my life and energy, in the best possible way. Within two days I received my first letter, from one of my old calligraphy instructors. Iku-hara Ryuji's hand was widely considered the finest in the Empire at the time.

The letter was as brief as it was cutting.

> *I wish you'd sent me only the hundred lines about Minami Shizuru. You are a creature of beauty; bleakness does not suit you.*

It hurt, of course—and then there was no one to discuss it with. If I told Iori that my latest work was ill-received he'd never let me hear the end of it. My father didn't even bother listening to me whenever I spoke about it.

So, there I sat, those two lines cutting through my stomach lining, my guts spilling out for all to see.

It couldn't be true, could it? Perhaps that was just his opinion. Perhaps others who had seen the things I'd seen would appreciate it.

But every day more letters came in deriding the thing, each one another needle in my flesh. It seemed this poem I'd been so enamored with was little more than an amateur's scribbling. Everyone seemed to agree that this was my worst work yet—with one equally unanimous exception: the depiction of that glorious warrior. My readers delighted in her. In letter after letter they commended me for capturing such a perfect image of that noble heroine, Minami Shizuru. Other poets seized that title, that imagery, and ran with it—by the end of that year there were at least a hundred works about the Queen of Crows.

Yet no one wanted to listen to me talk about my fear or my sadness, or my experiences at war. Only my longing for love interested them—only my observations on nature and beauty.

To know that something which had brought me such comfort met with such derision . . . it was as if the whole nation had watched me bleed before them, and not a single one offered to help. I was reminded, in the cruelest way, of the dying I'd seen at war—of that haunting look in their eyes. Dwelling on that memory left a sour taste in my mouth, no matter how relatable I found the image. A metaphor means nothing if it is misused. Who would dream of arguing that my suffering equaled that of a dying soldier's? No, I knew my place. This was ill-received poetry. I would live to write another day.

But to make matters worse, my father then fell ill. It was all very gradual—unexplained aches and pains—until the day he collapsed, howling in agony, while entertaining Doan Jiro. From that moment on the prognosis was dire. Healers are capable of any number of minor miracles—but in this instance there was only so much they could do. The poison in my father's blood would keep returning, over and over; any procedures he underwent now would only prolong the inevitable.

And so he chose to die.

Iori took it well. He began lording over the palace staff the moment our father told us of his decision. My brother strutted like a peacock down the Endless Halls, pronouncing to anyone who would listen all the things he'd change once he was Emperor.

It was not long before he got his chance. My father passed away in his sleep two days before the beginning of Ni-shen. I cannot say I was especially sad to see him go. The world would not lament the passing of Emperor Yorihito. His legacy—eight academies and a war—would long outlive him.

But during his last few days it was difficult to look on him without falling into despair. My father rode in General Iseri's army to conquer Xian-Lai; he was hale and hearty well into his old age. Yet the man who lay in bed before me was a withered husk. Even the most anemic branch of bamboo would be thicker than his arms. Gone was his trip-wire mind; he could no longer recognize either of his sons. All my life he'd bragged of Iori's physical talents and my mental ones—but in the end he was silent and still.

I did not miss the Emperor. But I would miss the man who raised me.

Despite miming his filial duty for years, Iori did not mourn. Our father's body was not yet cold the first time Iori donned the Dragon crown. Oh, he made a show of attending funerary services, but it was not hard to see the aura of joy about him.

His first decree was that, for all rights and purposes, our father died on the first of Ni-shen. Dying in Tokkar was too much of an ill omen; a coronation would go no better.

He was right on that account. Ascending the throne during the Brother's month would cast a shadow on his reign that death itself could not banish. In Hokkaro, where omens were everything, it was best to err on the side of safety. Wise, even.

His second proclamation was more in line his previous bouts of stupidity: a tournament to find the sixteen finest warriors in the land, who would then march beyond the Wall of Flowers to slay the Traitor. This was, to any Hokkaran, a just and righteous thing to do—the Traitor's foul creations were beginning to break through the Wall of Flowers. Shiseiki faced the worst of it, beset by demon attacks and the blackblood plague alike, yet there were other signs throughout the eight provinces. Shiratori's famed caverns full of gems were collapsing at an astonishing rate; Oshiro's golden fields returned smaller harvests every passing year; livestock throughout the empire were dying well before their time. That this was the Traitor's doing was not a matter for debate—all the theologians in the Empire were in perfect agreement.

Yet a force of sixteen heroes—mortal men and women—to slay a god? And he mocked me for being obsessed with stories! It boggled my mind. Did he think it would work? Or did he, like our father before us, believe in the spectacle of the thing more than its efficacy?

I will give him a little credit: the tournament served as a fine distraction from the nation's grief. A gathering of warriors renowned for their skill, dueling for the honor of saving the Empire? A fine plot for a novel, and a finer one to see play out before your very eyes. Though it cost an astronomical sum to put on, the tournament also drew crowds from all over the Empire.

Forced to attend his little show, I told myself that I might see something inspiring, but my heart was not in it. Inspiration was a distant memory.

Until, on the fitfth day of competition, my eyes at last fell upon her face.

At first, I had no idea who she was. Her opponent was Sugihara Gendo, who in any other era would go down as the most famous duelist of his time. Sugihara stood closer to our viewing platform and was announced far earlier than his opponent.

When she walked out onto the field—when I first saw her—it was as if I'd awoken from a long dream. As if nothing prior to that moment mattered. Who was this woman, cloaked in rough-spun robes humble even by a monk's standards? Who was this woman with a shaggy lion's mane of unbound hair? Though she stood in front of thousands of civilians and the Emperor himself, she held a pipe in her hand, curls of smoke coming up out of it.

I found myself leaning forward as she walked to the center of the field, where Sugihara Gendo awaited her. She took a drag from her pipe before stashing it away within her chest pocket.

"Ara, we've got a crowd!" she shouted, so loud and clear that I heard her without issue despite the distance.

"Who is this boar?" Iori asked. The city's governor, Kahei Junpei, who was in charge of the tournament and all the lists, shared our platform. He did not need to check his records; indeed, he could not hide his smile.

"That," he said, "is the Queen of Crows herself, Minami Shizuru."

My heart fell into my stomach. That was the woman I'd written about? How I wished I'd met her before I started writing! The woman before me was a staunch iconoclast, and I'd cast her as the height of Hokkaran monarchy.

I had to laugh. After this duel was over I was going to have to track her down and apologize!

"All right, you lot," she said. "Who do you think is going to win this match? Me, or Gendo-kol over there?"

Gendo-kol! As if he were a scholar, or a smith! I could not tell if she meant to insult him or if she simply didn't care which honorific she used. Either way I was entranced. Other competitors boasted—but none were as charismatic as she was. Her friendly country accent coupled with her relaxed posture made it easy to forget she was such a war hero.

I leaned forward, my eyes wide, my heart pounding.

The crowd erupted into cheers. It was hard to make out any particular winner with all the shouting, but the moment Minami Shizuru waved them off the whole crowd went quiet.

"They're excited! Gendo-kol, what do you say we make this more interesting, hmm? Every time I hit you, you've got to buy one of my famous bamboo mats."

"Bamboo mats?" sneered my brother. "She can't be serious."

"She is," said Kahei. "Haven't you heard of Minami bamboo mats? They've been selling them for the last five years."

I laughed, again, louder and harder than I had since the war. Bamboo mats! I knew of the Minami clan's financial troubles, but bamboo mats of all things?

Sugihara was also laughing. "Then I shall walk away without a single mat," he called. Next to Minami Shizuru, everything about him was stiff and old-fashioned, including his accent. "And what of you? For each blow of mine, what do you offer?"

Minami Shizuru grinned. I could not remember the last time I saw a noble grin in public. "Don't be so cocky!" she said. "How's this—if you can hit me even once, I'll run an entire lap around the palace, naked as the gods made me."

Sugihara did not hesitate. "Accepted," he said. He drew his sword, and Minami Shizuru followed suit.

Except that she wielded nothing more than a wooden training sword.

I could not believe my eyes. A wooden training sword? Against Sugihara Gendo? How was she going to parry with that thing?

And yet!

I watched, flabbergasted, as she dodged his most expert strokes. That woman turned herself to water right there in the arena. How else to explain the fluidity of her movement? One moment she was a laughing brook, swaying away from his sword; the next, she was falling rain landing blows on his arms and shoulders. All the while she was grinning, laughing, teasing him. When she ended the duel by breaking his nose, it was a mercy to the man's reputation.

In the end, Sugihara Gendo bought no less than fifty bamboo mats, and no one saw Minami Shizuru naked.

Over the course of five more duels she made the same wager. The results never changed: fifty mats sold, and not a lap taken. The winners of the tournament received ten thousand ryo each, but at this rate she was going to win that purse solely through selling mats.

And all this with a wooden sword! Where was the Minami clan's fabled Daybreak blade? That, too, I longed to see in person— though watching the endlessly entertaining Shizuru was its own reward. Kahei informed me that Shizuru and her brother traded the sword each day they were in competition.

"Where is he competing, then?" I asked. There were eight arenas spread throughout the city, though obviously the palace courtyard was the most prestigious. I'd seen Keichi dispatch two street thugs at once on the third day, now that I thought of it— and he was using the wooden sword. He was impressive, but he lacked his sister's effortless charisma.

"Out in the Harabana district," said Kahei. An hour's walk— and Minami Shizuru was not yet done for the day. As I looked out at her taking drags from her pipe, I knew without a doubt who I would rather watch.

I called for paper and a brush, and then for someone to carry my letter. To this day I remember it.

> *Minami Shizuru,*
>
> *Eight thousand apologies for misrepresenting you. I admit, I should have waited to write that poem until we met; your true self is far more interesting than my lines. Before you I am as awestruck and speechless as a schoolboy. Will you allow me the honor of your company after your final match of the day?*
>
> > *May the Fallen Son favor you today,*
> > *O-Itsuki*

I watched the servant run out from our platform, watched her weave through the crowds to reach the Queen of Crows. I watched her tear open the letter without a wink of care for the expensive paper. I tried to search her expression for any hint of her reaction, but it was difficult to do as far apart as we were. Sweat trickled down the back of my neck.

She flipped over the letter, shouted at someone for a brush, and scrawled something back. I was so eager to read it I stood and walked to the edge of our viewing platform, that I might receive it heartbeats earlier.

Her handwriting was as rough and untamed as the rest of her. Some of those characters were so badly done they'd paint a scholar scarlet.

But I loved them. Who else would dare to send me such a thing? It was so honest!

> Poet Prince,
>
> The price for my company is fifty mats and two bottles of plum wine. Afterward, if I like you, it'll be twenty-five mats and a single bottle. Impress me.
>
> The Queen of Drinking You Under the Table

Needless to say, it was a price I was more than happy to pay. That night, Minami Shizuru introduced me to a teahouse the city guard didn't dare go near—White Leaf, White Smoke. She did so on the condition that I keep a hat pulled over my face the whole time, and that I dismiss my bodyguards.

"And should I be attacked by an assassin?" I wondered. "Whoever shall protect me?"

"Are you as dumb as you are pretty?" Minami Shizuru replied. She smelled of smoke and sweat and wine and leather. "It's your brother they're after, everyone in the empire loves you."

"Do you count as 'everyone,' Minami-zun?" I said. There was an ease to being around her—I did not have to try so hard. She did not expect metaphors to drop out of my mouth as easily as honorifics.

She pulled the pipe out again—offering a quick glimpse of her scandalous tattoo—and bit down on the stem. Even so, she was smirking. "That is the question, isn't it?"

Though I badgered her to expand, to confirm one way or the other, I soon discovered her fluidity also extended to conversation. She'd turn my inquiry into a question about Yusuke the Brawler, or my inspirations, or my opinion on whatever painted opera the Fujino Theater Company was putting on. From there we'd branch out, like a river, into any number of conversations. By the time I walked her to her room at a local inn it was nearly Second Bell—but I didn't care.

I might have used all the luck in my life that night, for Shizuru agreed to see me a second evening. And then a third. And soon Minami Shizuru's presence became as essential to my nights as the moon, as the stars, as the breath in my lungs and the blood in my veins.

Being with her—meeting her even once—was the culmination of my life till then. Every experience I'd had—every sorrow, every joy—had prepared me for her. The first time we kissed I knew that I would ask her to marry me.

I resolved to ask her one evening as the two of us sat in White Leaf, White Smoke. Keichi was with us. I felt it was appropriate to have him there when I asked, in case he had any objections he wished to discuss with her.

But fate, as I have said, is a cruel mistress, and she had other plans that day. As we sat together, the three of us sharing our first round, we noticed an outpouring of people coming from the back of the teahouse. White Leaf, White Smoke was packed more often than not—a spot near a table was a treasured thing to have.

To see so many abandoning their hard-earned space did not bode well.

Minami Keichi sniffed. "I'll give it a look," he said, before setting off to do just that.

Shizuru finished her cup. "Better not be any problems," she said. "I like this place too much to see it shut down."

I followed Keichi with my eyes. The rough-cut crowd parted for him, for the most part, though he wore the wooden sword at his belt and not the Daybreak blade. "I'm certain it's nothing," I said. "Perhaps there was a spill."

When Keichi returned to us his face was hard. There was simmering anger in his brown eyes; thick ropes of tension flowing down his neck. "It's her," he said.

"Who is her?" Shizuru asked. "Keichi, don't be an idiot. Say what you mean or don't say anything at all. I don't know why I have to keep—"

"It's the Wall-Breaker."

My blood froze. Burqila Alshara. No one was particularly happy to see her competing in the tournament, yet no one could deny that she was one of the finest warriors alive. I'd missed her inaugural match due to a few of Shizuru's distractions, but I'd heard about it after the fact. She'd shown up on horseback. Qorin customs being what they are, she must have thought it would be acceptable.

The judges demanded that she dismount per the terms of the tournament. After a tense, albeit polite, argument with her interpreter she agreed.

Her opponent was a young man with a polearm who stained his trousers at the sight of her. When he charged her, she kicked him in the leg, pulled the polearm out of his hands, and bashed him over the head with it. As he lay bleeding onto the arena she pulled a slate and chalk from her chest pocket.

Are you going to deny the hole in your wall, too? Or only my skill?

Like Shizuru, she took everything we'd come to expect from honorable combat and turned it upside down. Unlike Shizuru, Burqila Alshara was responsible for the deaths of hundreds of Hokkaran civilians and a thousand soldiers; likely more on both accounts. And now she was sitting here in a teahouse in Fujino, surrounded by veterans who hated her more than they hated the Traitor himself, having a cup of warm fermented milk.

"I'm going to go give her a piece of my mind," said Shizuru. "Who does she think she is, coming here?"

"No," said Keichi. "We don't want a fight, Zuru, not here. If we get kicked out of this tournament, what are we going to do?"

"This is more important than the money," said Shizuru, which was the first time I'd heard her so much as hint at anything of the sort. She was already on her feet. My heart sank into my throat as I realized she had one hand on the Daybreak blade.

"Shizuru," I said, standing and following along after her. "Think about what you're doing. She's not your enemy anymore, she's not hurting anyone—"

"She's hurt enough people already," said Shizuru. And by then we saw her.

And, as with Shizuru, the Wall-Breaker looked nothing like I imagined she would. Instead of a hardened woman in her forties, covered in scars and the hint of coming wrinkles, I saw a girl at least ten years my junior. The baby fat clinging to her cheeks undermined the small scars pockmarking her brown skin. Instead of a pampered Hokkaran's finery, she wore a practical green coat in the Qorin style, embroidered with circles and squares in yellow thread. The coat intensified the viper green of her eyes, which now fixed us with silent expectation.

Her eyes were the trick of it. The rest of her was young, but those eyes had seen much.

All of a sudden Shizuru burst into laughter. "Which one of you idiots had the idea to prank me, hm? Someone told my brother that the Demon of the Steppes was here. You people think all Qorin look the same?"

Keichi, who had followed along after us, put a hand on his sister's shoulder. "Shizuru, that's—"

Shizuru didn't listen. As bold as ever, she pointed to the young Qorin woman with the sheathed Daybreak blade. "That's a child," she said, "who wandered off her mother's teat."

I loved the woman, but at that moment I was absolutely certain she was about to start a war. Yet how does one stop a hurricane once it's made landfall? The best I could do was stand at her side and pull her away if she tried anything.

All eyes fell to the Qorin woman. She pulled slate and chalk from her pocket. That was when I knew, without a doubt, that this was not going to be a good night.

Burqila Alshara was famously mute.

Apparently, this was all the confirmation of identity that Shizuru needed. She shoved the Daybreak blade back into her belt and launched herself across the table before I could get a hold of her. Time slowed like ice creeping through lake water as I saw my future wife punch Burqila Alshara square in the nose.

There was one wet pop, and then a moment of perfect silence.

And then—the explosion. The other patrons tasted blood in the water. Soon, two thirds of those who remained in the teahouse started swinging at one another. Cups and pots flew through the air, shattering, sending shards careening through the room. I held up my arm to shield myself as much as I could.

Burqila Alshara was no exception. She grabbed Shizuru's wrist, rose, and with one hand on Shizuru's back, shoved her right into the wall. To my horror Shizuru bounced backwards from the force of the blow. Blood ran down her chin from her now-split lip, glistening red as moist fruit.

But Shizuru was not yet finished. She tackled Burqila Alshara with enough force to send the two of them tumbling to the ground.

This was the worst thing she could have possibly done. Hokkaran wrestling was to Qorin wrestling as a wooden sword was to the Daybreak blade. And, though it was not so noticeable when she was seated, Burqila Alshara was at least two heads taller than Minami Shizuru.

Thus, the moment Shizuru took them to the ground, Burqila Alshara wrapped her long arms around Shizuru's shoulder and leg, and then stood up with Shizuru slung around her shoulders like a sack of millet.

"Shizuru," I shouted. "Stop this! You need to let it go; this isn't a proper duel, with rules—"

"I'm not a proper woman!" she shouted—still stretched across Burqila's back, mind you.

To her credit, Burqila did not continue their fighting until my little outburst was through. But as soon as Shizuru finished her boast, Alshara fell backwards, breaking the table with Shizuru's body, only to be confronted with a knee to the kidney.

"Get the magistrates," I said to Keichi.

"I'm not leaving her, you get them," he said.

I gritted my teeth. I, too, could not bear to leave her—yet there was no doubt someone needed to get help. I broke off for a moment to find the teahouse matron, who was hiding beneath a shelf of pots. She was the one I sent out to get the guard. As I spoke to her the crashing behind me continued. Shizuru's pained groans heralded the slap of flesh against flesh.

By the time I looked back, Shizuru was on top again. Any hope I had to see her triumph was soon dashed. Burqila rocked forward, scooped up Shizuru's arm, and twisted. In that moment I learned that broken arms sound very much like broken twigs.

She screamed, cursed, rolled off of Burqila. I was at her side in an instant, holding her hand, doing whatever I could to ease the pain. Sweat left a thin sheen on her body; her lips were dry and chapped. Next to us, Burqila Alshara knelt and wrote on her slate. I glanced up to see what she had to say for herself.

You should have submitted, old woman, before I had to break your arm.

I scowled. The worst thing was—she was right. Shizuru must have realized on her own. She, too, glanced over at the slate— and then she lay back down, laughing.

"Yeah," she said, "you might be right about that."

Behind us I heard the marching of Imperial boots. Barked orders to disperse followed not long after. The guards were coming— and yet Burqila Alshara did not run. As Keichi did his best to cobble together a splint for his sister's arm, Burqila Alshara scrounged up a plank of wood to help him.

I frowned. What was she getting at?

"Itsuki," said Shizuru. I turned my attention to her instead of the warlord helping us. "Next time I try to fight a Qorin, you talk me out of it."

I winced. "I tried," I said, "but you were an arrow in flight."

She laughed at that, too. In the haze of her injuries she gestured to Alshara, of all people. "Listen to him!" she said. "Arrow in flight. My poet!"

Burqila did not have time to react. The guards, by then, were on us. Without so much as asking what had happened, they seized Burqila. Apologies to Shizuru fell from their mouths like leaves from autumn trees.

Shizuru squinted. "Where are you taking her?"

What sort of question was that?

"To prison," said one of the guards.

Shizuru lurched up, yelping as she inadvertently put weight on her now-broken arm. "Wait, wait," she said. "I started this fight. You take her, you've got to take me, too, and I've got a feeling you don't want to take me in."

I could not believe what I was hearing. She was lobbying for Burqila's freedom? Burqila Alshara, the warlord? Even the woman herself raised a skeptic brow.

The guard looked to me for confirmation. I cleared my throat.

"With all due respect," I said, "it's true. Minami-zul started the fight. However . . ."

I faltered, for I could not bring myself to use my power in so corrupt a manner. The guard must have caught on to the situation from my awkward silence.

"Well, there's been a lot of property damage here, your Imperial Highness," she said. "Someone ought to pay for it."

"Of course," I said. I could already see the list of damages forming, and it would be longer than I was tall. "Rest assured, it will be taken care of."

"You heard him," said Shizuru. "Let her go! She won a fight, damn it, isn't that why we're all here? To win fights?"

Her voice was a little slurred from all the head injuries, but I got the feeling she'd make the same argument lucid. That was the most worrisome part of all.

The guards released Burqila. That fearsome warrior stood a horselength away from us, unsure of how to hold herself or what to say.

After a long silence, the captain bowed to us and departed. In so doing she snapped the tension of the moment like twine, and the rest of us were free to resume breathing.

"Hey, Burqila," said the concussed woman in my arms. "Teach me how to do that arm-breaking thing when you get a chance, yes?"

After all that fighting—that was what Shizuru wanted to say to her?

A smile broke out across Burqila's face like sunlight through storm clouds. She nodded.

And as we sat in the wreckage of the White Leaf, White Smoke teahouse, I thought to myself that it was a good thing I did not ask for Shizuru's hand that day.

For one thing, that hand was mostly useless at the moment.

And for another, with an introduction like that, there was no way Burqila Alshara was going to end up anything but Minami Shizuru's greatest friend.

A SCANT TWO days after this incident, I asked Minami Shizuru to marry me in the Imperial Gardens, beneath my favorite dogwood tree. To my delight, she agreed.

*   *   *

I WAS TO be proven wrong on the first account. Shizuru fought a great many of her most famous duels with her broken arm in a sling—after we got her to a surgeon. The woman outright refused going to a healer. As she put it, she didn't want to be responsible for my wasting several thousand ryo and ten years of someone's life over a broken arm. I should have expected nothing less from a woman who laughed in the face of death.

But—I was right on the second account. After that confrontation, Burqila and Shizuru's respect for one another only continued to grow. Soon, whenever we traveled, it was the three-and-one of us—Keichi, Shizuru, Burqila, and myself. Sometimes the two of them ran off together on some madcap adventure they'd later refuse to explain between tearstained bouts of laughter.

Burqila made good on her promise to teach Shizuru Qorin wrestling, and Shizuru repaid her with lessons in bare-handed fishing. Or tried to, anyway. It turned out Burqila had never been more than knee-deep in any water at all. The fact that fearsome Burqila could not swim brought Shizuru endless joy; it took two weeks of practice before Burqila could so much as doggie paddle.

Sitting on the banks of the Jade River, watching the Wallbreaker herself flounder in the water, Shizuru leaned on my shoulder with a grin.

And it was hard not to smile along with her—with them.

What a puzzling thing to behold, this newfound friendship. This woman who'd waged war on us took Shizuru out riding and drinking. She let us try to draw her bow and laughed at us when Shizuru could hold it back for no more than a second.

I admit, it did not feel quite right to me, to be so trusting of a woman who'd tried to kill us. And yet there was no end to Shizuru's enthusiasm for her.

That is my favorite thing in the world about Minami Shizuru—my favorite even among a host of favorites. I will never, I think, fully understand my Queen of Crows. Our cores are too different. She is iron and I am woven silk. We are strong in our own ways, but where I am soft she is rough. Or perhaps she is the silk, for she is far more flexible than I, who hold on to my grudges.

It is that difference that I yearn for. She is a puzzle I cannot figure out; she is a story with endless delightful little twists. Just when I think I've discovered all there is to know about her, she reveals something new.

It was only after our daughter's birth, for instance, that Shizuru admitted she was a fan of my poetry before we met.

I asked her, incredulous, what she thought when she read my long-ago war poem.

She tapped me on the nose.

"You're pretty, and your words are too," she said, "but nothing you've ever written about me has been quite right."

How many poems have I written about her? In some small way she lives in everything I've written since we've met—for she is always on my mind.

I suppose I will have to keep writing until I get it right.